Over the Breadth of the Earth

THE SAGA OF FALLEN LEAVES, VOL. II

J.L. FEUERSTACK

ILLUSTRATED BY ALANA TEDMON

Printed in the United States of America

ISBN 978-1-956019-46-9 (paperback)
ISBN 978-1-956019-47-6 (ebook)

**Canoe Tree
Press**

4697 Main Street
Manchester Center, VT 05255
Canoe Tree Press is a division of DartFrog Books

In memory of Thomas Wren.

"It's I'll be there in sunshine or in shadow…"
- Frederic Weatherly

AUTHOR'S NOTE

As stated above, this is a work of fiction. I have done my utmost to tread lightly regarding subjects that may provoke emotional responses particularly regarding depictions of religion, physical and mental illness, warfare, terrorism, genocide, and abuse. I hope you will take time to explore works of non-fiction pertaining to the various personas and eras that make up the history of our species. Finally, I encourage you to listen to the works of classical and folk music mentioned in this story (notated in italics) particularly when reading the chapters in which the songs are referenced. Although the story is fictional, my intent is to inspire thoughtful reflection while providing entertainment.

The More Things Change, the More They Remain the Same

"Death is my constant companion," Schitz[1] said.

The Demonic warrior sat cross-legged beside the banks of the River Styx. The peaceful waters calmed him. He watched them flow in their unending journey back to the Mortal Realm.

He'd been thinking about Anna, a love lost through cruel and ironic circumstances. His laugh was harsh, even bitter.

"Only I, the scourge of Hell, could fall in love with an Angel," he said.

He remembered Anna's face, contorted in the last moments of passion as they both reached the pinnacle of ecstasy in what she'd called "la petite mort."[2] When they made love in a desert oasis, he had finally understood the last of the Thirteen Steps of training: Surrender.

But what is complete surrender? he wondered. *Is it not Death?*

Another old acquaintance, but never one Schitz would ever call a friend.

I have introduced him to many an enemy, Schitz thought. *And he has visited me more often than I care to recall.*

Schitz stared at the island in the middle of the river.

I met Death for the first time face to face when I killed Vertigo on that very island. Would we have ever fought without Bubonic Plague's interference? What kind of a father goads his son into a duel, then watches while someone opens his throat?

Schitz felt the rough scar on his cheek, a jagged reminder of the first life he had ever taken.

A series of caves lined the opposite bank of the river. Legend

---

[1] Pronounced "Skits" – short for Schizophrenia.
[2] "The little death."

claimed that Bubonic Plague had gone there to die.

I hope it was slow and painful, Schitz thought. *You had me arrested on false charges. You rigged my trial. You ensured my banishment. Plague rigged everything. He wanted me to die but he settled for my exile, so I would be stuck on the far side of the world.*

His thoughts shifted to the other murderous presence in his life, the dark-haired Angel. She had killed his wife Rubella and slain his newborn son. The vixen of destruction had annihilated most of his friends, the band of Demons called The Free Thinkers.

I have seen so much of Death.

He stilled his shaking hands and looked back through the portal of memory. He recalled the battle in Babylon. He had possessed the king and driven him mad while Schitz's comrades slaughtered high-ranking Angels by the handful. He recollected the vicious fight in the shadow of the pyramids when the Free Thinkers charged into the midst of an Angelic feud. He remembered the bloodbath along the forest road at Teutoburg and combat at the summit of the Incan citadel. Schitz smiled.

I faced those harrowing moments and a thousand others with a steady hand. When Death arrived to eat his fill, I made certain I was not on the menu.

Schitz's chest swelled with pride.

I guided Death to feast upon the Angels and mortals alike when I led the Conquistadors through the New World.

For a moment, he heard the notes of a Spanish lute and the beating of drums. They morphed into the bugle and the fifes of the British Red Coat Army.

Ah, I laid waste to those who stood before me when I wore the King's crimson along the road to Quebec.

He saw decimated Angels fleeing along with the French forces they occupied.

Yet, I am not invincible, Schitz thought. Waterloo came to mind. He shivered in the memory of the carnage.

Death was everywhere.

He quivered and touched the spot where the musket ball had pierced his host's lung.

If I had not been quick, I would be dead, just like so many of those I led into battle that day.

Schitz focused on steadying his breathing. He zeroed his mind on a series of pictures. He could see faces sketched on parchment. Before Waterloo, he had ordered the Wraiths, Hell's Intelligence Service, to draw the likeness of the Angelic leadership. Of all the representations, one stood out: Lord Zinc II, Supreme Commander of the Army of Heaven.

He must be my primary prey, Schitz thought. *For even if Death is inevitable, and I must surrender to this reality, surely it is not a violation of the Thirteen Steps for me to focus all my energies to ensure He dines on Lord Zinc rather than me.*

Schitz slammed a clenched fist into his thigh.

And on the stone-faced bitch who murdered my family.

ZINC II WATCHED THE Eunoe River meander along its winding path through Heaven on the way back to the Mortal Realm. The pastoral scene of the riverside beyond the Great Hall should have offered Zinc a reprieve from the unending politicking and scheming of the Heavenly Houses. Yet, as he stood by the river's edge, all Zinc could remember was the visage of Uranium I, the late Lord of the Uranium House. His ghost haunted Zinc, the man who had murdered him and dumped his corpse in the river.

Why do I come here – to the scene of the crime? Zinc thought.

He kicked a small pebble and watched it break the water's surface. The rippled dispelled Lord Uranium I's image.

If only it were so easy to oust uncomfortable memories, Zinc thought. *I did not want to kill you, but your incessant scheming threatened the authority I fought so hard to win.*

Zinc was disgusted with Heaven's infernal politics. He thought back to his younger days – better days.

The Academy had been a blessed place. His academic prowess reinforced his high self-esteem and positive self-image even when he was continuously challenged and harassed by Peter and Samuel from the Gold and Silver Houses.

Of course, I dispatched them as well – my first taste of killing one of my own. Zinc winced, then recovered. *But they deserved it. I took what was mine, the right to live. It was not my House that rebelled against God.*

Still, when the tiny waves in the river smoothed over, he saw his classmates' faces in the glistening surface.

Someone's always getting in the way. I was building a monumental empire with Alexander and then that Demon with the scar on his face wrecked it by driving the Macedonian crazy.

Remembering the scar-faced Demon invariably led Zinc to thoughts of Rachael.

I miss her with an inconsolable hunger. I cannot believe she now shares Hydrogen's bed.

A paradox. His mistress now the wife of his friend. Lord Hydrogen, the Angel who had convinced the Demon Bubonic Plague not to kill Zinc at the conclusion of a duel during the Hundred Years War. Hydrogen, who had supported Zinc in sacrificing the Native Houses during the Spanish Conquest, an event that led God to appoint Zinc as Supreme Commander.

Hydrogen is my friend, Zinc thought. *And I need friends.*

He remembered his father, the man who had vanished while investigating how Gold had unleashed the powers of the Titans. He thought of his wife, Cecilia, killed in action on the eve of the Teutoburg disaster. And he thought about Uranium II – an ally who was not squeamish at all about having Angelic blood on his hands.

I have plenty of blood on my own hands, Zinc thought. He'd duped Iron III into taking command of the endeavor that ended in a wholesale disaster at Waterloo. In the aftermath, Zinc executed Iron III; Uranium II had dispatched Lord Palladium. Both bodies now kept Uranium I company at the bottom of the sacred river.

There were other enemies, but before Zinc could devise a plan for their demise, an itching sensation gripped at the back of his throat. It crawled through his palate and up into his head, where it squeezed his brain like a sponge. Zinc reached into his robe and withdrew a pipe.

"Damn – empty!"

I must return to the Isle of Neutrality and get more, he thought. *Perhaps I will see Spanish Influenza.*

The prospect of visiting the den of drugs and debauchery improved his mood – so did the prospects of reuniting with the violent, hedonistic Demon. They were not friends; Spanish had killed Zinc's sons in combat with the Black Death Coven.

That grievance aside, Spanish is a pleasurable acquaintance, Zinc thought. *He knows how to show someone a good, sordid time.*

Zinc looked over his shoulder as he walked from the river's edge. He knew the invisible hand of the dead would always pull him back to the Eunoe – no amount of drink, drugs, trysts, scheming, or fighting could change it.

I've built my throne out of the bones of the dead in that watery graveyard. The least I can do is come by and pay my respects. But that's enough for now.

The wind picked up, and with it, a chill to his body – or was it to what was left of his soul?

THE ROWS OF WEAPONS cast long, ominous shadows across the factory floor of the Springfield Armory. The eerie silence of the early morning hour stood in stark contrast to the typical drone and buzz that accompanied the day.

"Look at them all," Elise said.

She gestured toward the endless rows of stockpiled muskets. The deadly instruments were arrayed in neat rows; they looked like a deadly pipe organ.

"I wonder how many there are," Mephistopheles said. His voice conveyed little interest in his own query.

"Over one million," Elise said.

She longed to fill the awkward silence with anything, even

something as banal as an accurate assessment of the arsenal's capacity.

"I don't think they'll miss the few that we smuggle home," she said. She smiled but was unsuccessful in her attempt to elevate her mate's morose mood.

Mephistopheles grunted and unhooked two muskets from the wall. "Hardly worth the effort, really," he said, more to himself than Elise.

"Oh, come on," she said. "Why are you so dejected?"

A fleeting scowl formed across the elderly Wraith's face.

"I'm sorry, love," he said. "It all just feels so pointless. We worked so hard to train Titus. Against all expectations, he grew into a remarkable commander. Then your little rascal Schitz came up with that his tedious task, and we were required to render portraits of Heaven's leadership, an assignment we accomplished with phenomenal accuracy. Waterloo should have been our grandest hour. But our Lord Satan kneecapped us by cutting the number of Demons assigned to the cannons. The battle should have been Megiddo, the final victory. Regardless, the outcome should have been different – not the debacle we suffered."

"We gave as good as we got," Elise said. Her voice remained soft, but her tone warned Mephistopheles about the perils of criticizing the Demon she had attended for centuries.

While Mephistopheles grumbled, Elise feigned attention while she worked out the logistics of carrying more than one musket with her only arm.

Irritation crept back into her partner's expression. "Just carry the one, silly girl. It's not like we have a plethora of Demons waiting to train with them," he said. "Which is exactly the point, isn't it? Even if we had given the Angels a walloping, we don't have the strength to recover from the body blow they dealt us. Maybe if we had Bubonic Plague or Small Pox or Tetanus, we could, but now we have only the likes of Schizophrenia, Anorexia, and Spanish Influenza. We are weak and drawn down. And I... I am tired."

Elise grimaced at the prospect of abandoning either of the muskets she had labored so hard to lift. She rested both against the wall and embraced her mate.

"I know that it has been difficult," she said. "The forces of Heaven seem unlimited. Our forces, though fierce, are meager. What else can we do except keep fighting?"

"Here, I got this one," Mephistopheles said. He scooped up a musket in his free hand—two for me, one for you. Three is enough. Let's go home. We can leave the worrying for those that got us all into this mess. The Dark Lord we serve is almost as big an idiot as his brother who art in Heaven."

He laughed at his little joke.

Elise smiled and kissed him on the cheek.

"What was that for?"

"I think it's cute when you're blasphemous," she said.

WHERE CIVIL BLOOD MAKES CIVIL HANDS UNCLEAN

66 I t is evident to everyone on the Triumvirate Council that he is power-hungry."

Rabies and Schitz walked along the Ganges.

"More of your concern than mine," Schitz said.

He loved the ramrod posture and measured stride of the British officer he occupied, and the sharp, khaki tunic and trousers of his uniform.

Rabies sighed. "Elise said you might listen to me."

"She has been warning me about him for a while, but I insist that she not meddle in my affairs," Schitz said. "I do not see why I should be afraid of him."

Rabies stamped her foot like a petulant child. "You are the most senior Demon. You command respect even if Satan often fails to do so. Any Demon who wants control of the army will have to get rid of you."

Amusement trickled across Schitz's response. "You have a diabolical mind."

"Just promise me you'll be careful," Rabies said. "I've lost my mother and all of my children. I'd rather like to keep my last parent around."

Schitz stepped out of the mortal. "Come here," he said. He embraced his daughter. "I promise I will be as careful as my existence allows."

A tear ran down her cheek. "So, not careful at all then."

SKIN CANCER'S VOICE BUBBLED with excitement. "When the mortals charge, the Angels will have to move swiftly to keep up. If you can move along their row, I can drop them, one after the other in quick succession."

"Do you believe the Confederates will send the infantry tomorrow?" Schitz asked.

"They have to," Hysteria said.

Schitz took stock of Hysteria for a moment and was pleased to note the young Psychological's development. She was youthful and energetic, practical and pragmatic, intelligent but not overconfident. Schitz was incredibly proud.

"Why do you say that?"

"All throughout the war, the batteries have gone back and forth at one another," she said, analytical as always. "However, through my possession of General Meade's aide, I know that the Union artillery has been silent. The mortals and the Angels will believe the guns have been knocked out."

Schitz rubbed his chin. "And in the confusion caused by that misassumption, the Angels and mortals will be disorientated and vulnerable, caught off-guard."

His subordinates agreed.

"Not so long ago on the Plains of Abraham, we dealt a massive blow to the Angels by changing the dynamic of battle. We did the same thing at Waterloo. I believe that tomorrow may well be a day remembered as your arrival as a senior strategist. I only wish we had more Demons at our disposal."

Schitz cursed to himself. Satan's refusal to provide sufficient troops was maddening. The Dark Lord was still shaken by the casualties from the last great struggle.

"Do we expect any reinforcements?" Skin Cancer asked.

"The battle may attract a handful of small teams, but I doubt that any will arrive in time to be integrated into our plans."

"Are there any reports of Angels within the Union ranks?" inquired Hysteria.

"None yet," replied Schitz hesitantly.

He allowed silence to settle for a moment and then unleashed a bird call. A shadow slowly slinked along the outside of the white canvas tent. Elise appeared in the aperture like liquid smoke.

"Good evening, Mama," Schitz said. The attending Demons tried not to giggle at his uncharacteristic affection. "Are there any reports of Angels within Union ranks?"

"None yet, Commander," she replied with a faint smile.

The forces of Hell and Heaven jumped freely from side to side within an engagement before settling into a specific army prior to the onset of combat. Schitz knew if a small number from either side deviated from the trend, they could create an utterly chaotic situation.

"Well, that's good news; let us hope that it remains that way."

Elise looked around the room. "Good luck to you all," she said, then melted into the darkness.

"You're lucky to have your rearing Wraith," Skin Cancer said, "so few are alive. Unaffiliated ones can be less than helpful at times."

"True," Schitz said, but his mind was elsewhere. "Each of you commands a contingent of five." He bit the inside of his lip to stifle his frustration at his limited force. "I know for a fact that the Angels want to influence mortal events in this war. If the Confederates win tomorrow, the war will be over. Expect a veritable host of Angels tomorrow."

Schitz surveyed the faces of his two junior commanders before he continued. "If our strategy fails, I do not want us to sustain heavy casualties here. Therefore, and to increase my odds of being undetected, I alone will move forward. Hysteria, you and your team will remain with the guns while Skin Cancer's marksmen will remain at a distance. I will take up an advanced position between Cemetery Ridge and the Confederate lines and conceal myself."

"We'll cover you well," Skin Cancer said.

"I'm counting on it."

ZINC FAIRLY BOUNCED ON his way through the Great Hall. His greatest dreams had come true—his Angelic rivals' forces had been annihilated in the battle of Waterloo. Iron III's incompetence was on full display. But there was one remaining obstacle.

Lord Carbon VI remained cocky, and he enjoyed significant numerical superiority despite the additional support Zinc had added from Houses that were disbanded after the debacle.

"You will have to deal with Carbon VI in a different way than you did Iron III," Uranium II said. He was struggling to keep up with Zinc's lengthy strides.

"Indeed," Zinc replied. "I intend for him to break under the burden of command."

"How so?"

"He is a coward," Zinc replied. "I will put him in a place where he is forced to be brave. Then he will discredit himself. Ambition is not enough; it has to be backed up by an appropriate level of skill."

Uranium II grunted in disgust. "I'd just rather fight it out. I do not like the politics."

Zinc never faltered in his pace. "We are of the same coin, my friend," he said. "Just different sides."

Lord Barium gazed down at the mortal and Angelic reports spread across the desk of Major General George Pickett of the Confederate States of America. Flicking oil lamps illuminated the tent and cast dancing shadows on the canvas. Barium's eyes darted between directives from General Longstreet and communiques from Lord Carbon VI, who for the moment were one and the same. Barium assessed the situation.

Under his command were approximately thirty Angels. Lord Cesium stood over another thirty. Carbon VI had assembled the force as part of his strategic shift toward larger movements of Heavenly armies. He wanted to shake off the bad memories of the last time the Angels had departed Heaven in large numbers.

From his studies, Barium knew that in times past, all available Angels came to Earth in one giant phalanx and possessed scores of men. However, these formations had proved unwieldy. The Demons always nipped at their flanks. Carbon VI wished to revive the strategy with heightened organization. He had promised God a substantial victory over the Demons and an end to the American Civil War, a conflict sending multitudes to the River Styx daily.

Barium sat in solitude as he did before every battle, ruminating on his responsibilities to his God, his family, his men. The flap to his tent opened.

General Longstreet entered. "Good evening, George," he said.

Barium took in the gray and yellow uniform and the mortal's long, matted beard (though the Angel within was clean-shaven).

"Good evening, James," Barium said, rising to greet his dual commander.

The two shook hands.

Carbon VI (Longstreet) spoke in a pronounced South Carolina drawl. "I have promised God and the men a great victory tomorrow. I trust you will break their lines at Cemetery Ridge; Cesium will break their lines at Cemetery Hill."

Barium nodded.

Longstreet continued, "I will be farther to the South with a smaller contingent. We will occupy Little Round Top."

Barium nodded. "Yes, sir. I've read the dispatches."

Carbon VI brushed at something in his beard. "I am certain you have, General. I just wanted to see you for a moment; tomorrow is a monumental day."

Barium replied, "I understand that it is, but our reports suggest there are no more than fifteen or so Demons within the Union ranks."

"I know," Carbon VI said. "I aim to deliver a victory without casualties. As I'm sure you know, the strategy of Heaven has been to move away from large formations. But I believe, now more than ever, we need to return to the old ways. I have spent time studying the battle where Gold and Silver devastated the Demonic armies in Babylon. That was not a small contingent, but a sizeable fighting force. We have been so close with Alexander, Caesar, Khan, and Bonaparte."

"I am aware, Father," Barium said. He remained measured in his response, even when using the familiar address, "and I will do everything in my power to keep my men safe, believe me."

"I do, I do," Carbon VI said. He threw his arm around Barium. "Tomorrow, I will see you upon the field of victory. We will wipe our bayonets dry with the Union colors."

Pickett watched Longstreet depart the tent and disappear into the heat of the evening's darkness.

SCHITZ HAD NOT BOTHERED to take a mortal with him when he crossed the lines and climbed down to the narrow lane known as Emittsburg Road. There had been a time when standing between two colossal armies within the nakedness of the Celestial without a door in sight would have terrified Schitz. However, his experiences in Amazonia had rid him of the fear of extended stays within the vulnerable realm. It took a great effort without a mortal form, but he dug a small gulley beside the road. He lay in it and looked up at the brilliant array of stars spread across the night's sky.

He peered up at the serenity of the heavens and thought, *I wish Rubella could see me now. I have stepped beyond the simplistic leading of combatants; I now place my trust in the schemes and designs of those men and women I have trained and use their own insights to shape the greater strategy.*

He was proud of himself and the level of command and control he had established. His tutorage of Hysteria was already paying dividends and undoubtedly added to the legitimacy of the Psychologicals. For many reasons, Schitz was relieved that he had not created a coven of mental illness such as the Black Death or those who had recently started worshipping Cancer. He preferred his kinsmen to be open-minded, a link back to the original Free Thinkers. He never considered bringing Autism or Anorexia under his direct control. Yet, they developed into formidable psychological forces.

Schitz wondered how his compatriots were fairing in Vicksburg, in the Endau River basin, in Araucanía, in Shimonoseki, and along the banks of the Pra River; his colleagues all across the broad, forlorn world. He was grateful that all the soldiers of Hell were not his responsibility and vowed to do right by those under his command on the morrow.

Although he had his misgivings with the Triumvirate when it was first convened, the appointment of Demons of which he was fond, Wraiths he trusted, and a High Priest he had come to respect, made the Triumvirate more than tolerable. Even though he no longer had the authority he held during the Conquistador Conquest, he did not mind receiving missions from the Triumvirate.

Schitz looked up at the night sky and thought of how many had implored him to join the Council after Smallpox fell, but he knew he could never lead a venture with so many peers. When he was in charge, it needed to be a solo affair, not subject to another's whims. Schitz had supported Rabies for the Triumvirate Counsel and appreciated the strong link her position created between the Academy and those who would lead its graduates following their successful education.

Schitz was quite proud of Rabies. He was afraid of losing her; a weakness, but one he was more than happy to have.

UNDER A BLAZING JULY sun, a veritable sea of gray advanced under the command of Major General George Pickett.

Barium surveyed the Union battlements. He leaned over and spoke to a younger member of his House who had possessed the body of the General's attaché. "I requested that we position our own forces farther to the rear, but Carbon VI denied it, emphatically."

"Why did you ask such a thing?" the aide asked.

"We're exposed if they have any working artillery."

"I thought we knocked out their guns."

Barium shook his head. "I am concerned we are being sucked into a trap," he said.

"We could ignore Carbon VI's order."

"No," the Standard Bearer said. "In the mortal army as well as our own, orders must be followed. Come, let us leave this nice General to his fate. We are needed at the front."

SCHITZ HAD LADEN HIMSELF down with Hellish weaponry, two swords, two short swords, and ten throwing knives. He saw Angels in the first rank of the approaching rebels. The icy grip of fear threatened to strangle him. He was in a good position on the left flank of the Angelic presence. He crawled along the ditch.

The Rebels had crossed the grassy expanse through the sweltering, sunny day to the point where Schitz could make out facial features.

If you can see them, they can see you. He clenched for a moment, then realized the enemy forces were focused on their objective, not on him.

HYSTERIA PEERED OVER THE sight of the 24-pounder Howitzer.

"Load the canister shot!"

The gun crew atop Little Round Top armed the cannon with the cartridge containing hundreds of tiny musket balls packed in sawdust. She continued to adjust the sight and hoped the other gun crews would be as accurate as she.

The loader finished his routine. "Ready!"

Hysteria checked the other guns to her right manned by two of the Demons under her command. Each stood with an arm raised aloft. On her left, three more Demons commanded Union Howitzers. They signaled their readiness.

If only we'd had guns like this at Waterloo, she thought.

The sun's rays glistened off gold buttons and saber handles. Sweat ran down the nape of her neck. Her wool uniform was heavy and stank.

Hysteria raised her right arm. The Confederates were nearly on Schitz, but he would be safe from the mortal projectiles in the Celestial.

"Fire!"

Smoke and fire belched from the cannons and spewed death on the advancing infantry.

THE CANISTER SHELLS STRUCK the road directly in front of the Confederate lines. Schitz leapt from his ditch. The contents of the shells tore through the bodies of the mortals. The musket balls released from the artillery pierced lungs and hearts, cracked skulls, and ripped flesh from throats. Schitz's feet pounded the dusty road. He waited to draw his sword until he was nearly on the closest seizing Angel whose mortal had taken a shot to the heart.

Schitz cut down five Angels in a matter of moments, then encountered a cluster of unaffected, possessed mortals. They stood next to their fallen comrades. If the Angels stepped into the Celestial, Schitz knew he would have a fight on his hands.

SKIN CANCER AND HER retinue peered down the flip-up leaf sights of their Springfield Model 1863 rifles. Though the Confederates were too far away for the bulk of the Union forces perched on Cemetery Ridge, the foe was just within range of Captain Monroe's elite sharpshooters.

Skin Cancer issued commands in a calm, steady voice. "Each of you has your target, left to right." They lined up upon the Angels nearest to Schitz, the ones who had escaped the effects of the artillery.

SCHITZ CHARGED TOWARDS HIS foe at top speed. He knew he only had a few seconds before they recovered. Without warning, each soldier's head snapped backward violently, the uninvited guests from the barrels of the snipers' rifles found their marks. Schitz dropped his sword and unleashed five throwing knives in quick succession into the Angels felled by the artillery.

He reacquired his sword and set upon the Angels dropped by Skin Cancer's rifle brigade. He slit the last throat and reached the end of the mental countdown he'd started in the ditch.

Three... two... one... here it comes.

The ground heaved with concussions from Hysteria's battery. Schitz started the count again to keep pace with the battery. They would adjust their fire across the Angelic position.

Twenty... nineteen... eighteen...

With a blade in each hand, Schitz harvested Angels, a Demonic threshing machine. Mortals fell on all sides, shredded by modern instruments of death and Angels under Schitz's venerable blades.

Five... four... three...

"MOVE, YOU LAZY BASTARDS!"

Hysteria's voice carried over the roar of the surrounding batteries, all firing upon the Confederate formations. "Move."

The crew continued readying the next loads of canister shot at a furious pace. All the while, Hysteria adjusted the sights of the cannons, mentally calculating for the best location to place the shot.

SKIN CANCER RIPPED HER ramrod from the barrel of her rifle and pulled back the percussion lock before drawing down on the Angels. To her left and right, the sharpshooters drew a bead on their next targets. Schitz had reached the edge of impact from the last barrage. By Skin Cancer's count, the artillery was three seconds away from firing.

She weighed the options; if her shooters held their fire, the Angels might step into the Celestial where they would massively outnumber Schitz. If she fired, there would be no way to bring down any possessed mortals that escaped the artillery.

"Spread out your target, every other Angel, left to right," she said. "Fire!"

ANGEL-POSSESSED CONFEDERATES COLLAPSED TO the ground under the fire of Skin Cancer's snipers. Schitz drew his remaining throwing knives and launched one after another into the writhing Angels. As the final blade flew into its target, the unprotected throat of a flailing Angel, the next barrage of canister shells exploded. Men cried out in fear and pain. The Celestial reverberated from the concussions.

Two Angels stepped into the Celestial to avoid the barrage. Out of throwing knives, Schitz launched forward. The Angels drew their Celestial armaments and sliced at him. He blocked the blows, then drove his swords into them simultaneously. He left the weapons in the bodies and drew short swords. He made quick work on the Angels seizing from the artillery barrage. He killed the last Angel with a stroke to the base of the neck.

Schitz had lost the count, but he figured the encounters had lasted less than a minute. Hysteria's battery fired its third barrage. Skin Cancer's sharpshooters picked off enemy soldiers with systematic efficiency.

Within the Mortal Realm, a sea of gray rushed past Schitz even while death rained from the sky. The fallen lay strewn across the ground; the living continued to advance past into a wall rifle fire pouring forth from Cemetery ridge.

A similar scene of carnage unfolded in the Celestial. Mangled, dispatched bodies of broken Angels marked Schitz's grisly progress.

Schitz reckoned he had killed around thirty, an unheard-of feat; one owed as much to their lack of preparation as to his ferocity. In a single, unforgiving minute, Schitz had felled more Angels than his squad did on the Plains of Abraham.

Schitz's Notebook

Army of Northern Virginia

(Determined and tenacious troops.

They were highly professional and

a difficult adversary. Their defeat

at Gettysburg was some of

my best work.

He crossed his hands above his head, the predetermined signal for withdrawing from the Mortal Realm. While the Confederates rushed forward into a hail of Union fire and calamity, Schitz moved toward the rear where he would find a door via one of their tents. When he was carving the ancient symbols in the dirt below the entrance of the canvas lodging, the weight of his accomplishment hit him.

"B<small>UT WHY DID WE</small> withdraw?" Hysteria asked. Her voice sounded like a file on steel, ripe with agitation. The Return Ritual continued over her sidebar.

"We follow orders," Skin Cancer said.

"We had them on the run," Hysteria said. "We obliterated the Angels. We could have taken on the ones within Ewell's or Longstreet's contingents as well."

"Are you truly dissatisfied?" Schitz asked from behind the pair as he emerged from the portal and entered the queue.

A Priest looked at the whispering trio with irritation before returning to the Ritual.

"I just wish we had taken out more," Hysteria said.

A wistful grin cracked Schitz's lips. "The exuberance of youth," he said. "I promise you, it is far better to be alive after killing a few, than to kill one more only to fall dead."

Skin Cancer tapped them on their shoulders.

"Come, come, you all talk as though we have not served up a tremendous victory," she said.

Schitz's eyes betrayed his weariness even as he voiced his agreement.

I wonder what we could have done with twice as many troops, he thought.

Z<small>INC COMPLETED THE</small> R<small>ETURN</small> Ritual. There was a crowd walking towards the banks of the Eunoe. He looked at a young man next to him, a younger son of the Cadmium lineage.

"What's going on?"

"Decimation by Ordeal of the Carbon House," the young Angel said.

Zinc had never witnessed the spectacle, a punishment for cowardice.

The young man continued, "Apparently, Lord Carbon VI was not up to the task he faced at Gettysburg."

Although exhausted from the savagery of Vicksburg, Zinc navigated through the crowd to the edge of the Heavenly river. Across the expanse, he saw a dejected Lord Carbon VI holding a large spear. Opposite him was his younger brother bearing a sharpened stick.

Zinc heard voices all around him.

"A Standard Bearer who has displayed extreme cowardice is disciplined by Decimation by Ordeal."

"He must face every member of his own household in one-on-one combat."

"The disgraced Standard Bearer has a choice. He can die, or he can slay his entire House. Only those males who have been granted a charter for their own House, or females that have wed into another are exempt. All others, regardless of age or rank, must face the Standard Bearer. Even his retired grandfather, one-handed though he is."

Zinc winced at the reality.

Would a truly brave man choose to live by killing all his kin? he wondered.

Zinc watched the younger Carbon dodge the spear. After the Standard Bearer flailed away with a wild swing, the younger man charged. Lord Carbon VI recovered his balance and ran the spear all the way through his relative. The crowd gasped; the sibling shook, then coughed blood on the stone. The Standard Bearer pulled the spear free, then buried the tip in the young man's back.

Though he'd seen the gore of battle his entire adult life, Zinc shivered. A silken voice tickled his ear.

"How was Vicksburg?"

"Lady Hydrogen," he said. He bowed. "It was savage. The Demon known as Spanish Influenza was present. His wrath is like nothing I have ever seen." Zinc had seen another side of his Demonic drinking buddy, one he wished to forget.

She rested her hand on his arm—innocent enough, but Zinc's body pulsed with the desire born of lusty memory.

"I trust you and your men made a fair accounting of yourselves," she said.

"We took more than our share of them."

"I can't imagine you fared any worse than the debacle at Gettysburg," she said. There was odd amusement in her voice.

"What happened?" Zinc asked.

"Well, they say Carbon VI sent his troops out while he and his closest attachés maneuvered on their own. When the smoke cleared, half of his troops were dead, the other half never even saw a Demon. His own contingent was useless to explain what had happened. It smacked of cowardice, so God has brought back the Ordeal."

"Seems barbaric," Zinc said.

He hoped he did not display any joy in watching the systematic destruction of the Carbon legacy. Lord Carbon VI plunged his weapon through a young woman's throat.

Lady Hydrogen pointed. "Look there!" She removed her hand, but her touch lingered on Zinc's skin.

She was gesturing to the row of dejected Carbons who were lined up like so many cows awaiting the slaughter. Each was dreading the moment when it was time to cross the bridge to the island of death.

"That young filly, there," Rachael said.

A young Angel, barely old enough to have graduated from the Academy, awaited her turn. She was petite, delicately featured, thin, and attractive.

"You should marry her," Lady Hydrogen said.

"Why would I do that?"

"Married females are exempt from the bloodbath. They are joined to the House they marry. And let's be honest, you are not getting any younger."

He looked at Rachael, a look she knew all too well.

"It's not going to happen," she said. "Our time is past."

"Not by my choice," he said.

Oh, that sounded pathetic.

"It's just I'll always love you and... and I will always wish you hadn't chosen him."

"Darling," she replied, "the choice was never mine to make. I did as my father told me. Now you do as I tell you. Save the girl; it will be good for everyone's morale."

She pushed him forward.

Her voice was like aged wine, rich and intoxicating. "Go, my love. I release you from my affections. You must follow my command as repayment for saving your life."

"I miss you," he said.

"I know," she said. "And I will miss you for the rest of time. But we are just passengers in the carriage, we do not drive. Though it pains me to see you in the arms of another, I'd rather not see you alone."

Zinc pushed through the crowd. His anxiety grew with every step. He drew close and the appalling spectacle of slaughter faded—she was all he could see. She stood with quiet dignity, waiting her turn to cross the bridge.

He tapped her shoulder.

"I am Zinc," he said.

She looked at him. He took in her beauty; streaming blonde hair, full lips, steely eyes. She was not afraid.

"Yes, my Lord," she said. "Everyone knows your accomplishments. You instructed me at the Academy, but there were many students."

A gasp pulsed through the crowd. The penultimate member of the House of Carbon had refused to adopt a combat stance or take up a weapon. He was shouting at Lord Carbon VI.

"Hand me your spear and let this be over with. It is not our fault that this dishonor has been heaped upon our house."

The Standard Bearer, now entirely within the clutches of mania, ignored the younger's pleas and rushed forward. He shrieked, the sounds of Hell coming from the throat of an Angel, as he eviscerated his descendant.

The young woman looked at Zinc. "I regret our reunion was so, my Lord. But it seems I have an appointment from which there is no reprieve."

She put her foot on the bridge. Zinc grabbed her hand and dropped to one knee.

"Marry me!"

"To save my life?" Her question was blunt and without emotion.

"And to make both our lives better," he said. He shrugged. "Of course, later on, you can change your mind, and I can just kill you."

"Your sense of romance needs a little work, my Lord," she said.

Her expression had not changed. She looked like someone preparing for an afternoon stroll.

Zinc was suddenly aware that everyone was listening. Still holding the woman's hand, he bowed before God.

"Lord, I humbly ask your permission to marry this Angel."

There was a brief explosion of sound. It stopped abruptly when God raised his hand. A Red Sea of Angels made a path between the Lord of Heaven and Zinc.

With grave solemnity that did not match his sunny disposition, the Deity spoke. "Do you, Lord Zinc, Standard Bearer of the Zinc household and Holder of the Golden Halo, take this Maiden to be your wife, to love her singularly, to father Angels by her, and to protect and defend her until death or into eternity?"

"I do," Zinc said.

God turned to the woman.

"And do you, Maiden Carbon, take this Angelic Lord to be your husband, to love him faithfully and devotedly, to bear Angels by him, and to protect and defend him until death or into eternity?"

"I do," she replied.

"I declare you husband and wife. I further declare the conclusion of the Trial by Ordeal of the House of Carbon."

As though an afterthought, the attention of those assembled, including the bride and groom, shifted back to Lord Carbon VI. He stood bathed in the blood of his kin, his eyes wild and mad.

Odd, Zinc thought, *I began today, single, and this afternoon I am married. Lord Carbon VI began today the head of an ancient and well-populated house, and this evening he is bereft of kin.*

He turned back to the woman. "Excuse me, wife," he said. "I don't even know your name."

"Eleanor," she said.

DESPONDENCY CLUNG TO EVERY word when Schitz spoke. "I would understand if you decided that you wished to go elsewhere. If you fight alongside me, it will always be like this."

Hysteria and Skin Cancer looked at each other with bafflement, then back at Schitz.

Hysteria replied, "Sir, we are honored to fight alongside you, and I personally have dedicated my career to the Psychologicals. How can I not follow the school's founder?"

Skin Cancer nodded. "Our loyalty is with you, sir."

Schitz watched as various Demons departed from the Great Hall following the conclusion of the Medal Presentation. Schitz recalled the ceremony and spat on the ground in frustration. Two members of Spanish Influenza's contingent had received the Knight's Pentagram for their contributions to the victory at Vicksburg, five had gotten the Pentagram First Class, and Satan had thrown out Pentagram Second Classes like seeds to birds.

Schitz and his commanders had only received Campaign Stars for Gettysburg. Schitz glanced down at Hysteria's new Pentagram Second Class and rolled his eyes.

"They could have at least given you a First Class for our efforts, or more appropriately the Knight's Pentagram."

"We don't care about their medals," Skin Cancer said.

"The others weren't even acknowledged," Schitz said. He watched several of his junior Demons milling around the Great Hall their robes noticeably naked of awards. "What message does today send to them?"

"That they are alive," Skin Cancer replied, "and that through cooperation, planning, and cunning, a swath of Angels now lies beneath cold stone slabs."

"You fought well today," he said, "and you should be proud. Your precision saved my life and delivered us a huge success. I am immensely grateful and count you as astute in war as any holder of the Knight's Pentagram."

Hysteria beamed from ear to ear and saluted. He returned the salute and strode off towards his room.

What an odd day, he thought. *I began the morning lying in a ditch and ended the day overshadowed and barely acknowledged.*

Yet, he could see that he was developing his subordinates into capable tacticians; this made him happy. Schitz reflected on his own development; he had come a long way from a solitary fighter. Now he possessed the ability to command large cadres effectively in battle and to develop corps of fighters so that they might reach their full potential.

As he hopped onto the lion's skin that covered his bed, Schitz's mind whirled with schemes and ideas for the future. He felt motivated. He felt self-assured; he felt free of the past and its ghosts and ready for whatever Heaven or Hell had to throw at him.

THE BOTTLE SMASHED AGAINST the wall. Liquid trickled down the plaster and puddled on the floor.

Damn fine waste of Brew, Spanish Influenza thought.

Still, he looked for something else to smash. He had received nothing for his gallantry at Vicksburg. While others under his command had been feted—insignificant puffery to extend one of Satan's stupid pageants—Satan had ruined the festivities with one sentence, "We make these awards relative to the Vicksburg encounter despite his loss of two of our most valiant warriors, Cerebral Palsy and Dyslexia."

Soldiers die in battle, Spanish thought. *He could have recognized them with an award, but no, he had to sully my brigade's moment. And he made it sound like I was responsible.*

But the real problem was the theater of battle to which he had been assigned. True, the victory at Vicksburg sealed the Rebels fate, but Gettysburg... Gettysburg was the prize...Gettysburg won the headlines. Gettysburg was seen as the turning point. Its heroes were the bravest... the most resolute... the most valuable.

And of all the heroes, the one most lauded was Sir Schizophrenia.

He will not be as easy to dispatch as his wife, Spanish thought, *but I will not rest until he is dead.*

THE STRIDENT BANG OF hammers on nails echoed across what had been Savannah's Riverfront District. The locals now called the gentleman who stood before the large, southern live oak, "the ol' Haint." He did not mind so long as no one attempted to reenact the superstition of the American South that recommended scalding water as a means for repelling ghosts. It was generally assumed that he was a displaced son of the South, like so many cast far from home by the recently concluded War of Northern Aggression.

The Haint withdrew a folding knife from his vest pocket and began stripping bark from the tree. He was interrupted by a tug on the leg of his suit trousers.

"Mistah." The small girl's accent sounded like verbal molasses. "My mama said to offer you this here drink of water, on 'count of the heat."

The child wore a plain, simple dress, well-worn and faded. Her face was clean, her hair neatly braided. He was beset by a memory of his own daughters. He remembered Pulwabi combing their hair and teaching them how to cook. It was too much for The Ancient One. It was one thing to chase his soulmate with futility across the countless centuries; it was quite another to contemplate the varying fates the world had in store for his descendants. After his children had passed through the rivers of reincarnation, he had put them to rest in his mind. He could not seek them as he did Pulwabi.

"Well, I say, southern charm and hospitality are alive and well," he said.

The water was clean, cool, and refreshing.

"She also said to ask what in tarnation you are doing to our tree.'"

The Haint burst out laughing and handed her back the empty glass.

"Tell your mama that this tree was here when that flag over there," he said, gesturing to the pole of a military post across the street, "had only thirteen stars. Then it had more. Then it was the Stars and Bars. Now it's the Stars and Stripes again. And it will remain for a long time to come. No harm done."

"Don't reckon I am 'member all that," the child replied.

"Just tell her it will be fine."

Circades tilted his hat in the direction of the woman towards whom the child ran. He imagined she was less concerned about the tree and more interested in finding a replacement husband. The country was full of war widows.

He turned his mind back to his work and resumed carving his words into the trunk of the tree.

> *Many lifetimes were spent in pain,*
> *Searching for my soulmate only in vain,*
> *I crossed oceans and walked the world,*
> *As over the land, new flags unfurled,*
> *I felt in my solitude an invisible strain,*
> *As I crossed mountains and sailed the main.*
>
> *I've always known my soul was split in two,*
> *And no other lover was made for me but you.*
>
> *The wheel of life can spin however it sees fit,*
> *And we must be content to play our part in it.*

He closed his knife, wiped his brow, and meandered along the banks of the river.

"Oh, Pulwabi," he said, "how I miss you. What I would give to hold you in my arms and to gaze into your eyes."

He watched the city dwellers and their exhausted attempts to repair their ravaged city. And tears ran down his cheeks.

CHAPTER 2
A WATERY GRAVE

Rabies had just concluded academic lessons for the day when Anorexia arrived at the amphitheater. The five students in the current class blustered past her on their way to weapons training.

"You asked to see me?" Anorexia said.

"Yes, thank you for coming." She gestured for Anorexia to take a seat.

"It's been a long time since I sat in one of these seats—before you were even born," Anorexia said.

Rabies appreciated the sentiment but could not afford to be bogged in memory. "There is a crisis facing us," she said. "It is not just the scores of Demons we lost at Waterloo; it is the lack of new Demons we have as a result. There are five youngsters in the current class. The one before it had thirteen; the one before that sixteen."

"Many in this past generation died before having a child," Anorexia said.

"Yes. Gingivitis and Hemolytic-Uremic Syndrome wed shortly before the battle. Both were killed in action. We also had twins and triplets born on the battlefield that did not survive to return to Hell."

"The Angels have gotten extremely good at picking off our infants and their Wraiths," Anorexia said.

"Gulls on sea turtles," Rabies said, "but the real issue is this. They have already prearranged for Anthrax to marry Melioidosis. They have arranged for Cholera to marry Oral Cancer. Pancreatic Cancer has claimed the young lad Obesity once he is of maturity."

"Oral Cancer is ancient," Anorexia said. "She's two generations older."

"Precisely. We are putting a lot of pressure on these youngsters to rebuild our numbers. They would greatly benefit from... ah... some assistance."

Anorexia looked puzzled. When the point of the conversation hit, she flushed. "You wish to marry me off?"

Rabies made a conciliatory gesture. "I don't mean to offend. We simply have a lot of widows in Hell. If they—if you—would consider remarriage, we could see a massive increase in our numbers."

"Out of respect for my nephew, your loving husband who yet lives, I will forgive your naivety in understanding the heart of a woman who has lost her mate."

"I understand loss," Rabies said. She fought to control her rising temper. "I have buried four children, and many of their children."

"Yet, you do not add to our 'numbers' as you put it," Anorexia said.

"I was injured," Rabies said. Her cheeks glowed red. "The water of the Styx heals tissue but leaves scars."

"Oh, so should we marry Pneumonia off to one of the still fertile young Demons?" Anorexia asked.

Rabies did not know if her tears stemmed from anger or sadness.

"I'm just trying to do my part to help this blasted cause," she said.

Neither woman spoke for a while. They let the temperature cool.

Anorexia offered her hand. "I'm sorry, dear. I was overly defensive. You know I remember how happy your father was when you were born. You were your parents' little miracle after so much time trying to conceive."

Rabies took the proffered hand and smiled through her raging emotions.

Anorexia continued. "You know my father tried to marry me off many times before his death. Not many would even consider it a *remarriage* considering the lack of consummation—well, that doesn't matter. The point is that there is someone I love. Someone I would happily marry and have children by, but I am not in his heart. That is why I responded the way I did."

"I am so sorry," Rabies said. "Who could be so cold to you?"

Anorexia locked eyes. "Why, your father, Schizophrenia."

ZINC RECLINED IN A soft, comfortable chair and looked about at the numerous volumes in the reading room. Heaven had an expansive library, although many volumes went unopened for centuries at a time.

"I appreciate books," Zinc said. "They are a link to those who came before us. Take that volume there, the tear on the cover might have been made by a young Lord Sulfur. The page might have been dog-eared by Lead or Antimony, or even Gold."

"I suppose," Cesium said. Constance Silver stood beside one entrance; Zinc's bride, Eleanor Zinc, stood beside the other. Both women exuded a menacing demeanor as if the potential for great violence lay just under the surface of their delicate features. Zinc had been greatly surprised to discover that though petite, his new wife was a warrior—top of her class.

"I trust you understand our agreement," Zinc said.

Cesium started to respond... then stopped.

Zinc resisted the temptation to roll his eyes. "And once again, I find the need to impress upon you that a body will be at the bottom of the Eunoe. You simply have the choice of whose body it is."

"You... you want me to kill my father," Cesium said.

He then turned to his sister. "Eleanor, how can you be a part of this?"

"He would have killed me, Lawrence," she replied softly, "and he would have killed you, too, if you hadn't just received your own House and been exempt from the decree."

Zinc rose.

"My young lad," he said, "this is an opportunity. Your old man is reviled throughout Heaven, both for his cowardly display at Gettysburg and for the decision he made to save his life by sacrificing his family. He lost his honor by killing his kin. You must return it to him."

"By his death?"

"And in return, I will appoint you as head of all the Houses descended from Carbon, second only to Uranium II and me," said Zinc, as he slowly drew his dagger from its sheath. "Or I will present this generous offer to Cerium," he continued, as he rested the hand clenching the dagger upon Cesium's other shoulder, "but you know what that would mean for you."

"I'll do it," Cesium said in a whisper. "I'll do it."

Zinc sheathed the dagger and strolled to the window with the innocence of a newborn. He spoke over his shoulder.

"Then go; no time like the present."

Cesium stalked out, followed by Constance.

"Do you think she will do it?" Eleanor asked.

"She'll kill him without hesitation," Zinc said. "Everyone will assume the distraught, but estranged son killed his father in retribution, then died of wounds sustained in the attack. No one will ask too many questions. Cesium did not distinguish himself at Gettysburg either."

Zinc moved to the door. Eleanor shut it.

"Not so fast," she said. "Our business is not concluded."

Zinc kissed her. She pushed him away, a game she liked to play.

"Someone might come in," she said.

Zinc was already lifting her skirt.

"Then they might learn something," he said.

Outside the reading room, a Familiar approached intent on completing her work in the restoration room. With her hand on the knob, she heard the moans of passion from within. She dropped to a knee, peered through the keyhole of the door, and enjoyed the spectacle she would later share with her friends in great detail.

"LET US REVIEW THE strategy of targeting Angelic Leadership," Scarlet Fever said.

She looked out on her class. A *pathetic number of students— pathetic and frightening*, she thought.

"During the recent battle of Waterloo, your weapons instructor, Schizophrenia, led fifteen Demons, a squad three times the size of your class, against a contingent of one hundred and twenty Angels."

A wave of murmuring awe rippled through the room.

"I know," Scarlet Fever said, "very impressive. And the primary reason for his success was the work done by his supporting sharp-shooters, your Academic Instructor Rabies and the Demon Bornholm Disease. They knew the identities and appearances of the Angelic Lords they were facing. The price was dear. Although they killed over a hundred Angels, we sustained ten casualties, all from the group ahead of the snipers. Compare these results to Gettysburg. The same Demon, Sir Schizophrenia, was supported by a multitude of sharp-shooters and cannons. Under these circumstances, the Demons were able to ambush the enemy within their mortals and cut down thirty rank and file Angels without the loss of a single Demon."

More oohs and aaahs.

"Pay attention," Scarlet Fever said. "There is a heightened risk of failure when targeting Angelic Leadership. During the Battle of Waterloo, Anorexia attacked the Angelic Leadership with limited success and lost eleven Demons as a result."

A slender, gaunt Demon raised his hand.

"Yes, Anthrax."

"Does that mean that we have abandoned the strategy of targeting Angelic Lords?"

"Can anybody answer that?"

A brawny arm shot skyward.

"Yes. Cholera."

"The Triumvirate Council can provide instructions regarding any target or strategy. The key point of the lesson is to illustrate the high-risk nature of such a strategy."

"Yes, correct as always," Scarlet Fever said.

She immediately wished that she had simply answered the question instead of fanning the flames of the tension between the two Demons.

"Well, we will resume our discussion tomorrow," she said.

The gong sounded and the students filed out for physical training with Rabies. Scarlet Fever noticed Schitz walking through one of the hallways. She caught her old instructor's attention.

"A word, please."

"Sure."

He still had a muscular frame and his piercing eyes never looked better. Scarlet Fever felt a tingle of arousal. She understood why the young girls were mesmerized by the eligible widower.

"We don't have room for slow learners," she said.

"Go on."

"Anthrax has great potential, but it will go unutilized unless he can overcome some intellectual and martial shortcomings. You have never been bashful about your student days—how you were... ah..."

"Behind everyone else; a dullard, dense, untalented?" he asked. "Stop me when I get to the right word."

"Stop it," she said.

His eyes twinkled.

Oh, I bet he is a Demon in the bedroom as well, she thought. But she returned to the topic.

"Could you... would you... discreetly take him under your wing?"

Schitz mentally assessed Anthrax's pedigree, the son of Lymphoma and Brucellosis. His ancestry threaded back through Bornholm, Brain Cancer, Liver Cancer, and notably Spanish Influenza. Schitz had long pondered the position of the Demon of whom he was continually being warned, but Spanish Influenza was isolated.

Schitz's liaisons with the maidens of Hell had created a contingent of Demons who held a very positive view of him. Although he'd never recreated his entanglement with Bornholm, the woman appeared enamored with him whenever they crossed paths. Bornholm had saved his life at Waterloo. He'd returned the favor by selecting her as a sharpshooter. He could think of countless similar circumstances of Demons with whom he had shared intimate congress.

Spanish Influenza would not find an accomplice for any nefarious plot within the females of Hell. Schitz also had loyalty among most of the blooded males as well. Through the random assignments of the Triumvirate Council, most Demons worked with him in combat and came to respect and admire his prowess and ability to win battles. If Spanish Influenza attacked alone, he would lose; he would need support. A distant young relative would be a perfect confederate.

As Scarlet Fever pitched her idea for mentorship, Schitz was already formulating a plan to ferret out the ambitious Spanish Influenza.

"I'll do it," he said blandly, "but please get your colleague Rabies to back off with her incessant and obvious efforts to set me up with Anorexia."

Scarlet Fever chuckled. "She's your daughter and my superior. Surely I'm not fit for such a task."

"Take it or leave it, but that's my offer," Schitz said.

Scarlet Fever knew she was lucky to have a living mate in Typhoid. But in that moment of laugher and banter, with their eyes locked upon one another, she found herself increasingly enamored with the legendary warrior. She reflexively bit her lower lip. In her mind, she could see herself on her knees in front of him, servicing his every need.

She had heard from several girls that he was a voracious lover and a very distinct part of her longed to discover what they knew. Flushed with embarrassment and afraid her lust was suddenly very transparent, Scarlet Fever collected herself and bid Schitz farewell after agreeing to his terms.

A COLD WIND BLEW across Port Arthur, Manchuria. Even within the Celestial, Zinc could feel the frigid air. He had assembled the Standard Bearers of Heaven to the Russian leased port because all intelligence pointed to the outbreak of hostilities between the Russian Empire and the Empire of Japan.

Neither nation was heavily occupied by Hell or Heaven. Zinc wanted to use the conflict as a broad-scale training exercise for the Angels. Beyond the purpose of improving the lethality of the Angels, who were always less skilled than their Demonic counterparts, it also offered the opportunity for him to consolidate his hold over Heaven further.

To his great satisfaction, the circumstances surrounding Carbon VI's assassination and Cesium's death had been accepted on face value officially. Unofficially, more and more understood the power of his far-reaching, blood-soaked hand. The Angels were fearful of him; most importantly, there was no coalition of Houses vying for power. The few survivors of the Iron Houses had been seamlessly integrated into his House without much ado. Carbon had no survivors and the many Houses his line had founded were less than interested in challenging the established order.

In a series of swift and succinct maneuvers, Zinc had shattered any possible usurpers. He had arrangements in place with Uranium II, Hydrogen, and Platinum. He held sway over the newer Houses who knew that on a whim, he could easily kill them and claim their survivors as his subordinates.

For the first time in history, he sensed a unified and undisputed chain of command in Heaven. He sat at the top, then Uranium II, Hydrogen, Platinum... the rest. Survival for any House was predicated on adhering to his wishes.

Zinc knew the path to such a position was paved in blood and solidified in the sacrifice of his moral character. However, he saw his innocence as a necessary martyr for the essential outcome.

I would never challenge God, like Gold and Silver did, Zinc thought. *I have done this all so his army will be ready to annihilate Hell once and for all.*

"Now look at us," he said aloud to the Standard Bearers, "freed from politicking and dissension. Now we are ready for the next European war to usher in the last great battle. However, in the interim, we will train as never before."

AT THE BEGINNING OF the mortal Twentieth Century, devastating famine gripped the British Raj of India. The ragged, skeletonized wrecks of consumed, yet living, corpses lined the streets, gutters, missions... everywhere. Their vacant stares served as a grim reminder of the perils brought on by the absence of the monsoon. Malaria cut through the weakened mortal population like a scythe through ripened wheat.

"I touch the mothers here," Schitz said.

He lay his hand on the distended stomach of a poor woman waddling through the streets of Bombay, "and the child is born with my malady."

"I see," Anthrax said. He looked in awe at the expansive Mortal Realm.

"It's a big world, isn't it?" Schitz said.

Anthrax nodded.

"Soon, you'll be a part of it, and when we achieve the final victory, we will rule over it," Schitz said.

"I would like very much to see that day," Anthrax said with the solemnity of a priest at prayer.

"You will," Schitz said.

"I don't share your optimism." Anthrax had the natural cynicism of the young.

"Well, you're a lot like I was when I was your age," Schitz said, "and I turned out all right."

Anthrax laughed. "You say that all the time, but I find it hard to believe."

They continued to walk past the myriad of vacant living-corpses. Schitz reached out and infected a mortal with his disease.

"It is easier when their body is under such oppression," he said. "That man's madness will transfer to another almost immediately."

As predicted, a man who had been in possession of his faculties passed the afflicted and began to utter nonsensical ramblings. Schitz liked the bond with Anthrax. He had taken the youngster on as a protégé and taught him much over their time together.

Anthrax got his baptism under fire in Afghanistan, where the British battled the natives. Schitz and Anthrax fenced and sparred next to the Styx. Over time, the novice's natural talents bubbled to the surface. Schitz was pleased with the progress—and always happy to solidify another allegiance.

"My apprentice, I'm certain you recall that at the outset of our venture together I informed you of two conditions as prerequisites to your training."

"Yes," Anthrax said. He infected an Untouchable. "First, our training and our friendship were to be as secretive as possible."

The crowded street was full of the chatter of desperate people and the lowing of healthy, unmolested cattle.

"Second, you told me you would ask a favor of me. I agreed to acquiesce to it without question or explanation."

Schitz was interrupted by the angelic aura of a shrouded figure attending to the sick.

"There is no mortal fighting here," he said under his breath. "However, that does not mean that she might not break the rules."

Anthrax nodded. He felt goosebumps emerge on his arm as he contemplated the meaning of his tutor's instruction. They passed the Angel with crouching steps. She was a vicious-looking specimen. Asiatic in appearance, she had dark eyes and jet-black hair. She held Anthrax's gaze for a moment, then handed a metallic coin to the afflicted mortal, healing him.

Schitz pointed to the shadows further down the alleyway. "We are always watched," he said.

"What are those?" Anthrax asked. He beheld the shadows with fear in his heart.

"Familiars or Wraths. Always watching. If we attacked the Angel here, there would be Hell to pay," Schitz replied. Schitz turned his attention back to the Angel and winked at her as they continued past. The tension of the encounter melted away as the pair continued walking through the famine-stricken town.

"The favor," Schitz said, circling back to the previous conversation. "Would you say you are close to your betrothed?"

"Of course," Anthrax replied. "I've known Melioidosis since I was an infant. I love her deeply. I was relieved and pleased when we were selected for each other. We both were."

"Good," Schitz said. "I assume you are aware of my reputation with Academy maidens?"

Anthrax paused a second too long. "Of course," he said. His laugh was forced and nervous.

"Don't worry," Schitz said. "I will not sully your woman. But I want you to do this. Next time Spanish Influenza is near, you must threaten to kill me if I do not stay away from her. Channel the rage you would feel if anyone were to harm her."

Anthrax grimaced. "I will do as I have been asked." He paused. "I know I am not entitled to an explanation, but I would appreciate one."

Schitz smirked. "Spanish Influenza will undoubtedly approach you for some kind of duplicity directed against me."

"I would never conspire against you." The boy's voice was resolute.

"Oh, but you will," Schitz said, "and you will tell me every part of it."

"THE ANGELS ARE TRAINING like lunatics."

Mephistopheles quaked in front of the Triumvirate Council. The meeting was open to the public, and Spanish Influenza had decided to attend. He watched as the former commander, Titus, listened to the Wraith's report alongside the Demons Anorexia, Autism, and Rabies. He looked at Rabies with an ever-present sense of guilt. With her large eyes and pursed lips, he could see her mother in her features. For a moment, he found himself back in the orchard in the Levant. He could hear Rubella's voice as she tried to warn him about the Angel. He could feel the blade slicing into her abdomen. Images of her skinned remains smeared across his brain. He saw a tangle of muscles and veins laid bare under the hot near-eastern sun. There was something so haunting about the way exposed teeth appeared once the skin of the face was removed.

He shuddered and turned his attention back to the speaker. The senior Wraith continued.

"They have utilized the war between Japan and Russia to stage numerous mock exercises under real-world conditions."

"What a good idea," a Demon within the crowd of spectators commented.

"Why haven't we ever done that?" asked another.

Spanish Influenza reflected on the Angel's ingenuity. He grimaced as he contemplated the reality of facing Angels who had closed the gap in expertise between the two armies.

"What seems to be their primary area of focus?" Titus asked.

"Naval coordination," Mephistopheles replied. "They seem to be innovating the next generation of Celestial naval warfare. The age of boarding parties is over. They seem to be developing methods for inflicting casualties during duels that take part across great distances."

Spanish Influenza recalled Trafalgar with wistful nostalgia.

Oh, the age of sail, he thought. *Batter them with your cannons, corner them upon their vessel, board them by force, and lay them low; those were the days.*

"Have we attempted to impede these exercises?" Titus asked.

It was Anorexia, one of the most senior Demons who responded to Titus's question, prompting Mephistopheles to sit; Spanish Influenza beheld the Demon, his distant kin; she was quite attractive and thin. She exuded confidence and the aura of having physical strength far beyond her musculature.

"We have attacked some of their exercises," she said, "however, the need to avoid casualties has greatly restricted operations."

"It is a conundrum," Titus said. "We cannot catch up to the Angels in terms of repopulation. Yet, lowering their numbers poses an extreme risk to our already depleted forces."

"They will be planning for the next European conflict," Elise said. "They will expect us to contest that. Otherwise, they might succeed at their ever-present goal of uniting the mortal world under a single empire."

Spanish Influenza appraised the haggard expression of the senior Wraith, then shifted his attention to the Demon she had raised, Schizophrenia. He was not an unlikeable character. Many times, Spanish Influenza had felt as though he could respect and admire the senior Demon. Many times, he regretted sending Rubella to her demise. Yet, as he looked at the battle-scarred warrior, he knew that Schitz was the obstacle most directly in his path. He would not likely die in battle; if that were going to happen, it would have occurred centuries earlier. He was also not likely to be disgraced in defeat; he planned his endeavors meticulously, set attainable goals, and trained his subordinates rigorously. He had shown his steely resolve at Waterloo, where his ranks never broke or fled even though they had marched to their death. Schitz continually bathed in Angelic blood and drank deeply from the goblet of victory.

He is a formidable obstacle, Spanish thought.

The Angels were preparing for another European war. The forces of Hell were reeling from their decimation in defeating Napoleon Bonaparte. More than ever, Spanish needed a way to jump ahead of the Demons who were his senior. He looked once again at Schitz and noticed that he was standing particularly close to the Academy student, Melioidosis. Spanish Influenza watched as the weapons instructor whispered something; the girl blushed and giggled. Schitz ran his hand ever so subtly along her back.

He is relentless, and yet I have never seen him at the Isle of Neutrality.

Suddenly, Anthrax moved through the crowd of Demons, Wraiths, and Priests attending the meeting, and pushed his way between Schizophrenia and the young maid. The young Demon aggressively interposed himself between the senior and the female he was engaged to wed. Although, Spanish's first instinct was amusement at the plight of the youngster, he saw an opportunity—an enemy of his enemy.

"You seem to really have taken things in hand," God said.

The Eunoe flowed through Heaven, a soothing sight for the Ultimate Commander and his chief general.

"I don't always approve of your methods, but I am pleased with your success."

Zinc glanced at the river, his regular depository for Angelic corpses.

Uranium I, Iron III, Carbon VI, and Palladium are in there somewhere, he thought.

Having perfected a system of ambushing and disposing of rival Angels, he and Eleanor (fully in agreement with his scheme) identified and dispatched opponents with regularity. He sometimes suspected his wife was settling childhood scores instead of treason, but her willingness to assist him outweighed any trivial ethical considerations.

Regardless of the cause, Angels who were not emphatically supportive of both Zinc and Uranium II disappeared like so much dust in a high wind, as did Familiars who pressed too much to uncover their fate.

"You rule with a rod of iron," God said.

"I do what is required," Zinc said. His voice was flat and emotionless, much like what was left of his soul.

"Indeed," God said, "but what of mercy?"

Zinc stopped and bowed. "If I have done wrong, sire, I accept whatever punishment you would have me experience."

"Oh relax," God said. He tapped Zinc on either shoulder with his scepter as though knighting him. "You're doing a great job—one I do not wish to encounter. I always hated the infernal jockeying for power. And I think that is long dead now."

"Do you?"

"Quite," God said. He smirked. "It's all buried in the river."

A caterpillar of dread crept up Zinc's spine, but he did not speak.

"Look," God said, "if this is the cost of unity, I accept it. Just promise me you haven't dealt so roughly with your own brethren out of wrath."

"That would be ugly," Zinc said.

"I don't like ugly." God slowed his pace a little, a sure sign he wanted to be heard.

A sudden burst of confidence hit Zinc. "I could not have completed the realignment any other way."

"Next steps?"

"We want to pull the Demons into a pitched conflict where our superior trained Angels will defeat them once and for all."

"Can you do it?"

"Yes." Zinc met God's gaze and never wavered. "I have removed from our ranks any and all social climbers, any individuals whose interests were aimed toward personal advancement. We now have a corps of Houses focused solely on victory. They are all aligned with Uranium II and me."

"You overlook Platinum," God said. "He hates Uranium II."

"I control him," Zinc said, "and all the others. We will present the Demons with a global war. They will either have to come out and fight, or they will hide. If they hide, we will unify the world under an empire we control. Either way, Satan and his minions will perish."

"We are in a good place to execute such plans," God said. He walked a few steps in silence. Zinc knew better than to interrupt. Then, "I want you to give it ten mortal years before you execute. Plan every aspect of your strategy to the minutest detail. We cannot afford for this to fall through."

Zinc signaled his assent with a head bob. "Ten years will not give them enough time to replenish their numbers."

God adopted a dismissive tone. "Even if they do, such a hurriedly assembled force will surely be inferior to our newly trained cadre."

"The board will be set in our favor," Zinc said.

God veered off the path. The meeting was over. He called over his shoulder. "Finish this. I grow weary of the struggle."

THE SMOKE RING FLOATED through the air, perfect in symmetry until it dissolved into nothingness.

"Let's see Michelangelo try that!"

Spanish Influenza reclined on one of the leather sofas and looked at Anthrax.

"You whine too much, my friend."

Anthrax grimaced, then coughed. "What do they call this stuff?" he asked.

Spanish Influenza launched a series of three circles in a row. "Cerberus fur," he said. He leaned back and let the drug drive him towards numbness.

"They ought to call it Caesar's Ass," Anthrax said.

"More complaints," Spanish said. "Relax... take a few more hits. Sex is amazing on this stuff."

"None for me," Anthrax said. "This place makes me nervous."

He jerked his head at a cluster of male and female Angels who were drinking and smoking.

"They aren't here for combat, my friend," Spanish Influenza said. "They are here for the same purpose we are—get high and get laid."

"I'm married, and my wife is with child, triplets actually," Anthrax said.

"Your mate who made you a cuckold by means of the weapons instructor?" Spanish Influenza said. "The way I see it, you're free to indulge in anything you desire."

A shapely Angel pointed to Anthrax and made an unmistakable gesture with her tongue. He inhaled deeply from the pipe, and immediately regretted the decision.

"This stuff makes me dizzy."

"Don't fight it," Spanish said. "Now, back to the purpose at hand. You refuse to have sex even after your wife gave her maidenhood to Schizophrenia? You should be very angry."

"I am angry, but with him... not her. She was impressionable. He was fully aware of what he was doing, and he knew she was promised to me."

I need this dolt to trust me, Spanish Influenza thought.

"You know," he said, "when I rise to power, those who stand with me will be richly rewarded. I presume you would like to avoid the sort of suicide missions Schitz used at Waterloo."

"Is that a trick question?"

Spanish handed his pipe to a scantily clad attendant. "Another, please, and one for my friend as well." He looked at Anthrax. "When I lead the armies of Hell, I will use sound strategy, I will not needlessly sacrifice men and women for my own glory, and, as I mentioned, I will be very generous to my friends."

Anthrax's pupils looked like soup bowls. "I accept."

The two clasped hands.

"With the business out of the way, let's make some new friends— not the handshaking kind."

ORAL CANCER PLODDED THROUGH the South African bush and groaned. "I feel like a brood sow."

"It will be worse for our babies," Pancreatic Cancer replied.

Melioidosis shuffled alongside, her hands under her protruding belly. "How so?"

"Satan wants the swiftest repopulation Hell has ever seen," Pancreatic Cancer said.

Oral Cancer stopped walking. She panted for breath, hands on her knees. "Let's see," she said. "One mortal year for a Demon to reach academic age; four mortal years to finish the Academy." The timeline had accelerated drastically following the elevation of human consciousness. The maturation that had once taken centuries now took place over a mere handful of years.

Pancreatic Cancer patted her friend on the back and prodded her back into the march. "Satan wants the Triumvirate to determine marriages and have the pairs begin breeding even while they are in the Academy," she said.

"Doesn't that violate the Devine Dictum?" Oral Cancer asked. "Weren't we supposed to be able to choose our spouses?"

"There's a clause that allows the interests of Hell to supersede individual choice," Pancreatic said.

All three women shook their heads.

The little group was well protected; their unborn children represented the future hopes of Hell. The plan was to find the Boer commandos and launch an attack against a British outpost to allow the births to occur during combat.

Spanish Influenza led the defense contingent. His mind was elsewhere as they scouted the bush for the Boer holdouts, who had long been defeated by the forces of the Crown.

The Angels always grab the mortal empires, Spanish Influenza thought.

They came to the Boer outpost.

"Quickly now," Spanish said.

The Demons rushed into hosts. The occupied hosts ceased the

tasks and activities in which they had been engaged and stepped into the brush. The birthing process was brutal on the mortals. The possessed woman became pregnant—at full term—at once. She died following the birth.

The ambush was straightforward. The possessed Boers fired on the British forces with merciless accuracy while the possessed women shrieked in the pangs of labor and delivery. The Wraiths arrived and shepherded away the young. The minute the children were gone, the forces of Hell fell back to the camp where they constructed departure portals.

There were no Angels within the Crown Forces, and if there had been any Familiars observing, they kept their distance. Spanish Influenza stood in the queue waiting to pass the Priests as they performed the Return Ritual and thought about his ascension. By his count, he was the seventh oldest Demon. He was successor to his Aunt Cancer, the sole survivor of her cohort, who had been preceded by her Uncle Pneumonia and his wife Rabies. That duo was outdated by the siblings Autism and Anorexia, and of course, Schizophrenia. Despite being two generations younger than Schizophrenia, Spanish Influenza was rapidly approaching the apex of Hell's power. When he was a youngster, Bubonic Plague and others manipulated him, but they were gone, and he remained.

He passed the Priests, made the sign of the pentagram, and strode through the Great Hall. He glanced at the statues erected in honor of former victorious Demons: Fever, Tuberculosis, Bubonic Plague, Syphilis, Schizophrenia.

There was even one dedicated to Waterloo, a monument the Devil had been reluctant to authorize. Spanish stared at a marble Titus commanding a cannon crew comprised of Smallpox, Meningitis, Streptococcal, and Encephalitis. Spanish Influenza felt conflicted as he gazed upon the stone figure, representing his mother, who was interred below the monument.

I don't want to be a cold, lifeless lump of non-decaying flesh, I want to be in charge.

He knew he was considered to be one of Hell's fiercest warriors.

No one hated him enough to oppose his ascent to the pinnacle of power once Schitz was removed. Spanish Influenza thought about his confederate, Anthrax. The young Demon had just been announced as the valedictorian of his Academy class.

He's a marvelous choice. He's smart, talented, and a direct descendant of mine via Liver Cancer, Brain Cancer, Bornholm, then Lymphoma, and he hates Schitz.

Spanish Influenza touched his mother's marble brow and walked to his room.

My plan is perfect!

FROM INSIDE THE BODY of a parishioner, Anthrax looked around the interior of the confessional booth. "It is not always pleasant being in his company," he said. "He is a Demon of contradictions."

On the other side of the screen, Father Schitz said, "You're doing a good job. I'm certain you have gained his trust. You just have to hang in there. I don't believe he will make a move against me until the start of the next great conflict. As soon as I learn his plans, then you'll be out."

"I'm concerned," Anthrax said. He hoped his whispers could not be heard outside the small cubicle. "He is incredibly mistrustful of those around him. I believe he will develop schemes separate from whatever plans involve me."

"An astute observation and assessment," Schitz said. His voice reflected great pride. "I'm very impressed with the manner in which you comport yourself."

"Thank you," Anthrax said. "It's just a lot to deal with—new children, all the talk of the next war, and these machinations."

Schitz recalled the turmoil of his younger years and suppressed a laugh. "You have to compartmentalize your life," he said. "You cannot allow one concern to impact the next. When you are with your family, you must be with your family. When you are with Spanish Influenza, you must be with Spanish Influenza. When you are at war, you must be at war. Then find time to be with your own mind and your own thoughts."

"That's why you go by the river?"

"Absolutely," Schitz said. "The balance of mind is essential for the warrior. If you allow emotion and other concerns to pollute your mind, there will be no way for you to master your opponent. It is harder than it sounds, and I am in no way fully adept at it myself. However, understanding is the first step toward the completion of any task."

Anthrax sat with elbows on knees and chin in his hands. "Why did we meet in a church?"

"I love churches," Schitz said. He closed his eyes and envisioned the pillars and arches of the Cathedral of Notre-Dame de Paris in which they sat. "Besides, there's something enjoyable to me about traipsing about in the enemy's backyard."

Anthrax could not stifle his laugh. "If only you knew how similar you and Spanish Influenza are."

Schitz shrugged. "If he or I were slightly different, he probably would not be planning to kill me; unfortunately, that is the reality, and we will deal with it in due time."

Schitz put his mouth close to the screen. "Ten Hail Marys for your penance," he said.

He snickered and departed the confessional.

ZINC STOOD ALONG THE banks of the Eunoe and thought about the corpses he had deposited in the depths of the river.

It will have been worth it when we are finally victorious.

He squatted and let the water rush over his hand. By itself, even a few drops of water from the sacred river could drive an Angel mad. Its healing properties were released only when used to make Manna.

Zinc wiped his hand on his robe and put his damp fingers to his lips.

Aren't we all mad already?

CHAPTER 3

ENTANGLED

"¿Donde mierda estamos?"

Álvarez Cabrera, exhausted and irritated, muttered from the front of his cadre of soldiers.

"I have no idea where the fuck we are, Colonel," Lieutenant Rafaella Valencia said.

She peered over the barren Moroccan landscape. The soldiers had departed Melilla intending to outmaneuver the forces of Mohamed Amezian El Chadly; however, the night march had turned into a debacle. Unaccustomed to the rocky terrain, the soldiers struggled—their confidence and stamina bled out with every step.

Anaphylaxis groaned from within the colonel. "These mortals are idiots."

Next to him, Stomach Cancer responded from her host, the lieutenant. "I don't know if we're much better."

The young Demon leading the training foray glanced at his peer. She was smiling.

"What makes you say that?" he asked.

"Well," she replied, "the upperclassmen have been switching through this commander since we left the outpost, but nobody has taken the initiative to lead him away from this idiotic path. Now we are stretched out across the lowlands."

Stomach Cancer gestured along the dispersed file of Spanish soldiers. The bolts on their rifles glistened in the desert moonlight; their khaki uniforms were floating apparitions.

Rabies, the instructor on this exercise, snapped a sharp whisper from the Celestial.

"You two are always going back and forth!"

Stomach Cancer blushed. She was generally quite reserved even in front of her academy crush, Anaphylaxis.

"She makes a good point," Anaphylaxis said. "We are extremely vulnerable on this low ground; a lot of exposure."

Rabies looked about the canyon's sheer cliffs. Echoes from the crunch of leather boots and the clatter of weapons and gear resonated like pebbles shaken in a can.

"Not so stealthy, are they?" Rabies asked.

How in the world has a nation as mighty as Spain that marched across half of the New World deteriorated into this pathetic bunch barely in control of a small swath of North Africa?

She had the same concerns about her Demonic students. She had three academic classes in the field for a simple night march. Each one managed to put their hosts in a dangerous, indefensible position. There was no coordination; no one grasped the inherent risks involved with every trip to the Mortal Realm.

What has happened to the army of Hell? Since Waterloo, Satan has imposed tight restrictions on combat operations. The centennial approaches and still we feel the ripple effects in the Triumvirate Council.

Rabies turned her attention back to the youngsters she was entrusted with safekeeping. The Triumvirate's decision to assign marriage partners and force procreation at the first sign of puberty had resulted in a veritable explosion in Hell's population. Anthrax, Melioidosis, Cholera, Oral Cancer, and Obesity had produced a class of nine. Now there were three sets of triplets: Breast Cancer, Ebola, and Elephantiasis; Sinusitis, Dyscalculia, and Depression; Anxiety, Fibromyalgia, and Hypertension. This trio of trios produced its own class of nine: Streptococcal Pharyngitis, COPD, Muscular Dystrophy, Tay-Sachs, Multiple Sclerosis, Explosive Bowel Disease, Sociopathy, Atheism, and Communism. The matrons of Hell finally produced a class of double digits when they gave birth to Stomach Cancer, Colon Cancer, Marfan Syndrome, Charcot-Marie, Nieman-Pick, Keratoconus, Keratoglobus, Anaphylaxis, Hand-Schuller-Christian, and Wilson's Disease.

Hell now boasted fifty-five fighting Demons, only seven short of the pre-Waterloo level. Still, none of the twenty-eight occupying the column of Spanish soldiers had ever seen combat.

Rabies's sixth sense warned her of an ambush. She could feel the weight of eyes; the enemy's malicious intent pricked her like a pin.

She spoke to Stomach Cancer sotto voce. "The Spaniards are done for. I just don't know if there are Angels in their midst."

Rabies swallowed with trepidation at the thought of the Angels that generally occupied Northern Africa. The Wraiths had identified them as Thallium and Beryllium. Like the mortal inhabitants of the Sahara, they were neither as dark as their sub-Saharan counterparts nor as light as Europeans. Rabies recalled the well-known Angel that had mothered the Angels of the region—The Destroyer, The Demon Killer, or The Savage.

Her proper name was Lady Hydrogen.

Mauser Model 1893

The report of a rifle rang out over the canyon; a hailstorm of rifle fire followed. The Berbers held the high ground, and, as Stomach Cancer had noted, the Spaniards were at a distinct disadvantage.

"Protect any fallen," Rabies shouted. She ran forward in the Celestial, issuing commands to the Demons.

"Return fire on the ridge!"

It's an active training exercise now, she thought.

She stepped into the body of a Catalan woman and raised her rifle toward the cliffs, expertly dispatching a shadow perched on the valley's edge. Rabies appreciated the accuracy of the 1893 Spanish Mauser. Even more, she liked the quick reload afforded by the bolt action. She ejected the cartridge and considered the superiority of the modern weapon to its muzzle-loader ancestors.

Her assessment of the mortal weaponry was interrupted by the emergence of several hazy light auras on the cliffs overlooking the valley.

"Mierda!"

Rabies knew that a wholesale departure would invite pursuit from the Angels. Something clicked in her mind.

The Angels were not expecting this many Demons, and they have no idea these are all raw recruits.

Her orders were swift and decisive.

"Ebola, take your squad in the Celestial, fall back to the valley entrance and take the Eastern Heights. Anxiety, take your squad in the Celestial to the Western Heights."

The Demons she selected were nearly graduates.

'Sociopathy, COPD, you keep up your rate of fire on those possessed mortals over there."

Those were the best members of the middle class.

"Charcot-Marie and Colon Cancer, move towards the outpost and begin readying return portals."

She desperately hoped that all the cadets remembered the plan for evacuation from the area.

Those that had not been cut down by the initial barrage of Berber fire found cover behind boulders and began to return fire. Rabies saw an advancing contingent of four Angels. With the Demons she had dispersed to the flanks and the rear area, she was left with a unit of four. The Angels were visibly perplexed by the evenly matched squads. They usually enjoyed vastly superior numbers.

The Celestial conflict was clearly tipping in favor of the Demons. A quick glance up to the rocky heights above the valley revealed that the Angels were being pushed back on both sides. Rabies knew the Angelic thrust down the valley center was an act of desperation to cover their comrades' retreat. If the Demonic force continued unmolested through the valley, the Angels would have no escape route.

This is a delaying tactic, she thought. *If we back off after a skirmish, so will the Angels.*

Then...

A female Angel stalked across the field with arrogant self-assurance. Everything about her screamed, "I cannot be bested." A tremor of fear flicked at the base of Rabies's neck. She could not take her eyes off the wild eyes of the approaching specter. The Angel wore a tight robe; her toned physique was obvious. But what shook Rabies was the cape—familiar and sickening.

That's my mother's skin!

Rabies retched, her sickness coming as if from her shoes. She vomited until there was nothing left, then dry heaved several times. She chugged some water and immediately regurgitated it.

The sickness gave way to a growing rage, but Rabies did not forget the burden of command. She shouted orders to Anaphylaxis.

"Sound the retreat!"

The order echoed down the line. Rabies drew her Celestial sword and stepped toward the foe.

The encounter was ferocious and brief. The Angels accompanying The Destroyer rushed forward in unison. Rabies blocked the swipe of one blade, then another. She sidestepped a third thrust before driving her sword through the middle of an Angel's chest. A Celestial axe whooshed over her ducking head. When Rabies stood, Lady Hydrogen was glaring at her.

"I won't miss again," The Destroyer said.

Rabies was attacked by another member of The Destroyer's cadre. She tripped the Angel and flung him into his comrades, then rushed forward, disarmed another Angel, and stabbed him with his own sword. Slicing through his intestines, the blade remained in Rabies's hand. She was falling back with her students when she saw a Spaniard crouched against a boulder. It was a woman.

What luck!

She leapt into the mortal. Maria Arroyo—a good possession—then broke into a run across the loose gravel of the valley floor. Over her shoulder, she heard the footsteps of her Celestial pursuers. She was sure she could escape them in her host. However, she had seen this type of pursuit many times before; if her host were killed, the Angels would fall upon her in an instant.

Rabies zigzagged through the valley as a few Berbers fired in her direction. Suddenly, she spotted Anaphylaxis running towards her in the Celestial.

"I couldn't leave you," he said.

"Run, you idiot," Rabies shouted.

The youngster realized the situation he had stumbled upon and leapt into a mortal cowering behind a boulder. The two Demons exited the valley, still closely pursued by the Angels; a contingent of mounted Berbers approached atop galloping horses.

"Fuck, they'll shoot down these Spaniards," she said.

"From this distance?"

Rabies looked back. Lady Hydrogen was pursuing them in the Celestial, her sole remaining comrade having diverted his run toward the approaching Berbers.

"Pick off whichever mortal he possesses," Rabies said. "I'll lead the dangerous one away from you."

Anaphylaxes turned and dropped to one knee. Within his host, he was afflicted by the thoughts of Private Caceres, a cowardly excuse for a man, let alone a soldier. An older Demon would have been more adept at coping with a host's desire to flee, but Anaphylaxes was inexperienced. He was beset by the mortal's erratic thoughts. He felt the warm, wet sensation of urine running down his host's thigh.

The cavalry continued its charge. The Demon attempted to steady the shaken mortal; he aimed at the Berber most likely to be possessed by an Angel. He saw the Heavenly warrior's aura slide into the horseman and pulled the trigger as smoothly as he could manage given his host's panic.

"Hijo de puta," he said, cursing the mortal as the shot sailed wide.

He yanked at the bolt while the Angel fired from atop his horse. Anaphylaxes watched in horror as the Berber's shot struck Rabies's mortal squarely in the back.

The bullet felt like a hand reaching into Rabies's midsection and clutching her by the lung; a hot, merciless sensation of choking. She rolled out of the mortal, narrowly avoiding a departure seizure. She turned, drew her sword, and blocked a crashing blow from her pursuer.

Rachael's forward momentum carried her into Rabies; the pair bowled over in a heap. The Angel made it to her feet first and kicked Rabies in the ribs with a crunching strike. Through her winded agony, Rabies saw an unfazed Anaphylaxis running towards her.

"I'll kill him first and make you watch," Rachael said.

Despite the pain of her broken ribs, Rabies hauled herself to her feet and launched herself toward Lady Hydrogen. The Angel threw her to the ground. Rabies grabbed, caught a shoulder, and pulled Lady Hydrogen down as well. Rabies wrenched a hand free, drew a dagger, and sliced Lady Hydrogen across the torso.

The Angel shrieked. A sneer creased her face. Then she head-butted Rabies. Anaphylaxis arrived, out of breath and red-faced.

"Go!" Rabies shouted. "It's all right; go!"

Anaphylaxis fled the field. Lady Hydrogen punched Rabies in the head and chest. Rabies lay defenseless. Rachael held her sword aloft.

"I'll skin you like I did your mother. You'll make a lovely matched set. And just like her, you were undone by one of your own. At least I have the pleasure of stabbing you in the heart instead of the back."

From her vantage point in a cluster of shrubs, Elise heard the Angel's words with as much shock as though she had been struck by one of the Berber's rifles. She gasped and shut her eyes as The Destroyer drove her blade up to the hilt in Rabies's chest.

"I might not be able to fight her to save you," said Elise under her breath, "but I will save your body."

Rachael stood and turned to speak to her colleague who had arrived having just departed the Berber horseman. While they talked, Elise flashed across the open ground and spirited the body away. When she was safely hidden, Elise sat and gasped for air.

I do not know what to do with the information, she thought, *but now I know for sure that Spanish Influenza killed Rubella.*

ELISE CLUNG TO SCHITZ'S robe.

"There's something I need to tell you about Spanish Influenza."

"I have heard enough warnings about that pompous ass," Schitz said.

He didn't break stride and virtually dragged the diminutive Wraith across the Great Hall.

Else recognized his anger as a mask for his grief over Rabies's death.

"You lost your daughter, I know," Elise said. "I am as devastated as you, but you must hear this."

She lost her grip and skidded along the flagstone. "Please—I beseech you."

Schitz stopped. He bent over and helped the Wraith to her feet.

"I'm sorry, Mama," he said.

"I'm taking a group of them to the Kongo. The Portuguese are fighting the locals there."

Elise dusted off her robe. "Maybe with some luck, you'll encounter the Angel that killed Rubella and Rabies," she said.

"It's a training mission," Schitz said.

"I still need to tell you something," Elise said. "It's about Spanish Influenza."

"Don't bother," Schitz said. "I heard it all before."

He stormed off.

IT WAS A WARM, sunny day in June, and the streets of Sarajevo were lined with raucous crowds in anticipation of the archduke's visit. The morning had already been marred by violence. A bomb had exploded along Archduke Ferdinand's motorcade route and killed twenty.

Zinc and Uranium II walked abreast of the cars.

"How did you miss?" Zinc asked.

"I have no idea," Uranium II said from within the Celestial.

"It doesn't matter." Zinc was within the body of one of the Serbian assassins. "These morons have publicized the parade route to ensure a crowd. You would think the anarchists would be able to assassinate him even without our help."

"What's the plan?" Uranium II asked.

"Simple," Zinc said. "I'm going to shoot him. Keep an eye out for Demons Your bomb turned this into an active warzone. They can legitimately target us now."

Zinc felt vulnerable with only his fellow Supreme Commander and a handful of Angels. However, his operation to kill a mortal was not overly popular in Heaven because it sent souls to the Styx rather than the Eunoe. Though few loved the method, no one doubted the mission's necessity.

Zinc had spent years possessing various diplomats and heads of state to devise a spider web of alliances across the European map. These bonds would be the fuse. Once lit, the continent—no, the world—would explode. Zinc intended to supply the ignition spark.

"Quick," Zinc said, "possess that driver. He will say they are going the wrong way. That should stop them."

Zinc grinned as the black, open-topped Gräf & Stift 28/32 PS came to a halt a few meters from where he stood. He could feel the young man's heart pounding in his chest. The summer air warmed his skin. He heard the buzz of the crowd. He reveled in the moment.

This is the last instant that the mortal world and the Celestial Realm will be innocent of the ways of truly modern war, he thought.

The gravity of the moment made his steps leaden. He stepped into the street and drew a lightweight FN 1910 semiautomatic pistol. He raised the firearm and shot the archduke in the throat. With the shot still ringing and the crowd noise rising to a corporate scream, he sighted the duchess.

The mortal's mind rebelled. His host wished only to harm the heir to the Austro-Hungarian throne, not his wife. Zinc hungered for the additional shock that the double murder would provide.

Ferdinand was clutching at his jugular when Zinc fired into Duchess Sophia's torso. She flopped onto the beleaguered duke's legs. The two morphed into a heaving, exsanguinating wreck.

Zinc stepped into the Celestial. Freed from his control, the mortal attempted to turn his weapon on himself, but the crowd pummeled him into submission.

Having unleashed hell on Earth, Zinc, Uranium II, and their security contingent passed through a portal and returned to Heaven.

NEWS FROM SARAJEVO DROVE both the Triumvirate Council and councils all over the Mortal Realm into emergency sessions. Titus drummed his fingers on the table and cursed his existence. On most occasions, he enjoyed being the High Priest, but he hated when he was called on to serve as "Satan's Voice."

Somehow, I get blamed for this, he thought.

The table of the Triumvirate was surrounded by a mob of Demons, Wraiths, and Priests. If ever there was a time for an appearance by "The Man," this was it. Titus glanced toward the door to the Devil's chamber. No one emerged.

He began slowly. "It is the will of Lord Satan that this will be the last meeting of the Triumvirate Council."

Bedlam erupted.

"Order!" he shouted. "Our Lord recognizes the monumental struggle facing us in the days to come and has laid the foundation for an almighty victory by freeing you from the constraints of the Council."

Titus did not put much faith in the idiotic rationale for abandoning the Council, but he did his best to sell it. Perhaps Satan had lost confidence in its ability to deliver decisive victories. Maybe he did not want to choose Rabies's successor on the Council. Regardless, Titus was charged to present the new plan of organization.

Titus cleared his throat. "Before I continue, I would like to thank my colleagues who have served upon this Council: Erin, Desdemona, Mephistopheles, Elise, Anubis, Anorexia, Autism, and those who came before you. You have given yourselves in the crafting of worthy strategies, and I cannot thank you enough. It has been my honor to serve with you."

The clapping started slowly, a few solitary palms slapping together. The sound rose in intensity until the chamber shook with thunderous applause. Titus felt the corners of his eyes burn, and the back of his throat tighten.

The old Wraith Mephistopheles rose to his feet and embraced the Priest.

"Thank you for that," he said into his ear. "I would rather have your recognition than a Knight's Pentagram."

Titus raised his hand to reestablish decorum. He glanced down at the scroll on the table.

"Satan has handed down an ambitious and remarkable plan," he said. Those who had survived Waterloo, understood his sardonic tone. He continued, "The Mortal Realm will be divided into areas of responsibility. One will consist of Europe, Africa, and the Near East. The second will be North and South America. Asia and Oceania comprise the final area. Schizophrenia has been named the Commander of Europe-Africa-Levant. Autism the Commander of the Americas, and Anorexia the Commander of Asia."

Europe, Africa, & the Near East

Schizophrenia .... Commander

Pneumonia .... Europe Lieutenant Commander
Liver Cancer .... Squad Leader Eastern Europe
Melioidosis and Anxiety .... Eastern Europe Squad
Brain Cancer .... Squad Leader Western Europe
Cholera and Fibromyalgia ..... Western Europe Squad

Scarlet Fever .... Africa Lieutenant Commander
Leukemia .... Squad Leader Africa
Oral Cancer and
Hypertension .... Africa Squad

Hepatitis .... Levant Lieutenant Commander
Bornholm .... Levant Squad Leader
Obesity and
Streptococcal Pharyngitis .... Levant Squad

Schitz's attention perked up at his assignment to the most strategic and important regions of Europa and the Holy Land. He thought about the plan. There was still a Triumvirate of sorts in place. Satan had simply removed authority from the Wraiths and Priests. He had forced Schitz into a heightened leadership role, the equivalent of a seat on the Council.

Excitement welled up inside Schitz for the first time since Rabies's death. The challenge of commanding such a vital region with authority to make decisions, strategic and tactical, awakened within him the strong, undying drive to show the world his worth, to demonstrate that he was neither a dunce nor a coward. Schitz listened intently as the lieutenant commanders were named: Pneumonia for Europe, Scarlet Fever for Africa, and Hepatitis for the Levant all fell under his command. Cancer was named Lieutenant Commander of North America and Typhoid Lieutenant Commander of South America. Lung Cancer would assume responsibilities in South Asia, while Spanish Influenza, the Demon everybody insisted on warning Schitz about, was appointed Lieutenant Commander of the Far East.

Spanish has a very prestigious area to cover, Schitz thought, *vast lands in China, an emerging empire in Japan. He is not cunning enough to hide his ambition. I will see him coming and so will everyone else.* Next, the squad leaders were announced; Liver Cancer was to lead a squad covering Eastern Europe, comprising Melioidosis and Anxiety. Brain Cancer was to lead a squad assigned to Western Europe, consisting of Cholera and Fibromyalgia. Leukemia was appointed to the squad allocated to cover Africa, with Oral Cancer and Hypertension. Bornholm was assigned to lead the squad covering the Holy Land with Obesity and Streptococcal Pharyngitis. Schitz felt very happy with the Demons he had been assigned to command. He immediately realized that he had received none of the newest recruits. Although this was a relief, it also filled him with concern as to who would be commanding the most novice of Demons.

North and South America

Autism .... Commander

Cancer .... North America Lieutenant Commander

Pancreatic Cancer .... North America Squad Leader

Breast Cancer & COPD .... North America Squad

Typhoid .... South America Lieutenant Commander

Lymphoma .... South America Squad Leader

Ebola and Muscular
Dystrophy .... South America Squad

It was announced that Autism's North American Squad would be led by Pancreatic Cancer, who would lead Breast Cancer and COPD. His South American Squad would be led by Lymphoma, and contained Ebola, and Muscular Dystrophy. Anorexia's China Squad would be led by Anthrax and contained Elephantiasis and Tay-Sachs. Anorexia's Japan and Eastern Russia squad was assigned to Hysteria, who would lead Sinusitis and Multiple Sclerosis. Her India squad would be allocated to Dysgraphia and contained Dyscalculia and Explosive Bowel Disease. Her Oceania squad would be led by Skin Cancer and contain Depression and Sociopathy.

Schitz's attention perked up when he realized that Anthrax would be one of Spanish Influenza's squad leaders. He wondered if Spanish Influenza was favored by Satan. If such were the case, it would have the potential to complicate things greatly; it would raise the likelihood that Spanish Influenza could recruit Anthrax to his side through lucrative incentives and would mean that Spanish Influenza would have a large deal of freedom to act however he desired.

It is too much to be a coincidence, Schitz thought. However, the most surprising assignment to Schitz did not involve Anthrax; it was the creation of a Strategic Reserve which consisted of a squad led by Atheism that contained Stomach Cancer, Colon Cancer, Marfan, Charcot-Marie, and Nieman-Pick, and a squad led by Communism that included Keratoconus, Keratoglobus, Anaphylaxis, Hand-Schuller-Christian, and Wilson's Disease. Schitz was baffled by the conservatism of assigning the newest class to a reserve role on the eve of such a major conflict. Yet, the wisdom of such a move was apparent; the newest Demons were the least prepared and had just begun rearing children. They were of much more value to Hell continuing their procreation than they were dead upon the battlefield.

Asia and Oceania

Anorexia .... Commander

Lung Cancer ..... South Asia, Oceania Lieutenant Commander

Dysgraphia .... India Squad Leader

Dyscalculia and
Explosive Bowel Disease .... India Squad

Skin Cancer .... Oceania Squad Leader

Depression & Sociopathy .... Oceania Squad

Spanish Influenzac .... Far East Lieutenant
Commander

Anthrax .... China Squad Leader

Elephantiasis & Tay-Sachs .... China Squad

Hysteria .... Japan & Eastern Russia Squad Leader

Sinusitis & Multiple
Sclerosis .... Japan and Eastern Russia Squad

Strategic Reserve

Atheism .... Squad Leader
Stomach Cancer, Colon Cancer, Marfan, Charcot-
Marie and Nieman-Pick

Communism .... Squad Leader

Keratoconus, Keratoglobus, Anaphylaxis, Hand
-Schuller-Christian, and Wilson's Disease.

Autism rushed to Schitz at the conclusion.

"They always act like I'm stupid," Autism said.

"What are you talking about?" Schitz asked.

Autism moaned like a child being forced to eat vegetables. "They've given me half the amount they gave you and Anorexia."

"The Americas are easy," Schitz said. "Don't take it as an insult. Not much of this war is going to be fought there. Besides, we are undefeated in the Americas."

"Yeah?" Autism said. His mood lightened.

"Yeah," Schitz said. "I defeated Gold and Silver, we won the Spanish Conquest, Queen Anne's War, the American Revolution, and the American Civil War. You are set up for success."

"Thanks," Autism said. "Nothing like a little pressure."

Both laughed and Schitz waved for Anorexia to come over. Schitz looked at the siblings.

"I hope you both fully appreciate your new position. On the Council, the Wraiths and Priests were your equals. Now you are their superiors. Come," he said, "there is a lot happening, but we must take a little time to celebrate. Meet me at the river's edge in ten minutes."

The pair trotted off. Schitz called after them.

"And do not forget the Brew."

SPANISH INFLUENZA SAT ALONE within his new room. He found there was a considerable amount of peace that accompanied being a widower.

A partner is overrated when I can find what I need at the Isle of Neutrality and then return here for blissful solitude, he thought.

His official appointment elevated him to a room formerly occupied by Schizophrenia.

"Soon," Spanish Influenza said aloud, "this will not be the only thing of his I possess."

Others reveled in their promotions and assignments. Spanish Influenza spent his time comparing his strengths to those of his rivals. He was level in authority with Cancer and Scarlet Fever, two valedictorians and respected Academy instructors, as well as fellow classmates, Hepatitis, Lung Cancer, and Typhoid. Spanish Influenza thought of his Academy cohort. Many of them were still alive. In fact, they represented the highest number and highest percentage of living graduates of any class save those sheltered from combat.

"They are strong warriors," he said to himself. "When the older ones have died off, they will be the heart of Hell's Army."

He stood only two steps removed from supreme authority. First, he would become a commander, then the not-yet-created-rank of Overall Ruler. He did not dream of challenging Satan for power over Hell, even though the idea carried a certain appeal. He would be satisfied to lord over all the other Demons, and to report only to Satan.

Then I will never be helpless or powerless, he thought.

A knock on the door interrupted his scheming. He had requested all the literature available regarding the Angels frequently seen in China, Japan, and Eastern Russia. An ancient Wraith stood at the door. She clutched the leather-bound volumes in the grasp of her singular arm.

"They didn't have any full-bodied Wraiths available?" he asked.

"I volunteered to bring them," she said.

"Why?"

The withered old woman appeared to grow a few inches. Her smile was broad and devoid of anything other than malevolence. "To tell you this. I know you delivered Rubella to the Angel that killed her."

The books clattered to the floor. Spanish Influenza considered killing the Wraith. He imagined snapping her neck, but he knew Wraiths were quick. Besides, there was no telling who else knew.

"I might not have evidence," she said, "but I know what happened, and I will ensure that you pay the price for your treason."

He feigned indignation. "If you accuse me without proof, I have the right to challenge you to a duel. I don't think you want that, you deformed, old hag."

She's not told anyone, he thought.

"Indeed," she replied, "that is why you are the first to know. Once I have evidence, you will be the last to find out."

She melted away into the shadow beyond the doorway of his room. He scooped up the books on the Asiatic Angels.

"I have to focus," he said aloud.

He tried—for an hour. But the stress of his new responsibility combined with the crone's accusation dulled his brain. He could concentrate on only one thought: the available indulgences on the Isle of Neutrality.

Well, I am going to be busy. It would do me good to relax a bit before I assume command.

HEAVEN'S STANDARD BEARERS STOOD at attention before Zinc.

"There is only one way that this war is going to end," he said. "The forces of the Entente are going to cover the globe. Yes, yes, you are thinking, 'he has said this before.' And it is true; I have. However, it is a fact that it will happen, because essentially it already has."

Zinc pointed to a giant map that displayed the mortal world's various empires. "The sun never sets on the British Empire," he said, "and what's more, it doesn't set on the French Empire either. When we aligned those historically warring nations, we gained control of virtually all of Africa, as well as wide swaths of the Near East and Asia. Bringing Russia into the Triple Entente added the largest nation on Earth to the list."

Zinc pointed to France and her territories. "After the collapse of Napoleon, we held onto La France and her holdings. Now we have strategic positions in Africa and Indochina, even a foothold in South America." He pointed to Russia. "We engineered Russia's humiliating defeat in the Russo-Japanese War during our training exercises. This attracted the Demons to Japan but allowed us to consolidate our hold on Russia and mainland Asia." His pointer tapped England. "Here we were lucky. The losses we inflicted on the Demons at Waterloo meant they could not hold onto an empire within the Mortal Realm. Thus, we gained Britannia as well."

There was mumbled assent.

"When the Entente is victorious, we will control the globe within a loose framework of Empires and aligned nations; the Demons will be further decimated and unable to control any sizeable mortal army."

Thunderous applause echoed through the room. Zinc bowed and headed for the exit. Lord Hydrogen threw an arm around Zinc's shoulder with a level of affection that was still foreign to Zinc even though his old nemesis had been supportive in many dire moments.

"I feel positive about your plans, and I appreciate the level of trust you have placed in me," Hydrogen said. "You are giving me the opportunity to strengthen my argument for replacing Uranium II should the position become vacant."

Zinc tapped his nose, indicating that Hydrogen was correct.

"Africa will be an important part of this conflict," Zinc said. "It will be imperative that you drive out the remaining powers not aligned with the Entente, just like with the Boers."

"It will not be difficult," Hydrogen said. His teeth sparkled against the background of his dark skin. "The British and French colonial forces are disciplined, well equipped, and motivated. We will mirror your victories in Europe and Asia."

Zinc felt a shadow growing over his otherwise sunny thoughts.

"Is something wrong?" Hydrogen asked.

"It's just the Americas," Zinc said. "I have not accounted much for them in this plan."

"We don't have the best luck there," Hydrogen replied.

"It's true," Zinc said. "I mean, they killed all of the indigenous Angels, and there are still some Native mortals, yet the Angels are gone."

"Well, you had something to do with that, too," Hydrogen said.

"Yeah, yeah." Zinc rolled his eyes. "But still, I would like to incorporate a plan to claim at least the United States."

Hydrogen paused. "Perhaps... ah... Rachael? She was instrumental in crafting the entangling alliances that helped fuel this Great War."

"True," Zinc said.

He marveled at the detachment he experienced regarding his former lover. Eleanor had delivered him from Rachael's clutches. Now he could hear The Destroyer's name without cringing.

It was only late August and Schitz was already exhausted from the responsibilities of commanding the central theater of a global conflict. He had been rushing from one place to the next, coordinating with Scarlet Fever regarding the strategy in German East Africa, where they would fight the British and Belgians via guerilla warfare tactics. He had also liaised with Hepatitis about the need to defend the Dardanelles against the Allies via mines and artillery. This was followed by a meeting with Pneumonia to discuss the facets of the Schlieffen-Moltke Plan, where they would initially focus on the West before turning their attention to Russia. It was an exhaustive series of briefings and assessments during which he continually stressed the need to avoid casualties to his subordinates.

Although he was commanding a broad endeavor across multiple continents and fronts, Schitz did not wish to be separated from the action like the Devil. So, on the hot, humid August morning, Schitz found himself within the body of a junior officer of the German 4th Army, crouched over a map in the Ardennes Forest. Schitz looked up and saw Brain Cancer, the squad leader of Western Europe and her subordinates Cholera and Fibromyalgia.

Schitz had maintained his position as the weapons instructor for the Hellish Academy. However, he rarely developed strong personal bonds with students, even those which he bedded. He was only vaguely familiar with the members of the Western Front squad.

"What a glorious day it shall be," he said. "Let's play the introduction game. Youngest first."

The Demons encircling the map raised a hand. Fibromyalgia, an unusually skinny and gaunt lad, spoke first, "The Kongo Revolt."

All hands remained raised. Next Cholera, a husky male with rounded features, spoke. "San Juan Hill."

Fibromyalgia lowered his hand.

Brain Cancer tossed her long, blonde hair to the side and said, "The Spanish Conquest, pick any battle. I was there for them all."

Cholera lowered his hand.

"And I'll go with Teutoburg Forest, though I could go back much further than that," Schitz said.

As Brain Cancer lowered her hand, he continued. "In years to come, you will name this as the fiercest campaign you've seen. Though it will not be your first taste of combat, it will be memorable, and you will look differently on those who arrive after this campaign is concluded."

Schitz wished that his son-in-law were present for the battle, however, he had sent Pneumonia to protect a large contingent of Wraiths conducting reconnaissance in Lorraine. Had Pneumonia been there, he would have led the mission. Schitz wanted his subordinates to be leaders in their own right; independent thinkers. He turned to Brain Cancer.

"What is the plan?"

After further scrutinizing the map, she began. "The French will attack early, within the hour. The mortals' goals will be to break through, capture Longwy, and push east from there. The Ardennes is strategic. There will be a lot of Angels present to ensure French success. We have to assume considerable Familiars will be assisting such a sizeable force."

Involuntarily, those assembled glanced to the shadows among the trees.

Brain Cancer continued, "We know that your work at Gettysburg made the Angels antsy about long-range artillery. They will want to advance primarily within the Celestial, only using mortals as a last-minute shield should the need arise. I will make no efforts to hide my position among the German guns from the Familiars, to assure this eventuality. The rest of the squad will be here among the German troops at the foremost point of their entrenchment. They have dug in, expecting an attack and should be difficult to dislodge. We will be spread out so that all of us are not visible to all the Angels. When the Angels attempt to surround our flanks, the furthermost Demons on either side will feint as though they are falling back to regroup at my position. Then they will double back to catch them off guard.

"Hopefully, we can pick off one or two Angels. The Demon in the middle will drive forward. This will create an overextension within enemy lines. When the middle Demon reaches the French artillery position, he can send word to me, and I will annihilate the guns, thereby ensuring victory for our mortals. Then we will all flee to doorways within the town of Longwy or any other suitable location."

"How will we send word? By Wraith?" Fibromyalgia asked.

"Precisely." The speaker emerged from the shadows. The young Wraith broke into a self-assured smile. "The name's Josephine."

Schitz scrutinized the young creature—reddish hair and the body of a teenage mortal, which meant she was quite young. He wondered if she had seen combat before but decided not to ask.

"The plan is very well thought out," Schitz said. "It plays on information we know to be true about the Angels. It accounts for our need for a German victory and places Demonic safety at the utmost. In a very realistic sense, if things turn sour, we should all be able to escape with our lives, even if that means prematurely abandoning the battle."

Brain Cancer nodded, visibly pleased by her superior's assessment of the plan.

"Cholera, you take the left," Liver Cancer said. "Fibromyalgia, you take the right. I trust you with the center, sir."

Schitz smirked and turned his attention to the redheaded Wraith. "I guess you're with me, Josey." He patted her on the shoulder.

When she grinned, her face turned the color of her hair.

The battle commenced as Brain Cancer had anticipated. The French attacked in a hurried, disorganized manner without a preparatory artillery bombardment. Schitz sat in a shallow German trench and watched a mass of blue and red advance towards his position. A whistle sounded from behind him.

"Achtung! Achtung!"

Schitz raised his Mauser Gewehr 98 and sighted it on one of the leading Frenchmen, a non-possessed mortal, but an appetizing target, nonetheless. He pulled the trigger and watched with satisfaction as the man collapsed to the grassy earth beside the base of one of the many trees. Schitz worked the bolt and chambered another round. He scanned the trees looking for the auras of Angels. Around him, the early morning air filled with a thunderous cacophony of rifle fire. To his right, a machine gun crew opened up on the French troops from behind a Maschinengewehr 08.

Through the haze of gun smoke and flying debris, Schitz spotted several Angels within the Celestial. They moved behind the trees as they approached his position. Schitz knew he was vulnerable in a stationary position, but he held his ground and fired another round. Instinctively, he looked right and left, though his comrades were just out of sight. Schitz fired again, then ducked down in the shallow trench to reload. Incoming rounds kicked up dirt around him.

Schitz continued to fire on the advancing French. A bold trio of Angels advanced within the Celestial. Schitz stepped out of his host and grabbed one of the five throwing knives he had laid out on the edge of the trench prior to the start of the engagement. He hurled it toward his first target. Before it had found its mark, he had already grabbed the next knife. Schitz bit his lip in frustration—only two of three blades found their target. The remaining Angel fell back. Schitz stepped into another mortal infantryman and awaited the next onslaught from the Angels. He saw a great many regrouping around him.

"Perfect," he said aloud. He fired a round into a Frenchman. The mortal advance had stalled, and the Angels appeared to have stopped opposite his location, which meant their flanks were extended. Schitz hoped they would mount another direct assault, but they appeared to be maneuvering to surround him in the Celestial. Schitz glanced at Josephine. She huddled next to a crate of ammunition.

"There are a lot of them, so stay very close to me," he said. She nodded vigorously.

"Schnell," he said with a devilish grin. He leapt from his host and began a weaving run through the trees. The Angels were visibly taken aback by his sudden abandonment of a secure position. They froze for the critical moment. Schitz and the Wraith passed through a small gap in their formation. On the way past, Schitz hurled a throwing knife into the throat of the nearest foe.

His breath came in great gulps. "Thank goodness they're novices," he said.

"Why... is... that?" Josephine was panting.

"They might have killed us both if they were experienced enough to expect a charge," he replied.

The Demon and Wraith duo managed to evade their pursuers' half-hearted chase by taking a circuitous path through the trees of the Ardennes. They came upon the struggling, plodding advance that was the French artillery. Anticipating a swift advance, the French had determined to pull them forward after the infantry charge, a strategic blunder.

They should have barraged, Schitz thought. *You always barrage.*

Schitz withdrew a Celestial parchment from his robe and sketched a map of the French position. He shoved the paper into the Wraith's tiny fingers.

"They'll follow me, not you," he said. He saw a sizeable cluster of Angels emerge from the tree line. "Just make sure you get this to the German battery as soon as possible."

Josephine looked toward the Angels and back at Schitz with a quivering expression of terror.

"You've never been in combat before?" he asked. He placed his hand under her jaw. He pulled her face close and looked into her eyes.

"It's going to be all right," he said. His voice remained soft, his words confident. "Just get back to Brain Cancer, and it will all be over before you know it."

Along the edge of a clearing beyond the point of contact between the two armies, Brain Cancer stood within the body of the stout Fraulein Muller.

She shouted instructions to the gun crew manning three, 21 cm Mörser 10s. "Get those estimated coordinates dialed in."

The gun was a nightmarish upgrade of the classical nineteenth-century cannon. It still had wheels and a stock, but the barrel and the firing mechanism were very different from its predecessors that had seen action under Napoleon and Wellington. A fleeting shadow passed by the lieutenant and disappeared through the woods. Muller strode over to the field radio and raised the receiver while looking down at the parchment the Wraith had transferred from Schitz in the Celestial to her in the Mortal Realm.

After a moment of conversation, Brain Cancer moved from one gun to the next and dialed in the exact positions of the French artillery.

21 cm Mörser

Schitz had barely maneuvered a few hilltops away from the French guns when he felt the violent rumblings of shells pounding the earth. He could not see the effects but judging from the location of the rising black smoke, he knew they were tearing mortals and machinery to bits. He could envision the high explosives from the Mörsers detonating around the French guns, ripping men to shreds, and pulling apart their valuable guns. He turned and continued his flight toward the nearest possible location for a portal.

SPANISH INFLUENZA LOOKED OUT past the defenses of Tsingtao across the Yellow Sea. The late summer breeze intermingled with salt from the ocean. He closed his eyes and listened to the endless waves. He stilled his mind so he could best deal with the frustrating conversation he was having with his superior.

"Avoiding large-scale pitched battles is the commonsense way to implement our goals, and you're proposing the exact opposite," Anorexia said.

"That is what the reports from across the globe indicate we are doing," Spanish Influenza replied. "I've already submitted my proposals for many areas where we can stage localized rebellions against British rule or territorial expansion of the Japanese Empire. All I'm asking for is the opportunity to deal one surprise blow that will hit them harder than all of these pinpricks. We've been needling them; let's land one solid uppercut."

"How would you do it?" she asked. She suppressed a smile at her junior's ambition.

"By feigning the strategy we've so obviously adopted," he said. "I will send the Japanese squad aboard a ship. They will transfer to a German vessel when the naval battle that is sure to follow commences. They will engage in a hit-and-run attack at the Angels in the Royal Navy Squadron. When this happens, the Angels will expect a similar strategy from the defenders. The defenders will initially fall back, only to counterattack from within the defenses, again and again. By the time the Angels realize they are facing a pitched battle, we will have inflicted much more than the handful of casualties we produce through our hit-and-run attacks. Then will we retreat."

"I can see it working," Anorexia said. "Both sides tend to anticipate the other's next move. After a limited attack by the naval forces, they will be quick to assume a similar action from our shore defenders."

"Exactly," Spanish Influenza said. "We can make them pay dearly. This opportunity will only be available now; after the British dislodge the Germans from China, there will be next to zero probability for a large-scale battle. Then there will be plenty of time for your ambush tactics."

Anorexia laughed. "They're not *my* tactics."

As her giggle subsided, she was aware of Spanish Influenza holding her gaze for slightly longer than normal. She broke eye contact first and glanced down modestly. She felt his lips press against hers. Caught off guard but not put-off, she opened her mouth while he wrapped his arms around her body. After a moment, they separated.

He said, "I'm sorry; I just felt..."

She cut him off by kissing him again. Even as she enjoyed a level of physical intimacy she had never experienced before, she could not help wondering if he was manipulating her or genuinely enamored. She had avoided sex with Mononucleosis before his death and had not even considered anyone since. Now, she let go. Spanish Influenza's hands explored her body. He kissed her neck, then between her breasts. She was moments away from total submission—

She pushed away despite the aching between her thighs. "Okay," she said. "Stop, there is much to do. We will have time for this later. I promise. Right now, we need to win the war."

"Yes, Commander," he replied. His grin was one of partial conquest.

Once he had departed, Anorexia looked out across the port.

Why do I always seem to fall for notorious philanderers?

She had considered giving her body to Schizophrenia but resisted because she did not wish to be one of his endless conquests. In her mind, she saw Spanish Influenza.

Would it really be any better to be one of this playboy's multitude of lovers?

Painful thoughts ricocheted in her brain. *Do I want to die with the act still a mystery to me? I have waited this long; surely, I deserve it. I really want Schitz. Will Spanish Influenza be a worthy substitute?*

The sun rose over the port defenses.

"I am a commander in Satan's army," she said aloud. "I am not a schoolgirl. There will be time to satisfy the desires of the flesh later."

ZINC FELT PULLED IN a million different directions, and the war had only just begun. Reports flooded in from Africa, India, the Middle East, the Far East, North America, and all sorts of European locales. Some were simply warnings: Mexico might invade the United States. Others contained more specific information: the Germans initiated a guerrilla campaign in East Africa. Positive—Russia was mobilizing faster than anticipated. Negative—casualties in the face of a German advance; differing railroad gauges between Russian and European locomotives meant the Russians had slowed at the Prussian frontier.

The Demons appeared more agile and nimble than predicted. They popped up at every locale all at once despite their inferior numbers. Zinc feared he would lose the opportunity for a decisive battle. The enemy was difficult to pin down. He sent Abraham, now Lord Cadmium, to the Russian Army. Zinc hoped the Russians' superior numbers would deliver an easy victory to the last remaining son from his first marriage. Eleanor had borne twin boys who were currently in the Heavenly Academy.

Hopefully, we'll have this wrapped up by Christmas, he thought, *and there will be no need for my little ones to see the horrors of modern war.*

CONSTANTINE, THE ELDEST SON of Lord Cadmium (Zinc's least favorite son, Abraham), turned beet red. "This is an absolute disaster."

"I know," his father said from within the Russian officer. "I'm accustomed to supporting the Familiars in scouting, not commanding large forces."

"At this rate, by nightfall, there will be no Angels or Russian soldiers in Tannenburg fit to fight," Constantine said.

Abraham wracked his brain. He had outnumbered the Germans and the Demons substantially. He was certain each would retreat or face annihilation. Yet, both the mortal and Demonic armies had concentrated their forces and briefly outnumbered his forces in select portions of the battlefield. Cadmium's unwieldy mortal and Angelic formations were poorly equipped to deal with sudden attacks. When they responded in one place, they faced a withering assault in another.

"I don't know what to do," he said.

"Come, let us to the front to die with honor," Constantine said. "I would rather that than have to tell your father we destroyed his Russian contingent of men and Angels."

ANXIETY RUSHED ALONG A row of burning houses in Usdau. She weaved her way through the destruction in the Celestial. The Angels had adopted a defensive position, four in the Celestial, four within mortal troops. They trembled under the weight of yet another assault despite the odds being so heavily in their favor. Just as it appeared that Anxiety would crash into the lead Angel, she wheeled to the right and dove through the broken window of one of the burning houses.

At that moment, Melioidosis fired her rifle from within a German sharpshooter. A possessed Russian's head jerked back violently as the round struck him in the forehead. To the surprise of the Angels who were still focused on Anxiety's disappearance, Liver Cancer emerged from behind them, and hurled a throwing knife into the seizing Angel.

RACHAEL SCREAMED IN FRUSTRATION. "Fuck! How do they know my own countryside better than me?"

The Germans and the Demons within them had struck the British patrol mercilessly, then vanished into the bush.

"Come on, you lot," she shouted to the remaining King's African Rifles and the Angels within. "They must be nearby."

The sentiment proved correct. A hundred meters later, the lead scout was cut down by machine gun fire.

Rachael issued orders in Swahili. "Get in the bunker!"

She pulled one of her mortal soldiers down into cover. She gritted her teeth and watched in frustration as a pair of Demons within German infantrymen advanced under the cover of the burping gun. Her lead Angels stepped into the Celestial to avoid the gunfire only to be set upon by two Celestial Demons who emerged from a trench unnoticed in the thick grass. Both Angels died swiftly.

She abandoned her host and charged forward, but the Demons had departed faster than they had murdered her kinfolk. She stooped in the hot African sun and took in the butchered body of a niece and a distant cousin. For the first time in centuries, fear squeezed her throat.

"WE HAVE THEM ON the run!"

Lord Fluorine thrust a victorious fist into the air. He was watching Japanese troops storm the fortress at Tsingtao. His mood changed abruptly when he saw two Demons emerge from his flank. Fifteen minutes later, after an exhaustive and perilous struggle, the Hellish fiends withdrew. Fluorine yelled over his shoulder to his brother, Emiyo.

"They're like damned gophers, popping up everywhere!"

He heard nothing in response. When he turned, his worst fears were realized. His brother lay, open-mouthed, with a Demon's dagger impaled in his eye.

"SO, THESE ARE THE reports then?"

Satan scanned the scroll. "There's been action in France, Russia, Africa, and China, and yet, if I'm reading this correctly, only thirty Angels have been confirmed killed, maybe five more that haven't been accounted. Is that accurate?"

"Yes, my Lord," Mephistopheles said.

Why must I bring the reports? the Wraith thought.

Satan slammed the scroll to the ground. "Then why does everybody seem so amused?" He glared in turn at every Priest and Wraith in the room.

"The Co... co... commanders and Demons are in the field, so I'm n... n... not sure I can speak for them," Mephistopheles said.

"I mean all of you." The Devil gestured to the folks cowering in the corners.

"Permission to speak freely," the old Wraith said.

"Granted."

"We sustained no casualties. We prevented the Angels from rolling over the Central Powers and establishing a worldwide empire. My fellow Wraiths and I are deployed for specific battlefield intelligence, something at which we excel. We have no expertise in the formulation of effective global strategies."

Satan said nothing. Mephistopheles eyed him with caution.

"The plan to replace the Triumvirate with field commanders was ingenious," Mephistopheles said. He knew how to soothe the Devil through flattery.

"Perhaps in a few more months we'll be calling the mortal world ours," Satan said.

"We all hope so, my Lord."

The old Wraith saluted and left.

"WHAT AN INEXTRICABLE, ENTANGLED mess we've worked our way into," Uranium II said. He looked at the map again. "We have obligations all over the world; to help in one place, we must neglect another."

Zinc looked for a reaction. God sat on the throne, steely-eyed and stoic.

Zinc looked at Uranium II. "That is why you are the supreme field commander, and I am the supreme strategist, my friend," he said. He pointed to the map. "We have one section we must win, France. Victory there means we take out Germany. If we take out Germany, we take out the Central Powers. The Demons have clearly spread out across the world, so concentrating in France should halt the German offensive, allow us to clear their small contingent, and roll all the way to Berlin."

When he looked at God and Uranium II, he saw expressions of longing.

They both hope I am right, he thought.

"Where will you pull troops from?" God asked.

"Asia and Africa. We can ignore the Americas; the war will not spread there. We concentrate on France. Maybe we try to knock out the Ottomans so that we can send aid to Russia through the Dardanelles and prevent a complete collapse of their empire."

God stroked his chin. Uranium II scratched his head.

"We can turn this around," Zinc said.

Maybe, he thought.

CHAPTER 4

THE ZOMBIE

T he storm swept across the globe, but it concentrated its wrath
on the fields of France. Trenches on either side of the barren
death zone of No Man's Land filled like a storm sewer. Men who'd
managed to avoid metal projectiles and poison gas died in their
sleep, unaware of the flash flood surging from around the bend.

Schitz made agonizing strategic choices. He pulled Liver Cancer,
Melioidosis, and Anxiety from the Eastern Front to position them
on the line. He left his forces in Africa and the Near East in place.
The battles of the Marne and Ypres had been exhausting affairs. The
strategy of hit-and-run tactics they employed against the Angels
required great physical exertion; the longer the engagement, the
more taxing the effort. The era of the two-day battle had fled. Ypres

raged for over a month. The continual conflict left Schitz and his fellows drained.

The Angels had gotten better at expecting the strategies that had been so effective at the Battle of the Frontiers. Reports indicated that the Angels were pooling their resources at the Western Front. Schitz considered abandoning his efforts there to avoid a pitched battle, but the more he studied the nature of trench warfare, the more he realized there would be no grand battle like Teutoburg or Waterloo. There would be a series of continual, limited encounters across the lines.

He convinced his peers that France was the focus of the war effort. He summoned Autism from The Banana Wars between America and Mexico and placed him between Verdun and the Swiss border. He moved Anorexia and her contingent between Verdun and Amiens and placed his own forces between Amiens and the North Sea.

The year bled away, and casualties accumulated on both sides. On Christmas Eve, Schitz emerged from a dugout where he had been reviewing a series of German and Demonic dispatches regarding various situations along the lines. He noticed ice and frozen mud in the trenches and heard a cluster of soldiers singing *Stille Nacht*. The strains of the song wafted over the sandbags of the parapet and past the twisted wire of the pockmarked expanse separating the opposing forces.

Somewhere in the middle of No Man's Land, the strains comingled with the warble of English voices singing *Silent Night, Holy Night*.

Schitz had never seen a miracle—they were not part of Demonic training. But he witnessed one. Without any command, troops from both sides crawled from their trenches, not to kill each other, but to exchange pleasantries and small presents. A young mortal from the London Rifles offered Schitz a tin of tobacco. Schitz fumbled in his mortal's pocket and withdrew a small wooden box. It contained varying types of knives.

"You can use it to whittle," Schitz said.

Schitz knew that boredom in the trenches savaged the mind like trench foot did the body. Boredom opened the soul to fear, malice, and despair. Anything that could pass the time was more valuable than gold.

"Thank you, sir. Merry Christmas to you, eh, fröhliche Weihnachten," the boy said. His Cockney accent butchered the German. He embraced Schitz in a half hug and ambled away. One by one, the soldiers slumped back to their respective trenches with promises to maintain the peaceful coexistence on the morrow.

The next day Schitz navigated the maze of wire and shell craters. His jaw dropped. The mortals were playing football, smoking, and talking amicably.

"Peace has sprung up like an infection," he said aloud.

A voice behind him spoke. "Indeed."

Schitz whirled, ready to defend himself.

An Angel within a British officer stood five feet away. "What is the cure for peace?" the Angel asked.

Schitz fought the impulse to kill the Angel. Constant time on the battle lines in the Mortal Realm had weeded out any desire for liaisons with the folks from Heaven.

"We cannot fight now," Schitz said. "There are no hostilities. It would be in violation of the Divine Dictum."

When the Angel laughed, the soldiers paused and looked skyward. They thought they'd heard thunder.

"Fair enough," the Angel said, "but you do not hide your malicious intent very well."

"Why should I?" Schitz asked. He pointed to the shell-shattered earth, the mud, the smoldering rows of broken trees. "This is surely Megiddo. Is there a better time to fight than the end of all things?"

The Angel shrugged. "So, you're Schizophrenia?"

"The one and only," Schitz replied.

"They talk about you a lot," the Angel said. "The Demon of the Scar—you remain quite the mystery."

"Oh?"

"Well, no one has ever reported seeing you at the salons: the Isle of Neutrality or La Rue de la Croix Nivert."

"I have no need for such debauchery."

"Debauchery, no sir. Liberty is a far better word, but there are also important debates and stimulating conversation," the Angel said. "There may come a time when we do not butcher each other like animals. When that comes to pass, the seeds of the new order will have been planted at the gentlemen's clubs."

Schitz made a non-committal gesture with his head. "Well, an interesting thought," he said, "but if you'll excuse me, I think I'll be enjoying my own company now."

The Angel made no move to leave. "Silver," he said.

"Excuse me?"

"I am of the House of Silver. Jeffery Silver, to be precise."

"I thought your House was disbanded," Schitz said, "when—"

"When you ruined my father's face and killed my uncle?" the Angel asked. There was no malevolence in his voice. "That did not eradicate our House; it just made us subservient to another."

A surge of elation popped at Schitz's nerves.

Is Anna alive?

He suppressed the urge to ask. "In my kingdom, your whole family would have been put to death."

"Well, thankfully, our Master is more merciful than yours," the Angel replied.

"Good thing for you. Good day, Silver."

"Merry Christmas, Schizophrenia."

A PACK OF RATS skittered along the trench. Lord Cerium spat in disgust.

"You have lousy taste in holiday locations," he said.

Zinc speared one of the rodents with a bayonet. "What's wrong with exotic Constantinople?"

"Other than the fact that we're stuck here in Gallipoli?" Cerium asked.

Zinc retrieved his blade and tossed the rat over the face of the trench. It exploded from the impact of an overzealous sniper's bullet. "This has been a disaster, hasn't it?"

"To the utmost, sir," the young Lord replied.

"Have we taken many losses?"

"Massive, especially considering that we see so few Demons in the area," Cerium said, "however, whenever we encounter them, they seem to have our number, just like the Turks."

Zinc sighed. Gallipoli had been an embarrassing disaster. Things were not going well. Russia was a debacle. Hydrogen and Rachael were chasing their own tails in Africa.

"I'm thinking of pulling our resources from here, gradually. We are definitely leaving Russia," Zinc said.

"To focus on France?" Cerium.

"Yes. You've made a notable effort here, but if we can win in France, we will win the war."

"Perhaps I could be dispatched to the Holy Land and Mesopotamia," Cerium said. "If the Demons are focused here, there is potential for beating the Turks there."

Zinc thought for a moment. "Do it. Take a small contingent and see what you can accomplish. For my part, I will see what can be done in France."

THE DAY SETTLED ACROSS Northern France and the Low Countries like a wet wool blanket. The summer rains that intermittently pelted the village of Longueval and the forest of Delville Wood offered only momentary relief from the smothering humidity. The area could have been scenic— the picturesque rolling hills, the tangled copse of trees, the small narrow streets lined by tiny, utilitarian country houses lent a nostalgic and appealing allure to the French country-side; an image of peace and tranquility.

But the war had a different idea. Defensive trenches, machine gun emplacements, piles of materials, artillery bombardments, and the ever-present pall of death ruined the naïve rural expanse, unfamiliar as it was to shells, and gas, and bullets, and bombs.

The IV Corps of the German Imperial Army held the woods and most of the town. The divisions of XIII and XV of the 1st South

African Infantry Brigade occupied the southernmost portion of the town and the area leading up to the edge of the woods. The wide-scale battle for the Somme had begun two weeks earlier and was at full tilt as the massed armies of the British Empire and those of the Triple Alliance once again clashed in momentous, clattering battle.

Karl Werner hummed under his breath, a haunting tune he had learned at a younger age: *Der Tod in Flandern.* The corporal felt like the embodiment of death. He was festooned from his head to his muddy boots in a green smock. He peered through the holes cut for his eyes, an olive drab ghost. Werner crawled through the wire into No Man's Land under cover of night. He sat in the trunk of a metal tree built to conceal a sharpshooter's position. The compartment was cramped and uncomfortable. Werner raised his field glasses and scanned the barren expanse between the trenches. The scene was hellish, illuminated by the crimson light of phosphorous flares launched into the night sky by artillery crews. The rugged patch of wire and corpse-strewn expanse between the trenches was unoccupied.

Werner felt confident from his position in the iron outpost. At his feet lay several Stielhandgranate potato masher grenades. A Beholla M1915 semi-automatic pistol slept in a holster at his waist. Cradled in his hands was his most dangerous weapon, a Mauser Gewehr 98 equipped with an optical scope and a Maxim silencer.

Werner let the field glasses dangle from his neck. He raised his rifle and peered through the scope. Schitz appreciated the remark-able skill of the German marksman; it made his work even easier. Werner spotted a detachment of British troops making their way through the maze of obstacles. The scouts were surveying the German positions in preparation for the morning's assault. There were no Angels in sight.

Schitz felt no inclination to deny Werner his own objective. In fact, the Demon appreciated the challenge. The British troops moved and wove in a haphazard path several hundred yards from his position. Schitz peered through his Görtz scope. Schitz counted seven and settled the prongs of his gunsight over the midsection of the rearmost scout. Schitz had been on scouting missions. Both he and Werner knew the scouts were singularly focused on reaching the safety of their trench. They were attentive to their own steps and significantly less concerned about their comrades behind them.

Schitz continued to hum the eerie tune. Werner steadied his breath and assumed a stone-like stillness.

Der Tod reitet auf einem kohlschwarzen Rappen, er hat ein undurchsichtige Kappen.[3]

Werner squeezed the trigger. Through the scope, he saw the round strike its mark. The bullet caught the rearmost scout in the center of his spine, smashing one of his vertebrae before burying itself within the man's heart. Schitz grinned as the man reeled and collapsed to the ground unbeknownst to the rest of the detachment.

Wenn Landsknecht in das Feld marschieren, lässt er sein Toss daneben galoppieren.[4]

Werner absorbed the recoil of his rifle and adjusted his sight over the next scout. He pulled the trigger. The round struck slightly off its intended, central mark and tore through the soldier's left lung. The infantryman collapsed to his knees unable to breathe. Schitz pulled back the bolt of the rifle and ejected the spent cartridge.

Flandern in Not. In Flandern reitet der Tod.[5]

The column changed direction. The next target was perpendicular to Schitz when Werner pulled the trigger. The round caught the scout in the small space between his ear and the edge of his plate-shaped helmet. The bullet punctured the skull and tore through the man's brain before embedding itself within the far side of the skull.

Der Tod kann auch die Trommel rühren. Man kann den Wirbel im Herzen spüren.[6]

The only sound was the slight click as Werner worked the bolt. The spent casing sailed through the open rear of the tree and dropped to the wet mud, a perfect imitation of the dead man on the other end of Werner's muzzle. He re-sighted.

Er trommelt hell, er trommelt laut, er schlägt auf eine Totenhaut.[7]

---

[3] Death rides on a coal-black horse, He wears a transparent coat.
[4] When mercenaries march into the field, He lets his horse gallop along.
[5] Flanders in need, Death rides in Flanders.
[6] Death also can stir the drum; you can feel the whirl in the heart.
[7] He drums long, He drums loud, He drums on a skin of a dead man.

The remaining scouts were facing away from Werner's position. The sniper suppressed a giddy joy; he watched his next round find its mark in the center of a man's back.

Flandern in Not. In Flandern reitet der Tod.[8]

Schitz aimed at the next scout. At the precise moment of firing, the target stepped on a fallen branch. The round intended for his head tore through his midsection and punctured his liver and intestines.

Als er den ersten Wirbel geschlagen, da hat's das Blut vom Herzen getragen.[9]

Schitz watched the round pass through the intended target and clip the next scout in the column in the knee. His cries alerted the leader of the contingent, who dove for cover among the wire and fallen branches.

Werner swore, then worked the bolt. Schitz fished within the sniper's pockets and removed a clip of ammunition. He slid the set of five rounds into the chamber and locked them in place.

Nothing is ever flawless, he thought.

Werner remained calm.

Al ser den zweiten Wirbel schlug, den Landsknecht man zu Grabe trug.[10]

Schitz sighted the scope over the injured man's shoulder and pulled the trigger. He was too far away to hear the beleaguered man's scream but could see the man's mouth working in agony. Werner fired again. He struck the wounded man in his other leg.

Flandern in Not. In Flandern reitet der Tod.[11]

The precision torture finally got the better of the remaining soldier. The man broke cover and crawled toward his injured comrade. The squad leader had just grabbed the man by the collar when Werner pulled the trigger. The round punctured the man's helmet. He stiffened for a moment, then sprawled across the ground. The

---

[8] Flanders in need, Death rides in Flanders.
[9] As He hit the first drumroll, the blood departed from the heart.
[10] As he hit the second drumroll, the mercenary got carried to the grave.
[11] Flanders in need, Death rides in Flanders.

lightest of rain began to fall over the trenches. Schitz felt the droplets on his smock. He squared up the injured scout, then savored the moment.

Der Tod kann Rappen und Schimmel reiten. Der Tod kann lächlnd im Tanze Schreiten. Er trommelt lau, er trommelt fein: Gestorben, gestorben, gestorben muss sein.[12]

He pulled the trigger.

Flandern in Not. In Flandern reitet der Tod.[13]

ZINC PUMMELED HYDROGEN ON the back. "You've conquered most of Africa for us."

"I would have liked to finish the job," Hydrogen said. "It feels wrong, leaving them in my backyard."

"There'll be time to clear them out," Zinc said. "Right now, you are needed here."

Zinc gestured across the vast expanse of wasteland that was the Somme.

"My God, they have created Hell on Earth here," Hydrogen said.

Artillery shells intermittently interrupted the conversation. After a while, the pair ignored the munitions sailing overhead.

"War is different now," Zinc said.

They walked along a forward trench.

"There is a new dimension to battle—the air. Aircraft represent a marvelous innovation. There are bombers and fighters. There are reconnaissance planes that track the movements of armies. There are balloons to spot the impact of artillery. The Germans have massive airships that can travel great distances. The air is the most perilous form of combat for us. The impact from a crash is instantly fatal, even if one is within the body of a host. It is too traumatic,

---

[12] Death can ride the black and grey horse; Death can smile while dancing. He drums loud, He drums gentle: died, died, died, that's what it must be.
[13] Flanders in need, Death rides in Flanders.

as we discovered when our original aviators fell in high numbers. Hence, only the craziest of our side or theirs venture into the skies."

Hydrogen shook his head. "The mortals have surpassed even our limitations."

"Yes, they have," Zinc said. "Here on the ground, it has evolved into a complicated chess game of sorts. The armies are rarely close except during an offensive when a trench might be captured. That is rare. Most of the time they simply shoot across the lines or charge each other only to be mowed down. Our lot in this is complicated. Both sides send infiltrators into No Man's Land in the Celestial. If a side advances, they try to hit the advancing troops with support from their lines and then fall back. The advancing troops are generally not covered by their comrades in the trenches or by the artillery because there are no mortals for them to possess. So, they must be stealthy and flee after the initial engagement.

"Some of these experts have made it as far as the enemy's trench. From there, when they are so bold, they can be supported by their counterparts in mortal form and attack any possessed enemy. It is difficult to accomplish. Most of the time, there are quick Celestial exchanges in No Man's Land. Stepping into a mortal there means being shot dead virtually on the spot. Don't do that. If you encounter a Demon that has you at a disadvantage, fall back to the line. I tell you again, do not possess a mortal between the lines; it will end poorly."

Hydrogen indicated his understanding with a wave of his hand.

"Lastly," Zinc said, "though a fall from a great height will kill you, you can survive a smaller one. Some enterprising tacticians on both sides have developed something we call 'jumping the lines' whereby Angels or Demons leap from their pilot hosts at a low altitude and land behind enemy lines in the Celestial. This is mainly done to take out foes stationed with the artillery. Don't position your troops with the artillery crews indefinitely. Rotate them back to the trenches during periods when precise fire is not needed."

Zinc came across the slaughtered remains of a field gun's crew that had been set upon by the sneaky Demons.

"That's a lot to think about," Hydrogen said.

"It's just the tip of the iceberg," Zinc said. "There are tanks, gas attacks, tunneling, and all sorts of things to learn."

Hydrogen sucked at his teeth. "Right about now, I'm missing Africa."

"Yeah, me too," Zinc said. "But you've come at a decent time. This offensive will offer more traditional fighting. We should be taking some trenches and getting in close. By the time it settles down to normal, you and your Houses will be adjusted."

Hydrogen saluted. "I'm going to go brief my Angels."

Schitz sat in the shallow dugout of a frontline trench in the Somme. Shells whistled and exploded overhead. Both he and his Sturmtruppe host made quick calculations about the incoming whines and determined if they would impact nearby. Schitz checked the mortal's gear: ammunition, gas mask, grenades, pistol magazines, flare gun and flares.

The burden of command had wearied Schitz to a new level. There had been success. Liver Cancer had routed the Angels and Russians at Tannenburg. In like fashion, Bornholm devastated the British and Angels at Gallipoli. Leukemia exhausted the Angels and had apparently driven them out of Africa, at least for the time being, thus preventing the forces of Heaven from gaining the continent outright. In other sectors,

Schitz's Notebook

British Expeditionary Force

During the Great War, I often found my sights trained upon soldiers of the B.E.F. They were considerably more brave than their French or American counterparts. However, their officers showed an inability to lead them effectively, due to stubbornness or cowardice. I have an oddly pleasant memory of the Christmas Truce of 1914 and savage recollections of the Battle of the Somme of 1916.

Spanish Influenza won a massive victory over the Angels in China, even though the Germans had been driven out.

But those early gains had been replaced by the soul-crunching tedium of the trenches. Like a magnet, the Western Front had drawn the forces of Hell and Heaven together into an endless series of fierce engagements. The first death of the campaign had been Fibromyalgia. The Angels had developed countermeasures to the hit-and-run tactics so successful at the beginning of the conflict. The Angels sent pursuers along secondary routes through No Man's Land. During such an encounter, Fibromyalgia, zigzagging through the cratered landscape in the Celestial, came across two Angels and was cut to ribbons. As a counter move, Demons began placing stationary individuals along the routes of retreat. They engaged the spare Angels. The role was dangerous, and some newcomers, such as Explosive Bowel Disease and Sinusitis, were unprepared for the fast-paced nature of the encounters. Schitz could still see them lying in the mud, wide-eyed, with their throats ripped out. Their Celestial blood stained the wet, muddy ground.

Veterans fell alongside the newcomers. When the war machines of the sky arrived at the front, some of the boldest and most self-assured took to the skies despite the risks. Schitz remembered picking through the charred wreckage of a Fokker D.I. to confirm they could not survive a fall from height. It had been impossible to distinguish between the mortal and Demonic remains—both disintegrated on impact. Schitz could only identify Hepatitis because he had watched the takeoff.

Guilt sliced through his mind. He'd recalled him from the Levant to discuss redeploying troops from the Middle East. The old Demon was so taken by the new marvels that he refused to heed the warnings.

Obesity and Dysgraphia met their end when they fell from the sky as well, victims of vicious dogfights over the trenches. Elephantiasis, Tay-Sachs, and Sociopathy fell in intense exchanges because the Angels had captured the supporting trench and surrounded the front line's defenders before they could withdraw. The Angels had developed "Sleeper" squads. They could conceal their auras and appear not unlike Familiars. Melioidosis, Cholera, Depression, and Anxiety met their ends at the hands of "the trench ghosts." Each turned up as a gruesome corpse without explanation.

Since the Demons were vulnerable to "the Sleepers" in the Celestial, some forces of Hell sought refuge by remaining within mortal hosts. Those that did so often fell victim to "the Sappers," another horrifying unit of Angelic specialists. The Sapper strategy relied heavily on the Angels' numerical superiority. When the Demons curled up inside mortal hosts, the Angels utilized artillery or sniper fire against the possessed mortals. The Sappers then rushed forward, without regard to their own safety, to dispense with anyone in the throes of a departure seizure.

Such reckless frontal assaults resulted in high casualty rates among The Sappers, but the unit almost always killed a seizing Demon, which made the trade-off worthwhile. The near-suicidal tactic terrified even the toughest veterans.

The casualty list was staggering:

Killed in Action
(replacement)

Pneumonia *(Liver Cancer)*
Leukemia *(*)*
Muscular Dystrophy *(Anaphylaxis)*
Multiple Sclerosis *(Metastatic Cancer**)*
COPD *(Wilson's Disease)*
Melioidosis *(Colon Cancer)*
Anxiety *(Stomach Cancer)*
Cholera *(Marfan's)*
Fibromyalgia *(Charcot-Marie)*
Hepatitis *(Bornholm)*
Obesity *(Nieman-Pick)*
Dysgraphia *(**Renal Cancer)*
Explosive Bowel Disease *(**Pineal Cancer)*
Depression *(**Rectal Cancer)*
Sociopathy *(**Kaposi Sarcoma)*

* no available replacement
** green recruit from Academy, not yet trained

Schitz watched the grim cycle play out before his eyes. From within a Stormtrooper, he watched Charcot-Marie, Nieman-Pick, Hand-Schuller-Christian, and Wilson's Disease drop in the first day of the Battle of the Somme. There was no one else to summon to the front.

Who will be sacrificed next? he wondered.

The Demons did not want to cede ground. The Angels might use the gap to drive onwards to ultimate victory. Schitz and his colleagues held the line and bloodied the Angels whenever possible.

Schitz secured his stick grenades to this belt and recalled the intermittent successes. Spanish Influenza had developed a strategy of dropping into the Celestial from low flying planes and landing behind enemy lines without injury. He scored numerous victories. Hysteria was a feared ace in the Luftstreitkräfte. She flew alongside the notorious Baron Manfred von Richthofen and downed one enemy plane after another. In a special assignment with the Wraiths, Gangrene and Bovine Spongiform Encephalopathy targeted and assassinated several senior Angels.

It's not all doom and defeat, Schitz thought.

But with shells exploding overhead, Schitz's primary sense was foreboding. Anorexia had been severely injured by a Sapper; Spanish Influenza took her place. He was in every way on the ascendancy while Schitz, though commanding a huge proportion of Hell, felt stuck in the mud of a floundering career.

He knew Spanish Influenza's success would embolden the young Demon. Schitz was certain that Anorexia's life was in danger as well because there were no lengths to which Spanish Influenza would not stoop to gain power and control.

Schitz locked a clip into his freshly cleaned rifle and pulled back the bolt. The rifle was the only item not caked in a thick crust of mud. The haze of exhaustion clouded Schitz's mind, a blurry tunnel of fatigue and frustration.

His feet elicited squeaks from the uneven lumber planks that ran along the bottom of the dugout. The British offensive had stalled, and the job of the Sturmtruppe was to probe the lines for points of weakness through which to exploit a counterattack. Schitz would adhere to this mission so long as it did not interfere with his own. He walked along the row of infantry and saw the trio of Cancers he would be leading into combat: the battle-hardened veteran Liver Cancer, and newcomers Stomach Cancer and her brother Colon Cancer. Schitz watched Liver Cancer's host drain a flask before donning his helmet. It was a day just like any other in the relentless killing fields.

Schitz climbed the rough, wooden ladder leading out of the forward trench and stepped over the parapet. In daylight hours, his host would have already been shot dead. The Stormtroopers slithered behind him through the maze of barbed wire. Schitz navigated around broken tree husks and puddle-filled craters, bypassing corpses of friend and foe alike, and advanced his host toward the fateful end of all soldiers.

As dawn broke over the line, Schitz lifted his field glasses and scanned the British position. Covered in mud, the gray uniforms of the Germans blended well with the early morning hour. They were close enough to see the slightest movement within the British front line. Schitz raised his rifle and lay the sights over a British soldier, then another, then another. He did not see any Angels. He defaulted to his mortal's objective. To assess the strength of the British, they had to probe. Schitz selected the bit of flesh just above the collar of the drab green uniform. He pulled the trigger. The rifle molested the fragile morning peace.

Weeks later, the post arrived at a tiny row house in the East End. Martha Evans had always believed her husband William would return home safe from the war. She had known him her whole life; she felt an unseen bond with her childhood love, the boy she swooned over since the time his cap fell over his forehead. When the post from the War Office arrived, she knew it had been an error, a clerical mistake. There were other stories of such instances. Surely it was another William Evans who lay still and alone in a foreign land, not her Will.

Before William Evans's heart stopped, his squad launched a ferocious barrage of return fire in the direction of the enemy. Multiple 7.7mm Vickers machine guns raked the hillside from whence the shot had originated. Enfield rifles popped over and over and hurled round after round at the foe. For all the expenditure of hot lead, most of the angry response simply tore into the hillside. The rest sailed over the prone Germans. Schitz raised himself slightly and sighted his rifle at the midsection of another uniform.

When the post arrived at the small cottage in Hampshire, Matt Wilson was reclining in a wicker chair in his vegetable garden and admiring the morning's labor. Lizzy tended to her flowers. He read the bulletins about the brave lads at the Somme every day and was anxious for word from his son Matthew Jr. When the old postman handed him the yellow telegram from the War Office, Matt felt an unseen hand clutch him by the throat. Marvin's face was unsmiling from underneath his postman's hat. The trio stood frozen in awkward silence until Lizzy's wailing broke the spell.

Schitz ejected the spent cartridge of the bullet that had taken young Matthew's life. The resistance was fierce and unwavering; this was not a portion of the lines in which to attempt a breakthrough. The Stormtroopers disengaged moments before mortar rounds began pummeling their position.

Moving farther along the lines, Schitz and his colleagues engaged a British outpost from an advantageous position. Here he sent a missive reading "I deeply regret to inform you..." to a young widow from Manchester and an elderly mother from Newcastle. He sent a round through the skull of an orphan from Cornwall whose sister would receive the letter. Again, resistance was too heavy for a successful attack from the regular troops. Schitz shoved another clip into his rifle and pushed the bolt back into place.

Eileen O'Brien-Downing had spent much of her life in Birmingham, but she felt little affection for the British other than the dashing lad she had wed. She balanced her youngest on her lap and burped him while she thought of her dashing Shawn in his sharp uniform. Part of her was glad he was in France and not her native Ireland. At least she did not have to choose sides.

A knock sounded at the door; she called for her eldest Collin to answer.

"It's some kind of telegram," he said.

"Take your brother," she said.

She heaved the mewling infant into her son's hands and ripped open the notice from the War Office. She collapsed on the cottage floor.

"Oh, thank God," she said, "he's been wounded, but praise Jesus, he's alive and on his way home."

Schitz cursed. He'd gone for a headshot, but the British soldier turned his head at the last moment, and the round merely shattered his lower jaw. The stretcher-bearers carried Shawn Downing away from the thirsty specter of Death. Schitz and his men continued to exchange fire with the British. Determined to execute a shot to the temple, Schitz dropped an amateur footballer from Ipswich whose family was not as lucky as Mr. Downing's. He put one through the heart of a Sunday school teacher from Southampton, and another into a cartography enthusiast from Nottingham.

This is the place, Schitz thought.

He watched his squad exchange fire with the Brits.

This is the weak spot.

The morning sun stood in full splendor over the Somme. The officers in the trenches awaited the signal to attack. Schitz inserted a blue smoke canister into the flare gun and fired it aloft.

Whistles sounded. Schitz knew enough of the Western Front to understand their advantage would soon be challenged by every artillery gun the Tommies had in range. He maneuvered his troops along the British flank. To their great luck, they came across a largely unoccupied defile. After a brief exchange of gunfire, which sent a few more notices out from the War Office, they had taken up a position perpendicular to the attack. When the surviving British infantry retreated to their support trench, Schitz and his troopers lay down a withering fusillade. Schitz reached to his belt and pulled out a "potato masher." He unscrewed the bottom of the stick grenade, yanked the cord, and hurled the explosive. His vision was still hazy, but he saw the geyser of dirt and several stricken mortals flying into the air.

With the first and second British trenches captured, he blew a shrill note on his whistle and issued a warning.

"Gas! Gas! Gas!"

Seasoned fishermen foretold gales with less precision. No sooner had he sounded the alarm than artillery shells fell across their position and spewed thick clouds of yellow gas. The troops donned their gas masks with the efficiency born of necessity and experience.

Schitz also anticipated the British counter-offensive. The ferocity of the close-quarter combat exceeded anything Schitz had ever witnessed. The Demon's mind was as cloudy as the poisonous air.

He hurled another grenade and charged the British position. There were at least ten Angels in the squadron of Brits that emerged from the final reserve trench. He threw his remaining grenade at a blockhouse almost fifty meters away, a throw no

Schitz's Notebook

9/10

Model 1915 Stielhandgranate
-170g charge -pull cord detonation
-Highly accurate, handle prevents excessive rolling
-Good for clearing out buildings, dugouts, c. bunkers

mortal could make. The grenade flew through a slit window with the accuracy of a Walter Johnson fastball and exploded.

Schitz pointed to the remaining machine gun post and signaled for Liver Cancer to maneuver behind it. Then he stepped into the trench and fired into a mass of British soldiers and Angels. The first shot dropped a mortal host to the trench's muddy floorboards. The mortals engaged each other hand-to-hand. Schitz drew his semi-automatic pistol and fired several well-placed shots into the British soldiers. He stepped into the Celestial a moment before his mortal was shot multiple times in the chest.

In the Celestial, Schitz was a veritable blur. He drew his sword to block the lead Angel's thrust. He spun and kicked another solidly in the ribs, before bringing his blade back across a third. With a mighty shout, he raised the blade above his head and plunged it into the chest of the first Angel.

He hurled himself forward along the trench into a somersault. Halfway through the tumble, he drew a throwing knife in each hand. He popped to his feet and buried the weapons into two onrushing

Angels.

To his right, Liver Cancer laced the area with machine gun fire and forced more Angels into the Celestial. Schitz heaved his remaining throwing knife into the air directly above him. He pulled his sword from the impaled Angel and drove it into another foe. The Demon whirled in a roundhouse kick, striking the descending knife and hurtling it into the throat of another Angel.

Momentarily unarmed and still faced by a handful of Angels, Schitz sidestepped a sword thrust and arm-locked his attacker. He used the momentum of the sword to spin, then dug his heels into the ground to stop the movement. The sudden halt accompanied by an upward twist broke the attacker's arm. Schitz relieved the Angel of his sword, then stabbed him. The surviving Angels' attacks grew more frantic. They tried to protect their vulnerable comrades. A female Angel tripped and fell on top of Schitz. She raised her weapon, a wicked-looking knife. Schitz head-butted her, then ran her through.

Schitz slid along the ground and kicked a male Angel in the groin. Schitz pulled him to the ground and began punching him in the face with unremitting ferocity. He drew back to administer his fifth consecutive strike when he felt a hand on his shoulder.

Earth & Water

Stomach Cancer spoke in a soft voice. "He's dead, Schitz. You can't kill him anymore." She gestured toward the mortal German infantrymen, most of whom were staring in his direction. A Bavarian corporal, obviously younger than the others by nearly a decade, leaned over and retched.

Schitz stood up, straightened his battle tunic, and said, "Please, excuse me." He traced the symbols in the muck, then scooped up water from a puddle and opened the portal.

He left the front for a moment's reprieve.

"How are you feeling?" Spanish Influenza asked.

He leaned over Anorexia's bed.

"The water of the Styx works wonders," she replied meekly, "but I fear you will have to carry on in your new capacity for a bit longer."

Spanish Influenza smirked. She knew him well enough to recognize that he reveled in the power of his new position. He leaned down and kissed her. He felt her body arch up toward him and caressed her small breasts over her robe.

"I thought I would never get the chance to do this again," he said.

"It would seem we were almost wrong when we said we would have time for this later, weren't we?" she said, though speaking was a struggle.

Spanish Influenza had a sudden thought. *She might be willing to have me now.*

With the precision of a psychic, she said, "I want to, darling, I do, but I don't want my first time to be while I am rendered such an invalid."

"Of course," Spanish Influenza replied before he kissed her again, "and now adieu until the time is right."

She smiled in a girlish fashion and curled up within the sheets of her bed.

Spanish Influenza departed Anorexia's chamber feeling euphoric. On the way down a connecting corridor, he nearly collided with Schizophrenia.

"Ah, you're looking rested," he said. "Is the war won?"

Schitz made a half-hearted effort at a salute. "Hardly, but I did, in fact, get some well-deserved rest," he said. "What are you doing here?"

Spanish Influenza noticed Schitz's glance toward Anorexia's room.

Does he have feelings for her? Has he had her?

His mind whirled in a sudden, inexplicable rage. He steadied himself and remembered the scroll in the inside pocket of his robe. He'd cashed in every chip he had with the Lord of Darkness and gained Satan's agreement to a bold plan, something Spanish hoped would end Schizophrenia once and for all.

"I was briefing with my former commander," Spanish Influenza said. "We reviewed some matters. I am certain that you are aware that I am acting as commander of the Asian detachment."

"I am," Schitz said.

He stepped toward Anorexia's room. Almost involuntarily, Spanish Influenza obstructed his path.

"She is resting," he said. Before Schizophrenia could protest, Spanish added, "Besides, fellow commander, I have urgent orders from Lord Satan pertaining to both of us."

"Oh?" Schitz sounded both annoyed and interested.

Spanish pulled out the scroll and tapped it. Schitz did not read it but saw Satan's signature at the bottom.

"Satan wishes all of his senior commanders to become skilled aviators," Spanish Influenza said. "He fears the Angels will acquire a strategic advantage, and you, my dear sir, have not yet taken to the skies."

Schizophrenia said nothing. His face remained blank, but his eyes displayed someone who was formulating a plan.

Spanish Influenza recognized the look and realized—to his delight and horror—that soon he would either be the undisputed leader of the Demons, or he would be dead.

ANTHRAX STOOD BESIDE THE Albatross D.II and watched the flight crew complete the pre-flight procedures. Anthrax, like most Demons, thoroughly hated flying, but today he was on a mission. He could hear Spanish Influenza's voice and his diabolical instructions.

Once again, Anthrax cursed all humankind for the invention of powered flight.

"All ready, sir," the stocky crew chief said. "Happy hunting, sir."

Easy for you to be cheery, Anthrax thought. *No one ordered you to ram your plane into one piloted by Hell's most illustrious Demon.*

The crew chief's voice rang out over the field. "Contact!"
The engine coughed and the wooden propeller began to spin.

HIGH ABOVE THE BATTLEFIELD, Schitz drank in the knowledge of the aviator he was possessing. Suddenly, he was infused with a knowledge of physics and geometry and engineering that astounded him. He pushed the heavier-than-air crate of wood, canvas, and metal effortlessly through the air and shouted aloud at the marvel he was experiencing.

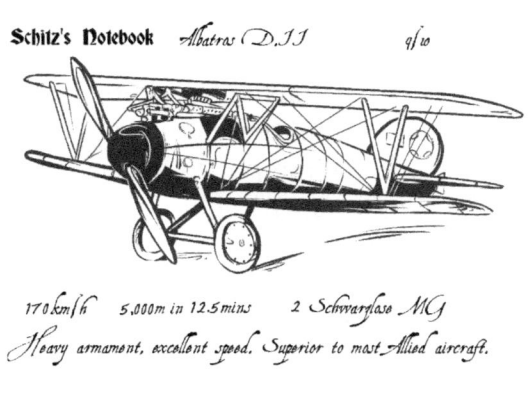

Schitz's Notebook   *Albatros D.II*   9/10

170 km/h   5,000m in 12.5 mins   2 Schwarzlose MG
Heavy armament, excellent speed. Superior to most Allied aircraft.

If I am to die, he thought, surely, this is the way to go—high above the muck and the mire I have known for so many centuries.

Before takeoff, Schitz sent a Wraith with a message for Josephine to meet him at the aerodrome. He also sent instructions for Anthrax. Without knowing which aerodrome Spanish Influenza's supposed confederate was departing, he hoped the messenger would find his protégé in time.

SPANISH INFLUENZA TIPPED HIS Albatross into a dive and joined the Germans in an attack on a flight of RFC Sopwith Pups. He was close enough to see the Royal Flying Corps roundels and the scarf of the British pilot fluttering in the breeze. The British pilot swerved to avoid the fire from Spanish Influenza's machine guns. The Demon was aware of the foe's wingman lining up behind him. Spanish Influenza also knew that Schitz would be targeting the British wingman.

"Now it is all up to Anthrax," he said aloud.

SCHITZ'S HEART POUNDED. HE watched the black-crossed Albatross sandwiched between the two, olive drab Sopwiths. Had he been unaware of Spanish Influenza's scheme, he would have been entirely focused upon protecting his vulnerable comrade just like the RFC pilot ahead of him. Because he knew about the ambush, Schitz scanned the skies to his flanks. Only when he felt the mind of his mortal host screaming for him to pull the trigger did he focus on the Sopwith in his gunsight. Schitz pulled the trigger.

Wood and canvas shook under the discharge of the guns. He watched with glee as holes stitched along the forward portion of the enemy biplane. When the plane's engine began to emit a thin trail of gray smoke, he eased off the trigger and returned his attention to the possibility of a threat.

He saw a German fighter at one o'clock on a collision course. Schitz blocked out his mind's protestations and climbed into the Celestial atop the plane's top wing. With a fleetness born of desperation, he ran along the top of the plane and leapt into the air. A moment later, his feet met solid canvas as he landed on the Albatross piloted by Anthrax. He knew he only had a split second before the two German planes collided. He threw himself out across the abyss.

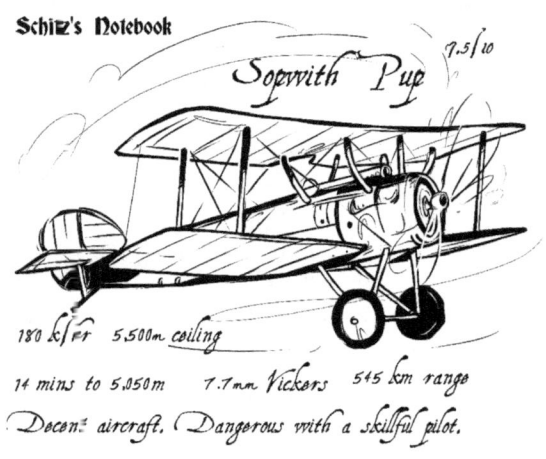

Schitz's Notebook

Sopwith Pup

7.5/10

180 k/hr   5.500m ceiling

14 mins to 5.050m   7.7mm Vickers   545 km range

Decent aircraft. Dangerous with a skillful pilot.

He felt the terrible sensation of falling but also the pull of the mortal Brit piloting the damaged Sopwith. When the undercarriage of Anthrax's Albatross demolished the top wing of his old plane, Schitz was already within his target's body.

He let out an uncontrolled "Wahoo!"

He guided the wounded Sopwith down onto a grassy field in a manner that was as much crash as it was landing.

FROM A LOWER ALTITUDE, Spanish Influenza watched the accident. All had gone according to plan; Anthrax had accidentally clipped Schitz—collisions happened all the time—and while the other Albatross had not crashed, it was sorely wounded and would never survive a landing attempt.

But Spanish wanted to be sure. He climbed until he was positioned underneath the struggling aircraft. He waited, one... two... three... and savored the final seconds of the only obstacle between himself and absolute power.

He dropped back and sent a lethal burst of machine gun fire into the biplane's sputtering engine. He rolled into a climb, careful to avoid a collision. By the time he looked over his shoulder, the fighter was in a death spiral.

I wish I could have seen his face!

FROM THE REMAINS OF his biplane, Schitz watched Spanish Influenza's duplicity. The senior Demon shook his head.

Now he has crossed the line.

In a flash of enlightenment, Schitz realized why he had ignored Elise's warnings and those from others.

Vertigo... I've fought the stigma of killing a rival for eons. I refused to kill someone with ambition because he "might" have me in his sights.

He watched the plane he was meant to be piloting slam into the ground and evaporate in a fireball. He raised his hands at the command of the German soldiers who took his host into custody.

He stepped into the Celestial and took a moment to appreciate the sight. The Germans treated the British pilot like a dignitary—he was a prince of the air.

"All this butchery, and yet they converse as though they were long-lost friends," he said aloud. "Spanish Influenza will not be as fortunate."

SPANISH INFLUENZA STRODE THROUGH the Great Hall, a conquering hero returning home for his reward. He hummed the strains of *Preußens Gloria*. He crossed the Great Hall and made his way to see his beloved.

I should dampen my mood ever so slightly considering our great national tragedy, he thought.

He opened Anorexia's door. She was sitting on her bed holding her brother Autism's hand. Their foreheads touched—a portrait of grief.

"Is it not terrible news?" Spanish Influenza said. "A most tragic occurrence."

From a darkened corner came a voice—a familiar voice—the most horrific sound Spanish Influenza had ever heard.

Schizophrenia said, "News of colleagues falling in battle is always tragic."

An ice pick of terror seized Spanish Influenza's throat and rendered him speechless.

"I..."

"I know," Schitz said. "You are overjoyed to see me and surprised, no doubt, since you watched my plane auger into the dirt."

"Precisely," Spanish said, hoping against all reason that the trio of commanders was assembled for some reason other than the attempted assassination.

Anorexia would not look him in the eye—all the confirmation he needed.

Schitz's voice was calm, a killer's whisper. "Be man enough to admit what you've done, sorry, what you tried to do."

Spanish Influenza flinched. "How?" was all he managed to say.

"Nothing with which you need to be concerned," Schitz said. "We are here to deal with your treachery. No one outside of this room, other than your confederate, knows what happened. Who was he, by the way?"

Spanish Influenza contemplated protecting Anthrax's identity but decided it was pointless.

"Anthrax."

"Well, I'll have something in store for him," Schitz said, "but this is about you. You are hereby banned from combat operations anywhere on the globe. Busy yourself with a pandemic, or something else that serves our Lord and our people. I will deal with your treachery in my own time. Now, get the fuck out of my sight."

Outside the door, Spanish Influenza realized the worst punishment of all.

I will never again hold Anorexia in my arms.

SCHITZ SAT AMONG THE dirt and debris of the dugout, leafing through mortal and Demonic reports.

"Do you hear that, sir?" Renal Cancer asked from within the body of a young scout.

Schitz was taken aback by the Demon's exuberant smile. Her bright face stood in stark contrast to the rat-infested, waterlogged trenches just beginning to show the signs of impending winter.

"I don't hear anything, actually," Schitz said.

"Exactly," she said. "The guns have gone silent; it's over."

Schitz had heard rumors of a ceasefire but had been too overworked to pay attention. He removed a sturdy pocket watch from within the breast pocket of his host's uniform.

"Eleven-eleven," he said, "on the eleventh day of the eleventh month. How peculiar."

He looked at the young Demon within the mortal woman. "There won't be much of a reprieve for us; unlike that soldier you're within, we just pack up and find another conflict."

"I know," she replied with less jubilation in her voice, "but I suppose it's nice to have survived this one when so many didn't."

"Indeed," Schitz said.

He fished through the stack of papers strewn about the officer's rough desk and retrieved a ledger. In the years since the Somme, they had lost Scarlet Fever, Typhoid, Bovine Spongiform Encephalopathy, Bornholm, Dyscalculia, Streptococcal Pharyngitis, Marfan's Disease, Keratoconus, Keratoglobus, Tularemia, Insomnia, Chronic Wasting Disease, CHHF, CHIKV, Hantavirus, and Powassan Virus. Some of the names were simply words on the paper, fresh-faced recruits who never stood a chance against the machinery of Heaven. Others, he could see vividly.

He recalled Typhoid, forever positive and upbeat. He thought about Bornholm, first in a passionate embrace as he enjoyed her young body, but also later when she saved his life at Waterloo. He remembered countless hours debating scholarly points with Scarlet Fever after the pupils had been dismissed. She always called him Dunce—an inside joke based upon his confession of his own lack of academic prowess as a student long before she had been born.

"So, did we win, lose, or draw," Renal Cancer asked.

He broke from his trance.

"That depends on who springs back to their feet quicker," Schitz said.

He knew they'd bled Heaven severely over the years. The Wraith Josephine, with whom he enjoyed regular romantic liaisons, frequently told him of the vast casualties they were heaping upon the Angels. Still, as he perused the parchment containing the names of the living, a quick glance revealed that fifteen of the thirty-eight surviving Demons were essentially children forced into service quite prematurely.

Renal Cancer glanced at the names on the list. "How is it that some Demons are named after mortals?" she asked.

"Well, when we possess a mortal with The Strain, you know, those who remember past lives and can see into the future, we often get a fleeting glimpse of the future as well, or so I'm told. For some Demons, the experience of possessing a strain carrier is very impactful, and they are drawn to the names of the mortals that will one day eradicate a sickness, or at least discover it."

"It seems counterintuitive," she replied, "to celebrate the mortal that benefitted from your child's future demise."

"I think it's a taunt," Schitz said. "A challenge to live beyond what was seen. The future still must be written, even if some part of it was seen. I believe we can always change what has been foretold if we work hard and sacrifice."

"Regardless, there are going to be an awful lot of cured diseases soon," she said, glancing at the list of the dead.

"Possibly," Schitz said, "but remember, a Demon's death only means that humans have the potential to identify and cure the disease the Demon propagated. It's two separate parts, and sometimes it takes humans millennia to put the two together. Take me for instance; I've been in so many mortal minds that the humans know my name. Yet, because I live, there remains no cure. The Demon Lyme Disease died centuries ago, but mortals have not identified her, so they remain afflicted even though she is dead. However, because she is dead, the potential for a cure is possible. Someday they will be able to cure it or at least effectively treat it. Until then, she lives on beyond the grave, a deadly echo upon humanity."

"It is fascinating," Renal Cancer said. "I missed a lot because I was rushed to the battlefield."

"There will be some time to learn now," Schitz said.

He looked at her and saw the all too familiar glint in the eye of an Academy girl—one interested in "the challenge."

"Come," he said gesturing for her to leave her mortal host.

The mortals took a moment to reflect on the end of the war while Schitz and Renal Cancer celebrated in their own way in the corner of the dugout.

Zinc walked beside Eleanor within the body of Prime Minister Lloyd George.

"Well, I would say we finally have our global empire in this League of Nations," he said. They strolled through the gala of heads of state and assorted nobility. Zinc's attention was briefly drawn to Uranium II who was within the body of the Chinese President, Sun Yat-sen.

"I would have preferred that the United States had joined," she replied.

She placed her hand discreetly against his back and whispered to him. "This empire, though expansive, is filled with many broken nations. We, too, are heavily strained with loss. It will fall to you to rebuild our Earthy presence and our Heavenly army so that we can once again face the forces of Hell."

'Yes, my dear," Zinc replied. "The premature conclusion of the Great War gave both sides some reprieve, but this peace is just an intermezzo. I promise you the second act will be more vigorous and conclusive than the first."

From within the Prime Minister's wife, Eleanor smiled with salacious intent. "Your second acts usually are."

Chapter 5

A Grim Intermission

D ust covered almost every surface in the New York City dive, at least the places they could see in the dim light.

"This has all been very difficult on me," Anthrax said.

He squinted to read Schitz's expression—passive.

"I know," Schitz said. "I can never thank you enough for what you've done."

"The least I could do," the junior Demon said. "All the one-on-one training you gave me kept me alive in the trenches. I owe my life to you."

"As I owe you mine, my friend." Schitz raised his glass of dry gin. "Cheers, to survival."

The two Demons drank, then signaled for refills.

"I need to figure out how to deal with this," Schitz said.

"It's going to be hard to kill him," Anthrax said. "He has already recruited Encopresis and Ganser Syndrome."

"I don't know them," Schitz replied.

He was still teaching at the Academy, but his interest in the new class was minimal.

"Little wonder," Anthrax said. "We have a population explosion."

"True," Schitz said, "but neophytes die quickly. Our success in the next war will depend on the experienced fighters."

Anthrax nodded. "Spanish Influenza is doing quite well with his epidemic," he said.

Schitz took a slug of his drink and grimaced. "This is not very good," he said. "I prefer Brew."

"Me too," Anthrax said, "but I'm still ordering another round. This stuff is weaker than water."

Schitz considered his next words with care. "I believe Spanish Influenza is trying to manufacture a response to his current position. I need you to dig around a little, find out what he's up to. Then, I will release you from this perfidious assignment."

Anthrax's eyes glowed. "Done! I would like to spend more time with Breast Cancer and Ebola."

When Anthrax mentioned his children, Schitz thought of Rabies. A pang of regret stabbed his gut, a sensation he tried to drown with more gin.

"You were valedictorian," Schitz said. "I could use an associate professor at the Academy."

Anthrax rapped the table with his knuckles. The noise made something skitter across the surface. Neither Demon minded. Even in its deteriorating state, the bar was better than anything they'd experienced "over there."

"That would be a dream come true," Anthrax said. His smile was uncontained. "Working with you, shaping the next generation, I can't think of anything better."

"It's settled then," Schitz said. "I hear our friend is headed to Russia. Find out what he's up to, and I will deal with him once and for all."

Zinc sat beside Eleanor at the meeting table and glanced across at Uranium II, Hydrogen, and Rachael.

"We must accept a grim reality," he said. "We have built an organization that controls the widest swath of the Mortal Realm we have ever controlled. We have Angels within armies stretching from Brazil to Siberia, across the African continent, and spanning the vast stretches of Asia. As far as we can tell, the Demons have gone to ground. In general, the Eunoe is flowing strongly with peaceful, mortal souls."

"So why is the reality grim?" Uranium II asked. "We should be preparing to crush the last remnants of our foes in a final, glorious battle."

"That is the problem," Hydrogen said. "Countless times we have laid the Demons low, yet they always recover. This time will likely be like the others regardless of the gains we have made."

"We should launch an attack upon Hell itself," Uranium II said.

Silence rolled across the room like a thick fog.

"It's possible," Uranium II said. "We can employ the Familiars to ascertain the symbols requisite to traverse into the Demonic Realm. Once we have the entry code, we will rain Heavenly fire on them and wipe them from existence. My plan is not without precedent. Do you not remember the Devil that assaulted us in Heaven ages ago?"

Zinc shook his head. "Such a strategy violates one of the core principles of the Devine Dictum. We must fight in the Mortal Realm during a human conflict."

Uranium II chased his idea, a dog in pursuit of a juicy bone. "If we win, what difference does that make? The Divine Dictum would be rendered moot."

"The powerful neutral entity who brokered the agreement is still extant," Rachael said. "Do you wish to anger him?"

A scowl traversed Uranium II's brow. Rachael could have sworn she heard his teeth grinding. Not noted for his judicious nature, Uranium II charged ahead.

"He hasn't done anything except wander the world for millennia," Uranium II said. "As I heard it, he is chasing the latest incarnation of his lover."

Zinc raised a hand to quiet the discord beginning to bubble at the table.

"Let us agree that we will explore the viability of Uranium II's plan with the understanding that we will not act unless we are certain of success. In the interim, we must also plan for a conventional victory. I will entrust those details to you, Lord Hydrogen." Zinc turned to Uranium II. "You may develop the details of your proposal, but," his voice took on a steely edge, "do nothing without my expressed permission. Am I clear?"

"Yes, my Lord."

The meeting adjourned. As the attendees departed, Hydrogen pulled Zinc aside.

"Your co-commander is insane. He could cost us everything."

Zinc waved his hand as if to swat a troublesome gnat. "Don't worry, I'll keep him in line, or I'll install you in the position."

After a half-hearted salute, Hydrogen left. Zinc took Eleanor's hand and began the walk home.

Uranium II or Hydrogen, with whom shall I side?

SCHITZ SAT BACK IN his chair and stared into space. The Wraith's words echoed in his ears like the report of the cannonade at Gettysburg.

"I'm sorry, Josephine," he said, his voice barely registering. "Say that again. I could not have heard you correctly."

His lover stroked his hair. "It is true. Both Spanish Influenza and Anthrax were killed in action around Yekaterinburg, apparently in an engagement with Angels from the Dysprosium House."

"I've never even heard of them," Schitz said. His voice was unfocused, his thoughts full of the last conversation he'd had with his understudy.

"I thought you'd be happy that Spanish Influenza was dispatched so serendipitously."

"Yes," Schitz said, "but I hate to lose someone as valuable as Anthrax."

Josephine continued her attempts at cheering him. "Well, if it's any consolation, the clique Spanish Influenza assembled was growing quite strong. It is in your best interest that they are gone."

Schitz closed his eyes. He was about to dismiss Josephine, when she said, "Elise seemed overjoyed with the outcome; I'm saddened to see you so upset."

"Elise?"

"Of course," Josephine said. "She was the one who sent me to Russia to do the assessment and retrieve the bodies."

Schitz's eyes narrowed. "Oh, how interesting."

THE BRASS BAND FILLED the parade route with a lively marching melody. Schitz enjoyed the *Präsentiermarsch von Friedrich Wilhelm III.*

No one can write a march quite like the Germans, he thought.

The music filled him with euphoria, purpose, and determination. Schitz was sure Otto Weinberger, the artillery officer he had possessed, felt the same way about the bombastic refrain. His steps along the parade route felt light and fell in rhythm with the march.

Swastikas covered the city of Nuremberg. The old brick buildings sported red, white, and black ornamentation wherever the eye chose to glance. Beautiful women lined the streets, and young, bright-eyed children gazed at the parade in awe. All along the route, spectators raised their right arms in salute.

The spectacle struck a chord of nostalgia. Schitz remembered the Roman triumphs, one Caesar after another in a chariot pulled by a quartet of perfectly matched, white steeds. He thought about the man he was indwelling. Artillery was so much more mobile now than in the last war. It was coordinated with infantry movements and aerial assaults to form something called "Blitzkrieg."

I have a lot to learn, he thought.

So many differences. Fighters were faster and more maneuverable; bombers flew higher and rained desolation; ships slunk along under the water and dealt death; warships with bigger guns bombarded fortifications from miles offshore.

The "war to end all wars" had not accomplished its purpose. Schitz reminisced about the Angel he had met during the Christmas truce. They'd longed to kill each other, but without active Mortal conflict, they'd been forced to talk.

Must be like the Isle of Neutrality I keep hearing about. He looked outside. *I wonder if that Angel lived.*

Schitz's thoughts were ambushed by a trio of jovial Angels—two possessing the men on either side of him, and one behind.

"Ready for action?" the one on his right asked.

"No, he's not ready," said the one on his left.

"What are you doing all by your lonesome?" came from over his shoulder.

The Angels spoke in Latin to conceal their conversation. Schitz kept his expression placid.

They will not goad me into anything.

"Your side has no hope, you know," the Angel behind him said.

"You should just give up." This was the one to his right.

They sound young, Schitz thought, *barely children, and a little too eager to be tested.*

He remembered being naive and idealistic. He looked straight ahead.

Propaganda Poster

The sabers and cannons thirst not for blood alone, but also for youthful exuberance and innocent ideals.

"What's your malady?"

"Why are you being so rude?"

"Can't you carry on a conversation?"

Schitz did not recognize any of the youngsters and was certain he would never see them again. Ignoring their buzzing interrogation, he drank in the fanfare of the rally. Shortly the parade would lead them to the Zeppelinfeld.

Schitz was eager to hear the charismatic, excitable German leader, Adolf Hitler. He'd been so lost in thought he only realized the angels had departed when the band launched into *Die Fahne Hoch*.

Probably in search of someone more interesting.

Fifteen minutes later, the author of *Mein Kampf* launched into a lengthy tirade. The assembled hung on every word. His speech started at full blast and built in intensity; a verbal maelstrom.

"The National Socialist Party has created the tremendous. Not our business leaders, not our professors and scholars, not soldiers, not artists, not philosophers, thinkers, and poets have pulled our people back from the brink but only the political soldiering of this party."

The crowd erupted in cheers, angry and strident. Schitz thought of his own struggle; the truth seemed universal. Leaders had not kept Hell relevant, nor had trainers, or soldiers only concerned with survival. He—Schitz, the ultimate eternal warrior—he was to be lauded for Demonic success.

"The party's action is just about to begin. Its continued importance, however, will be measurable by the world after us. Everything else will perish but not the party."

Schitz considered everything that had fallen away. A tremor of enthusiasm rippled through the Demon. All the effort throughout centuries had led to this moment. The little man with the ridiculous mustache sent shock waves of renewal and reinvigoration through Schitz. The mortal could not have orated better if he'd been possessed by a Demon. The speech continued.

"I but have to take up position in this context against the thinking of the bourgeois, which often puts it in the phrase: 'Yes, Der Führer, yes, but the party, that's something else.'"

The crowd giggled at the Führer's imitation of the bourgeois. He shifted into a higher oratorical gear.

"No gentlemen, Der Führer is the party, and the Party is Der Führer."

Yes, Schitz thought. *That is truth in all its nakedness. I am the cause, and the cause is me. I am the undisputed leader of the Demons. At the end of the Great War, I was appointed leader of the High Command— the elite group of the three oldest living Demons. I am their Führer!*

Motivation burned in him; a raging fire of industry and purpose. He tuned into the voice once again.

"Just as I feel only as part of the party, the party feels only as a part of me. When I will close my eyes, I do not know but that the party will go on living and stand upon all people, upon the weak and the strong, and that it will shape the future of the nation successfully; I believe, and I know that!"

Schitz cheered and joined in the raucous symphony of "Heil Hitler."

For the next several months Schitz heard nothing but *Die Trommel Schlägt und Schmettert*, the Drums Bleat and Blare.

Die Trommel schlägt und schmettert Rataplan, dondiribon.[14]

'Gentleman," Schitz said (he was possessing the body of an infantry officer), "the Kar 98 bolt action holds a five-round stripper clip; maximum range, 500 meters."

He slid a clip into the rifle. The metallic click of the bolt chambering a round brought him to near orgasmic levels of euphoria. He heard the steady pop... pop... pop of rifles on the range.

Der Hauptmann murrt und wettert.[15]

He stood in front of Waffen SS troops and shouted over the chatter of automatic gunfire. Rain pelted his camouflage poncho.

"The MG 34, a potent weapon. Up to one thousand rounds per minute but watch out for overheating."

Rataplan, dondiribon.[16]

A salty ocean breeze washed over Schitz's face. The U-30 represented the Kriegsmarine's newest class of U-boat.

"She has a speed of 17.7 knots and dives to a depth of two hundred and thirty meters."

His naval officer beamed from ear to ear. He pointed across the choppy Baltic waves. "They'll never know what hit them."

---

[14] The drums beat and blare, *Ra-ta-plan, don-di-ri-bon (vocalized sound of drumming)*
[15] The captain grumbles and rails,
[16] *Ra-ta-plan, don-di-ri-bon (vocalized sound of drumming)*

Fahnen knattern hell, Wehen in dem Wind.[17]

Departing Bf-109s roared down the tarmac.

"That's right, Feldmarshall," Schitz said. He stood in a hangar and addressed possessed senior Luftwaffe figures. "The E-3 variant sports two MG 17s above her engine, and an MG FF in each wing, superior firepower to anything the RAF has to offer."

He punctuated his assessment with a devilish grin and issued a command. "Start her up!"

Schitz put his index fingers in his ears; his scarf whipped about in the warm breeze.

Frisch voran Gesell, Komm mit uns geschwind.[18]

Schitz walked past the assembled Demons. They looked young and hungry. They never broke formation. Their eyes remained locked ahead. He'd learned sword and shield techniques here. They were about to learn how to arm a Tellermine 35 anti-tank mine.

Es gilt die neue Welt.[19]

Schitz struggled to keep his eyes from bulging. He could not believe what he'd just heard from General Kurt Student of the newly formed Fallschirmjäger.

"We parachute out of planes into combat?" Schitz asked.

"Jawhol, Herr Major," the General replied. "Blitzkrieg demands that the infantry be as swift as all the other forces, and now the Luftwaffe's soldiers have the means to make a quick strike at the heart of the enemy."

A far cry from chariots in the desert, Schitz thought.

Die neue Zeit kommt morgen, Rataplan don diri don.[20]

---

[17] Flags rattle bright, Fluttering in the wind.
[18] Brisk companions ahead, Come with us swiftly,
[19] The new world is at stake.
[20] Tomorrow is a new era, *Ra-ta-plan, don-di-ri-don (vocalized sound of drumming)*

The ground shook and jostled the binoculars Schitz held to his eyes. Before the 8.8cm Flak cannon fired another 88mm shell, he focused the glasses and scanned downrange.

"Hit!"

He tried to make his report sound routine, but he could sense the obvious enthusiasm in his voice. The bright, young faces of the gun crew beamed with satisfaction. Schitz's heart pounded in his chest.

Soldat kennt keine Sorgen, Rataplan don diri don.[21]

"You gentlemen have the fine honor of driving this behemoth into battle," Schitz said.

He glanced over from the assembled soldiers and tapped the side of the Panzer III medium tank. The metal was cool and firm beneath his palm.

'Fifteen millimeters of armor all around," he said, "and yet speeds of forty kilometers per hour on the road."

Hinter uns vergeht, Was noch gestern galt,
Rote Sonne steht Abends überm Wald.[22]

8.8 cm Flak 18-36

Schitz shouted at the squad of panzer-grenadiers that was running along the dirt trail through the forest. "Keep moving!"

Gear and weapons were jangling; each man jogged at an impressive pace.

---

[21] A soldier knows no grief, *Ra-ta-plan, don-di-ribon (vocalized sound of drumming)*

[22] At our rear elapses, what yesterday accepted as true, red sun rises, Evenings over woodland.

Und morgen ist neue Zeit.[23]

Schitz's black leather boots clicked on the bunker's concrete floor. He stepped into the presentation room and was greeted by the other generals. Outstretched on the massive table before them lay a map of Europa with countless tiny flags marking the deployment of various units. They talked about troop movements and coordinated assaults with electric intensity.

Die Nacht steht schwarz im Dunkeln, Rataplan don diri don.[24]

The Wehrmacht officer made no attempt to conceal his pride. He patted what looked like an enormous typewriter.

"This is Enigma," he said, "history's first unbreakable code machine."

Schitz remembered when Roman codes were as simple as off-setting each letter by three places. Now there were rotors and electric wiring, a composite of scientific ingenuity that would cloak the movements of great armies.

Doch unsre Sterne funkeln, Rataplan don diri don.[25]

Schitz peered through the telescopic gunsight and whispered, "One thousand meters."

The rifle cracked and recoiled heavily into his shoulder.

His spotter's voice was calm and quiet. "Dead center. Excellent shot, sir."

Feuer weit und breit, Leuchten übers Feld.[26]

Schitz stalked behind the firing line. The air was saturated with the smell of burning powder and alive with ejected brass casings.

---

[23] And tomorrow a new era transpires.
[24] The night remains black and dark, *Ra-ta-plan, don-di-ri-don (vocalized sound of drumming)*
[25] But our stars glitter, *Ra-ta-plan, don-di-ri-don (vocalized sound of drumming)*
[26] Fire far and wide, Glaring over the fields.

A junior Demon shouted to be heard over the glorious racket. "What do you think?"

"What's not to love," Schitz said. "It weighs less than four pounds and fires at a rate of five hundred rounds per minute. The MP40 is every combat soldier's wet dream."

Und die Männlichkeit, Stirbt nicht in der
Welt, Unser Herz ist fest und jung.[27]

"Never forget," Schitz said to the cadet Demons from the Celestial Realm while they possessed an artillery crew, "no matter how much firepower you have at your disposal (he gestured to the 3.7 cm Flakzwilling anti-aircraft cannon still smoking from the earlier drill), we will always have to be skilled enough to kill the Angels with these." He pointed to an array of dirks that festooned his belt. "You must be prepared to leap out quickly and fell them with a single, well-placed thrust."

Kamerad laß uns nur ziehen, Rataplan don diri don.[28]

"Gotcha!" Schitz's voice resonated with delight as he placed the gyro gunsight of his fighter over his training partner's BF-109. A wide grin spread across the mortal pilot's face. He banked away, then dove toward the ground.

Scheust du auch Not und Mühen, Rataplan don diri don.[29]

"Faster! Faster!" Schitz's demands for increased pace from his paratroopers were as unrelenting as the hill they were attempting to climb. The sun assaulted them without mercy.

---

[27] And the manhood won't die in this world, our hearts are hard and young.
[28] Comrade we may only march, *Ra-ta-plan, don-di-ri-don (vocalized sound of drumming)*
[29] You dread troubles and adversity, *Ra-ta-plan, don-di-ri-don (vocalized sound of drumming)*

Neue Welt ist not.[30]

"Eyes right!"

Schitz snapped his head to the side and saw the Führer's arm outstretched in salute. A contagious fire pulsed in the man's eyes.

Und sie bricht herein, Woll'n beim Abendrot, überm Berge sein Dann trifft auch uns die Ruh.[31]

The marching echoed in his head long after the parade had concluded.

SCHITZ SAT, CONTENTED, IN the shade of the Parisian café.

"Germany might be building a war machine, but you still have to come to France if you want the best wine and cheese," he said with a smile. He laid his cigarette on a porcelain ashtray and lifted his glass of merlot. Elise smiled demurely.

"I can't drink much wine nowadays," she said softly. "It goes right to this old head of mine."

Her wrinkled lips creased with a smile. Schitz shuddered at how old and frail she had become. The rules did not seem fair. Demons and Angels aged to around the maturity of a human thirty-year-old and remained there until killed. Wraiths aged to the maturity of a human eighty-year-old before leveling off.

"You're not that frail," he said.

Elise batted away his reply with her one remaining hand. "Pish, posh," she said with a smile. "No one said I was frail, just old, but I can still pull you by the ear."

Schitz laughed and leaned his head back. He closed his eyes and

---

[30] The new world is misery.
[31] And you break inside, by sunset glow you want to be across the mountains, then we will have serenity.

enjoyed the cool breeze kissing his face, the hustle and bustle of the City of Light. He drank in the aromas of breads and cheeses, the popping hiss of music from a record player in the window of an apartment above the café.

"C'est la vie, Mama," he said.

He scooped up his cigarette and took a long pull.

"It is a beautiful day," Elise said without much enthusiasm. "I've always liked it here, maybe because of the name, the Champs-Élysées..." Her voice faded into nothingness.

"But you're wondering why I asked for you to meet me," Schitz said.

"Well, you don't exactly call on me too often nowadays, my young lord," she replied.

It struck Schitz as odd how she still considered him young after countless centuries. "It is important to savor these moments, Mama," he said in a voice much softer than his usual bark. "The next war... it will be," he paused, "massive."

The cigarette burned out. Schitz frisked his double-breasted, tweed suit for another.

"Wars are always massive," Elise replied dismissively, her voice heavy with sadness.

Unlike him, she could not possess a youthful host. Instead, she sat before him dressed as the elderly woman she was, though in modern enough clothing so as not to draw attention.

"Is it all that bad?" Schitz said.

"Who do you think you are fooling?" she asked. "Every corner of the map will be engulfed in flames. I worry for you now as when you were little."

Schitz shrugged and would have replied but his gaze fell on a stunning redhead draped in a tight green dress.

"Fashionable," Elise said.

"Ah... sorry," Schitz said with a bashful smile. "It's just, I've kind of gotten accustomed to all that war entails. I am a seasoned warrior. One takes pleasure where one can."

"You are no longer a regular soldier," the Wraith said with a strained voice. "You're second only to the Lord on High; you are the Supreme Commander of his armies from now until the day... until the day you fall, or the day we win, whichever comes first. Now the Angels will hunt you without mercy. You cannot bed every woman you see; there are spies everywhere."

Schitz lit another cigarette and drew in the calming smoke. He held it for a long time, then blew it from his nose.

"Mama," his voice suddenly very stern, "we will win, we will win in the next war, garantis."

"Garantis? Vous ne garantis rien," she said and raised her glass of wine to her lips.

Schitz saluted her with his glass. "Well, don't bet against me. I've been learning a lot."

"I never would, Son," she said. "I'm just very taxed. This war, it's all anybody can talk about."

Schitz drained the wine. "That's part of why I wanted to speak to you today," he said. "There's a rumor that even the Wraiths are going to be used in a combat role."

"It's no rumor," she replied. "There's been a decree to that effect."

"Why wasn't I informed?"

"I believe Satan informed us first to give us time to come to grips with our fate," she said softly. "What hope do we have against the squadrons of Heaven? It would seem we're to be sacrificial spoilers, Sir Francis Drake's burning ships, if you would."

"But surely the Lord doesn't require anything from you," Schitz said, aghast.

"And why not," Elise replied with resignation, "am I somebody of note?"

"You are to me," he said. He touched her hand. "I'll ensure you have no part in this folly."

Elise did not even attempt a smile. "You are a good son. I would be proud to have borne you, but please, worry about yourself."

"Well," Schitz said. "that was the second reason I called you. I have the inkling that there's a half-breed in the High Command, maybe more than one."

"That's a very serious situation," Elise said, "and an accusation you should not level without certainty. If you accuse without irrefutable—"

"I know the punishment for false allegations," he said. "The accused can demand satisfaction, and the Priests would be outraged."

She leaned across the table. She looked around for prying ears. "But if there's proof, there'll be nowhere in Hell or Earth for them to hide. The Lord considers half-breeds an unholy abomination; so does the king of the Angels."

"What should I do? I cannot lead the squadrons into battle with turncoats alongside me. In their very nature, half-breeds are... dangerous beyond belief."

He took another deep drag from his cigarette.

No wonder humans like these so very much, he thought.

Elise leaned back a little. "Let's start with why you feel this way. Are you sure you're not getting paranoid?"

A steely glare settled over Schitz's face. "A healthy degree of paranoia can be the closest of friends," he replied.

"Yes, that's right, I did teach you that; nevertheless, you'll drive yourself batty looking for a rat if one does not exist."

"But you don't deny the possibility of such a thing."

"Of course not. It has happened before."

Now it was Schitz's turn to check for eavesdroppers. "Well, to answer your question, at the end of the last war, there was a string of suspicious deaths."

Elise looked suddenly alarmed.

Schitz continued, "Spanish Influenza was poised to assume the role of Supreme Commander, instrumental as he was in all aspects of the Great War. He led in every imaginable way—strategy, innovative technology, battlefield kills. He was going to be quite a challenge to the three senior commanders, myself included."

Elise said nothing, but Schitz could see her facile mind at work.

"He was killed in Russia in a mop-up operation," Schitz said. "After all the battles across Europa and the Near East, he died in a skirmish with the Red Army, claimed by an Angel of virtually no notoriety."

"These things happen," Elise said. She filled her glass.

"They do, but this seemed too perfect. It changed the appointment of the Supreme Commander."

"To you," Elise said, "not the worst outcome."

"I suppose," Schitz said.

He was distracted again by the redhead in the tight dress. She smiled at him; an invitation?

"Get your head out of your pants and focus," Elise said. She was not smiling.

Schitz was grateful that the waiter's delivery of a fresh bottle distracted his old caretaker for a moment. The Demon regrouped. "It also changed the dynamic of the High Command. I have long since perfected my art. I don't need to kill humans to send fear through humanity; I can break their minds at will, I can turn them stark raving mad. They wander into the darkness by the millions at the flick of my hand. I bring to the High Command the first Psychological-based Supreme Commander in the history of Hell. It elevates the other Psychologicals: Panic, Anxiety, Depression, Anorexia, Autism—all gained massive credibility over the Cancers and other physical ailments."

"So?"

"Think about it. With authority, the rats can conceal themselves. With Spanish Influenza in charge, they would be more vulnerable to discovery. When you're on top it's very easy to deal with those who find you suspicious, not so much as a subordinate."

"He was very power-hungry," Elise said. They sipped wine for a while. "Did you ever take all of our warnings seriously that he was a threat to you?"

A mysterious look painted his face. Little did she know about the dogfight and mid-air collision over the Western Front.

"He was ambitious, successful, competitive," she said.

Memory transported him back to the pitching deck of His Majesty's Ship Temeraire as it fired upon the French Bucentaure. Spanish Influenza strode across the swaying boards, boots clacking and gear jangling, pistols in hand, and saber adorning his belt.

"The Angels are trapped there on the French ship of the line," he shouted to Schitz. "A gold coin to the Demon with the most bodies when we capture the ship."

The ocean spray receded as quickly as it had arisen, and Schitz returned to the café. "He was... a warrior, and I suppose he could have been dangerous if I did not always control my surroundings. Why?"

Elise looked relieved. "No reason," she replied.

"Are you all right?" he asked.

Elise composed herself. "Yes, I'm fine, just tired. I think I should return home."

Schitz tossed back the remainder of his wine and stood. He embraced the Wraith with great affection, shocked by how frail and skeleton-like her body felt.

"I'll head to the washroom," she said, "I should find enough water there."

She gestured to her ever-present satchel of earth that hung from her waist. Schitz smiled and dropped a wad of bills on the table. As his Wraith headed into the café Schitz was uncertain of his next destination. He drifted aimlessly across the street and entered a sweets shop. He was pleasantly surprised to see the woman in the green dress. He walked down the aisle to where she was inspecting a package of dried cherry candies.

"Excuse me, Miss," he said.

When he squeezed past her, he brushed his hands along her hips. Her body was lean and fit. She exhaled audibly and rolled her head to the side as if in ecstasy.

"What are you doing here, Monsieur?"

She pushed her body into his; subtle, but hardly by accident.

"Looking for something sweet," he said.

Her lips, cloaked in crimson lipstick, curled into a devilish smile. "You're quite forward," she said.

"I take what I want," Schitz said.

All subtlety aside, he slid his hand up from her waist along her rib cage until his thumbs rested under her generous breasts.

She responded by pressing her thigh against his crotch. Her eyebrows arched—he was fully aroused. "But how can you take what is offered to you freely?"

Schitz moved closer. She opened her mouth and licked his lips. The kiss left no questions about what was going to happen.

They barely made it through the door of Schitz's flat. Her body was intoxicating, voluptuous. Schitz explored every inch; her ivory skin, her heaving cleavage, arching pelvis.

Flushed with wine and passion, he pushed her, face down, onto his small writing desk lifted her dress to her waist. He did not care that the blinds were open. He entered her from behind and grabbed a handful of her long, thick hair.

"Look at the view while I fuck you."

"I can't keep my eyes open," she said. She was already gasping for air.

"Do as I command, or I will stop," he said.

Her voice took on a commanding tone. "If you stop, I will have to kill you," she said.

He obeyed... for a long time.

THE SHEETS OF THE small bed were warm. A cool breeze wafted into the tiny flat. The room's only illumination came from the dying rays of another Parisian day.

I've taken quite a little holiday, Schitz thought.

He looked next to him at Madalyne's naked body. The strains of *Mon Legionnaire* filled the apartment, a melancholy little tune.

"It's a little apt," Madalyne said. She licked his ear.

"Hmm," he said.

"The singer does not know much about her lover," she said. Schitz said nothing.

"I like it, though," she said, "although it is so sad; it makes me remember, just like you do."

Despite every inclination to resume their lovemaking, Schitz stepped out of bed. "What do you mean?"

"I know it might sound crazy," she said, uncoiling into the space Schitz had vacated, "but ever since I was a little girl, I've had memories. They are memories of other times, other lives, déjà vu—they are overwhelming, clear, and intense beyond measure."

Schitz knew all about "The Strain"; a bloodline of humans able to recall portions of their past incarnations, albeit some more lucidly than others. That was part of what had attracted him and Madalyne to each other. He now realized they were both aware of their journeys across millennia—they looked at one another and saw a kindred spirit.

"What do you remember?" he asked.

A bashful look crossed her face. Schitz felt a twinge of regret for his inquiry. "Ah, a lover, I surmise," he said, shocked at how much dejection he heard in his voice.

Like a slinking wisp of smoke, Madalyne rose and pressed her naked body against Schitz. She kissed him with intent, then whispered, "We're here now; that's all that matters."

Inwardly, Schitz groaned. He knew he could not stay in this body for much longer. His thoughts were already becoming disorganized; he risked losing the focus required to open a portal or to leap with precision. Then there was the potential danger to his psyche.

"Yes, mon chère," he replied, "and we're in need of dinner."

He pulled on his trousers and shirt, then began searching for his tie. Somehow Madalyne was ready before he finished his half-Windsor.

What a beauty.

She dragged her fingers across his stubbly face and walked out of the apartment. Schitz was happy that his host owned an automobile. He fished in the pocket of his suit jacket for the keys to the Citroen. He opened the door for Madalyne. Something registered in his subconscious on the way to his side of the vehicle.

He whirled and looked up the street—two Demons. He did not recognize their hosts, but he immediately sensed hostile intent.

He dropped to one knee as pistol rounds peppered the car's fender and side panels. Schitz grinned and pulled the Walther PP from the small of his back. Any Demon who had graduated the Academy should have hit Schitz, but neither of his assailants anticipated his ability to afflict the minds of their hosts. Schitz's instantaneous mental interference had been just enough to throw their shots wide.

The city street that moments earlier had been serene now reverberated with of the chatter of gunfire. The Demons were each armed with a pair of M1911s. They emptied their clips and reached for spares. Schitz centered the solitary bar of his Walther PP's iron sight over the head of the Demon to his left and squeezed the trigger. An oozing hole dotted the man's forehead. Before the target fell, Schitz pulled the trigger again.

With ruthless instinct, he stepped out of his host and retrieved a throwing knife from his belt with each hand. The two Demons, vulnerable and defenseless, seized beside the slumped heaps of their former hosts. The steel vipers in his hands hissed on their way to the targets and fanged the Demons in their respective carotids.

Schitz watched until they twitched no longer.

Fuck! I can't jump back into Jacques.

He saw an elderly man crouching against the façade of a building across the street, apparently paralyzed with fear. *He'll have to do,* Schitz thought.

Encopresis and Ganser Syndrome, he thought. *Two of Spanish Influenza's retinue.*

He scooped up one of the discarded 1911s, walked to the car, and fired two shots into Jacques's midsection. He slid behind the wheel of the Citroen and looked at Madalyne.

Terror etched the beauty's face.

"I'll explain in a moment, my dear," he said.

He cranked the car and backed into the street. He drove away in the opposite direction of the approaching sirens.

Half a kilometer away, Schitz slowed the sedan and spoke.

"Don't worry, don't worry," he said. "It's me, Jacques, well not that my name is Jacques, but it's me. Your name is Madalyne DuPont; you grew up in Aaras; you have a small mole very high on the inside of your left thigh."

He stole a glance and was relieved to see a calmer expression on his lover's face. Then he looked at her heaving chest. Lust boiled within him.

A car horn blared. He'd drifted across the center line. He swerved back into his lane and was immediately snapped back into reality.

What the fuck? Who tried to kill me? Who has the balls to attempt such a thing in direct violation of the Divine Dictum?

He weighed the consequences of confiding in Madalyne, the mortal.

"Why not," he said.

"Pardon?" Madelyn's voice shook; whether from fear or anger, he could not tell.

He took a deep breath.

"I need to tell you something," he said. "Something incredible— frankly unbelievable."

"Go ahead," she whispered.

"My name is Schizophrenia Incenderos Nervosa, but most people call me Schitz. You said that you remember your past lives. Well, you've had many past lives; in all that time, I have had only one. My kind—"

"Your kind?" she asked softly, as though falling asleep.

"Yes... ah... I am... well, you would call me a Demon. I have only one life, and I have spent it in an unending cauldron of ceaseless war against those you would call Angels. As in all war, everybody believes they are on the just side, but for now, right and wrong have little bearing. I will simply say that I was born on a barren plain amid the clatter of swords in the time of Zargon. I came of age during those early years of humanity. Ever since I have participated in one side or another of every human conflict in history. There is a docu- ment... it's called The—"

He stopped.

Broad strokes, he told himself. *Keep it simple.*

"Never mind. Let's just say there are rules. God and the Devil are in a constant battle for control of this world. Each has a vast army. But one of the biggest rules is that we must always conceal our exis- tence from humanity."

Madalyne had recovered her fire. She sat straight, eyes boring into Schitz.

"But you are talking to me now. Wouldn't that be a violation, or penalty, or something?"

"Absolutely," Schitz said. "But something is wrong. I was just attacked during a time of peace. That's not supposed to happen—ever."

"Why are you different... why are you suddenly old? Is this your real form?"

"No. I don't want to explain it all, but I had to leave Jacques. Human hosts are not reusable. We are generally stronger than a human's psyche. We can enter their mind, control their body, speech, and actions; we have access to their memories. They have minimal recollection of the time we are within them, and they are held responsible for the actions we take—ah—on their behalf, as it were. When we possess a human, we cannot be killed. It is only when we are outside of their body in the Celestial Realm that we can be killed."

"Explain, please?" Her voice was once again weak.

"It's a place where we can see both the human world and our own domain, and it's the only place where we can die. My side believes that our victory is the only way for the world to know peace. When the war is over, we will no longer need to afflict humanity with our diseases. There will be tranquility. You and I can be together, forever, if we make that happen soon."

Never in his millennia-long life had Schitz ever intentionally violated the Dictum. Panic clutched at his throat. He was uncertain of the mechanism by which divulgences were reported, but he was certain he was burned and would be subject to a death warrant from either side.

After a life of work—a lifetime of lifetimes—I will be disavowed, he thought. *But she is worth it. Perhaps there is no way for anyone to know that a mortal has gained knowledge of the conflict, that I have violated Clause 3. In that case, we can remain together while I pursue the final victory.*

Schitz relaxed. He'd never known such peace. He took a moment to appreciate the serene countryside. Night was falling, and the hills and fields reflected the amber hues of the dying sun.

He eased the Citroen down the country road.

Schitz glanced at Madalyne. Her head slumped forward. He'd seen the unnatural pose before far too many times.

He reached across and raised her heavy head. Just below her delicate collar bone and exposed by her plunging décolletage, Schitz saw the telltale circle of a bullet wound—an errant round.

He unleashed a howl of anguish and continued to shriek until the only noise he could make was a choking croak of pain. Only after he positioned Madalyne as though she were sleeping and parked the car at the side of the road did Schitz realize he had never broken the Divine Dictum. Accidental and/or purposeful divulgences could be remedied without breach if the offending party ensured the death of the knowledgeable human before said informed human passed on, documented, or in any way preserved the knowledge obtained. Stumbling along the road, intoxicated by his grief, Schitz wondered whether any of his tale had seeped into Madalyne's ebbing conscious.

Several miles down the road, he recovered sufficiently to reflect on the events of the afternoon.

Elise was too eager to entertain my ridiculous theory of a half-breed in a position of authority. She knows the blood lines of Anorexia and Autism better than I do. She was trying to throw me off the scent—she was behind the death of Spanish Influenza and Anthrax.

He kicked a stray stone and stopped. Anger boiled inside, a burning fire of rage that could be quenched with only one thing; blood.

I don't care that Spanish Influenza is dead, he thought. *That's one less rival, one less dangerous enemy. But Elise cost me a dear friend and she indirectly participated in Madelyn's death. I warned Elise many times not to interfere with my affairs.*

His rage was displaced by a cold, calculated resolve.

My friend and my lover are gone. Someone is going to pay.

Chapter 6

The Marksman

"Their focus is fixed upon Poland at the moment for certain."
Uranium II almost always spoke with confidence, even when he was wrong.

"Soon, they will be drawn in deeper. The war will expand. France, then England, will join the fray."

"I agree," Zinc said.

Uranium II unfurled a parchment on the meeting table. His pride was evident. "I have prepared the documents and assessments. My Familiars have been most industrious. They now know the signs and incantations to open a portal to Hell. They have even charted a rough map of its layout. It is very similar to the geography of Heaven, about five square miles overall."

He indicated different areas with extravagant flourishes of a brass-tipped pointer.

"There are high unpassable mountains to the South from which flows the river Styx. Immediately North of the mountains is a series of swamps that give way to rolling grassy hills. The Styx bisects the land mass. To the East is their Great Hall, a massive structure, presumably their training grounds and living quarters. The Familiars did not dare get too close."

Zinc pursed his lips and stroked his chin.

Impressive recon, he thought.

Uranium II continued, "On the western bank of the Styx, there is a dark and twisting wood; it is called Limbo. The entirety of the realm is surrounded by a celestial sea. Joined by the Styx, it plummets off a chasm to the Mortal Realm. Unlike our world, which is illumined by the sun, Hell's source of light is Earth's moon. Our forces must be prepared for perpetual nighttime."

Uranium II looked around the table. God, senior Familiars, his sons Lord Fluorine, Lord Bromine, Lord Tantalum, and Lord Osmium, as well as Lord and Lady Hydrogen, Lord Lithium, Lord and Lady Zinc, and Zinc's sons from his two marriages, Lord Cadmium, Lord Scandium, Lord Gallium, and Lord Germanium were fixated on the map with varying degrees of excitement and concern.

"The woods of Limbo represent the best place to initiate the assault," Uranium II said. "From there, we can construct a rudimentary bridge to cross the Styx and storm their Great Hall."

Everyone awaited God's reaction. He took his time, as he did with all deliberative matters.

"I believe the primary objective of this incursion should be to find and eliminate my brother," he said. "If we kill him, we can likely expect the surrender of Hell and the conclusion of this conflict. This is an extreme risk, perhaps even a violation of the Divine Dictum. Are we prepared for this assault to be our undoing?"

Again, there was silence.

Finally, God spoke again. "Having said that, I believe the plan is well-conceived and well worth the risk."

No one else felt the need to share an opinion. The attendees filed out. Zinc made a point to walk out last, with Uranium II.

"The absence of your brother and all of the Standard Bearers he has sired was more than noticeable," Zinc said.

"Platinum is not my issue," Uranium II said. "I am not my brother's keeper. Besides, he is heavily involved in the most recent Sino-Japanese war."

"Hardly a good reason," Zinc said. "There seems to be no Demonic involvement in that conflict but considerable casualties on our side."

Uranium II snapped a response. "You never seem to have a problem spilling Angelic blood!"

"Only when necessary," Zinc said. "But if you recall the circumstances leading to your installation as Lord Uranium, you recognize I make no accommodation for an Angelic civil war."

"Circumstances are far different now," Uranium II replied. "The way you broke Iron and Carbon has all of Heaven in lockstep with you. Even if there were those who would seek to usurp your authority, the Great War drained the Houses substantially of any of the older fighters. The new generations all see you and me not as targets to overcome but as revered Ancestors, pillars of the Heavenly order. Once I have dealt with my brother, stability will be fully secured."

"And yet, you leave yourself vulnerable," Zinc said.

Confusion painted Uranium II's face. "How?"

"You know how dangerous Heaven can be. Except for meetings like this one with the senior leadership, I am always shadowed by Constance Silver and Anna Gold."

He gestured over his shoulder. Uranium looked at the menacing females a few strides to the side. Zinc continued, "I have an expanded security detail, Familiars who keep an eye on the Angels around me. You should consider the same."

"Maybe you're just paranoid," Uranium II said. "Or maybe you have more enemies. My greatest foe is my brother. In time, I will end him, but right now, the focus of all must be on our incursion into Hell. It offers us a great opportunity that must not be squandered."

T<small>ITUS WALKED WITH</small> E<small>RIN</small> along the banks of the Styx, a rare moment of blissful privacy.

"You've taken to carrying a sword, my love?" she asked.

"Since we are now sending the Wraiths into combat, I may well be next, even though I was dismissed from the military," he replied.

"It feels as though it is the end," she replied. She gazed at the river. Her eyes were moist and wistful. "Hold me once outside the secrecy of our chamber, please."

For as long as he could remember, he had been forced to keep his relationship with Erin a secret. Priests were forbidden to engage in carnal relationships by church doctrine. Priests were the offspring of Demons and Wraiths, conceived during a ritual overseen by Satan and only conducted when the Dark Lord deemed the need for more members of Church leadership.

Still, Titus and Erin had maintained their secret tête-à-tête for so long, it felt more like a marriage than a love affair. He pulled her closer to him, certain that the Wraiths and the Purists were occupied with other matters more important than observing two Priests strolling along the river's edge. He enjoyed the luxury of feeling her body against his while outside the confines of his chamber.

Erin stiffened.

"Is someone watching?" Titus said. He pushed her away, a little less than gently.

"No, my love. What is that... look!"

He followed her pointing finger. A wooden bridge spanned the Styx. Rows of Angels walked in single file—one after another like ants on a stick.

"This cannot be," the Priest said. "It is forbidden." He pushed Erin again, this time launching her in the direction of the Great Hall. "Run, girl! Run for your life! Tell every Demon, Priest, and Wraith you encounter to arm themselves and get here at once. And tell Satan to lock himself away."

He blew her a kiss, then ran toward the bridge, drawing his sword.

At the terminus, Titus encountered an Angel of broad stature with features like a mortal Asian. The Angel was driving wooden stabilizing spikes into the ground with a hand sledge. When the Angel saw Titus, sword in hand, he withdrew a wicked-looking axe from behind his shoulders.

Titus swung his sword. The Angel blocked the telegraphed move easily but lost his balance and fell backward into the incandescent waters of the Styx. The Angel howled and screamed in panic until his comrades pulled him back onto the bridge. Titus seized the initiative and attacked. He hacked at the flimsy structure, apparently made in haste using lumber from the forest of Limbo. It was lashed together with rope. After a piece broke away, Titus jumped across to the edge of the bridge, grabbed one of the guide ropes and began yanking on it. The back-and-forth motion made the bridge sway. The Angels, still trying to recover their comrade, clutched for any handhold they could find.

Titus rushed forward and swung his sword at the lead Angel. He struck the Angel's sword. The impact pitched the Angel into the water. She screamed as if she were being boiled alive.

Titus knew the Angels would not try to surround him. The water of the Styx was mother's milk to him but injurious to citizens of Heaven. The Angels recovered their scalded friends and retreated.

Now overconfident, Titus feinted the attack. He was struck in the chest and stomach by arrows fired from the far shore. Though sorely wounded, he crawled back towards his homeland and hacked away at the remaining guy-line until it severed. The bridge collapsed into the Styx and carried the Priest along.

Titus felt the restorative effects of the water. He recoiled when one of the writhing souls carried by the current careened into him but regained his composure and pulled the arrows out of his body. He swam to shore and took refuge behind a bolder to avoid another attack from Heaven's archers.

A host of Demons arrived at his position.

"Well fought, Your Holiness," Autism said. "Thank you."

Autism plucked an arrow from the ground. "I didn't think there were ranged weapons in the Celestial," he said.

Titus extended his hand. "Give that here," he said. "I believe these fools have just ended the war in our favor."

THE BOARDROOM OF THE insurance company overlooked Manhattan. Within his light gray suit, God stared across at the marvel that was New York City. The endless flow of souls along the streets below reminded him of the Eunoe.

He glanced away from the window to his solitary companion, Gertrude, a senior Priestess of the Heavenly Church, and the foremost expert on the Divine Dictum.

"I should kill Uranium II," God said.

"I was under the impression that you despised capital punishment. Even the Decimation by Ordeal allows the guilty party a choice," Gertrude said.

God scowled. "I said I *should*, not I *will*," he replied. "At the very least, I should demote him, but his battlefield prowess is almost unmatched. Besides, according to the reports, we experienced a wretched case of bad luck. What are the odds that a Priest and his mistress happened upon our army at its most vulnerable, right before they snuck across the river and into the heart of Hell's capital?"

Gertrude shook her head. Before she could respond, the door creaked. The Devil strolled in wearing a fashionable white suit over a starched, light blue dress shirt, and a matching paisley tie and pocket square. He was accompanied by a Priest dressed in the traditional black robe of Hell's clergy.

Everyone sat at the conference table. After a few awkward moments of silence, God spoke.

"Well, Brother, you are looking healthy."

"To your disappointment, I'm sure," the Devil replied.

Before anyone else spoke, a solitary figure entered the room and closed the door behind him. He was tall and dressed in an immaculate charcoal suit. He stood at the head of the table and spoke in a grim voice.

"This meeting will be brief; you will each present your information. My determination will be instant and final."

God hoped no one else heard him gulp.

The efforts of centuries hang in the balance. So many lives have been squandered—they could all have died in vain.

The three deities had last met when they drafted the Divine Dictum. Circades had not aged, but his appearance had changed in some manner, though God could not identify exactly how.

The Devil's Priest spoke first. "We are here today because the forces of Heaven, under the command of the one who refers to himself as God, have breached the central tenant of the Divine Dictum—that all conflict be contained to the Mortal Realm." He tossed a handful of Celestial arrows up the conference table. "Additionally, they have produced weapons banned by the Divine Dictum."

Gertrude rose from her seat. "What constitutes conflict?" she asked. "A conversation? The movement of troops? I would contend that the only acceptable definition of conflict in our context is an action resulting in violent death or severe, irreparable injury. Did any Angels or Demons or other living beings die in the events mentioned by the members of Hell? The answer is a resounding 'no.' No one died. Were any maimed? No. We are willing to accept censure for the creation of the banned weapons. We made them... we will accept the consequences."

That's the end, God thought. *There is nothing more to say.*

Circades leaned on the table. "I accept that the presence of Angels in Hell is a novel experience. However, I can hardly see why I should be bothered with this matter. Surely, conflict is any time you are in proximity to each other. Let's say this: you will only be in proximity to each other in the Mortal Realm. In the Celestial, you will maintain distance and you will stay out of each other's abodes. As to punishment, I will not hand victory to Hell over such a minor thing as this."

God sighed audibly in relief.

Circades continued, "Still, I would like to see this resolved. Heaven, you will turn over to Hell fifty percent of the Angels that participated in the incursion, and they will be dealt with as Hell sees fit. Punishment for Hell, you will cede the area occupied by the Angels while in Hell to Heaven."

Satan erupted. "Why should we be punished?"

Circades eyes grew dark. "For wasting my time."

IN THE DAYS FOLLOWING the meeting with the Titan, Heaven secured its position in Limbo and began clearing much of the forest to construct a fortress. The Standard Bearers chose which Angels would be sent across the river.

The subsequent bloodletting was a pageant of gore. The sacrificial Angels, sent in canoes built of the felled trees of Limbo, endured all manner of torments. Their colleagues in Limbo watched a systematic orgy of retribution—torture, humiliation, rape, and, finally, murder.

From atop a parapet, Uranium II took in the end effects of his venture with grim bearing.

"I will take to the mortal world," he said to Zinc, "where I will deal with Platinum once and for all. Then we will have our final victory over these heathens."

THE GREAT HALL OF Heaven was typically serene and majestic regardless of the state of Heavenly affairs within the Mortal Realm. This was not, however, the case in the late spring of 1940. Injured Angels filed through the portals at an alarming rate. They bypassed the Return Ritual in search of lifesaving Manna. Haphazard combat groups were thrown together without clear objectives or instructions. The Demons appeared to be everywhere all at once. The pandemonium and lack of strategy heightened the sense of dread that weighed heavily in Zinc's stomach. He had a foreboding premonition of impending disaster.

Zinc overheard a cluster of Angels arguing over the merits of operating in large or small groups. The young Angels appeared petrified at the notion of combat. They ceased the discussion and snapped to attention at his approach.

A junior Angel signaled for permission to speak. Zinc gave a haphazard wave.

"Where do you think we can make the most impact?" the youth asked.

Zinc glanced at the young soldiers, ten in all. He recognized none of them.

"Have any of you seen combat prior to this war?" he asked. He hoped they could not see his frustration.

One of them responded in a reedy voice. "I saw action at the end of the Great War and during the Russian Revolution."

"Good," Zinc said. "I can use you."

The group appeared to perk up with the knowledge he would be going with them.

"I was supposed to be conducting a reconnaissance of Manchuria or Manchukuo, or whatever they are calling it these days," Zinc said, "but I can put that off for a little. We'll go to the Ardennes."

Angels and Demons were neutral in the wars of men. They imbedded themselves in the forces of any army where they thought they might enjoy a tactical advantage. Still, Zinc was heavily invested in maintaining the empire he had sought to build despite the frustration brought on by the failure of the League of Nations.

Consequently, for better or worse, Heaven found itself tied to the countries who identified themselves as the Allies. Zinc readied the men knowing they would seek out Belgian, French, or English forces to possess. It did not matter much to Zinc that the Allies were in retreat. He only sought to slay the Demons he encountered.

Zinc saw the irony of his position. The mortal Allies were as inept at halting the spread of Germany and Japan as the Angels were at handling the Demonic forces. His decision to lead the neophytes had been spontaneous and driven more out of irritation than wisdom.

He had assigned Uranium II, Hydrogen, and Rachael to a more experienced squad then charged into battle once again.

The German army traversed the Ardennes in a pincer movement—General Reinhardt in the North, Generals Kleist and Guderian in the South. Their forces would eventually link up in the vicinity of Montcornet. Along Reinhardt's line of advance stood an assortment of French infantry. They had been deployed along a nameless bridge that spanned one of the region's many rivers. Zinc and his ten Angels encountered the contingent of French forces along the river's western bank beside a narrow footbridge a few hundred meters south of the Germans. The French infantry carried mainly aging bolt action rifles. They had only two machine guns.

Zinc assessed the situation.

The Germans are already in possession of the larger bridges. Their armor will cross there. The French are virtually surrounded. We can assay the German troops, offer token resistance, and then surrender.

From within the commanding French lieutenant, he addressed his men. "Gentlemen," he said, "we can either sit here on our asses or do something for France. Let us show the Germans we are not yet whipped."

He struck out over the footbridge; the men fell in behind. They threaded their way through the thick, pathless expanse of the forest. Zinc saw a gray-clad figure and raised a hand. The men halted.

Zinc raised the iron sights of his MAS Modèle 36 rifle and pulled the trigger. The report of the rifle was accompanied by the impact of the recoil into his shoulder. The enemy soldier collapsed to the ground. A collection of gray shadows dropped to the ground. Flashes of light blinked from the distance and the crashing of incoming rifle fire resounded through the woods. Zinc's squad fired in the direction of the enemy.

"Avance!" he shouted.

This is a minor force, Zinc thought. *They are tasked with securing the flanks while the main unit moves along the road.*

Zinc led his men towards the enemy. Leaves crunched underfoot. Incoming fire snapped tree branches. Bark exploded on all sides. The foe scattered as he and the squadron of inexperienced Angels led the French forces toward the road. When they reached the tree line, Zinc saw the main body of the German forces moving along the road toward a large bridge. He scanned the Germans for Demonic auras.

An Angel moved along the tree line to his position.

"I don't see any Demons, sir."

"No," Zinc replied. "Pass the word—machine guns target the light vehicles. Infantry will storm the tanks."

The Angel nodded and moved back along the line. Zinc watched two machine gunners set up their Fusil-mitrailleur Modèle 1924 M29s on their bipods, one on either side of him. Zinc still did not see any Demons but decided that the time to assault the road had arrived. He reached for the whistle at the lieutenant's neck and placed it between his lips. The metal was cold; his mouth was dry. He raised his rifle and aimed for one of the foes riding on a German tank. The whistle's shrill blast cut the air like an audible razor. Zinc fired, worked the bolt, then broke cover.

The French machine guns chattered like deadly chipmunks and cut through the exposed troops and lighter vehicles. The infantry clamored up onto the tanks, raised their hatches, and dropped grenades. Zinc had just hopped to the ground when he heard a muffled explosion.

They're all dead.

His orders came with a certainty born of experience.

"You men, move down the road—half on either side. Position one gun facing east and one west. The rest of you form a perimeter."

The men fanned out around the scene of the ambush. Dead infantrymen and burning vehicles littered the road. Zinc looked at the wreckage. He always found it pointless to kill mortals. He wished the ambush had yielded better results, but he knew he had to accept whatever battle he encountered.

Machine gun fire along the eastern-most road interrupted his thoughts. Contact with the enemy. Incoming rounds kicked up dirt. The infantrymen fired in a constant stream at the approaching ghostlike gray images. A shell exploded a few meters from Zinc. When his vision cleared, he looked west; German tank. The western machine gunner opened fire on the supporting infantry. Within a matter of minutes, the French position deteriorated from precarious to untenable. The enemy came from all sides and opened a withering volume of fire. French soldiers fell all around. Zinc prepared for a withdrawal.

It would be nothing for the Angels to move through the German troops and open a doorway. Zinc saw the head of a possessed Frenchman explode—a bullet to the forehead. Instinctively, Zinc stepped into the Celestial while his fellow lay seizing upon the ground. A dark blur moved from behind one of the immobilized German vehicles that were scattered across the road. A Demon set upon the hapless Angel.

Zinc shouted to his compatriots. "Demons in the perimeter!"

He rushed forward. The Demon ducked behind a smoldering German vehicle. Zinc approached with caution. When he peered around the rear of the half-track, the Demon was already gone. Zinc circled the wreck and was met by an onrushing sword. He blocked the blow with his own blade and stepped to the side. The Demon was a lithe female with flowing red hair and steely blue eyes. She raised her weapon as though to strike at Zinc but, at the final moment, jumped into a nearby mortal.

Zinc was certain the Demon was cornered. Several other Angels arrived in the Celestial. Two of them stepped into mortals to fight the Demon. The redheaded devil pulled the pin on a grenade and dropped it to the ground, then stepped into the Celestial. One of the mortal Frenchmen went down with a bullet in the gut.

Sniper—she's working in concert with a sniper!

The Demon stabbed the stricken Angel in the throat with a Celestial dagger and avoided an onslaught of blows from the other Angels with acrobatic dexterity. She pulled her head back just in time to dodge Zinc's throwing star.

The grenade exploded, and although it offered no threat to the Angels within the Celestial, it jarred their vision. The last possessed mortal rose unevenly to his feet, shaken by the grenade. He was struck in the head by a bullet. Zinc glanced to the tree line.

Where would I be?

The redheaded Demon had struck the seizing Angel with a throwing knife in the commotion and was fleeing the scene.

Zinc whirled to the remaining Angels. "Get her!"

It was a textbook maneuver; half the Angels pursued in the Mortal Realm and half in the Celestial. If they were lucky, they might catch her, regardless of her skill. Zinc broke pursuit and ducked behind a disabled German tank.

If the sniper is focused on covering his compatriot, he won't notice me, Zinc thought.

Skin Cancer sat comfortably in the crux of the large pine tree and surveyed the engagement through her telescopic scope. Slowly she moved the crosshairs over Stomach Cancer.

"She's good," she said aloud, familial pride heavy in her voice, "very good."

She pulled the trigger and dropped the final mortal pursuer. Slowly, in a sweeping motion, she brought the scope back to a disabled tank. She was certain she had seen an Angelic aura. The foe had not appeared. She lowered her rifle and peered through her binoculars. She kept up her scan. Her finger never left the trigger.

Zinc reclined against the trunk of a massive beech at the edge of the tree line. He heaved and wheezed, feeling the exhaustion of the Frenchman he had possessed. The lines had broken, and most of the few surviving French troops were in the process of surrendering. He knew that his moment to catch the sniper was fading; he could not risk engaging outside of the confines of mortal conflict. After all, who knew what Wraiths or Familiars were lurking in the woods along the path of this advancing army.

He noticed the slightest glimmer of unnatural reflection from a treetop barely a hundred meters ahead. With shaking hands, he raised his rifle and centered the notch of the forward sight over the camouflaged cluster from which what appeared to be a rifle emerged. He pulled the trigger and rushed toward the Demon that fell from the tree beside the dead Wehrmacht sharpshooter. Zinc flew through the Celestial to the seizing Demon, his sword prepared to strike.

The distance was too far. The Demon recovered from the seizure and sat up.

Not the redhead, but I'll have to take her on, Zinc thought.

One-on-one, odds fell to a Demon. However, Zinc was not recovering from a departure seizure, nor was he seated. The Demon deflected a crashing blow from Zinc, meant to decapitate her. Zinc kneed her in the chest. The pair fell to the forest floor in a heap. The Demon sliced Zinc across his ankle. He howled in agony but rolled to his feet and faced the foe. The Demon was heaving and clearly winded. Zinc struck with a savage blow, disabling his foe's right arm. The next blow ended the contest, a thrust to the stomach.

Earth & Air

Zinc's leg was severely injured. He glanced around and found a stick. He leaned it on a large branch, knelt, and traced the ancient symbols in the dirt of the forest. He grabbed a fallen bough and fanned air over the symbols while uttering the requisite incantations. The portal opened. Zinc hoisted himself to his feet and out of the Mortal Realm.

STOMACH CANCER FLITTED THROUGH the dense Ardennes woods. Evading the pursuing Angels was easy. She had abandoned her mortal cloaking and felt utterly unencumbered as she made her way through the brush. Temptation whispered in her ear: *You can kill more of them.*

She suppressed the urge and remembered the voice of the supreme commander. When addressing her cohort, Schizophrenia had said, "We will acquire victory not through sacrificing for our cause, but in making Angels sacrifice for theirs."

Stomach Cancer knew that an engagement resulting in the death of three Angels was a successful encounter. She stopped to catch her breath and listened in the stillness of the darkened wood; they were close, but she had time. Beneath a broken branch, she knelt on both of her knees and traced the ancient symbols in the earth. She began the incantations as she removed a small canteen from her waist and poured the water over the symbols.

The portal opened, but the sound of pounding footsteps told her that a solitary Angel was closing the gap. She closed her eyes and surveyed the scene in her mind's eye. She was well in front of the others. She knew the approaching Angel was a woman from the gait. Stomach Cancer waited until the Angel was nearly on her, then rolled backwards.

Her back struck the Angel's shins, vaulting the foe into the air. The Demon scrambled along the ground and locked the Angel's sword arm with a half nelson.

Stomach Cancer drew a dagger from her waistband and whispered to her captive, "You were too rambunctious, too eager; look what it got you."

Seemingly undaunted, the Angel shouted her Lord's motto in defiance. "Caelum Prævalebunt!"[32]

Her words gurgled into incomprehensibility when the Demonic blade severed her windpipe.

Earth & Water

Z<small>INC HATED THE TASTE</small> of Manna and grimaced as he consumed the white, flaky medicinal bread.

He spat to clear the chalky taste, then watched the wound to his ankle heal even as the Manna dissolved on his tongue.

Never ceases to amaze, and gag me, he thought.

He waited for the junior Angels. When they arrived, they were visibly despondent. The young male who had previous combat experience stepped closer when Zinc beckoned.

"A moment please," Zinc said.

He placed his arm around the youngster's shoulder and pulled him to the side.

"What is your House and your position within it?" Zinc asked.

"I am a lesser brother from the house of Cadmium," the youngster replied.

"There was nothing lesser about you today, son," Zinc said. "You honored your House, and you are well on your way to being a leader of Angels. You must not be dejected in the face of your comrades. Defeatism is as much of an illness as any malady that the Demons inflict."

Zinc brought his attention back to the group. "Did we catch the redhead?"

"No, sir," they said in unison.

"Everything is fine," Zinc said. "You distracted the sniper long enough for me to shoot her. She appeared to be a senior Demon; there were many notches on her sword. You are as much a part of that kill as I am."

Zinc produced the blade he had taken off Skin Cancer. The youngsters marveled at the long line of hash marks etched into the Demonic blade.

"Believe it or not," Zinc said, "one to four is not a horrible ratio for us nowadays. More importantly, you have gained experience and are more seasoned for it. Rest up for a bit and prepare for a return. Head back to the battle for France. There will be Demons to engage along the Wehrmacht's axis of advance."

SATAN SCOWLED LIKE HE always did when hearing a report—even a good one.

"We're rolling over them on most fronts," Schitz said.

The two stood in the middle of the unending bustle of Hell's Great Hall. The Demons and Wraiths rushing back and forth exuded confidence and high spirits. A Wraith approached the Dark Lord and his most senior officer, saluted, and handed Schitz a scroll. Schitz felt his eyebrow twitch involuntarily.

"What is it?" the Devil asked. His impatience was evident.

"It appears we've lost Skin Cancer," Schitz said. "She fell in the battle for France."

"There will be losses," Satan said. He showed all the compassion of a man who's just stomped on a cockroach.

"On a happier note, the youngster Stomach Cancer seems to be making a name for herself. The report claims that she felled four Angels."

"Four to one isn't a great return, but acceptable now and again," the Devil said.

"We can sustain such losses for now," replied Schitz, "as long as we continue to bring down Angels at the current rate overall."

Schitz saluted and walked away from Satan. He had more pressing obligations than listening to his cantankerous Lord.

THE THÉVILLE AERODROME WAS approximately ten kilometers from the outskirts of Cherbourg and a mere stone's throw from the Channel. The smell of the surf cascaded across the airfield, taking with it the thin wisp of smoke rising from Lieutenant Fredrick Schmidt's cigarette. Lost in thought, Schmidt mechanically raised his hand to his mouth and inhaled another drag. He closed his eyes and let the breeze convince him that he was in a peaceful place—at least for a moment.

He exhaled and looked out across the night.

Or is it morning now, he thought. *I really need to get some sleep before the sun rises.*

Schmidt's thoughts froze at the idea of "tomorrow." His muscles tensed, and his upper lip trembled slightly.

Tomorrow is a mystery, today is today, he thought. The words to an old folk song filled his mind with nostalgic memories.

Schmidt lit another cigarette and peered across the open expanse of the airfield. The landing strip was peaceful and haunting. The moon lit the hangars and equipment sheds of Jagdgruppe 27 with an eerie light. Schmidt could almost make out the sentries quietly traversing the flight line, silent as Wraiths.

Schmidt did not need the light of day to know his elegant mistress awaited him in the second hangar. Lilith was sleek and lithe, nimble and flirty, sensual and mysterious. The Messerschmitt featured four 7.9-millimeter guns in her wings and an engine-mounted, 20-millimeter cannon. With Schmidt in her cockpit, she was vicious and lethal.

Four black rectangular bars emblazoned on the yellow of Lilith's rudder a few centimeters from the Swastika that adorned her tail declared the enemies Schmidt had downed. He blew out another long gust of smoke and looked up into the dark heavens. Schmidt's thoughts were reluctantly and violently wrenched back to a different scene.

"Achtung, Achtung; Spitfires low at three and nine o'clock! They're closing on the bombers!"

The captain's voice crackled over Schmidt's radio, puncturing the crone of his engine with staccato bursts that shifted between muffled babbling and ear-blasting directives. Schmidt looked down to his right and saw the Spitfires, a mix of olive drab and evergreen, closing in on the squadron of Heinkel He 111 bombers that his flight was charged with protecting. Schmidt's skin tingled; sweat beaded on his brow; his collar suddenly grew sticky around his neck. The Brits were in a bad position; they were out of range of the vulnerable bombers and had failed to spot his squadron flying high cover.

Schmidt's stomach tightened with the expectation of the hunt. He knew the bombers carried high explosives designated for specific enemy targets and his fellow countrymen, his fellow aviators. The Heinkel He 111s lumbered along with all the speed and maneuverability of lazy cows.

Schmidt was flying lead in the fighter group. He would engage the enemy fighters while his wingman, Lt. Otto Landt, covered his six o'clock. Schmidt pushed his plane into a dive and recalled the sensation of teetering at the apex of a roller coaster. The bottom dropped out, and with it, his fear. Nothing mattered but a whirl of calculations. He flew by feel. His left hand eased back the throttle to correct his airspeed. His right hand made intermittent adjustments to the stick while the Messerschmitt snarled towards the target.

Schmidt judged his speed, the Spitfire's, his rate of descent, the distance to the target, the angle of fire—all in a matter of seconds. He calculated the degree of deflection needed to lead Spitfire into the path of his fire.

Schmidt squeezed the trigger on his control column and watched the phosphorous tails of the tracer rounds fly from Lilith. The bullets cut through the sky, their white tails a wake of impending death. Schmidt watched with sinister delight as the tracers bored into the wing and fuselage of his target. Bits of metal flaked away from the Spitfire; a wisp of smoke appeared.

Schmidt adjusted his course and aligned his Revi C/12D gunsight in front of the Spitfire's path, and fired his 20mm cannon. The right wing crumpled; a piece of paper held too close to a flame. The enemy aircraft started to cartwheel through the sky; a slow-motion ballet of defeat with only one possible outcome.

The bright blue English sky in his mind melted away and the dark night returned as Schmidt snapped back to the present. It could easily have been him falling from the sky like Icarus. Yet here he sat, alive, one kill away from ace status. Schmidt took one last deep pull from his cigarette, then flicked it into the darkness. His joints ached as he slumped toward his bed—unusual pain for a young man but an affliction well-known to those who crammed their oversized frames into undersized cockpits day after day.

Schitz appreciated the advantages he gained from possessing such knowledgeable mortals. Air combat remained a terrifying specter to the forces of Hell. Within a combat aircraft, a Demon or an Angel could do massive damage. When the accuracy of a Celestial combatant was paired with a dive-bomber, a fighter, or a bomber aircraft, the effects to troops on the ground or at sea were devastating. But the risk of death was immense. Yes, there were parachutes. Sometimes, there was the option of possessing another host on the ground or in an undamaged plane but the odds of saving one's life in a damaged plane were low.

The Battle of Brittan had been a cagey affair for the forces of Hell and Heaven. As far as Schitz knew, neither side had managed to kill a member of the other contingent. Only mortal aviators had fallen under their guns because Celestial combatants took to the air with great trepidation. Schitz knew that the experience he'd earned would not go to waste. There was already talk of a campaign to the East.

He slipped out of the aviator and watched him limp up the barracks' stairs. The lieutenant had much more to do the next day—this might be the final night of rest in his young life.

THE VILLAGE OF LUSHNO was not sizeable on any map but it was the only place in the world that mattered to the Demon AIDS. His entire existence currently consisted of the small pit of sandbags surrounding Fritz Christen's 108mm anti-tank gun. Christen's detachment of the Waffen SS Division Totenkampf, the infamous Death's Head Division, had been wiped out to the man from a withering barrage of rifle fire.

Christen managed to repel the Soviet skirmishers with several well-placed rounds from his Kar98 rifle, all while incoming rounds whizzed by him like angry bees. The young soldier was certain that he would be killed any moment, but he held firm to his training. When he had manned the anti-tank gun and fired a well-placed shell amongst the Russian infantry, the attackers had temporarily withdrawn. The Angels in the Celestial Realm had not.

Now they stood around the possessed Christen and awaited the trapped Demon. AIDS was baffled to find himself in such a position—a treed opossum. He could not run; he could not attempt to fight six Angels simultaneously; he was stuck. The Angels tried to shake his focus by taunting him.

AIDS fired the anti-tank cannon once more. The recoil set off a paralyzing whine in his ears. He saw the turret of yet another Russian tank jolt upward, flames engulfing the armored vehicle.

One of the Angels hissed at him. "We're going to kill you slowly for making us wait."

AIDS ignored the catcall and raised his Kar98. He fired another round and struck the closest Russian in the chest. He chambered another round before the soldier hit the ground.

The heckling continued.

"Are you too scared just to pop out and face us?"

"He's a frightened bitch!"

"Come out and fight like a warrior, you sissy!"

AIDS pulled the trigger three more times in succession, sending three more letters to grieving mothers and wives; he was not in the habit of missing. More incoming fire sent Christen ducking behind the small pile of sandbags. He reloaded his rifle and began firing again. The sun beat down without mercy; the wind was a dry cough. AIDS was in a heightened sense of awareness. He felt everything— the slightest movement of infantry even hundreds of meters away, the mechanical groaning of enemy tanks, the breeze raking his face, every bit of dirt on his boots, the spent shell casings somersault- ing through the air each time he yanked back the bolt of his rifle, the hiss and pop of incoming rounds—everything came to him with magnified clarity.

He saw the Angels' lips moving but blocked out their jeers. Instead, he focused on a muzzle flash emanating from a first-story window, squared his weapon, and spewed death from the barrel of his weapon.

A MILE FARTHER AFIELD from the entrance to Lushno, the Wehrmacht sniper, Maximillian Hessler, scanned the landscape from his perch high atop a massive oak. His mountaineering shoes dug into the bark. The scout had applied leaves and sticks to the mesh covering his helmet. His rifle was swaddled in dull canvas; every reflective surface had been coated in grease. Not even the most discerning eye could differentiate between Schitz and the upper reaches of the mighty tree. Cradling his Kar98 in his left arm, he surveyed his surroundings through his binoculars. Schitz saw AIDS and marveled at the young Demon's composure. It was an interesting balance. As long as the lone survivor killed Russians at range, the Angels could not move in to slay him. The Angels needed a single round from a member of the infantry or a tank shell to take out the pugnacious Demon.

Karabiner 98 Kurz a.k.a Kar98

A perfect encapsulation of the Demonic cause, Schitz thought. Outnumbered, outgunned, but denying Heaven the ultimate victory because of our innate savagery.

He smiled and began to whistle Chopin's Nocturne in E-flat major, Op. 9, No. 2. Panning away from the town to the east, Schitz picked up a massive formation of troops moving across the open countryside towards the town. He let the binoculars dangle from their neck strap and peered through his telescopic sight.

"Sixteen and a half," he said aloud, calculating that the foe was just under the length of seventeen football fields or one thousand seven hundred meters away. The man's execution was delayed only by his lowly rank. Schitz navigated through the mass of infantry until he found the commanding officer. The Demon ran the calculations— the east wind, his elevation, the enemy's distance, the bullet's path. When he reached a pause in the *Nocturne*, he pulled the trigger.

Schitz had aimed for the officer's eye but was slightly off. The bullet smashed into the officer's cheekbone and plowed through his skull. Fragments of metal and bones bored into the roof of the man's mouth on the way to his brain. The officer's head snapped backwards, and he crumpled to the ground. Schitz resumed whistling the *Nocturne* and sighted the next soldier. Within every army, be it Russian or German, Heaven's or Hell's, the infantryman's response to incoming fire was to go to ground, the worst possible response for the Russian troops.

Schitz reached an appropriate part of the *Nocturne* and pulled the trigger. The rifle cracked and the neck of the prone soldier exploded. Arterial spray doused the ground around him. The Russians began firing in all directions, attempting to suppress their invisible tormenter. The Russians' weapons were not out of range; however, they could not identify a target due to Schitz's distance. Even the rounds aimed toward the tree fell short and harmless.

More whistling; more devastation. By the time he had killed ten of the soldiers, the Russians began to run towards the town—fish in a barrel from his position. His only concern was whether he had enough ammunition. He loaded another stripper clip into the breach of the rifle and fired again, calmed and inspired by Chopin's brilliance.

Schitz growled when he misjudged the distance and gut-shot a soldier instead of hitting the man's heart. Schitz decided to let the soldier wither into oblivion.

Schitz turned his attention back to the junior Demon. He watched yet another Soviet tank explode in flames, a victim of AIDS's deadly accuracy with the anti-tank gun.

A crooked smile spread across Schitz's face.

I wonder how long the kid will hold out.

AIDS FELT BLOOD TRICKLE down his face; a round had grazed his forehead.

"We're getting close now."

AIDS fired a haphazard "fuck you" at the Angels. He was tiring of their blather. But he returned to his task in the waning light. He fired. Another Russian flopped to the ground close to a burned-out tank.

AIDS took a deep breath and scanned the carnage around Lushno.

SCHITZ CONCLUDED HIS WHISTLING concert and lowered his rifle. The last infantryman clutched his heart and fell.

'Fifty-seven," Schitz said aloud.

The column had been reduced to a pile of corpses strewn across a blood-soaked field. Schitz shouldered his rifle and crawled down from his treetop lair. He stepped into the Celestial and watched the sniper wander toward the west. Just before Schitz headed to Lushno, a random artillery shell blew the sniper to pieces.

Better him than me, Schitz thought.

AIDS SWEPT HIS RIFLE from side to side in anticipation of more enemies. To his surprise, a guttural sound of agonized choking met his ears. He looked over the sandbags and saw two of Angels collapsed upon the ground, the handle of a knife protruding from each of their throats. The remaining Angels froze, perplexed.

The attacking Demon held complete command of the surroundings. He withdrew two blades from his waist and impaled two more Angels. The remaining three Angels looked about as though they were determining whether to run or fight. They opted for the latter and raised their weapons a moment too late.

AIDS watched his unknown confederate dispatch the remaining trio in three smooth thrusts.

The Demon tugged his sword from the last Angel. "Well, you were a lot of help," he said.

"Ah... uh... sorry, sir," AIDS said. "I've never seen anything like that."

"It's nothing, kiddo," the Demon replied. "You did well this afternoon. Figured you could use some help." He extended his hand. "Schizophrenia."

"You are everything your reputation purports," AIDS said. He grasped Schitz's hand with both of his. "I'm Auto Immune Deficiency Syndrome."

Schitz laughed. "That's a mouthful."

"My friends call me AIDS."

"Mine call me Schitz. And you can let go of my hand."

AIDS stepped back, embarrassed by his naïve enthusiasm. "Thank you again," he said. "I was certain I was dead; surrounded, nowhere to go. All I could do was keep my host alive and hope."

"Exactly how you were trained," Schitz said. "Now, come on. Let's get out of here."

"Pity," Schitz said, looking at the last Angel he'd slain. "She was pretty."

Schitz made the symbols upon the ground before the entrance of a vacant house. Dead soldiers were strewn about the first floor. Others were lying along the street beside what had once been mighty armored vehicles.

Schitz looked around. "Very nice work," he said.

He unplugged his canteen and poured water over the symbols.

"Thanks," AIDS said.

It was all he could think to say to this living legend. The portal opened, and they went home.

AFTER THEY COMPLETED THE Arrival Ceremony, Schitz turned to AIDS.

"Take today's experience and keep it in your locker, so to speak; remember the circumstances that led to you getting cornered. Consider what you could have done differently. Then get some rest and get back out there."

The junior nodded and headed off in the direction of the barracks.

A stern voice came from behind. "How many did you get today?"

"Six or seven," Schitz said.

Schitz looked at the Devil with his typical combination of loathing and desire for recognition.

"We have to keep pushing. Big things are happening this year. We can break their back if we can just land the decisive blow."

Always pushing—always in a hurry to sacrifice others for your cause, Schitz thought.

"Our men are tired as well," he said. He hated how Satan spoke as though he had been part of any real fighting.

"If the Germans capture Moscow, the war in Europe will fizzle out. They'll negotiate peace with England and America. We have to move while we have the initiative," the Devil said.

These are not the old monarchies, Schitz thought. *No one will stop fighting and redraw a map. The ideologies of Capitalism, Fascism, and Communism are locked in a battle of annihilation. They will fight for decades to come.*

He looked at Satan. "The Angels I killed today were sitting in a circle around one of our newer soldiers, waiting for his host to get killed," he said. "They were inexperienced novice—"

Satan interrupted. "And yet they trapped our warrior. Is he of inferior quality?"

"No," Schitz said; he purposefully did not add sir. "The newer soldiers on either side are relatively easy to dispatch. We cannot calculate how close we are to victory simply by the number that we kill. It matters how many skilled veterans we're getting. Also, we put ourselves at risk when we overexert and expose our own veterans to losses."

Satan waved a dismissive hand. "A kill is a kill," he said. "What's important is that we are doing well on all fronts. We need to press them now. Their veterans will fall like their novices."

Seeing that he was getting nowhere, Schitz saluted and stepped away from the conversation. Upon reaching his room, Schitz collapsed on his bed. He did not need to sleep the way a human would, but he appreciated being off his feet. Schitz had no way of knowing that the repercussions of the day would echo deeply into his life. All he knew was that it had been another productive day.

Schitz had been spilling Angelic and mortal blood for so long it barely impacted him. But something peculiar clung to the corners of his mind. He could not quite place what stood out about the Angels he had killed that day. He stared blankly at the ceiling until the scene returned to his mind's eye. He had virtually strolled up to the cluster of Angels as they fixated on their prey. He almost felt bad for them as he ambushed them.

They had been so young and naïve. Then it struck Schitz in a moment of realization: the Zeppelinfeld. These were the Angels that had interrogated him during the march.

"So, I did see them again."

He laughed aloud.

And I guess I gave them an answer after all.

THE LIBRARY EMANATED GERMANIC order and discipline both in the arrangement of the books and the general sense of organization. Fritz Christen smiled as he returned a copy of *L' Inferno* to its correct location. He smiled slightly as his attention shifted to the glass case containing his Knight's Cross of the Iron Cross. Though a frail man in his nineties, the decades that had aged his body had done nothing to diminish the clarity of his memory of the day he'd earned his award. Fritz remembered it as though he were still in the uniform of the Third Reich.

I was lucky to survive, he thought. *It must not have been my day to die.*

"WHAT ABOUT LARGER CONTINGENTS," Uranium II asked, exasperation heavy in his voice.

"We've tried that," God said. His indignation was clear. "There was once a time when we sent out all of Heaven within one human force; it was too unwieldy. Surely you remember those instances. The Demons nipped at our heels; our force was too cumbersome to command."

Uranium II threw his hands into the air and sighed aloud.

'I believe the problem is training," Zinc said.

"Elaborate," God said.

'We've made training too simple. Our fresh graduates do not match up to Hell's newest soldiers. Our sophomores do not match up to theirs. Only our veterans can stand as equals. Our advanced training during the Russo-Japanese War created superior soldiers, but we lost too many of them during the Great War."

"But we have numerical superiority," Uranium II said.

"It's not addition," Zinc said. He was growing agitated. "This is a matter of multiplication. Five times zero is still zero, fifty times zero is still zero. Our training is zero."

"I do not believe we have the time or the resources to overhaul our training regimen," God said.

Zinc held his response.

I am not in the presence of a peer, he remembered.

"But I have come to the same conclusion," God said. "Our training has let us down. The Angels we are sending out into the field in this conflict are far below the level of those from previous generations. When this conflict is over, we will tear down our training regimen and rebuild it from the ground up."

Zinc felt a sense of relief. God was not finished.

"So my question to you, my two Supreme Commanders, is this: how are we going to survive until the next conflict?"

Uranium II jumped in with his usual confidence. "The humans," he said. "I will give them such an awe-inspiring weapon that they will end the conflict."

God closed his eyes for a moment to compose himself. Zinc looked at his liege, who had taken to wearing a gray suit in accordance with the times. By outward appearance alone, it was difficult to comprehend that he was the Lord of all Creation.

God opened his eyes and spoke. "Do you see any problem with that plan?"

Uranium II shrugged and glanced from God to Zinc. Zinc sympathized with Uranium II, a brilliant battlefield commander but someone promoted to a level above his capacity for evaluation.

"The Divine Dictum," Zinc said.

God nodded. "We have already paid for your flagrant disregard for the laws which bind us."

"But what clause does my idea violate?" Uranium II asked indignantly.

"Such a weapon would likely cross the line regarding the requirement to conceal our existence from the humans," replied Zinc.

"No, it wouldn't."

"It's debatable," God replied, "but the idea is not worth forfeiting the entire war with Hell."

"But—"

God cut him off. "Something else... find another way; something not so risky. Your venture in Limbo nearly invoked The Ancient's wrath. Please try something within the bounds of our accord with Hell."

A thought passed through Zinc's mind, ruthless and frightening. A slight quiver ran through him.

"Perhaps," he said.

"Spit it out!"

"Perhaps, we could establish an order of the veterans and rather than disperse them with the others, they could be combined into one fighting force like the specialty squads in the last war but on a grander scale. We would utilize the rest of our troops as bait. When the Demons attack, the veterans swoop in to destroy them."

Uranium II made a sound akin to a human passing a kidney stone. "We're guaranteed to sustain heavy losses," he said.

Zinc's expression never changed. "Yes. It will essentially be a purge, but it will bleed the Demons dry before we are annihilated, which we surely will be if we continue utilizing our current strategy of propping up ineffective units with veterans. This way we can target their best troops, as we did with the Black Death."

"Create the order," God said without hesitation. "Just ensure that those Angels losing their lives to this strategy have not sacrificed in vain."

And for the first time in a long while, Zinc felt the full weight of command.

Chapter 7

O Cursed Be Them Cruel Wars

Schitz's Notebook

Type VIIB

7.5/10

Length-66.5m Draught-4.74m

Range-16,112km Depth-250m 14 Torpedoes or 26 TMA mines

-Deadly to surface ships. Most effective when used in groups

-Vulnerable to aircraft and destroyers

The gale tossed the U-boat like a schnauzer trying to break a rat's neck. Captain Prien rested his hands on the ice-encrusted railing of the bridge while the submarine bobbed along the surface of the North Atlantic. Prien liked the rocky waves and salty sting—he was at home when the ocean spit into his face. He rubbed his hand across his beard and thought about the many months he'd been at sea—many months removed from the warmth and comforts of home; many months of canned meats and biscuits. Many months to wonder how his wife occupied her time; many months to arrive at this moment.

His silent assassin of a craft floated perpendicular to the lumbering convoy. The captain watched the warships that guarded the convoy with disinterest. Although they posed a threat to his boat, the corvettes and destroyers were not Prien's target. His U-Boat was hunting the merchant ships that were packed full of arms and supplies bound for England.

Schitz was not fond of U-boat patrols. They took him away from the land actions he considered far more critical to the war effort. However, wherever there were Angels, he was obliged to fight. From within the Kriegsmarine captain, Schitz felt spine-tingling anticipation. The captain was fixated upon the merchants; Schitz's interest focused on the nearest warship. He knew there was a contingent of Angels aboard the Royal Navy's corvette.

Advancements in mortal technology had consigned the act of boarding enemy vessels to the attic of antiquity. During the Russo-Japanese War, the Angels had perfected the art of placing fighting units on ships on either side of an exchange. Once the salvos began, they could engage the Demons quickly. The Demons learned how to counter the tactic during the Great War.

Schitz had missed the Battle of Jutland[33], but he knew it had been a frenetic affair during which Angels (presumed to be exclusively aboard His Majesty's vessels) emerged from every position aboard the Kaiser's ships. The handful of Demons assigned to the German naval squadron had been lucky to escape with their lives—and with a broader understanding of how the Angels intended to fight.

Schitz descended the slippery ladder from the conning tower.

"Captain on the bridge!"

The captain intended to fire two torpedoes at the merchants. If Schitz could possess the weapons operators effectively, he could accomplish Prien's aim as well as his own.

Schitz left a message in the captain's mind, then jumped into the navigator. While possessing the navigator, Schitz embedded instructions that fit his plan. Schitz stepped into the Celestial and rushed through the cramped corridor to the forward torpedo room.

---

[33] May 31 – June 1, 1916

He needed to influence each of the crew members to achieve a very precise outcome.

After he pulled the levers to fire the torpedoes from within the weapons officer, Schitz raced back past the control room and climbed the ladder to the conning tower within the Celestial. He arrived in time to see the effects of the "fish." A ball of fire shattered the pitch-black darkness, then a second. The first torpedo had struck a merchant amidships with fatal effect. The second fish drifted wide and hit the corvette towards the stern, destroying the propellers and tearing a gaping hole in the keel.

Schitz grinned.

Did my part, he thought. *Now it's up to the Demons stowed away on the corvette.*

While the crew of the wounded craft scrambled to abandon ship, the Demons and Angels would be free to engage in a bitter struggle. Schitz returned below decks to craft a return portal to Hell.

"All in a day's work," he said. And he chuckled while he descended the ladder.

ABOARD THE ROYAL NAVY corvette, Hysteria led the neophytes Conduct Disorder and OCD along the length of the sinking ship within the Celestial. The frigid Atlantic air washed over them while they made their way from compartment to compartment in search of Angels. Before long, the youngsters mirrored Hysteria's confident attitude.

They encountered a group of five Angels within Royal Navy sailors. With the boat settling ever lower into the violent sea, the Angels faced a choice: remain in the mortals and risk seizing should they die in the water or step into the Celestial to confront the Demons and risk combat at an extreme disadvantage. The sailors were unarmed, which offered no opportunity for the Demons to kill them within the Mortal Realm.

Schitz's Notebook *HMS Resolution*

8.5/10

Length-182.9m Draught-10.2m
Range-12,960km Speed-41k/h
4 twin 58mm guns 14 152mm guns

Excellent for protecting convoys, somewhat out of date for sea battles.

Hysteria heckled the Angels. "We're ready and waiting."

The contingent from Heaven was not game. They saw a support vessel steaming to pick up survivors and slipped into the water, leaving the Demons alone with their taunts.

"Maybe next time, tutz," one of them shouted as he leaped into the water.

Hysteria cupped her hands around her mouth to project her voice. "Enjoy your swim, cowards!"

"All that for nothing," Conduct Disorder said.

"Well, we sank two of their ships and got some good practice," Hysteria said. She shrugged. "Come on, let's open a door before this thing goes under."

NATASHA IRON THOUGHT SHE had married well when she joined one of the founding Houses. She tried desperately to recall the pride and hope, the anxious anticipation of physical and emotional intimacy with her new husband, and the honor of being a lady of an ancient House. But the memories of her blissful wedding day had long since evaporated on the white-hot burner of reality.

Once widowed, she remarried one of her late husband's nephews.

Passed along the line like a cow, she thought.

Still, the boy was not terrible, and she had grown to feel an odd sort of affection for him. By the time she was widowed again, her House was already a vassal of Zinc. Interest in marriage to her disappeared.

Zinc was not a bad overlord. Mostly he treated his vast multitude of chattel with benign neglect. However, he was a Supreme Commander and their overlord. His lesser Angels obeyed his orders without question, so when commanded to the ramparts of Limbo, Natasha acquiesced.

There were worse postings. This one was far away from any combat. However, any type of appeal began and ended there. The bleak landscape of perpetual twilight and a constant Demonic presence depressed and frightened her.

The matron of Iron looked across the iridescent blue of the Styx and saw the bodies of the Angels that had been executed in accordance with the decree. They'd been nailed to crosses as an affront to the Messiah. She shuddered at the thought of the horrors the departed faced prior to their deaths.

Natasha feared the Demons would attempt to retake the barren land of Limbo. She longed for her time at the citadel to expire, even if it meant a return to the front.

"Anything is better than this," she said.

COMBAT ALWAYS BROUGHT TO Uranium II the sensation of elated focus. Now he crouched next to Zinc in the brush overlooking a nondescript rice patty in a sector of China controlled by the Empire of Japan. Uranium II preferred the Marxists' guerilla tactics. He scanned the well-equipped troops armed with Soviet rifles and machine guns and recognized the future of the Chinese mainland. Uranium II had read reports about the sister and brother team who oversaw Hell's reserve troops. According to the rumors, Atheism and Communism never entered a combat arena, but Uranium II could feel the strong effects of each fiend on the mind of the mortal he possessed. Anyone who denigrated the values of belief in God and individual responsibility represented a dangerous foe.

"At least this will finally be over today," Zinc said from within the commander of the guerrillas. Uranium II had known his colleague for a long time. He'd watched how Zinc suppressed any who attempted to outmaneuver him—by whatever means required. He operated with a brutal political efficiency that Uranium II knew only on the battlefield.

Zinc never flinched in his approach to Uranium II's brother, Platinum. After assessing the snowballing losses in the siblings' escalating conflict, Zinc demanded a meeting with Platinum and his sons to broker a peace treaty. Platinum had refused; he feared a trap. Zinc used the insubordination as justification to issue a death warrant for treason.

Under the authority of the warrant, signed by God, Zinc had summoned his forces, a veritable horde of unincorporated Houses who were his vassals.

"I imagine you need these forces on the Eastern Front," Uranium II said.

Zinc grunted. "On the Eastern Front, on the Atlantic, in Africa, in the skies over Europe, take your pick really."

Uranium II pursed his lips. "I appreciate your part in ending this affair."

Zinc's response was flat and tinged with bitterness. "This conflict has claimed many of my House and my sons' Houses. You don't have to thank me. Once this is over, take your forces to Europe."

"Absolutely," Uranium II replied. "I relish the chance to be fighting Demons again."

Uranium II watched a Japanese patrol emerge along the country road. It was a mixed outfit of light vehicles and infantry. The Angels within their ranks, led by Platinum, were ready for combat.

Although Platinum had ignored Zinc's purported peace overtures, he would not ignore a challenge from Uranium II for a fight.

"He won't expect us to be here supporting you," Zinc said. "Engage them, then fall back. Then, we will attack."

Uranium II signaled his assent. He took a deep breath and listened to the birds calling and the insects humming. He thought about how he had betrayed his father and his brothers. His religion told him that they were gone. Yet, part of him longed for absolution. *Grant me victory, that we might end this family rivalry with honor,* he thought. *Oh, most esteemed ancestor, Cobalt, give me strength to defeat my insidious brother and his children. Thank you in advance for granting me the honor to end their lives with my own hand.*

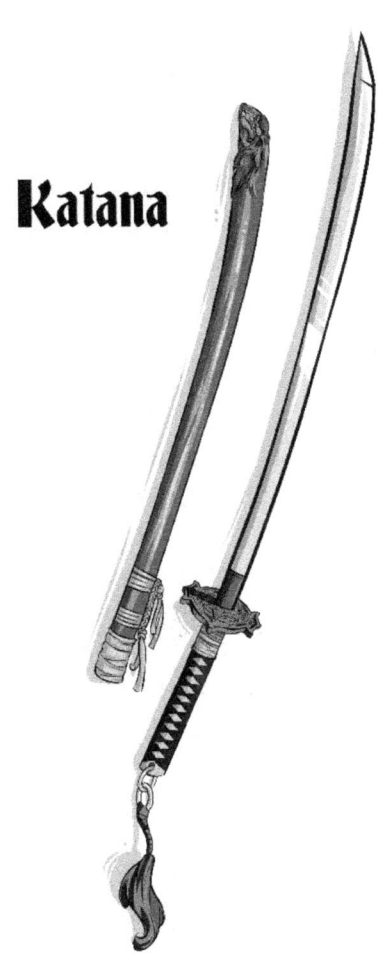

Katana

Uranium II assayed the advancing Japanese troops, their khaki uniforms, and their imperial flags. He raised his rifle.

The battle erupted in savagery. Rifle and machine gun rounds ripped through air and flesh. Grenades exploded. Within the Celestial Uranium II and his sons, Fluorine and Bromine, rushed forward into the opposing ranks. Tantalum and Osmium covered them from within mortal troops and lay continuing fire on the Japanese soldiers.

The Celestial assault mirrored the mortal one. The attackers initially exacted heavy casualties from the patrol.

178 • OVER THE BREADTH OF THE EARTH

Angels under the command of Platinum, Silicone, and Selenium fell like acorns from an overripe oak. The Chinese mortals peppered the imperial troops; a rout appeared inevitable. However, the Japanese forces were staunch; despite the ferocity of the onslaught, they maintained their position. Machine guns from the vehicles began zeroing in on the guerrillas; the infantry regrouped and poured out a stream of accurate rifle fire.

The ambush broke down as the Chinese began sustaining heavy casualties. From across the edges of the brush, the irregulars collapsed under the Japanese fusillade. Uranium II's forces suffered losses when Platinum's reserve (Cadmium, Ruthenium, and Dubnium) arrived along the flanks within the Celestial. They possessed Chinese troops and caused havoc as they began to engage the forces of Tantalum and Osmium.

Casualties from the Angelic and mortal battle mounted; the guerrillas and Uranium II's forces retreated towards the wooded area beyond the road and the rice paddies. Uranium II drew back as per his instructions, but he seethed. He loathed the dishonor of yielding ground to the foe.

The Japanese, like Platinum's Angels, sensed the possibility of victory. Discipline broke. Uranium II looked over his shoulder to see a Japanese officer charging forward with a pistol in one hand and a samurai sword in the other.

Then, it all changed. Just as the Japanese and Platinum's forces reached the dense woodlands, the combined forces of Mao and Zinc emerged and began to cut them down. What had looked like a sure victory for Platinum's warriors suddenly morphed into a fight for their lives. Imperial forces fell one after another, cut down by rifle fire. Angels slumped to the ground within the Celestial, where Zinc's forces were swift to restrain them or slit their throats.

Rifle in hand, Uranium II searched the fray for his brother. He spotted Platinum a hundred yards removed and directing troops from within the body of a Japanese officer.

Uranium II stepped forward within a Chinese foot soldier. "Platinum!"

His mortal raised a rifle. Platinum hoisted a semi-automatic pistol. Both mortals fired. A piercing bolt of white-hot agony burned through Uranium II's chest. He stepped into the Celestial and watched as his bother slid out of the Japanese officer, who had been shot through the midsection and collapsed.

Uranium II drew his katana and charged. The two engaged in a whirling series of feints, strikes, and parries. Then Platinum made a mistake. He overcommitted with a swipe. Uranium stepped back. Platinum lost his balance. Uranium II whipped his blade across his brother's midsection. Platinum collapsed to the ground, screaming.

His sons rushed into the duel, but their attack was more enraged than organized. Uranium II blocked a strike from Silicone before cutting his throat. He sidestepped a blow from Selenium and ran him through. When Cadmium charged, Uranium II grabbed his wrist and wrestled the young man to the ground. Uranium II wrestled the young Angel's weapon away and decapitated him with it.

Horrified by the slaughter of his family, Dubnium screamed and flung himself toward Uranium II, who ducked and drove his shoulder up under Dubnium's rib cage. Dubnium flew into the air and landed barely two paces from his disabled patriarch, Platinum, and nearly atop his slain father, Cadmium. After kicking away any weapons within reach, Uranium II stood over Platinum. He had envisioned the moment many times and always imagined a long speech.

But eloquence failed him.

"So much blood, Brother," he said. "This could all have been avoided but for your pride."

"And your treachery," Platinum said. His voice rasped through bloody bubbles.

Uranium II raised his sword. "I simply have the will to rule."

His sword fell and Platinum's head rolled past Dubnium. The boy whimpered and retched.

"What say you?" Uranium II asked. "To whom do you owe loyalty other than God?"

"I, in honor of my life, pledge my loyalty to you," Dubnium said.

"And your House and its holdings?"

"Forfeit to you."

"No," Uranium II said. "They remain yours so long as you bow to me. This is all I have ever asked. Am I unreasonable?"

He hoisted the gasping lad to his feet.

"No," Dubnium said.

He grunted and lowered a knee to the ground. Uranium II looked over his shoulder at the twisted forest of bamboo, red pines, and fir trees. Every surviving foe dragged to some semblance of obeisance, either bowing or kow-towing. He saw Zinc, bathed in blood. Zinc winked, then cocked his head in a mock bow.

Uranium II considered the carnage, the broken bodies, the shattered futures, and smiled.

It is over, he thought.

THE CANTEEN EMITTED THE sickening, familiar aroma of all dives at closing time—a mixture of stale beer, cigarette smoke, and leftover fried food. Slightly alluring, slightly revolting, delicious nastiness. A solitary figure maintained vigil. Slumped on a chipped stool, Lieutenant James Green rested his left arm on a battered, out-of-tune piano. His fingers strolled along the yellowed keys. Green's old friend had survived spilled drinks, billiard balls, and the weight of many an unwelcome reveler. Green stabbed at the keys with his right hand and sang along with a voice so quiet, he could scarcely hear it himself.

"Rule Britannia, Britannia rule the waves, Britons never, never, never..."

Green trailed off before completing the chorus. A shudder started in his extremities and rushed into his core. The hubris he associated with the end of the chorus seemed too much akin to tempting fate to utter aloud. Instead, Green reached for the glass of Scotch perched atop the piano next to his worn Royal Air Force cap.

"I should get some sleep before tomorrow," Green whispered.

The familiar sting of whiskey slid down his throat and spread through his body.

Tomorrow, he thought. He began to mumble, "Tomorrow and tomorrow and tomorrow creeps in this petty pace from day to day."[34]

He always quoted Shakespeare when he drank too much. "But what tomorrow does a young man at war have to look forward to?" he said with a slur intelligible only in his own mind. "Well, at least ole Willie got the sound and fury part right."

He shouted loud enough to make the bartender look his way. "Signifying nothing!"

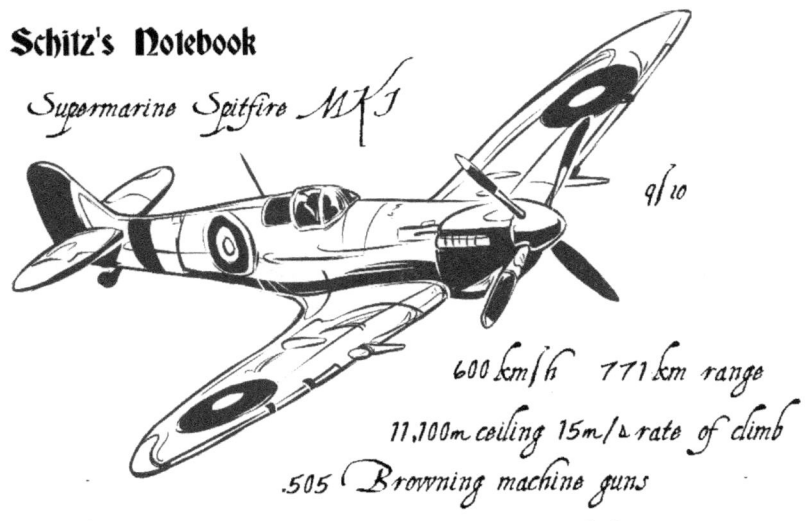

Schitz's Notebook

Supermarine Spitfire MK I

9/10

600 km/h   771 km range
11,100m ceiling 15m/s rate of climb
.505 Browning machine guns

A reliable fighter. Successful defending England during the Battle of Britain. Not overly durable. Acceptable for aircraft carriers. Armament slightly lacking

Suddenly his right hand was no longer at the piano keys. Green clutched the stick of his Spitfire I. His muscles were tensed and

---

[34] *Macbeth,* Act 5, Scene V.

trembling. The squadron leader's voice exploded over the radio.

"Messerschmitts! Break, break, break!"

The Jerries bounced them a mile or so off the Isle of Wight. Green swore and banked hard to the right. The Germans had a knack for dropping out of the sun. He broke left and searched the sky for the enemy.

Fuck! I can't see them.

Nausea constricted his throat. The cold chill of sweat beaded his forehead. Hail banged against Green's fuselage.

Not hail; bullets!

A German fighter overcooked its approach and cut right in front of him. Green urged his Spitfire into position and held his breath until the GM 2 reflector gunsight aligned along the Bf-109's engine. He depressed the trigger on top of the stick. He was too close to miss. Clunks of metal tore away from Messerschmitt's cowling. He watched the German fighter nose over. Smoke gave way to flames and Green followed the trajectory of the wounded aircraft all the way into the Channel.

That's four, he thought.

His elation was short-lived. Where there was one bandit, there would be others. He wiggled the stick left, then right. The plane barely responded.

I'm going to have to coax this shot-up crate back to base.

He turned towards home. If he had to fly, Zinc liked the Spitfire; quick and responsive. And Green was an excellent pilot. With his business in Asia concluded, Zinc was back in Europe in an RAF squadron. The Battle of Britain had concluded in a British victory. However, there was still much for the Angels to learn and a great many more air battles to be fought.

The action off the Isle of Wight had been one of several dustups between the Luftwaffe and the Royal Air Force. Zinc, like most sensible Celestials, held a great fear of flight but the war demanded that he and others learn the art of aerial battle. If the Demons gained the upper hand, the results would be disastrous.

Green wandered back to the present and drained his Scotch. He left the glass on the piano, then wobbled up the stairs to his room, coaxing himself "home" like he'd cajoled his wounded Spitfire.

Come on, old man. You can make it.

When he reached the doorway, he realized he'd left his cap atop the piano.

Well, it'll still be there tomorrow, he thought.

Zinc had left the young pilot at the base of the stairs.

"Come morning time, he'll have bigger concerns," Zinc said.

He slipped the cap onto his head, a worthy souvenir for his bedchamber.

CANCER SAT ON THE roughhewn throne made from the few trees that had once lined the leeward side of the Styx. The cult that had grown around her started prior to the Great War when a general observation emerged that Demons named in her honor tended to have a high rate of survivability. Cancer was the sole survivor of her class. Lung Cancer was the sole holdout of her class; Liver Cancer was one of two remaining from his cohort.

Within the next generation, Brain Cancer was the last standing from her class as was the case for Oral Cancer. Only two other classmates survived with Breast Cancer—the fraternal twins, Stomach Cancer and Colon Cancer, represented two-thirds of those yet living from their group. From within the Great War cohort, Metastatic Cancer, Renal Cancer, Rectal Cancer, and Endometrial Cancer had all made it. The youngest generation contained the Demons Gallbladder Cancer and Fallopian Tube Cancer. Additionally, Cult members Leukemia, Lymphoma, and Kaposi Sarcoma remained.

Cancer wore a crown of evening primrose. The yellow flowers wrapped around her head were common in Hell's countryside; they bloomed at night. Around her thin neck lay garlands of white Brugmansia and moonflowers, also common to Hell's flora. A wooden scepter not unlike Satan's rested in her lap. It was festooned with night-blooming jasmine. Around the base of her throne lay a pile of purple and white night phlox.

"I am overjoyed that we are able to convene. Once again, I can report there are no casualties amongst our brethren," she said.

The members of the Cult of Cancer smiled at one another as they reclined on the grass. The war severely limited the opportunity for such gatherings. The senior academic instructor following Rabies's demise, Cancer had found herself overwhelmed with training such a massive class. The newest cohort numbered thirty-six. Cancer savored the rare moments when she could rule over her adherents.

"We don't have much time," she said. She rose and allowed her robes to fall to the ground. "Let us now enjoy our moment of communion."

The concept of remarriage existed within the Demonic community, though many avoided it. Cancer wanted her cult to serve as a physical and mental outlet for her followers, many of whom were widows and widowers. As membership had expanded, some Demons with living spouses and some married couples, such as Renal Cancer and Kaposi Sarcoma, had joined her ranks. Cancer encouraged all members of the coven, regardless of marital status, to participate freely in carnal exchange. She found freedom and equality in the unconfined way the Cancers bonded with one another at the most intimate of levels.

Bared before her adoring adherents, Cancer remembered a time when she had felt sullied by the act, a time when she felt defiled for giving herself to Satan only to be discarded. Now, she beamed with radiant splendor, and she recalled the Academy sisters who restored her pride and self-confidence. From that foundation, she had reclaimed the power to lead her willing and consenting followers through the cult's ritual. She was no longer afraid of shame or criticism; she was truly free and, in turn, gave this freedom to her adherents.

Later, after the ceremony, Cancer found herself on the soft glass along the riverside reclining between the brothers Metastatic Cancer and Pineal Cancer. She was exhausted from the attention she had received from the twins, but she considered her place in the world.

The global war was draining. Asperger's and Delirium Tremens had fallen on the Eastern Front. Pelvic Inflammatory Disease died in air combat over the Reich.

This war is different. There are not as many pitched battles like the old days. This conflict simply drips blood every day.

She closed her eyes and listened to the flow of the Styx running endlessly back to the world.

I hope my people continue to stay safe, she thought.

For the first time in many years, she thought about her husband, Greed.

I miss him so much, even after all these years.

She pushed one of the brothers to gain a little distance. Such proximity to a naked demon while recollecting on her late husband seemed... gross.

I hope that the peace of the final victory is better than what we have seen thus far, she thought. *I am so weary of war.*

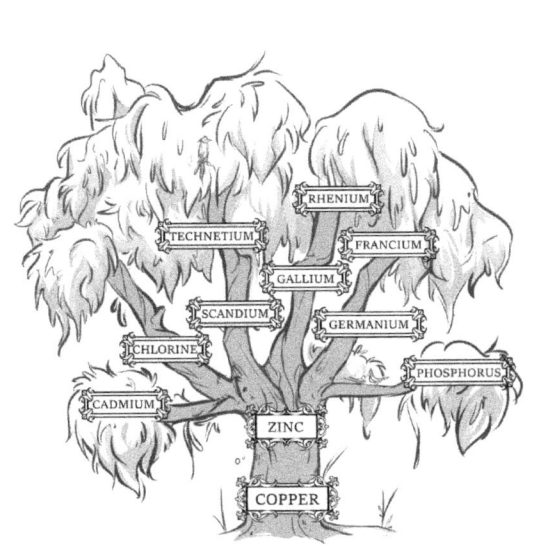

ZINC STOOD A LITTLE taller as he watched his grandsons receive their ceremonial swords, representative of their Houses, Technetium, Rhenium, and Francium.

He whispered to Eleanor. "I'm so proud of them."

His sons had married daughters of Uranium II. Consequently, his grandchildren all displayed an interesting mix of occidental and oriental features.

"They are handsome lads," his wife replied, "but you must afford them a greater involvement in the war."

Zinc grimaced. "It's just been so costly. I keep recalling the single combat with the Black Death. I don't want to go through that again."

"I know," she said, "but they need to assume authority. They are my sons and grandsons, too. I do not wish to feed them to this slaughter, but we must dispatch of Hell, and our heirs are the ones to do it."

There was truth to her words. Zinc nodded as he looked upon the Standard Bearers of the other newly incorporated Houses: Astatine from Lanthanum, Promethium of Helium. Lanthanum had been productive, siring Helium during the prior Grand Gathering. Neon, the descendant of Cerium, had founded the Houses of Neptunium and Curium. Hydrogen's son Beryllium had established the House of Krypton. His father, Hydrogen, had sired Actinium and Radium.

"Heaven is very balanced at the moment," Zinc said. "I do not believe that we have to be political in looking out for our descendants' future."

"When the mortal world is ours, there will be much to hand out," she answered. "There were other Celestial wars before this; there may be others yet to come. The Ethereal and those mystical beings within it stand beyond our understanding. We might have to conquer that realm as well. You must put our sons and Abraham in a position to inherit much from the Lord when our victory arrives. There may yet come a time when factionalism and discontent grow with the Heavenly ranks."

Zinc marveled at his wife's ability to discern the future. Once the ceremony concluded, Zinc approached his assembled sons.

"Gentleman, Lords, I congratulate you upon this day!"

He smacked Rhenium and Francium on the back and smiled at Technetium.

"It is an honor to expand our Houses," Germanium said.

Although he was grinning, Zinc perceived a dark shadow passing across Abraham's face. Zinc knew that his sole surviving son from his first marriage harbored little love for his half-siblings. But he was weak and dared not invoke his father's wrath by confronting them openly.

Does he have his father's cunning? Zinc thought. *I cannot be undone by feuding children.*

Scandium addressed Cadmium. "Abraham, I'm certain you will sire a House soon as well."

Abraham smiled and nodded quietly. He had a good relationship with the eldest of Zinc and Eleanor's children.

Perhaps, I can capitalize on that, Zinc thought.

He addressed the group. "I wish we could celebrate in the old ways, drinking Elixir and telling tales long into the night until even the most ancient among us slept like Academy pups. Alas, this is not to be. There is an urgent meeting. The Elite Squad is preparing for further action, and I would like you all to attend."

Zinc settled his gaze on Cadmium and repeated. "All of you."

Eleanor is right. I cannot afford to protect my descendants. They need to claim their rightful place and the only way is in combat.

THE DESERT WINDS WHIPPED the sand into a frenzy and did nothing to cool troops of the Afrika Korps. Erwin Rommel perused an array of maps spread across the hood of the Kübelwagon. He evaluated both the British and Angelic positions along the road to El Alamein. From within the field marshal, Schitz weighed the potential outcomes for the mortal soldiers and the Demons under his command. The assessment for both was grim.

There had been victories along the push across Libya and Egypt, but the forces were exhausted, and the British, with their Angelic occupants, were regrouping to protect the Suez Canal. The operation called for many more than four Demons, but Gangrene, Ebola, and Bipolar Disorder were the only colleagues available. The strategic reserve overseen by Communism and Atheism was depleted.

Schitz determined to augment his forces with a multitude of Wraiths. The intelligence gatherers would be called upon to attack the Angels, a more elegant way of saying "suicide." Schitz put Josephine over the Wraiths. She had aged past the point of youthful attractiveness; she looked like a mortal in her mid-fifties. Still, he felt a connection with her; they had known each other a long time.

Ah, the bonds we form, he thought.

He looked at his subordinates. He had trained them all at the Academy and fought beside them in various battles and campaigns. He did not know them well, and he did not care. He missed Rubella, not only his first love but his first good friend. He missed Anna; she of the passionate and impactful affair. He missed his good comrade Conjunctivitis. He missed Anthrax.

Rage bubbled within him. Except for Elise's unsolicited meddling, Anthrax would still be alive.

He signaled to Bipolar Disorder. "Call forth the Wraiths."

The Wraiths appeared moments later and stood in formation at parade rest. Twenty by his count, varying in age and gender.

The wind continued to whip. He felt the sting on his face. He squinted into the unrelenting assault of the Saharan sun.

"Wraiths of Hell," Schitz said, "the order of the day calls for you to identify and engage the Angels ahead of our advance. Such a task has never been assigned to your people before. But you are the descendants of Titans. Your ancestors were so formidable that they were bred with humans to dilute your potency. I call upon you now to reach back to your ancestry. Today, you must be Titans once more."

Schitz allowed for his words to hang in the air. "Elise," he said. She appeared next to him and stared into his face with her doleful eyes.

Surely, she knows this is not good, he thought. *But does she know how bad it will get?*

He leaned close. "You did this to yourself," he said. "Anthrax was a friend of mine. I placed him next to Spanish Influenza, but you didn't know that."

Bitterness crept from her voice. "I'm sorry," she said. "I was only trying to protect you."

Schitz made a motion as if shooing away a pesky insect. "I made you promise not to interfere in my dealings, Wraith."

"Ah," she said. She would not look at him. "No longer mama, am I?"

"No," he said. He returned his attention to the formation.

"Today, you will either kill those before you, or you will fall under their weapons. How many of you have taken a life?"

No hand raised. He shoved Elise forward a step.

"This one here," he said, "she has taken many lives. So now you will take hers or she will take yours."

Silence strangled the group. Elise drew her Celestial dagger. She glanced between Schitz and her fellow Wraiths with wild eyes.

"I have given an order," Schitz said. He stepped away from his surrogate mother. "Wraiths, attack!"

The front row of the formation charged Elise. With nimble fleetness, she sidestepped and parried the initial onslaught of blows. However, the odds were too much against her, and within a few moments, she was caught by one of her compatriot's blades, then another, then another. Each thrust of Celestial steel cut through her flesh and elicited an awful howl. Eventually, she collapsed to the dusty ground in a quivering heap. The Wraiths were clumsy in their work and had dropped Elise with injuries that were only fatal upon accumulation.

She lay upon the ground, heaving for breath. None of the Wraiths possessed the stomach to deliver the final coup de grâce. Schitz considered ending her suffering but could see nothing in his mind but Anthrax's smiling face. He watched her tortured breathing—impassive.

A moment later, she was still. Schitz grabbed one of the Wraiths who had struck down Elise and lifted him from the ground by his throat. He shook the small creature violently before tossing him to the ground. Schitz slapped another across the face.

He screamed and kicked Elise's corpse.

"Yes! That is combat. That is death. Inflict it on your foe or embrace it for yourself. It is that simple."

The Wraiths were wide-eyed and had long ago abandoned their neat formation. Schitz saw fire in their eyes. They were still afraid but had been awakened to the reality of their purpose.

He pointed east toward the British positions. In a calm, even tone, he said, "Attack."

"We should have a better name for ourselves," Rachael said.

The Elite Squad sat among the various desks and chairs of the Heavenly library's reading room. Zinc looked up from a remarkably detailed folder entitled *Autism*. He was amazed at the work conducted by the Familiars. One passage was particularly detailed: "The Demon enjoys herring and sardines when he possesses mortals." The folder contained a family tree and many other pieces of useful information. Such information proved critical when they hunted the Black Death.

' So, what shall we call ourselves?" he asked.

"I've always been a fan of Saint Patrick," Lord Uranium II said. "He drove the serpents out of Ireland."

"There's a similar line in our anthem," Abraham said. "*With each serpent, we slay.*"

Zinc suppressed the to urge to roll his eyes and wondered exactly how many serpents his academically inclined son had slain.

"The Order of St. Patrick, then?" he asked.

"Here, here!"

Zinc did not share in their joviality. "Let us remember that while we have created this order to kill the most ancient and deadliest of Demons, our comrades in arms are dying in scores. We must act with haste."

"The Cancers should be our next target," Lord Hydrogen said.

"If we can kill them, we shall weaken the other ancient Demons, and they will be more vulnerable."

Zinc's attention was drawn to Rachael. She seemed angered by her husband's statement. He knew her well enough to know that she longed to kill the Demon known as Schizophrenia.

"Agreed," Zinc said. Any hint of friction between his old flame and her spouse amused him.

Geranium raised his hand. "This report says a cluster of them are anticipated in Stalingrad."

"There are a lot of Demons and a lot of our forces in Stalingrad at the moment," Beryllium said. "It might be difficult to pinpoint their location"

"I think a Stalingrad operation could be useful," Eleanor said. "The Familiars should be able to provide us with the requisite details."

There were two stacks of folders on the table: those targets already dispatched and those still at large.

Zinc tapped the larger of the stacks. "The war is entering its third year," he said. "Most of our enemies still live. Let's change that."

Everyone stood and left. He turned to Eleanor and recognized the gleam in her eyes that sparkled before a challenging mission or in moments of passion—wild, hungry. Under his breath, he began to sing.

> O Elly love, O Elly, the rout has now begun,
> and we must go a-marchin' to the beating of the drum.

Eleanor snapped at the air as though to bite Zinc. Her gaze was deeply erotic. Zinc continued with a broad smile.

> Go dress yourself all in your best and come along with me.
> I'll take you to the war, me love, in high Germany.

The old tune carried on in Zinc's mind as the Order of St. Patrick set about clearing some of the deadliest of serpents. The burned-out factory building rose over the industrial section of western Stalingrad. Once a prominent landmark, bombs and shells had reduced it to a hulking ruin. The Soviets and Angels fell back through the rows of discarded, damaged equipment.

Lung Cancer led a squadron of Demons forward within Wehrmacht hosts. They crossed in front of the ruin.

> O Willie love, O Willie, come list' what I do say,
> My feet they are so tender I cannot march away.

From the rafters of the building, Scandium peered through the scope of his Mosin–Nagant and Cadmium through his field glasses.

"She is just past that furnace," Cadmium said.

"Roger," Scandium replied.

e

A shot rang out and the German officer collapsed to the ground. A secondary, Celestial assault appeared on the German flank as Lord and Lady Hydrogen led an attack against the German position. The fighting was intense, though brief. The Demons were determined to protect their fallen leader. Rachael spun a throwing star into the seizing Lung Cancer, but not before several Angels from the House of Hydrogen and Beryllium had fallen. Having achieved their objective, the Angels withdrew.

> And besides my dearest Willie, I am with child by thee,
> not fitted for the war, me love, in high Germany.

Jasper Gittens had smoked most of his life. He was not expecting a positive report when the oncologist entered the room at the university hospital.

'We have good news, Mr. Gittens," the young Asian doctor said. She was dressed in a crisp lab coat. Various ribbons adorned her lapels. "You have responded very well to the chemo. We should be able to remove all of the remaining malignant tissue when we operate."

Jasper inhaled deeply. He coughed a little. "Well, I'll be damned," he said.

The doctor laughed. "Not yet," she said.

> I'll buy for ye a horse, me love, and on it, ye shall ride,
> and all my d'light shall be in riding by your side.

Within Russian soldiers, Zinc and Eleanor ran along a shallow trench towards a Waffen SS Tiger I tank. The gun crew led by Uranium II would not be able to kill the tank, but an artillery round had smashed its tread. The tank was immobile, vulnerable. Lady and Lord Zinc leaped over a trench and rushed toward the tank. Rifle fire whizzed past them.

Eleanor remained within her mortal host and opened the tank's hatch. She dropped a grenade inside. After the explosion, Zinc dropped into the smoky interior and dispatched the seizing Oral

Cancer and Gallbladder Cancer. He popped his head back out of the ruined tank and was met by a grinning Eleanor.

> We'll stop at every alehouse, and drink when we are dry,
> be true to one another, get married by and by.

"Normally, we would have to remove the entire gallbladder," the doctor said. "However, this innovative treatment has allowed us to remove only the tumor."

Mary Anyongo broke into a smile. "So, I can still eat spicy foods?"

The doctor chuckled and held up both hands. "Well, one step at a time," he said.

> O cursed be them cruel wars that ever they should rise,
> and out of merry England press many a man likewise.

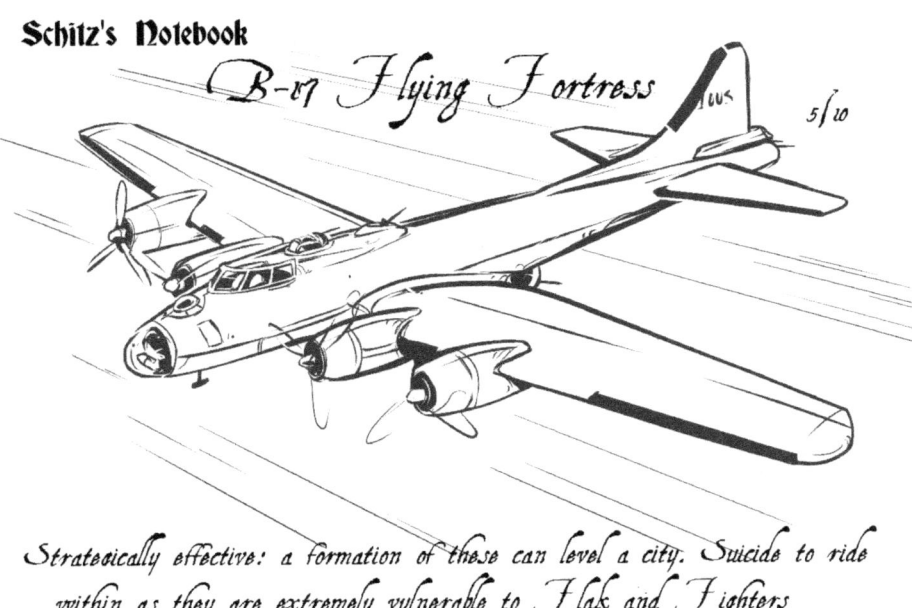

Schitz's Notebook

B-17 Flying Fortress 5/10

Strategically effective: a formation of these can level a city. Suicide to ride within as they are extremely vulnerable to Flak and Fighters

Inside the P-40's cockpit, Gallium shouted into his mic. "Look out, look out; on your right."

They had jumped Brain Cancer and sent her flaming back toward the earth. However, the vengeance of the remaining 109s, and Demons within, was fierce. Gallium looked on helplessly as his brother Germanium's fighter broke apart, the wing shredded by cannon fire.

"Fuck!"

Gallium sailed alongside the formation of B-17 Flying Fortress bombers. The Germans had already downed Boron in the dogfight, and now another Lord had spiraled to his death.

"Well, at least we got that Cancer," Gallium said.

He pushed his fighter into a dive and calculated the way home.

They took her true love from her, likewise her brothers three,
and sent them to the cruel wars, in high Germany.

The Director looked at Samantha Reed. "Just tell your story."

The young woman wondered which would be more terrifying: brain surgery or shooting the commercial. She took a deep breath, looked at the camera, and adjusted her headscarf.

Three fingers... two... one... a point. "Thanks to Saint Agatha's and its dedicated staff, I have a second chance at life."

Me friends I do not value nor me foes I do not fear,
Now me love has left me, I wander far and near.

Zinc and Eleanor ambushed the German patrol and cut down Liver Cancer and Fallopian Tube Cancer along a muddy Russian road. Farther away, however, Cancer herself recovered from her departure seizure before Eleanor and her dagger could reach her. Zinc watched the Demon roll away from his beloved wife. The razor's edge of Eleanor's blade buried in the ground inches away from Cancer's head.

Cancer whipped her leg into Eleanor's ankle. When Lady Zinc fell, Cancer stabbed her in the chest and sprinted away.

Zinc arrived a moment later. He collapsed over his beloved. "Hang on, we'll get you Manna."

She might have said, "I love you," but the blood rushing from her mouth turned her words into an unintelligible gurgle.

She closed her eyes and Zinc wept uncontrollably.

> *And when me baby it is born and smiling on me knee,*
> *I'll think of lovely Willie in high Germany.*

The professor pointed to the image on the screen. "At first, it was believed that fallopian tube carcinomas were very rare," he said. "Recent research, however, indicates that many instances of ovarian cancer may have originated in the fallopian tubes before spreading to the ovaries."

The classroom full of future oncologists took notes.

> *O Polly love, O Polly, the rout has now begun,*
> *And we must go a-marchin' at the beating of the drum.*

Zinc looked over the folders of the Cancers and other senior Demons slain by the Order of St. Patrick—Gangrene and Hypertension. His strategy bloomed at a great cost. Rank and file Angels fell at an alarming rate. But the biggest loss was his. He thought of Eleanor and hummed without joy.

> *Go dress yourself all in your best and come along with me,*
> *I'll take you to the war, me love, in high Germany.*

SCHITZ STRODE THROUGH THE Great Hall at a loss for ideas. Word had just arrived that Stomach Cancer and Colon Cancer had been killed in action in Sicily.

He focused his wrath on a bedraggled Cancer. "What the fuck is going on?"

"I just lost two dear friends in Russia," she said. "Get away from me." She put her hands on Schitz's robe, whether to push him away or to embrace him, he could not tell.

"Pull yourself together," Schitz said. "We have no time for sentimentality."

Cancer wiped her face.

Schitz noticed a youngster watching them.

"You there," he said, "come over here."

The youngster blushed at having been caught eavesdropping.

"Where do I know you from?" Schitz asked.

"Lushno."

'Ah, you are AIDS," Schitz said.

"Yes, sir."

"Listen to me," Schitz said. "We need to spread out the Angels' focus. I've read reports that something of an internal bust-up took place in the Far East, and Japan is basically vacant. I need you to open a second front there. Do everything you can to draw Angelic forces away from Europe. Take five Demons with you. I promote you to lead them."

"Yes, sir," AIDS said,

He executed a crisp salute and ran from the Great Hall.

"Can you do that without Satan's permission?" Cancer asked.

Schitz's laugh echoed from every wall. "Fuck it! At this point, what do we have to lose?"

Chapter 8

Bleeding Out

S chitz sat alone in his room and gazed out the window. He contemplated the vast map of the world above and below the Earth. His thoughts drifted to the problem at hand. Much like the forces of the Third Reich, Schitz's ranks were being bled dry by a technically inferior, yet numerically superior opposition. When the Germans rolled over Europa, the Angels were as impotent as the Allies. The training, the drills, the preparations had all paid off in Hell's favor. Angels fell like wheat to a reaper; all signs pointed towards the final victory and the peace of Hell's eternal reign over Earth. Schitz focused on the river. Uselessness and failure clung to him like tar.

"How many times," he said to the wall, "how many times, in my lifetime have we been so close?"

He remembered all the times he thought Hell was on the verge of annihilating Heaven: God's schism with Gold and Silver, the Black Death movement, the Seven Years War, the Great War. Each held such promise; each proved a disappointment.

He began to wonder about the Parisian redhead. Schitz remembered his rash dive into the love affair. Had he chosen to abandon his cause for a life with her, he would now be in no worse a state than he was in the summer of 1943. He groaned as he recalled the moment the bullet meant for him cut her down.

Sadness fell on him with the heavy thud of recognized failure.

This is never going to end, he thought. *The ultimate victory is out of our grasp. All my soldiers will continue to chase this chimera and all my soldiers are doomed to die.*

Schitz shook his head to clear the despondency. Victory was no longer his concern; he needed to avoid the final defeat.

"How? How did we get here?"

He thought about Satan—an absolute tyrant and an abysmal tactician. The Dark Lord preached abandon; he practiced reluctance.

Every time we've needed a bold move, he has failed us, Schitz thought.

That fool, that absolute and complete simpleton, he doomed us all.

One by one, the best fighters Hell had produced over eons had fallen to the Angels. The dam holding back his frustration and anger broke and Schitz slammed his hand against the wall. He wrenched open his door and shouted into the hall.

"Elis—" He stopped in the knowledge the one he'd called "Mama" was gone. "Wraith!"

A scrawny male Wraith appeared out of nothingness. "Yes, commander?"

"What is your name?"

"Malchus, sir."

"Malchus, I want the records of all fallen soldiers in the last year who were over three hundred years old at the time of their death and all of the kills we've claimed over the same period of time."

"Sir," the Wraith said. He saluted, bowed, and disappeared as quickly as he had arrived.

Schitz had an idea, but he needed evidence. Heaven was sacrificing its lesser soldiers in hopes of bleeding off Hell's superior and most experienced fighters one by one. The Angels knew better than to send their veterans against the Demonic best. It would have been no contest. The forces of God simply played the long game.

After all, eternity is a very long time.

A knock at the door was followed by the scraping sound. A ledger slid under the door. Schitz lifted the leather-bound index and poured through it.

"It's working," Schitz said. "It's the only way they can win. They have been throwing their newer and weaker units away and focusing on our best. Even our greatest cannot survive every battle, every time."

Schitz collapsed on his bed, his despair now fully replaced by a deep sense of urgency. He needed to turn the tide immediately. Schitz collected his Celestial weaponry then rushed to the Great Hall. He saw Malchus and grabbed him by the shoulder.

"Malchus, pass along this order. No matter where they are, have every veteran you can find return to Hell immediately. Make sure they know the command is directly from me."

"Yes, sir," Malchus said.

A familiar, rusty hinge of a voice bounced off the walls. "What are you doing?"

Schitz answered without turning around. "Saving the war, my Lord," he said.

He counted five beats, then pivoted. The Lord of Darkness wore his usual maniacal countenance. "These are still my divisions, and I am still their supreme authority, now answer my question," Satan said.

Schitz inclined his head. "I have broken down our recent losses and determined that the Angels are employing an ingenious strategy designed to gut us. I can turn the tables."

The Devil's upper lip curled. "If we're losing men, it is because they are weak," he said.

Schitz remained direct and emotionless. "Regardless of the reason, in the next few days, I will deliver an unprecedented tally of Heavenly losses. I will concentrate our remaining veterans and overrun their counterparts."

The Devil's response was quick and angry. "You will not put all of my veteran units in the same place; you will get them all killed and then surely the war will be lost."

Schitz groaned. "Curse the incompetence of those who lead without the skills or understanding of the tasks of their subordinates."

Satan exploded. His voice crackled with rage. "I could have you executed!"

"You might as well if you handicap us."

Satan dialed back the anger. Despite his flaws, he knew Schitz represented the best of the best.

"In the battlefield, the tactics are your responsibility," Satan said, "but you will not field all of our remaining veterans."

Schitz feigned resignation. "As you will have it, Lord." He paused. "I must remain here to belay the order."

Satan scowled and trudged off.

ZINC AND URANIUM II stood at the altar before God and the Priests.

"The strategy is working well," Zinc said. "We are whittling away at the most notorious Demons. Unfortunately, we have paid the price in heavy casualties. We've even lost some of the members of the Order of St. Patrick."

The murmurs ceased under Zinc's stern gaze. He continued, "We are close to breaking their backs, but we are vulnerable to a crippling defeat ourselves. I have concluded that we must put all our resources towards the destruction of their head Demons, not simply their veterans. We must finally destroy Schizophrenia, Autism, and Anorexia, the Triad of ancient Psychologicals."

From behind wild eyes, Uranium II looked scruffy. "Easier said than done," he said.

"What do you propose?" God asked.

"I still believe it is not a violation of the Divine Dictum for me to give the humans a weapon by which to end the war. It will be a miracle of science, not a supernatural one," Uranium II said. "We can consolidate our gains and continue from there. We will rebuild faster than the Demons. In the next war, we will be safe to complete the slaughter at our leisure. We can render their head ineffective, instead of being bitten trying to cut it from the snake."

Several of the Priests moaned. God glared at them, then at Zinc.

"You will not jeopardize our entire cause by exposing us to the harshest penalty in the Divine Dictum. I task you both with killing the head Demons. Drop the hammer."

SCHITZ STOOD IN THE Great Hall.

"Gentlemen and Ladies," he said, "I have called you away from your various ventures because our very existence is in peril, far greater peril than ever before. The sinister forces of Heaven have disregarded the lesser cards and waged a relentless campaign against the most esteemed of our ranks. While we have slaughtered innumerable foes, we are hemorrhaging from all sides. We must turn this pattern on its head and bleed their best and brightest."

Thunderous applause told Schitz he had galvanized the assembled. He pointed to Malchus.

"Travel to the Eastern Front where there is a rapidly approaching German offensive. Make sure that you are followed."

"Sir?"

'You heard correctly. Make no effort at stealth. Certainly, a Familiar will begin to tail you. Let the Familiar overhear that I will be meeting Autism to plan an assault here," he said. He pointed to a map of Kursk. "This is where the Soviet defenses will be at their highest, the perfect opportunity for the Angels to launch an ambush. Autism, you will already be there. You must both make the communication appear genuine, something exposed out of haste and not as intended deception."

Autism and the Wraith nodded in unison, saluted, and began to make the requite symbols to open a portal to the Mortal Realm.

Schitz resumed his instructions. "The rest of you will arrive only at the time of the ambush. I am certain the Angels will attack. Until then, remain out of sight."

Schitz handed out maps.

"You will arrive exactly at 0945 hours. You cannot be seen until the moment you enter the fray."

Several Demons began to mutter. Anorexia spoke first.

"You will be leaving yourself exposed. If the plan deviates even slightly, the Angels will have you."

"I know," Schitz said. "I am the required bait for this plan to succeed but I firmly believe we will triumph if everyone does things right."

Schitz walked from veteran to veteran, clasping each one upon the shoulder or by the hand. "Today, we will reverse the tide of the war. Today we will take back our own destiny."

With that, Schitz stepped through the portal provided by Autism and Malchus.

C<small>APTAIN</small> O<small>RESKINA</small> <small>LOOKED</small> <small>AT</small> the sunset from behind a large artillery piece. The hot, dry night was heavy and oppressive.

This endless Steppe could swallow a man's mind, he thought.

He knew the enemy lay to the west, far beyond the protective sandbags and the slat-lined trenches. The Steppe was so different from the captain's Ural Mountains. Zinc exhaled and tried to suppress his host's apprehension. He lit a cigarette, then ducked down into the trench in case there were enemy snipers nearby. The harsh smoke from the Belomorkanal filled his lungs and calmed Angel and human alike.

Zinc relished the moment. He was simultaneously giddy and anxious. By every indication, the coming day would deliver the most valued foes within the ranks of Hell. Zinc knew the fight would be dangerous and brutal—this was very likely the last sunset both he and the mortal captain both were likely to see. Zinc felt a momentary pang of jealousy.

When he dies tomorrow, he passes through the river of reincarnation and gets to live again, he thought. *When I go down, I turn into nothingness.*

Zinc pushed back against the most ancient of enemies, fear.

I will not die tomorrow.

Uranium II rounded the turn in the trench as the last rays of the sun cut across the barren field in sickly crimson hues. He had possessed the captain's lieutenant and fit the part of a less than satisfied, nervous junior officer.

"Are you certain of the plans?" Uranium II asked.

"The guns are pre-sighted; the tanks are in reserve out of view and waiting for the signal. We will clear the field of whatever Demons come across that plain tomorrow."

Uranium II chewed on his bottom lip. "I hope you know that my difference of opinion with you only comes from my nature as a soldier. I would be nothing if I did not say what I thought was correct. That aside, I trust you, and I will fight with you tomorrow side by side as your brother-in-arms and your friend, as always."

Zinc accepted Uranium II's outstretched hand. In an instant, the staunchness of his comrade banished all doubt from his mind.

Zinc smiled. "Tomorrow, my friend, we will win a great victory together."

THE PANZERGRENADIERS OF THE 1ST SS Division Leibstandarte Adolf Hitler began to move forward towards the Russian lines early the next morning. The sun rose behind the Soviet positions. Boots trod over the dusty ground and through the high grass. The grenadiers were battle-hardened men; Schitz admired their resolve as he boarded a light armored Sd. Kfz. 251 half-track. The mechanical beast lumbered forward, a great armored dinosaur flanked and proceeded by infantry. Schitz looked over his squad: Autism and a group of Phobias.

He yelled to be heard over the whine of the diesel engine. "We have no spare bodies in here except the drivers and the gunner. When we make contact, I need you out and into the lead infantry. Remember, we will encounter token resistance in the trench. Once we take it, the Angels will counter. We'll have the jump on them. Move quickly and take the trench faster than they anticipate. They want us buried in there."

RADON WAS STILL UNCERTAIN of what the battle held in store. He peered through the sight of the heavy artillery piece and wondered if he possessed the requisite mettle to hold his own. Although a recent graduate from the Academy, he had been offered admittance in the Resurrection Program. He was a descendant of an unincorporated house. He could become a Standard Bearer through admirable service.

He wondered if his fellows would support him. There was a cliquishness in Heaven's army, considerable friction between "the Regulars" and The Order of St. Patrick. The view of the approaching enemy through his field glasses made his eyes bulge. The lead vehicle brimmed over with Demons.

His pulse beat like a machine gun.

They're fish in a barrel, he thought.

Radon heard the order and fired the artillery piece.

THE SECOND HE SAW the first plumes of smoke erupt from the Russians' heavy guns, Schitz gave the order.

"Out!"

The shell impacted the ground a few meters ahead of the troop carrier and sent lethal shrapnel tearing through the air. The Demons leapt from their hosts into the grenadiers at the same time mortals jumped from the half-track as well. The infantry rushed across the open field toward the Soviet lines. Machine gun fire spit from the trenches and flayed vital organs. The German troops returned fire.

Schitz and his Demons swapped from body to body as they closed the gap, frustrating the novice Angels who tried to follow the moving targets. Soon the surviving grenadiers were close enough to hurl their potato masher grenades into the trench. Schitz possessed the leading infantryman shortly after he threw a grenade into the enemy position. Prone with the dirt pressed against his face, Schitz waited for the explosion.

Two seconds after detonation, he hauled the soldier to his feet and raised the sights of his sub-machine gun. Schitz fired across the closing expanse, ripping 9mm rounds into the foe. When he reached the edge of the trench, he brought down two possessed Russians who were uncertain whether to step into the Celestial or to engage from within their mortal confines. He cut them down in a hail of fire and then set upon them in his true form, stabbing at them with a short sword.

Schitz jumped into another German soldier and aimed his gun along the line of the trench. The foremost grenadiers began reorienting the artillery pieces along the line of the trench. They paid no mind to the fire coming from the Soviets. Schitz continued firing. Bullets plinked off the artillery piece. Everything was going the way he'd drawn them up. The undisciplined Russians and Angels were indecisive in selecting targets and could not repulse the infantry. They had only managed to knock out one of the half-tracks.

The surviving two Sd. Kfz. 251s opened a withering volley of fire on the second trench. The surviving Russians beat a hasty retreat. Schitz glanced around. His heart pounded against his chest and he grinned from ear to ear. The initial assault was an overwhelming success. The Angels were killed, and the guns captured—all faster than predicted.

The extra Phobias had thrown off the novice Angels who got so excited they could not prioritize the multiple targets. A moment later, a squadron of T-34 Soviet tanks rolled over the hill to the south a few hundred meters away. Schitz counted eight. He spotted at least fifteen Angels in the iron behemoths and the supporting infantry. His pulse ratcheted up another notch. The slaughter he had outlined was about to unfold.

ANOREXIA SAT IN THE turret of the squadron's lead Waffen-SS Division Tiger I tank. She checked her watch and chattered in her headset to confirm that the other tanks anticipated a correct arrival time. Anticipation grew. Anorexia heaved open the cover of the turret and peered through her binoculars.

"Amazing," she said.

Schitz and Autism each manned an artillery piece. Various Phobias followed orders and fired. A squadron of five Soviet tanks leveled a barrage on the artillery position. Three tanks burned at the crest of the hill. The ground ahead of Anorexia overflowed with Angels. She did not hesitate.

She shouted her orders to the gunner. "One hundred and fifty meters, dead ahead, zero elevation, fire on the lead!"

"UNBELIEVABLE!"

Zinc slammed his palm against the periscope of the T-34 Soviet tank. According to his intricate plan, he and his tanks were meant to catch the German infantry and half-tracks in the open. However, upon his arrival, he found the Demons already in possession of the trenches. Worse, they had enjoyed sufficient time to turn the artillery pieces in his direction.

"Fuck!"

He recalculated.

He tried to reassure himself. "We still have a numerical advantage," he said.

He peered through the sight of the main gun. The tank rocked and swayed.

I might as well be drunk.

He fired three rounds only to have the shells sail wide of the target.

If we stop, they'll use our tank for a barbeque pit.

He heard another shell clank into the breach.

He roared into the air. "Come on, Zinc! Come on!"

He tried once again to center the sight over the captured gun.

CLUMPS OF GRASS AND dirt flew into the air but there was no damage to Schitz's position from the wayward tank shells. His mind reeled with calculations primarily centered around the arrival of his reinforcements. He hoped they would arrive soon.

He sighted the artillery piece on the lead tank. The dark-green, hulking leviathan seemed close enough to touch through the scope. He saw smoke and fire belch from the tank's side. Despite the fatal blow, Schitz fired and watched as the artillery shell hit the front of the T-34 and launched the turret into the air as though the Soviet steel were paper.

From the west, Schitz spotted an arriving Tiger.

The reinforcements.

He looked at the surviving grenadiers. "Forward, repel the Bolsheviks."

The German infantry rushed out of the trench and began exchanging rifle fire with the Russian foot soldiers pinned down by the shelling. Schitz charged forward, his MP40 distributing death with every squeeze of the trigger. He saw the last Soviet tank burst into flame and raised a triumphant fist.

These were more experienced Angels. Half the Angels had already stepped into the Celestial; the others remained in human form. Schitz wished he had more than Autism and six Phobias to take on what he now counted as twenty-one Angels, presumably all elite veterans.

In his periphery, Schitz perceived his reserves were still a distance away. He gritted his teeth.

His voice cut through the cacophony of battle. "My brothers, the moment is now!"

He led the Leibstandarte into close-quarters combat. Schitz and the Phobias alternated bodies, jumping from one soldier to the next. Every time they stepped into the Celestial, they faced a fierce exchange with an Angel. The resulting melee was a spectacular display of strategy centuries in the making.

Schitz mowed down the nearest Russian with his submachine gun and stepped into the Celestial. When he raised his arm to hurl a throwing knife toward the seizing Angel, he was forced to sidestep a thrust from an Angel already in the Celestial. Schitz deftly avoided the foe and stepped into the safety of a new grenadier. At the same time, the active Angel moved to engage a Phobia who'd attempted an unsuccessful thrust toward the Angel's back. The Angel deflected the blow and stepped into a German. The Phobia stepped into a Russian.

Schitz reentered the Celestial and scrambled up one of the burning tanks. He crouched for a moment and hoped an Angel would be brought down nearby. A flash of light to his left. He dropped his head just in time. The Angelic throwing star grazed his scalp.

Schitz slid over the side of the tank and saw Autism engaging two Angels in the Celestial. Autism fell and the Angels raised their swords to deliver the killing blow. Schitz launched a pair of throwing knives. The first buried in an Angel's throat just below his jaw. To Schitz's amazement, the second knife sailed over the head of its intended target.

Autism used the opportunity to slice his attacker's leg. The Heavenly soldier buckled and leapt into a passing grenadier. Schitz stepped into a nearby officer and fired toward the host of the fleeing Angel with a semi-automatic pistol. His shots sailed wide. As the host dropped his empty magazine, Schitz stepped back into the Celestial. He drew his sword and assessed the scene. Every duel was incredibly complicated; they reflected the experience of the combatants.

Schitz moved through the Celestial, his eyes darting between friend and foe on the supernatural chessboard. For the first time since his battle with Gold, he experienced the delight of battle, the exhilaration of a true contest. The world seemed to slow down. Gunfire sounded as though underwater; the howling of dying men and Angels were mere whispers. He felt attuned to the hot, dry breeze and the Steppe below his feet. He believed he could do what he had promised. He could save the war.

To this point, casualties among the grizzled warriors had been light: two Phobias... two or three Angels. Anorexia and the reinforcements finally arrived. An Angel chomped at Schitz with a wicked-looking sword. When Schitz deflected the attack, the Angel threw a knife before stepping into a mortal. The blade grazed the top of Schitz's already wounded head.

Schitz judged the distance and launched his own knife. He aimed for the empty space to the Russian's left. The Angel stepped out of the Russian to avoid being cut down by a grenadier and directly into the path of the hurtling blade. The knife buried into the Angel's chest.

Schitz rolled across the dusty ground and arrived at the prone Angel. He retrieved the knife and plunged it into the Angel's throat. Just in time, he flipped sideways to avoid the Heavenly blade aimed at his head. It crashed into the dirt.

Schitz opted to avoid the Celestial and stepped into a grenadier. As he anticipated, the aggressive Angel, unfamiliar with all the tricks of combat, turned and took a human body to continue his pursuit. Schitz immediately jumped into the Celestial and ran the Angel through with his katana.

Schitz stopped to breathe next to a burning tank. Autism came up beside him.

"Run from this tank to the one over there," Schitz said. He pointed. "I'll be right behind you. Cut down the Angels as you go."

Confusion painted Autism's face, but he did not hesitate. Schitz raised his MP40 and lay the sight directly in front of Autism's path. Schitz unleashed a hailstorm of 9mm rounds and cut a path of carnage, four Germans and five Russians, through which his colleague raced. All but one of the dead were occupied by either an Angel or a Demon.

Autism swung a tomahawk. His run through the line of seizing Celestials mirrored the Angel of Death from the mortals' story of the Exodus. Autism opened the skulls of Angels like they were overripe melons. He left the seizing Demons unharmed.

Schitz dropped the possession of the sub-machine gunner and drew all his remaining throwing knives from their scabbards. The seizing Demons on the ground drew attacking Angels like honey attracts flies. Schitz loosed his knives in one single throw. In an instant, five Angels, who'd been intent on finishing the wounded Demons, met their demise. He stepped back into another grenadier.

Autism jumped into one of the few remaining Russians at the end of his run and looked back in amazement. Schitz started to wave but was suddenly aware that he was looking up at the sky. *Am I hallucinating?*

ZINC'S LEG THROBBED. HE'D jumped into an infantryman precisely when the tank exploded, but his new host caught a piece of the disintegrating T-34 tank in his left thigh. Zinc lay with his back against the treads of the smoldering hulk.

Within the Celestial, he could see through his human cloak to the blood oozing from his own separate wound. The artery was intact, but the injury was severe and required an expedited return to Heaven. The human was not in a much better state. He had been shot in the stomach; his intestines and kidneys were lacerated. Without emergency surgery, he would die. Zinc had a professional's appreciation of the skill displayed in the encounter. Though his side was taking casualties, he had held the hope of turning the encounter into a hard-fought victory.

To his deflated bewilderment, a volley of fire had cut down a portion of the field with deadly accuracy. A Demon who trailed the gunfire bashed in the heads of the fallen Angels.

Zinc punched the dry earth at his side at the sight of skulls caving like shattering eggshells, one after another. But Demons were seizing as well. Hope rose when he saw Angels breaking from their individual engagements and moving to strike upon the fallen Demons. Then, as though struck down by a higher power, all the Angels collapsed to the dusty Earth—dead.

How can anyone make such a throw? Zinc wondered.

Zinc raised his Kar98 rifle and shot the soldier housing the Demon. The man fell to the far side of the tank and disappeared. Zinc watched Uranium II, the sole remaining Angel, rush to the scene.

No one other than Schizophrenia himself could unleash such destruction in a single throw.

Zinc wondered if, at that very moment, Uranium II was killing the famed, scar-faced Demon.

THE BULLET HAD STRUCK SS-Rottenführer Klingelhofer in his left cheek just under his eye. It punched through his zygomatic bone then redirected and cut a path between his first and second vertebrae. Schitz realized why he was looking at the sky. His human had been shot. As the Rottenführer expired beside him, Schitz experienced the agonizing trembling of the departure seizure. He could see the area around him, but he could not move.

Earth & Water

The sense of vulnerability made him nauseous. In disbelief, he saw an Angel towering over him, lifting a sword high in the air. He could not scream; he could not move; he could not fight. Schitz tried with all his mental power to move away from the path of the descending sword but to no avail.

How cruel, he thought. *This is my greatest victory, and I am ended forever.*

He closed his eyes and remembered Anna's thirteenth lesson: surrender. He felt the blade touch his throat, but it was the flat, the broad edge. Schitz opened his eyes. It was not the Angel's blade against his throat but Anorexia's. She'd blocked the strike.

Anorexia threw herself into the Angel. The pair disappeared while Schitz's seizure continued. After what seemed like an eternity, all pain ceased, and Schitz felt his strength return. A familiar, feminine hand raised him to his feet. Anorexia leaned forward and kissed him on the lips—with intent.

"Glad you're still here," she said.

Schitz's legs wobbled. Anorexia supported him.

"Glad to be here," he said.

His field of vision blurred. He knew he was not at full strength.

"Please find me a door," he said. "I can't be out here like this."

He was vaguely aware of Autism's arrival; he braced Schitz.

"Come on," Autism said. "We can use the hatch on that Tiger tank to get him home. Then we can attend to the others."

"The others?" Schitz asked.

"The field is ours," Autism replied, "but there are many wounded. I've never seen anything like it in all my life."

"That was a battle for the ages," Anorexia said.

She slipped Schitz's arm over her shoulder and did not seem to mind when his hand fell across her breast.

The trio staggered to the nearest Tiger tank. Schitz still felt the horrifying sensation that he would lose consciousness. He felt certain he would vomit at any moment. Anorexia made the requisite symbols in the dirt around the hatch of the tank and Autism began the ancient incantations while she lit a match.

As they lowered him into the tank, Schitz said, "See to the others."

Stepping back into the Hellish Realm, Schitz was still beset by the unknown malady. A cold, naked terror grabbed at his body.

What if I am dying? he thought.

He wondered what had happened to him. He gestured for the Priests to bring him a beaker of water from the Styx. Breaking from the hymn of arrival, a Priest brought Schitz the healing drink. He sipped it with shaking lips and immediately felt restoration spread through his body.

The Priest looked at Schitz with puzzlement in his eyes. "You were injured, commander?"

Schitz's Notebook

Waffen SS Panzergrenadier Rottenführer Klingelhofer

These troops were disciplined and professional. Far superior to their Soviet counterparts. Though outnumbered they were resolute and unwavering in their fighting morale. With these soldiers I accomplished perhaps my greatest tactical accomplishment.

"I seized when my mortal was struck down," Schitz said.

The Priest nodded. "I would imagine you have not experienced the rigors of a seizure in centuries."

"True."

"It's a miracle that the shock did not kill you," the Priest said.

"I didn't know that that was a possibility," Schitz said. "But, as you said, it's not anything I have worried about in a long time."

The Priest checked Schitz and appeared satisfied with the progress of the healing. "You build up a tolerance to seizing the more often you do it."

Schitz forced a half-smile. "I have no intention of going through that again any time soon."

"Well, the worse is over now," the Priest said, "at least for another couple of centuries."

Schitz hoisted to his feet and staggered down towards his room. "Let's hope," he said. "Let's hope."

"So, you shot the Rottenführer," Autism said.

He was addressing the mortal possessed by Zinc. The surviving panzergrenadiers had assembled around their injured comrade and listened intently. Zinc's host was an SS-Untersturmführer, the highest-ranking among them. It was clear the mortals sided with Zinc's host.

"Yes," Zinc replied. "Apparently, he lost his mind; he shot Hans, Gunther, and Fredrick. He shot them all dead."

"It's true, sturmscharführer," one of the non-possessed grenadiers said.

"Jawhol, sturmscharführer, I saw it as well," another soldier said.

Autism and Anorexia were the only Demons still in the field. Autism cursed his bad luck. The mortal's injury hid the Angel's aura, so he had not been finished off during the fighting. If more Demons had been present during the mop-up, they could have possessed all the surrounding humans, deemed Zinc a traitor for killing the other Germans, and executed him. Alas, this was not to be.

"I had no choice, sturmscharführer," Zinc said.

Autism was sure he saw a faint smile flicker across the Angel's face from within the injured soldier.

"Take him to the field hospital at once," Autism said.

He sighed as he stepped into the Celestial.

"There's nothing we could do about that one," Anorexia said. "He's just lucky. Maybe he will bleed out before he gets back to Heaven."

Autism shrugged. "One can only hope."

"Only two of them got away—that one and the one I got off Schitz," Anorexia said. "All in all, we brought down nineteen Angels. We only lost three junior Phobias; Claustrophobia, Autophagy, and Seasonal Affective Disorder."

Autism stepped up to the Tiger's turret.

"Ready for a hero's welcome?" he asked.

"That's the spirit," Anorexia said.

She dropped through the hatch and passed through the portal in the process.

SCHITZ SAT UP IN bed. "Come," he said.

A jubilant Anorexia bounded into his bedchamber.

"They finally gave it to me!" she said.

She fairly pranced around the room. Schitz's eyes picked up the gleaming medal at her neck.

"The Knight's Pentagram," he said. "I'm proud of you."

Schitz stood, slowly. Anorexia dialed back her celebration.

"Are you feeling better now?"

"Yes, I am, thanks," Schitz said. "And I mean it; I am so happy for you. You've earned the award three times over now."

"And you deserve this," Anorexia. She tossed a medal into Schitz's lap.

Schitz stared at a Knight's Pentagram with Crossed Swords. He'd only seen it awarded a handful of times. The last instance was when he was part of the Free Thinkers.

"Titus said to give it to you," Anorexia said. "He called a peace overture from Satan."

She grinned from ear to ear and stepped closer to Schitz. She smelled of flowers and musk. An uneasy silence enveloped the room.

"I... I never thanked you sufficiently for saving my life," he said.

Anorexia leaned forward. "What constitutes sufficient thanks?" she asked.

She flicked her tongue across his lips. He felt warmth rising and thought about running his hands over her thin frame. But he stepped back.

"I cannot give you what you want."

Schitz hated the anguished gaze that met his eyes. He cursed himself as he watched tears form in the corners of her eyes.

"Just once," she said. She placed her hand on his chest. "Just once, let me be the one who pleases you."

She closed her eyes and rubbed his chest. Her other hand slid down his torso.

"Just once," she said, her mouth by his ear. "It's all I've wanted for as long as I can remember."

The pleading aroused him.

"I wish I could," he said.

"I don't understand," Anorexia said. She was beginning to pout. "You have slept with more than your fair share of maids after Rubella."

Indignation rose, but Schitz stifled it. He raised his palms.

"Let me explain," he said. "Sit down for a second."

He patted the bed. She sat beside him with her arms folded across her chest like a disappointed child.

"It is true," he said, "I have had my dalliances, but I have never replaced Rubella with any of those women. I have not given any part of myself to them. Each time I considered it, that woman has died." His voice cracked a little. "The way you love me... the way you love me. I don't deserve it. It's amazing. If I were to be with you, I would give all of myself to you, and if anything were to happen to you..."

He didn't realize he was crying until Anorexia wiped his cheek.

"I have to keep you at a distance," he said. "I cannot lose you—"

"That's unfair. Don't I have a say in this?"

Schitz chuckled. "Actually, you do not. I am the elder... I am in charge."

She huffed in disgust. Schitz suddenly remembered his time with Anna at the oasis.

"Let's do this," he said. "Lie here with me."

The two reclined onto his bed in a lovers' embrace. Satisfaction spread across Anorexia's face.

After a long while, Schitz spoke. "So, how awkward was my absence?"

Anorexia convulsed in laughter. "It was grossly obvious. Everybody kept on insisting they should go and get you. They applauded your bravery, and your miracle throw is now the thing of legend. Last I heard someone tell the tale, you brought down a dozen Angels with only four knives! Ha!"

She laughed so hard she started gasping for air. "Satan was furious, but there's nothing he could do. You sort of left out the part about his not approving your mission."

She slapped at him with both hands, beating on his shoulder while she cackled. Then... the mood was serious.

"I understand we can't be together, but I have waited for you my whole life."

Her words slammed into Schitz with more weight than any bullet.

"You mean, you've never?" he asked.

"Never," she replied.

"What about while possessing a human?"

"Never."

"What about Mono?"

"Never."

She waited... he waited... the silence grew oppressive.

"I deserve to feel like a woman," she said.

"I really don't deserve you," Schitz said. "But consider this a one-time, never to be repeated, post-award celebration."

He kissed her mouth, then her neck... her chest... her stomach. He opened the folds of her robe, baring her smooth sex. Instinctively she raised her knees on either side of his head.

Anorexia's grip upon the lion's skin blanket turned her knuckles white. Her body went rigid. Then she surrendered to a sea of ecstasy.

They held one another for hours. Finally, Schitz broke the silence.

"I'm sorry, that we cannot be more to each other."

"You fool," she replied. "This is the most wonderful day of my life. I'll always love you, Schitz, and I'll always have this moment with you."

Schitz drank in the moment.

He was home.

He was safe.

He was at peace.

And he offered no resistance when Anorexia climbed on top of him.

G<small>ALLIUM OFTEN WONDERED IF</small> he had been rushed into The Order of St. Patrick because of his father's position as Supreme Commander. He no longer wondered after Kursk. From that day, he knew the task was beyond him. They had intended to kill the ancient Demon Autism, and everyone in his company, but the ambush had devolved into a wholesale Angelic slaughter. A heavy despondency settled on the young Standard Bearer when he looked across the rows of those assembled for the funeral. Heaven had lost its very pillars; legendary names such as Lord Hydrogen and his sons Beryllium, Indium, and Thallium had fallen. Lord Uranium II's sons Fluorine, Bromine, Osmium, and Tantalum died. Gallium's brother Scandium was gone. Neophytes named Radon and Hassium never had a chance. And there were other sons and daughters of nobility. In all, The Order of St. Patrick had lost seventeen of its members. The Resurrected sacrificed two. Twenty additional regulars did not return from the fighting around Kursk.

All that death for three Demons, he thought. *What a waste.*

Incense permeated the air; so did the distinct odor of fatalism. Everyone thought the Demons were on the run. Then, they had rallied and decimated the Angelic ranks.

Gallium put his arm around his wife and whispered. "We all thought we were going to kill Autism today."

She put her delicate hand on his shoulder.

"You fought bravely, my love," she replied. "Yours was a lack of fortune, not of valor."

Gallium wanted to believe her. He looked at their eldest son, Rhenium. The boy had not taken part in any missions with the Order. Now, looking at the youngster's ashen face, Gallium doubted his son would ever desire such a posting.

Gallium shifted his gaze to his father. In a short space of time, the elder Angel had lost his wife and two of his sons. He appeared drawn and weathered.

He looked defeated.

Looming over the Great Hall, a new statue, a work by the Familiars, depicted an Angel driving its sword into a mighty serpent.

The figure featured large, outstretched wings pierced by arrows, one for each fallen member of the Order.

It looks like a Celestial pin cushion.

At the funeral's conclusion, the formations disintegrated. Gallium overheard numerous conversations.

"In the old days someone else would take over after something like this."

"Did you hear they are going to make Lady Hydrogen the Standard Bearer of the Hydrogen House rather than unincorporating it?"

"Do you think he will marry her now?"

"Did you hear about the Demons in Japan?"

"I understand Uranium II is leaving Europe to fight in Asia."

Each snippet of gossip pitched and battered Gallium. In addition to the fighters of the Order of St. Patrick, the solidarity of Heaven was a casualty. He gazed into his wife's almond-colored eyes and pulled her close.

"Oh, Hinata, what will we do?"

"You will fulfill your duty as a Lord and a warrior as you always have, my love," she replied.

"Duty seems to have taken on a different meaning today," he replied.

EVEN FROM AN EARLY age, Levy had exhibited abnormal strength for a Wraith. When the Wraiths were sent into battle, he seemed a natural choice as a fighter but his conspicuous might was relegated to a more mentally scarring task. He was appointed the head of the newly created cadre known as The Gravediggers.

Despite the name, they did not dig graves at all; their task was collecting bodies. Prior to the Second World War, ad hoc retrieval committees were assembled following battles such as Teutoburg or Waterloo, however, the steady stream of war-torn Demonic bodies created the need for Levy's division.

The day outside Salerno had begun like countless others. Reports arrived regarding any action in which Demons had been killed or where they had not returned with their fellows. The Italian engagement presented a mixed bag. Diogenes Syndrome was confirmed as Killed in Action. Pineal Cancer and Narcolepsy were unaccounted for following an engagement with numerous Angels.

Levy and his confederates, Sabrina, Marcus, Kathy, and Theodore interviewed any available Demon or Wraith that had been in the area. The Gravediggers assessed both likely locations for the fallen and any potential hazards they might encounter. Once completed, the team traveled to Salerno.

They had found Diogenes Syndrome curled in a fetal position. She appeared peaceful, almost sleeping. Levy had learned that such poses were often assumed when the departed succumbed to multiple wounds that combined to bring about death. Sure enough, Diogenes was cut all over her supple body. The Wraiths worked in teams of two, alternating responsibilities.

Levy carried Diogenes, and Sabrina opened the portal. Sabrina then carried the next corpse. While Levy delivered the first corpse to the Priests so they might prepare for the funeral, the others began the search for those yet to be recovered.

They found Pineal Cancer hacked to pieces. Unlike Diogenes, he was in a state of visible dismay. His eyes stared vacantly into nothing; his head had been nearly severed from his body; his robe was covered in blood. Kathy did her best to keep the corpse in one piece as Marcus opened a portal.

The most disturbing type of find occurred when they located Narcolepsy. The young Demon began to groan when Sabrina lifted him. Despite two collapsed lungs, the results of deep stab wounds to the chest, and a depressed skull fracture courtesy of a blunt instrument, the Demon clung to life.

Sabrina broke open her vial and poured waters from the Styx over the fading Demon. "Bring more water, quickly!"

The healing powers of water from the Styx rapidly diminished once transported out of Hell. Within a matter of hours, it turned into regular water. But in this case, there were still trace amounts of therapeutic properties.

The Wraiths rushed to the warrior's side and doused him in water while Sabrina began dragging him towards a portal Levy was opening. Before Levy inscribed the first symbol, he heard Sabrina's doleful voice. "It's too late. He's gone."

"Are you sure?" Levy asked.

Sabrina nodded. Levy winced; he hated being there when they died. They had found Erotomania within the wreck of a Bf-109. His host had died on impact. But despite shattered bones and organs savaged by the crash, the Demon clung to life. When they tried to pull him free, Erotomania screamed in pain. His lower torso was wedged in the wreckage.

The memories haunted Levy. At El Alamein, they had retrieved scores of Wraiths, dispatched by the Angels after an attempt to disrupt the Heavenly lines. As night settled upon the desert sands, The Gravediggers discovered the dismembered pieces of approximately twenty Wraiths from around the corpses of Gangrene and Bipolar Disorder. Gangrene died from a single sword thrust through her back; Bipolar from a throwing star to the jugular. But the Wraiths had been cut to ribbons.

The excavation was grisly work. For dismembered Demons, The Gravediggers used wicker baskets to hold body parts, one for hands and arms, and another for feet and legs, and still another for heads and torsos. The Priest then tried to pair the morbid jigsaw together to form a discernible individual for interment. Levy had nearly fainted when he felt something squish beneath his feet. In the moonlight, he looked down to realize that he had stepped on a Wraith's disembodied eyeball.

In addition to the parade of Demonic death, Levy and his crew saw an overabundance of felled Angels. At Anzio, The Gravediggers picked through the Italian countryside to find the corpses of Manic Episode, Conduct Disorder, OCD, and Trench Foot. At the same time, the Familiars were retrieving at least sixty fallen Angels. Sometimes there was conversation.

One of the Familiars lifted an Angel whose head had been sawed in half. "Whoa, look at what they did to this one!"

Levy grimaced.

Moments later, he extricated an Angel from beneath a Demon's body. The two were intertwined with their hands on each other's throats. "Here's one of yours."

But nothing could prepare Levy for the horror of the Normandy Invasion and the subsequent battle in the hedgerows. The contest for the beachhead left Levy and his crew digging through shell craters and damaged blockhouses for the corpses of Transient Tic Disorder, Pica, and Kaposi Sarcoma. They were all felled defending against the Angelic and Allied invasion.

Water from the Styx

But at least the battle for the beach, though brutal, reflected some semblance of organization. The butchery in the hedgerows was chaotic and savage. Mortal and Celestial combat broke out at every bend of the maze of vines and ditches. A tank would break through a copse of tangled vines and trees only to be knocked out a moment later by a Panzerfaust. The Angels and Demons hacked one another to pieces.

Even as Levy and his crew moved in to retrieve the dead, another assault erupted. A mortal invariably opened up with machine gun fire from a concealed position. Angels suddenly renewed their attack through a gap in the Celestial. Airpower and artillery pummeled mortal troops from both sides.

Wraiths fell alongside Celestials. Kathy was killed by an Angel's throwing knife. Levy wondered if she had been targeted, then decided nothing mattered except the outcome. He carried her unrecognizable pile of flesh home over his shoulder.

Schitz's Notebook

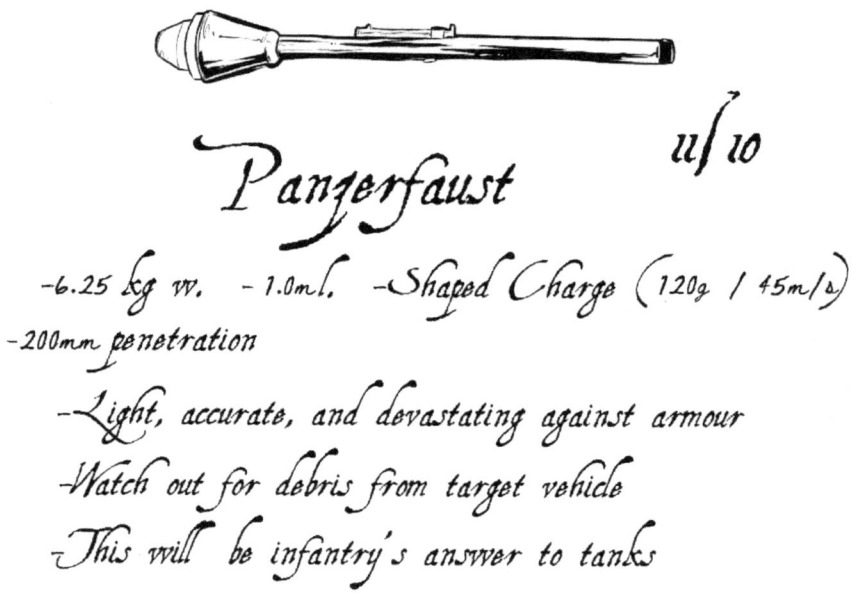

Panzerfaust u/10

-6.25 kg w. - 1.0mℓ. -Shaped Charge (120g / 45m/s)
-200mm penetration

-Light, accurate, and devastating against armour
-Watch out for debris from target vehicle
-This will be infantry's answer to tanks

The hedgerows proved cataclysmic. The surviving remnants of Hell and Heaven shattered their forces against one another. Levy watched as Schitz threw everything he had, veterans, neophytes, Wraiths, even some Priests, at the Angelic forces. On the field of battle, the commander appeared more of an animal than a Demon. Levy had just handed the limp body of Fregoli Delusion to Sabrina when he observed Schitz leading a contingent of Waffen SS infantry along a trench. He sent two youngsters, Huntington's Disease and PTSD, into a gap in the hedge. The young Demons began firing their submachine guns from within their hosts. Moments later, the duo of Demons was set upon by a barrage of fire from a substantial American force. Soon after, a flood of olive drab uniforms emerged from the gap.

Levy screamed when the Angels struck down Huntington and PTSD as they retreated. From either flank, Schitz and his confederates fell upon the Angels. They mowed down the Americans with

MG 42s and made short work of the Angels. The combat took only a matter of moments.

Levy and his crew, now with the new arrival Marsha, collected the dead. Cancer's name, the myth once held up as the salvation of the Demons, came across Levy's desk on a list of those missing in the hedgerows. When he headed to the Great Hall to conduct his interviews, Levy saw Satan grab Communism and Atheism by their horns. He was bellowing like a castrated bull.

"There is no strategic reserve for you to oversee. You will link up with our forces, and you will find Cancer alive."

Levy decided to follow the pair into the field. Unfortunately, neither Atheism nor Communism was prepared for the horrors of combat. For too long, the pair had looked after Demons and spent their time infecting the minds of men. Both were ambushed and dispatched by Angels within moments of entering the fray.

Levy watched a pair of Angels confront them within the Celestial. Communism was cut down forthwith. Atheism managed to jump into a mortal crouched in a trench. A moment later, attacking mortals arrived, and her host was cut down by fire from a Thompson submachine gun. The Angels finished off the seizing Demon with brutal efficiency, slitting her throat. She was still shaking when Levy reached her. He opted to save his vial of Styx water for Cancer.

Maschinengewehr 42
a.k.a MG 42

The hunt for the legendary Demon proved frustrating. First, they located the body of a female so disfigured that she was unrecognizable. Upon their return to Hell, assessment reports determined that the body belonged to the neophyte, Binge Eating Disorder. The Demons and Wraiths took to the Mortal Realm once more.

After clearing a trench of American troops, Schitz signaled to Levy and his crew that the grisly hunt was concluded. The Wraith had seen a great deal in his time, but what lay before him shook him to the core. The trench had been part of a defensive line containing a Flak 88mm gun. The Germans had defended the gun fiercely. It had served them well and knocked out countless tanks and other vehicles from underneath the camouflage netting that obscured it from Allied airpower. When the American infantry attacked, the Angels were within them. They paid dearly for the assault.

The Germans had counterattacked, desperate to save the artillery piece. Judging by the aftermath of the battle, the position had changed hands within the Mortal and Celestial Realm several times. The trench overflowed with dead mortals of both armies and Angelic fallen. The Germans eventually re-secured the area—a pyrrhic victory. The 88mm cannon had been destroyed in the melee.

Within the rows and rows of dead Angels, Levy and his crew found the body of Cancer as well as those of her followers Rectal Cancer, Renal Cancer, and Leukemia.

"They died hard," Schitz said as he passed Levy within the Celestial.

"This was a veritable slaughter, sir," the Wraith replied.

Levy felt uncomfortable talking to the Demon, but also excited to be speaking to such a legendary figure.

"I would imagine you have seen your share of slaughter," Schitz said.

"Probably still less than you, sir."

"You don't have to call me sir; Schitz is fine," the Demon said.

Levy knew most of the stories about Hell's commander. He was unsure what to think, but he was thrilled with the face-to-face.

"It will be a blow, losing her," Levy said. He pointed to Cancer's inert form.

"Indeed," Schitz said. "I fear for our morale after days like today. Even though we broke their veteran killing squad, our losses are severe. It is not possible to make up for the experience Cancer and her followers offered."

Dread spread through Levy's gut. If Schitz spoke so negatively about the losses, surely the conflict was unsustainable.

"Forgive me," the Demon said, "we must remain positive. I just lost a close friend today, Hysteria. She was manning another one of these guns farther up the line. She was always very good with artillery."

"I'm sorry," Levy said. "Where can I find her?"

"Oh no, I brought her home," Schitz said.

"Thank you, sir... I mean Schitz."

He stared at his boots and searched for something to say.

Schitz was done with the conversation. "Well, Levs," he said, "let's see what can be done, shall we?"

He patted Levy on the back and stepped into a passing infantryman. Levy watched in awe as the Demon walked away along the trench.

CHAPTER 9

A MIRROR IMAGE

The early April Baltic air was still cool at the operational area around Usedom. The breeze, interlaced with sea salt, blustered across the airfield, and battered the small glass panes of the wooden shack used as the Ready Room where pilots were briefed on the details of the upcoming missions. The sun blazed in a bright alabaster sky. It would have been a beautiful day, were it not the last for so many countless men and women on either side of the Oder–Neisse Line.

Schitz's Notebook

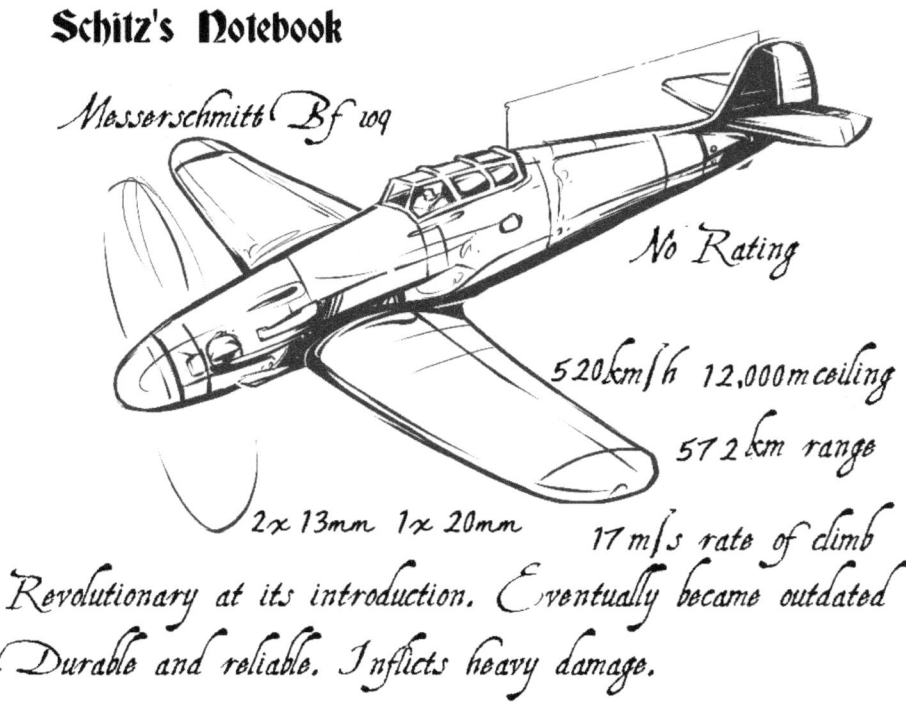

Messerschmitt Bf 109

No Rating

520 km/h 12,000m ceiling

572 km range

2x 13mm 1x 20mm 17 m/s rate of climb

Revolutionary at its introduction. Eventually became outdated Durable and reliable. Inflicts heavy damage.

Major Hammerstock never worried about grandiose projections or figures; he never considered the weight of good or evil. He was primarily concerned with keeping his few remaining planes operational and his even smaller allotment of pilots alive. If somehow his depleted portion of the crushed Luftwaffe delayed the Soviets a few hours, well, that was a bonus. Schitz found the Major's mind fascinating. Other than a brief stint combating the lumbering fortresses of the American 8th Bomber Command in the Defense of the Reich Campaign, most of the major's airtime had been on the Eastern Front since 1941. The major was a hard man with over a century's worth of kill-bars on the tail of his Messerschmitt. He had downed as many enemy aircraft as the model number of his plane, 109. On the rare times he displayed all his medals on his uniform, Hammerstock found it difficult to remain upright. Now, even though the end of the war moved closer with every day, Hammerstock was still flying, still killing.

Schitz felt the complex and convoluted notions of patriotism, survival instinct, and the paternal feeling toward one's command colliding within the major, things too akin to his own thoughts. Schitz recognized deep despair weighing down his mind and the physical pains brought on by a lifetime of physical strife. He groaned when the pilots filed into the room, downtrodden yet youthful.

They are a different breed, he thought. *Warriors everyone.*

Schitz considered his own dilemmas and allowed the major to confront his. The war had been planned meticulously, from the ramping up of Demonic numbers to arming the Wraiths. There had been painstaking training and strategizing. Schitz wondered as to the purpose of the monumental effort. The forces of Heaven and the forces of Hell had smashed each other with such lethality that a moderately sized, fresh contingent from either side would easily sweep aside the scattered remnants of the foe. Of course, neither side could field more than a scattered, demoralized husk of a fighting force at this point.

He looked at Anorexia. She and her possessed human offered a curious story. The pilot, Susan von Lowe, was a ghoulishly thin aristocrat. She received private flying instructions before the war on one of her father's personal aircraft. In the dying stages of the conflict, she cut her hair and dared any official to reject a willing and capable volunteer. When Lieutenant Voss perished behind Soviet Lines in the Winter of 1944, Fräulein Lowe took his place in the squadron and began her career with a clear understanding of the approaching apocalypse.

Four months and countless sorties later, she had four confirmed and ten probable kills to her name. The title of ace had thus far eluded her, and she gave her mechanics no rest. She drove them like one of the pharaoh's overseers to ensure her craft was flight-worthy whenever possible.

Anorexia had been with Schitz from the beginning. He remembered her birth. Elise was a friend to Anorexia's Wraith. Schitz shook his head to banish Elise from his mind. He gazed at Anorexia. Despite their singular tryst, she was essentially his sister. They shared a closeness born of similar circumstance and familiar history.

Schitz spoke through the major.

"Today's mission will be the same as yesterday's, and the day before that, and the day before that."

The pilots grinned even though the major began every briefing in like manner.

"We do not control the skies over the lines, and for every enemy we shoot down, their factories spit out ten more, or twenty more, whatever it is." He looked around the room and let his eyes settle on von Lowe. "I do not say this out of cowardice or defeatism; it is simply the reality. It would be foolish and unpatriotic to throw your lives away pointlessly. We are using an aircraft that was the top of the line five years ago. Now we turn slower, we dive slower, and have less powerful guns. We are outnumbered, but … (the assembled hung on his every word) …we are the Luftwaffe. We will always be the Luftwaffe. No matter how outnumbered our men or outclassed our machinery, we will outmaneuver and out-execute our opponents. You will, as always, split into groups of two when we get to the front. The lead will lure the Russians over our lines; his wingman will shoot down whatever he can. Then you will break for home. Stay alive; the Fatherland will need you tomorrow."

The pilots filed out into the blustering spring air and walked briskly to the flight line. Hammerstock tapped von Lowe on the shoulder.

"I'll fly lead today for our section as long as you think you can cover my ass."

The young pilot's expression brightened at the proposition of flying in the position most likely to score a kill.

"Thanks, Schitz," Anorexia said. "I know she'll like that."

Schitz laughed. "I just want to make sure we don't get too deep over Soviet territory. Sometimes I wonder if it's you or that aggressive fräulein in charge up there."

Anorexia unleashed a wry smile. "Sometimes, I wonder myself."

"I mean it," Schitz said. "Be careful up there."

The crew chief and his crew stood at attention next to Anorexia's plane. Schitz stepped onto the wing. Then the major climbed into the cramped cockpit of his Messerschmitt.

The engine roared to life and the bird taxied to the edge of the runway. The nerves never abandoned Schitz when it came to combat aviation. If his human were killed underwater, he would seize and float to the surface; he could not drown. If his human were killed in a fire, he would seize and walk away; in the Celestial he could not burn. But if his human died in the air, and he fell, death was unavoidable.

But the evolution of war required even the most reluctant of Demons and Angels take to the air. Schitz took a small margin of comfort in knowing that he was an unnaturally skilled aviator. When he paired himself with an ace, he was nearly untouchable.

Schitz pushed the throttle forward and felt the rush of exhilaration as the small, light plane skipped across the field and lifted from the ground. In a matter of minutes, they reached the front lines. Schitz cursed under his breath. They were too low. He surveyed the heavens for bandits. Out of the sun emerged a cluster of rapidly approaching shadows. A more inexperienced pilot would turn or dive, but the Russians and Angels would expect that reaction. Instead, Schitz maintained his heading and reduced the throttle.

Tracer rounds cut through the air in front of him. Having thrown off his pursuers' aim, Schitz banked into a turn. He slammed the throttle forward and dove towards the German lines. The lead Russian over-cooked his approach and ended up in front of Schitz. He was so close, Schitz could count the rivets on the underside of the wing.

Schitz maneuvered the gyroscopic gunsight over the middle of the Yak-9 and depressed the trigger. The aircraft's frame rattled as the rounds left his plane, and Schitz watched the tracers stitch through the enemy craft. A thick black cloud of burning fuel oozed from the tail and the plane tumbled towards the Earth.

The remaining Soviets were still behind him. Apprehension gnawed at Schitz's stomach and he wished he still had Anorexia on his wing.

She had veered off when they reached the front to avoid falling prey to the same attack. The Royal Air Force learned that lesson the hard way early in the war by flying in tight V formations where they were chewed up by eager Luftwaffe fighters. Now, with the enemy bearing down on him, the Demon hoped his compatriot was not too far away.

Schitz led his pursuers back over German lines when he recognized the unsettling sensation of incoming fire finding its mark. He knew his plane could be rendered inoperable at any moment. He nosed over slightly, dove, and glanced over his shoulder. He could see the closest emitted the aura of an Angel.

Schitz smirked. "Let's play ball."

Banking on the arrival of his wingman, Schitz pulled back on the yoke and raised his plane into a steep climb. When he looked back again, he saw one of his pursuers falling to the ground alight with flames. A second Russian was breaking away, pursued by the Luftwaffe's newest ace. The Angel had not anticipated Schitz exposing himself with such a dangerous action and passed underneath him.

Schitz hooted in delight.

I'm fighting a virtual rookie!

He pushed the control column forward and to the left, nimbly snapping his plane into a barrel roll. His enemy, overly reliant on his technical advantage, realized his error and compensated by throttling forward and entering a sweeping turn. His hubris of trying to speed through the shortest route to his enemy's rear, left him vulnerable.

Schitz's mind processed a turbulent array of calculations—the different airspeeds of both crafts, the angle of the arc between himself and his foe, and the drop of his machine gun and cannon rounds. He knew he would only have a limited window of opportunity before the Yak-9 escaped.

Schitz absorbed the calculations, then relied on his natural intuition. He adjusted his craft and unleashed a barrage of machine gun fire. Phosphorous tracers pierced the sky. They disappeared into the forward portion of the Yak-9's fuselage, the vital area containing the engine. Schitz adjusted his gyroscopic gunsight and pulled the trigger for the cannon. The metal skin covering the Yak's engine buckled with the impact of the shells.

The Angel leveled the Yak-9. Schitz considered aiming the more powerful shells at the cockpit. He remembered Tetanus, and his repetitive oration.

We've come a long way since we dealt the fatal blow solely hand-to-hand, Schitz thought.

Schitz leveled his 109 behind the Yak-9, careful to avoid the black smoke, oil spray, and metal fragments flying from the wounded bird. The Yak-9 was dead in the air; and soon the propeller stopped spinning entirely. The Angel's luck could not have been worse. When he started his turn, he was more concerned with the dogfight than escape, and his dying plane had drifted farther into German territory.

A black shadow on his periphery distracted him. A jubilant von Lowe rocked her plane's wings from side to side as she pulled alongside.

He keyed the radio while keeping a close eye on the Yak-9.

"Congratulations, ace," he said.

His fellow rocked her wings side to side again and responded, "Horrido!" without any effort to conceal her feminine voice. "Two down on this side of the lines, infantry will confirm for sure."

Schitz gave a thumbs up. "This one's done for," he said. "I'm going to escort him down. I'm fine. Now, head back home."

THE CRAMPED COCKPIT OF the Yak-9 was as close to Hell on Earth as Zinc could remember experiencing. The engine was dead and burning, the control column unresponsive. In every sense, he was a captive passenger. To make matters worse, his pursuer had been joined by his wingman, banishing all hope that any reinforcements would be arriving.

What horrible luck, he thought. *There are woefully few senior Demons left, and I run into a pair of them.*

To his surprise, one of the 109s sped up and pulled alongside. A youngster with a petite, small face, waved exuberantly to him before gesturing happily towards the ground. Confusion was replaced by anger. Zinc realized the meaning of the foe's gesticulations; he was going to hit the ground... and die.

Zinc started to raise his middle finger, but the 109 rolled over and disappeared. Zinc punched the control panel in frustration.

He screamed in frustration and anger. "Why? Why did I survive all I have only to die like this?"

He hated the thought of not existing, the idea of ceasing to be. He felt like a rat trapped in a burning can. When his enemy fired, the pilot would die, and Zinc would seize and die on impact with the ground. He felt unprepared, unready, lost. There was no possible relief.

But he refused to weep.

The claustrophobia of the cockpit pressed in on his lungs. The ground came closer in agonizingly slow motion.

This is taking too long, he thought.

He turned around. The enemy was still flying behind him, passive.

Maybe he's out of ammunition.

Zinc's entire body warmed—the sensation of throwing back a shot of strong liquor. He glanced at the altimeter. He was just above the minimum height from which he could deploy his parachute. He unlatched the lever to the glass canopy.

SCHITZ FELT LIKE A damsel plucking the petals from a daisy.

"Shoot him down. Shoot him down, not. Shoot him down. Shoot him down, not," he said aloud.

The gunsight still hovered over the Yak's fuselage. Then he saw the canopy of the cockpit open.

He reached up and beat on his own canopy with fiendish delight. "That son of a bitch really wants to live!"

Schitz was not sure how he would cope with certain death. He avoided such considerations whenever possible. Schitz checked the gunsight and pulled the trigger. The opened canopy exploded into shards of shattering glass. Sparks flew from the cockpit. He laughed maniacally when he saw the pilot's hand retreat like a frightened prairie dog into its hole.

Schitz's boisterous shout echoed inside the cockpit. "What are you going to do now, brave Angel?"

ZINC YANKED HIS ARM away from the canopy.

"Damn, he's still armed!"

But he felt an odd optimism.

"If he wants to play with me like a cornered mouse, I'll force his hand," he said.

Zinc braced himself against his seat with his arms on the side of the open cockpit. Cold air brought tears to his eyes. He hoped his altitude had not dropped below the minimum height for parachute deployment. He gathered his legs under him as best he could, the launched himself over the sidewall of the cockpit. His mortal's leg buckled and bent outward in an unnatural position. He landed on the wing of the Yak.

Zinc looked up. The fighter lumbered through the air. The enemy craft looked close enough to touch. The Demon adjusted his craft.

He's going to fire, Zinc thought.

Time froze. Zinc saw the steel blue of the Demon's eyes; he felt the throbbing of his mortal's broken leg, the brutal cold of the wing under his hand, the whipping wind.

And he braced for the impact of machine gun fire.

"THIS IS TOO EASY," Schitz said.

He eased the tension on the trigger. Hammerstock's thoughts were not helping; stuff about "honor."

"The man fancies himself a knight of the air," Schitz said.

He had an idea. He rolled the 109 into a split-s and dove for the ground.

ZINC STARED IN DISBELIEF as the 109 dove away from him. Had the Demon now run out of ammunition? Had the foe given in to some sort of sense of fair play? Did his enemy have a more sinister plan in store? None of it mattered to Zinc in the moment. With one final parting pat to the wing of his faithful aircraft, Zinc launched himself over the edge and heaved the chord on his chute, hoping against hope that he was still high enough for it to deploy safely.

SCHITZ LOOKED AT HIS wrecked Messerschmitt and burned with embarrassment. He had tracked the falling airman well, beat him to the ground, and identified a country road to use as a runway, only to have the landing gear buckle upon hitting the ground. He walked off the effects of impact.

The plane was less fortunate. It would never soar again. The engine was destroyed, one wing dangled from the frame. He inspected the punctured tail.

"They'll think I was fucking shot down," he said. "Total humiliation."

Schitz gazed up at the descending airman and instantly understood what was going to happen. Ten seconds later, in open countryside along a dirt road, his foe's parachute entangled itself high in the top of the only tree one could see for miles in any direction. Fabric tore, tree limbs cracked, but the aviator came to a stop a full thirty feet off the ground.

Schitz shouted up to the Angel. "So, Icarus finally lands!"

"Now what," the Angel asked.

Schitz shrugged. "I suppose that's up to you."

"Meaning?"

Schitz spread his arms. "Well, you could jump down, and we could try to kill each other. Or... we could have a talk."

A look of incredulity painted the Angel's face. "Why would I want to talk to you?"

"Well," Schitz said, "perhaps you would like to know why I didn't kill you when I had the shot."

"No," the Angel said. "You just fucked with me; you shot at the canopy."

"Would you have preferred that I blow you out of the air?"

"I guess not." The Angel was visibly confused—and growing more irritated by the second. "But why do you want to talk?"

Schitz squinted in thought. "In truth," he said, "I guess I was bored. Our kind talked once upon a time. We would lay down our arms and have conversations in gentlemen's clubs. Probably before your time."

"You presume too much. For all you know, I am older than you," the Angel said.

Schitz shouted his bona fides. "Verdun!"

The Angel laughed. "Sharpsburg."

"Waterloo."

"Saratoga!"

"This is getting old," Schitz said. He rubbed his neck to relieve the tension of craning upward. "Teutoburg Forest."

"Ah," the Angel said. "Alesia."

"Fair enough." Schitz paused and waited until he thought he saw a smile spread over the Angel's face. Then, "Thermopylae."

The Angel bobbed his head. "I only have one more," he said. "Halule."

Schitz executed a sweeping bow. "You got me. I should have shot you up there. That was around when I was born."

The Angel chuckled from his branch. "Me too."

"It's been a long time since I played that game with anyone," Schitz said.

The Angel's laugh was loud and genuine. "But nowhere near as long as you've been around, old man."

Schitz sighed. "I suppose."

Neither spoke for a long time. Schitz scrutinized the countryside. He'd long looked over the landscape but realized he always saw real estate in terms of tactics... troop movements... battlefields. Now, for the first time in a long time, maybe for the first time ever, he took in the sights and admired what little beauty had been left unscorched, unexploded, or un-mangled. The vacant peace of the empty road-side seemed odd given the surrounding cauldron of conflict.

Finally, he spoke. "I can't believe how long we've been fighting."

"I know," the Angel said.

"Have our paths crossed before today?"

Schitz shrugged, "Possible... actually, probable."

An odd sensation stirred in Schitz's brain.

"I feel... how do I say this? I feel I have every reason to hate you or to fear you. After all, your kind has been trying to kill me since the day I was born."

"Not a sentiment with which I am unfamiliar," the Angel said.

"Fair enough," Schitz said. "But, oddly enough, I no longer see any benefit in either sentiment. If I am completely honest—"

The Angel interrupted. "Is that possible for a Demon?"

Schitz raised his middle finger, but he was smiling. "Don't waste your sweet Heavenly breath by trying to convince me that all your colleagues are without duplicity."

The Angel returned the single-finger salutation, then said, "Point taken."

Schitz returned to his original thought. "If I am being completely honest..." He waited for another interruption. "I don't care about you much either way." He paused and lit a cigarette. "What about you?"

"Well," the Angel said, wiggling a little in his harness, "I just don't want to die, and I thought I was dead up there." He pointed skyward. "You had me."

"I sure as Hell did," Schitz said.

Both men laughed at the weak joke before Schitz grew serious again.

"I don't want to die either," he said. "My fear pretty much dictates everything I do all the time." He corrected himself. "Well, except for at the start of this latest mess. Everyone on my side thought we were destined for the final victory. For a little while, I was more concerned with the grand scheme and less about my own well-being."

"And what does the final victory look like on your side of the fence?" the Angel asked.

Schitz took another cigarette out of its pack and took a long drag. "Well, I guess we believe that once we have exterminated the Angels, the River Styx will dry because the cycle of human reincarnation will end. Humans will live forever, and we will be their absolute rulers."

The Angel chortled with more cynicism than humor. "That sounds incredibly similar to our version of the end of the conflict."

"Schizophrenia," Schitz said.

"As I suspected," the Angel said. He drew his right index finger along his cheek to mime a scar. "Your reputation precedes you. I'm the Standard Bearer of the House of Zinc."

Schitz executed a swift bow. There was no sense of mocking. "Nice to meet you, Your Lordship."

The Angel saluted. "Well, thank you for not taking the shot."

He immediately understood he had crossed some sort of line. Schitz looked oddly offended.

"I meant no insult, Sir Schizophrenia," the Angel said. "If we are not friends and you cannot receive my thanks, then accept the appreciation and respect of a rival."

The pair watched a formation of Messerschmitts fly overhead.

Schitz ground his cigarette under his foot. "Do you live with a certain sense of futility?" he asked.

The Angel hung silently from the tree and twisted in his harness. "How so?"

"Well, can your side mount any serious operation right now? I'm not asking for tactics. I want your impression."

The Angel's response came with surprising speed and transparency. "Honestly? No."

"See," Schitz said. "Neither can we, so I have a proposition if you are willing to listen."

The Angel slapped at his harness. "I am the epitome of a captive audience."

"How about..." Schitz stopped and looked around. "Ah, I propose an accord. We agree not to kill each other but to supply one another with information so we may effectively..." he looked around again, "deal with our personal enemies."

"So, you propose treason," Zinc said.

Schitz shook his head. "No, I propose survival. If we continue along this path, neither of us will live. You nearly got me on your first pass, and I had a more than adequate opportunity to dispatch you. Things may not always shake out so very neatly." He lit another cigarette. "I didn't get here without making a few enemies within my own ranks, and I'm pretty certain it's the same for you. Why not work towards our primary goal—staying alive?"

The Angel closed his eyes, whether in thought or prayer, Schitz could not discern. For his own part, he smoked and looked around. He wondered if God and the Devil might show up at any moment to extinguish not only the conversation but both its participants.

Zinc opened his eyes. "This can't happen again," he said.

"What do you mean?" Schitz asked.

"This," Zinc said. He moved his arms in a sweeping gesturing. "All of this; this insane global war of mass annihilation. There was a time when a great war came about every couple of centuries, but it was always regional in nature. This conflagration is global and will not end without significantly more bloodshed. Once this is over, it has to stop."

With a distinct feeling of relief, Schitz nodded. "So, we will provide balance," he said. "Mankind will never again face annihilation, our sides will remain in check, and as the fruits of our efforts, we will enjoy the advantage of shared information."

Worry wormed its way across Zinc's face. "But how will we communicate?"

Schitz replied, "My friend, one in every hundred humans is infected by Schizophrenia. It might not seem like a lot, but—"

"That's a staggeringly high amount; you must be very proud," Zinc said.

Schitz hunched his shoulders and held his palms upward in an "It's what I do" gesture. "Well," he said, "there are schizophrenics everywhere but very few people know that they are all connected in one channel of seemingly random, meaningless thoughts. Even without possession, all you have to do is talk to one and they will tell you what every other schizophrenic is saying or thinking."

Zinc's eyes betrayed skepticism. "How is that possible? All those millions of people are surely thinking different things. Aren't they talking to different people?"

Schitz looked like a proud parent whose child just hit the game-winning homerun. "That's the beauty of it," he said. "When I'm not tapped in, so to speak, they are free to do whatever they want within the bounds of their insanity. Once I go near one of them, the conversation becomes universal."

"Will it work for me too?"

"As long as I will it," Schitz said. "Still, even though I doubt anyone will listen in, we should speak in code for security purposes."

"A question," Zinc said. "Why create a secret network of communication if you had nobody to speak with?"

"I was lonely, I guess, or bored, or both."

"Fair enough," Zinc said.

"This is a good and workable agreement," Schitz said. "We can both stay alive. Don't get second thoughts—or try to screw me over."

Zinc remained silent.

"Well," Schitz said, "for what it's worth, I give you my word to keep this accord, although there may come times where I may need it to appear to others that you are my enemy."

"Understood," Zinc replied. "And I pledge to keep our covenant as well."

"Shake on it?" Schitz said. He extended his hand upward.

"All joking aside," Zinc said, "will you help me? It's a long way down."

Schitz was already headed down the road. He called over his shoulder. "You'll figure a way out; you've been getting out of tight spots for centuries."

THE COLD STONE WALLS of the Führerbunker were depressing. The state of Deutschland was worse. Schitz made his way through the bunker alternating between possession of soldiers and assorted members of the high command. It amazed the Demon to see the withered and decrepit shape of the broken leader of the Third Reich.

How is this the man from the Zeppelinfeld? Schitz wondered.

Schitz ascertained two haunting facts. The man had never been possessed by a Demon or an Angel; all his accomplishments and failures were his own, and he, like many others, was now a victim of Schitz's malady. Schitz felt a pang of grief that this powerful leader had succumbed to his illness.

"It is the cost of my genius, that a man I might admire can fall to my own dark arts," Schitz said aloud. "Another defeated leader to add to my tally."

"What? Who said that?" the Führer asked.

The only answer was the silence of an empty room.

CIRCADES LOOKED IN FRUSTRATION around the insurance company's boardroom.

"This is the second time in very quick succession that you have called me to a meeting," he said. "I am intrigued that your brother is not here."

God coughed awkwardly. He looked at his legal counsel, then back at The Ancient.

"This is an internal matter of clarification, but I thought it warranted your attention via a sidebar," God said. "A subordinate of mine—"

Gertrude jumped in. "Without our knowledge or authorization—"

"Yes," God said, "without our knowledge or authorization imparted a great deal of information about us to the mortals. He went crazy.

I thought it was a clear violation of the Dictum. However, I do wish to spare his life."

In the manner of many attorneys, Gertrude struggled with remaining quiet. "And to report it properly to avoid any sanction," she said.

Circades cracked a rare smile and said, "Gertrude, you remind me of someone I knew once."

"I hope it was someone you held in high regard," she replied.

"The highest." He sounded almost flirtatious.

Gertrude blushed and looked away. The Ancient resumed his serious demeanor and looked at God.

"By the letter of the law, you must sentence him to death," Circades said. "But you do not need to kill him instantly. Use these symbols and the corresponding incantations to accelerate the Atrophy. He will die unless he completes great exertions to reverse it. This will fulfill your obligation and allow you to spare him."

Circades sketched several ancient symbols and a series of phrases upon a sheet of paper.

God shrugged as he glanced at the sheet of paper. "Is this a loophole?"

"I assume you are familiar with the language of the Titans?" Circades said.

"I am," God replied, "thank you."

"Thank you for not evading your obligations," Circades said. He turned and walked toward the door.

"Seems fair," Gertrude said as she watched The Ancient depart. "Uranium II works back his debt, or he dies. Radiation has brought much suffering to the world. Now maybe some good will come from it."

Schitz and his young counterpart walked side by side in the Great Hall. They paused before the statue of the Demonic Redcoat.

"That must have been quite a day," AIDS said with reverence in his voice.

Schitz looked at the statue. "It was a long time ago," he said. "Besides, we cannot rest on our laurels."

AIDS straightened his posture as if being inspected. "I'm honored that you agreed to take me on."

"It's a little unusual for me," Schitz said. "I oversee the new cadets in weapons training, but I rarely agree to polish a full-fledged Demon."

"Why did you?"

"I would like to say you are the brightest of the up-and-coming talent. You are the only up-and-coming talent. The work you did driving that Angel mad, the one with the atomic bomb, was very impressive," Schitz said.

AIDS beamed at the compliment.

Schitz continued, "Additionally, your disease is elegant in its complexity. It does to the body what mine does to the mind. You and I think alike; we will work well together. Also, more than ever before, the last conflict showed the Devil that Hell requires my replacement. I am training you to take my place."

AIDS bit his lip to keep from shouting, then said, "It is an honor. I will do all in my power to live up to your expectations."

Schitz groaned inwardly. He admired AIDS and recognized his strengths, but the thought of being shackled with a mentee was debilitating. Schitz briefly considered handing him over to the other side, but then took a pause. AIDS was young but had survived many battles during the Great War and the Second World War. If he fell now, it would raise questions, and Satan would surely pair him with another protégé.

No, Schitz thought, *annoying as it may be, keeping him alive is a necessity. Besides, having a gutsy upstart may prove useful.*

AIDS stood rigid and motionless.

"First," Schitz said, "knock that shit off. Be yourself. I don't need you at attention; I don't need all this 'great honor' stuff. Save that for when someone builds a statue of you."

AIDS visibly relaxed. "It just seems like the real deal right now, like I have the chance to advance. Who doesn't want that?"

"Ah, so you're ambitious," Schitz said. "It can be a vice or a virtue, depending on the results. So, Mr. Ambition, where shall we do a run together? There's a civil war in Greece. There's a revolution in Indonesia. Perhaps we can head to a re-colonization in French Indochina? There's also some kind of war going on in Iran as well. So, where to?"

"Let's go to Greece," AIDS said.

"Greece it is."

THE LOCAL ARTISTS IN the community of Arab immigrants had taken to calling him Zil because he had never been observed putting up his various designs. To them, he was a ghost. Within the post-war community of young street artists, he was the most idealized, the most sought after—he was the man in the shadows. That night several of his followers strode the cobblestone streets in front of Notre Dame.

"Look," one young man said, "the paint is still wet."

They stared at the stone façade of a small café and read the script.

> *I knew you once in the city of lights,*
> *Alive at peace between the two great plights,*
> *As the strains of a record hissed and popped,*
> *Sat in a cafe, I felt as though my heart stopped,*
> *Hand in hand on those bohemian nights,*
> *Below the tower and other memorable sights.*
>
> *You gave me such peace in a world of strife,*
> *In a moment with you I could live a whole life.*

"I wonder what it means," another of the youngsters said.

They walked into the night. Circades, clad as a drifter, smiled from a bench, unobserved, and watched the paint dry as he thought of what it would be like to finally find Pulwabi.

Chapter 10
A Deadly Wager

The city of London was still a living wreck of bomb damage, but life pulsed through the city with the steadiness of the Thames—even in the dead of winter. Young men, grateful to be alive after the global war strode along the city's streets in heavy coats accompanied by vivacious women sporting furs and long gowns. The January cold did little to dent the spirits of those still enjoying the emotional warmth of a new year, a year of peace and prosperity. Cheers to life and victory could be heard from the East End to South Kensington.

Zinc walked alone through the North London crowd on his way to the Royal Opera at Covent Garden. Two young women in fashionable hats and chic dresses visible from under their coats smiled broadly at the unaccompanied Angel's host.

They passed and Zinc thought, *It is good to be young and alive.*

His enjoyment was tempered by the collaboration with the Demon Schitz. It had already paid dividends, but it added an extra layer of complexity to his life.

Zinc entered the Opera's glamorous, ornate hall.

Odd, he thought. *Shortly after the conclusion of the most devastating war in human history, they have chosen Die Zauberflöte. I guess Mozart is universal.*

Communication with Schitz had gone well through the connection of schizophrenics, still, the Demon wanted a meeting. The Angel ascended the stairs and glanced at the attendees. He entered a private box.

Schitz was already there, eyes glued to the stage.

"Is this what you do for holiday?" Zinc asked.

"Sometimes," Schitz replied. He did not turn or offer any greeting. "All work and no play makes Schitz a dull Demon."

Zinc tried to stifle a laugh but could not. "I must be very dull then," he replied.

"To quote someone with whom you have more than a passing acquaintance, 'Thou hast said,'"[35] Schitz said.

This time Zinc roared. "Hearing you quote that particular source is more than a little odd."

"What can I say," Schitz said, "I am a man of many parts." He finally looked at Zinc. He lowered his voice; the performance had started. "Oh, there is no Mrs. Zinc. She would have been more than welcome."

He gestured toward several unoccupied chairs.

Sadness tripped along Zinc's heart for a moment. "There was..."

"Say no more," Schitz said. "Your face betrays a sad tale. I can relate. And I apologize. I guess the situation is not uncommon among our kind."

Zinc hurried to the point. "So, why did you want to meet? The messages are working just fine."

"They are indeed," Schitz said. "I simply believe a multiplicity of communications will help to cloak our... uh... partnership."

Zinc looked through the crowd. He did not recognize anyone.

"What if we are seen together? Both the Familiars and the Wraiths are quite accomplished in gathering intelligence."

"Were you tailed?"

"No," Zinc said. His tone was more defensive than he liked.

"Okay, neither was I. We are both seasoned professionals. There are no Wraiths or Familiars here."

He turned to the stage and closed his eyes as a soprano soared through an aria.

Zinc tapped his foot. "Why are we here?"

"I have a conundrum," said Schitz with a smirk. "Oddly enough, our arrangement, the source of my conundrum, also allows me a sympathetic ear."

Zinc sat and waited.

"Anyway," Schitz said obviously disappointed by Zinc's refusal to engage in banter, "I have a protégé—"

"AIDS," Zinc said. "I've read about him. A real go-getter; a force to be reckoned with."

---

[35] Matthew 26:64

"Precisely," Schitz said. "I can't decide whether to give him up to your side or to protect him."

"Interesting," Zinc said. "Go on."

Schitz continued to stare at the stage. His interest in the soprano went far past anything musical.

"The thing is this," he said, "his constant presence is annoying, but I have grown rather fond of him."

Zinc exhaled sharply. "Now we are accounting for sentiment?"

Schitz shrugged. "Sentiment has nothing to do with it. I wonder if giving him up to you will knee-cap my side."

"Who do you want for him," Zinc said.

The minute the words escaped his mouth, his stomach churned.

Now Schitz turned, his eyes ablaze—the fighter who never yielded.

"It's not who," Schitz said. "I will require at least two-thirds of your fighting force."

Zinc fought the impulse to gasp. "Big ask," he said and hoped he sounded nonchalant.

"AIDS is going to be a big player. His body count of both humans and Angels will be massive. This is your chance to intervene."

Zinc listened to the music and weighed the options.

"You want two of every three Angels," he said. "I can't make that deal."

"Okay," Schitz said. "I'll deal with him as best I can. If—"

Zinc jumped into the discussion. "If you can't, then approach me again—at a substantially reduced price."

"So, you are open to negotiation," Schitz said. "Let's move on to a deal we can agree upon, shall we?"

"I'm listening."

"We should reduce the total number of Angels by fifty percent," Schitz said.

"Thirty."

"Forty."

"Twenty-five," Zinc said.

I've got him hooked, Zinc thought.

Schitz showed his teeth, white, gleaming, lethal. "You are a bastard, aren't you? Okay... I'll make it one-third. That's quite a bargain. I'll send you the mirroring number of Demons that matches your thirty percent draw down when I get back to Hell."

Zinc's skin tingled. "I hope you are not planning on short-changing me with the Demons you offer me in return."

The play reached the intermission. Schitz turned to Zinc. "You know I could have easily killed you when you were stuck in the tree. Instead, we developed this accord founded in trust. If you trust me with your life, surely you can rest assured that I will not shortchange you. I said I will tally the exact number of Demons to balance the equation, and it will be fair."

Zinc nodded, his face burning a little from the chastisement. They did not speak again until the curtain rose for the second act. Schitz spoke.

"I'll be back in Greece in a week's time. We can meet in person then. In the interim I will use the channels to give you the names you will be harvesting. I will give you the locations when we convene in Greece. You, in turn, will do the same."

Zinc considered the cold and calculating nature of it all. "That sounds like a plan," he said. "You know what?"

Schitz held up a finger. "Quiet, this is my favorite part."

Zinc peered down at the stage where a towering female character loomed over another woman in a menacing manner.

"The wrath of Hell," Schitz whispered. "*The Queen of the Night* aria."

"First, you tell me to shut up; then you want to talk?" Zinc said.
"Shh."

The soprano began.

Der Hölle Rache kocht in meinem Herzen,
Tod und Verzweiflung flammet um mich her!
Fühlt nicht durch dich Sarastro Todesschmerzen.[36]

---

[36] Hell's vengeance boils in my heart, Death and despair blaze about me! If Sarastro does not through you feel the pains of death.

Schitz turned to Zinc with a large toothy grin.

"I see why you like it," Zinc said.

Schitz nodded. The soprano continued,

Sarastro Todesschmerzen So bist du meine Tochter nimmermehr.

So bist du meine Tochter nimmermehr,[37]

She began a brutally difficult series of elaborate arpeggios.

> *Ohhhhahhhahhhahhhhhhh, Ohhhhahhhahhhahhhhhhh,*
> *Ohahhahhhahhhhaaaaa, Ohhaohahoaahaha.*

Zinc had heard the aria many times—a mother threatening to disown her daughter should she refuse to commit murder.

It's a little spot on, Zinc thought.

> *Meine Tochter nimmermehr,*
> *Ohhhhahhhahhhahhhhhhh, Ohhhhahhhahhhahhhhhhh,*
> *Ohahhahhhahhhhaaaaa, Ohhaohahoaahaha.*
> *So bist du meine Tochter nimmermehr.*
> *Verstoßen sei auf ewig, Verlassen sei auf ewig,*
> *Zertrümmert sei'n auf ewig, alle Bande der*
> *Natur. Zertrümmert sei'n auf ewig, A*
> *lle Bande der Natur.*[38]

The audience broke into applause. Schitz oozed from his seat and departed the box with a pat on Zinc's shoulder. "See you soon, Zinky,"

"I'm sure you will."

He decided to stay and watch the remainder of the opera. He settled into his seat and was engulfed in a comingled sense of loneliness and relief.

---

[37] Then you will be my daughter nevermore.

[38] My daughter nevermore. Destroyed be you forever, abandoned be you forever, destroyed forever be all bonds of nature.

THE AMBUSH OF COMMUNISTS and their solitary Angel had gone well. Schitz ambled past a road sign that indicated the direction of Athens and glanced at the bodies. Both the Demon and his partisan host, Nikos Gekas, were satisfied.

"The Communists don't have much of a chance," he said to Tileos Papadpolis, the head of a local group of partisans who had never disarmed after the war.

Zinc looked back at Schitz from within Tileos. Schitz handed him a detailed list of the Demons he would be claiming, their locations on specific dates, and other useful information.

"Where's your little protégé?" Zinc asked.

"At another ambush site," Schitz replied.

He looked at the list he'd gotten from Zinc. It listed details of Heavenly dispositions, their movements, and other vital information. Schitz gave a thumbs up, waved, and began walking towards Athens.

All the way he hummed *The Queen of the Night.*

Der Hölle Rache kocht in meinem Herzen.[39]

Schitz hurled a hand grenade into the middle of the French patrol from his lead position among

the Viet Minh fighters who crouched in the dense brush of the jungle.

Tod und Verzweiflung flammet um mich her![40]

---

[39] Hell's vengeance boils in my heart.
[40] Death and despair blaze about me!

Zinc leapt out of the Indian infantryman and cut down a Pakistani officer. Shrapnel flew and rifle fire reverberated across the Kashmir Valley.

Fühlt nicht durch dich Sarastro Todesschmerzen.[41]

Schitz ducked. The flight of Israeli Spitfires led by AIDS strafed the Lebanese position. The senior Demon charged toward the enemy's position and the seizing Angels who had been cut down by the aerial machine gun fire.

Sarastro Todesschmerzen.[42]

Zinc glanced down the row of Malayan Rebels. The jungle shook with the impact of each 5,000-pound bomb dropped by the Australian Avro Lincolns. He shouted to Uranium II over the roar of the explosions.
"Intel says they'll be coming straight for us after the bombing."
He raised his old bolt action rifle and peered down the iron sights.

So bist du meine Tochter nimmermehr.[43]

"Got you, you bastard!"
Schitz leered from the cockpit of his MiG-15 and watched the Angel's F-86 Sabre fighter catch fire and begin to break apart over the Yellow Sea.

So bist du meine Tochter nimmermehr.[44]
Zinc blew his whistle and another human wave attack surged towards enemy lines. He kept pace with the Chinese soldiers who hurled themselves at the UN force's machine guns. He glanced down

---

[41] If Sarastro does not through you feel the pains of death.
[42] Sarastro death pains.
[43] Then you will be my daughter nevermore.
[44] Then you will be my daughter nevermore.

at a crudely drawn map indicating the Demons' locations. Incoming fire struck the snow around his boots. He pressed forward.

Ohhhhahhhahhhahhhhhhh, Ohhhhahhhahhhahhhhhhh.

Schitz depressed the trigger on Chinese Type 66 mine. Ball bearings tore through the Cuban Government troops. AIDS emerged from the roadside in the Celestial and set upon the seizing Angels with grim efficiency, cutting them down, one after the other.

Ohahhahhhahhhhaaaaa, ohahahahahhahahahahaha.
Meine Tochter nimmermehr.[45]

Zinc tracked the fleeing Wraith's path with his rifle sight. He squeezed the trigger and the Wraith collapsed. The Demonic infant in its arms had barely struck the hard, dusty Algerian ground before it was skewered by Uranium II's short sword. The child's mother had died moments earlier by the same method. Over the newborn's death squeal, Uranium II grinned across the expanse towards Zinc as the withering effect of Uranium II's Atrophy healed ever so slightly.

Ohhhhahhhahhhahhhhhhh,
So bist du meine Tochter nimmermehr.[46]

Schitz fired a round from his pistol into the chest of the British soldier who was leading the Sudanese Defense Force battalion, then set upon the fallen man with a machete. Schitz's sun-roasted skin turned purple when it was bathed in crimson blood.

Verstoßen sei auf ewig, Verlassen sei auf ewig.[47]

---

[45] My daughter nevermore.
[46] Then you will be my daughter nevermore.
[47] Destroyed be you forever, abandoned be you forever.

Zinc glanced down at a map of the Suez Canal marked with both Egyptian and Demonic positions. The lumbering troop transport brought him and his British paratroopers closer to the Sinai.

Zertrümmert sei'n auf ewig, Alle Bande der Natur.[48]

Schitz walked along the line of Egyptian battle tanks and issued orders for the interdiction of British airborne units to the mortal soldiers and the annihilation of Angelic units to his subordinate Demons.

Zertrümmert sei'n auf ewig, Alle Bande der Natur.[49]

Zinc stepped out of his North Vietnamese sapper and swung his Celestial sword down on the head of the seizing Demon. He stamped her face and pried the sword free. Facial bones cracked and the Demon's final breath came in a rattle.

Ohhhhahhhahhhahhhhhhh,
Alle Bande der Natur.[50]

Schitz walked through the rugged country bush in the body of a Cuban soldier next to a column of captured CIA-backed irregulars.

"Well, I'd say this Bay of Pigs idea went particularly well," he said under his breath to the nearest prisoner.

"I'd say so," Zinc replied. He marched with his host's hands atop his head, fingers interlocked.

"We'll meet up next in Tunisia," Schitz said. "Something's about to kick off there."

Zinc nodded, stepped out of the doomed prisoner, and began walking East. Schitz abandoned his Communist soldier and headed in the opposite direction.

---

[48] Destroyed forever be all bonds of nature.
[49] Destroyed forever be all bonds of nature.
[50] All bonds of Nature.

Wenn nicht durch dich Sarastro wird erblassen!
Hört, hört, hört, Rachegötter, hört, der Mutter.[51]

SCHITZ LOOKED AT HIS bowl and groaned. "I've always hated North African cuisine."

AIDS shoveled the steaming concoction into his mouth like a locomotive hungry for coal. "I'll eat yours if you don't want it."

Schitz grimaced as his host chewed. "My human likes it," he said, "and as I've told you before, keeping your host fit can mean the difference between not seizing and seizing. If this man is shot in the liver, I'd prefer him not to be starving."

AIDS did everything but lick the bowl. "What was it anyway?"

"Goat, I think," Schitz said. "Disgusting little animals."

AIDS giggled. "Perhaps I just ate one of our Lord's pets." When Schitz did not react, he scowled. "Oh, come on, that was funny."

"Not if it's true," Schitz said. "He'd skin us alive."

"Good point." AIDS looked at Schitz's half-full bowl with something akin to lust. "Why are we here? The French have taken Bizerte; most of the action has died down."

Schitz felt the familiar anxiety he experienced whenever AIDS sniffed around too closely to his coordination with Zinc, an ever-present headache. Schitz took in the picturesque North African scene. The adhan crackled through a loudspeaker and summoned all Muslims to prayer. The atonal shriek blared from every corner of the city.

"When in Rome," AIDS said.

They rose to their feet, shouldered their rifles, and headed toward one of the city's innumerable mosques. Schitz noticed a bedraggled beggar in a doorway. He approached her to drop a coin in her basket and heard the unending stream of schizophrenic thoughts passing through her mind. He had no trouble picking out Zinc's message.

---

[51] If not through you Sarastro will turn pale! Hear, gods of revenge, hear the mother's oath!

"Reports from our intelligence indicate your presence in this region as well as all of the targets you were provided. I have found success in this campaign. Do we still need to meet?"

Schitz focused on the woman, her ragged clothes, gapping mouth, and wild eyes. If not for his affliction she might be a contented grandmother who meddled in her family's affairs and gossiped with her neighbors.

He interjected his reply into the stream of her babbling consciousness. "No, not alone. Aim for a face-to-face in Berlin next month."

His coded message concealed within a clever taunt. When he returned to AIDS's side, the younger demon scrutinized him.

"Something you want to ask me?" Schitz inquired. He made sure to sound irritated.

"I'd just like to learn the language," AIDS said.

"There is no language," Schitz said. "The afflicted hear random words coursing through their mind. The mutation cannot be cured, and I get credit toward avoiding the Atrophy. You should know; you modeled your malady after mine."

Schitz could see the skepticism in his colleague's face.

"Seems like there's more to it," AIDS said.

They rounded a corner and directly into a Tunisian roadblock devastated by French artillery. The bodies of the Tunisian soldiers lay in the sun, twisted and crumpled in the heat. They were burned beyond human recognition.

Schitz clicked his teeth. "God is good," he said.

The Central Intelligence Agency officer, Craig Walters, stared at the jungle of the Katanga Region of the Southern Congo. Schitz had little choice but to stare with him. From behind the wheel of the deuce-and-a-half truck, he heard the faint notes of reggae. The lyrics referenced Armageddon.

Schitz thought about the "phantom" haunting Africa. The villagers referred to the specter as "The Destroyer." He'd not encountered her in a long time but was certain she was alive. Neither had he worked up the courage to ask Zinc about her.

A gaggle of rebels approached him. They toted their Kalashnikov rifles as if they were carrying lunchboxes to school.

"You're long away from home there, white boy," one said.

Walters smirked. "We're not in the Bronx; all I see are niggers with guns."

The lead rebel laughed and kicked dust on one of Walter's combat boots. His manner was jovial. He looked at his comrades and said, "Don't let his appearance fool you. Dis' one's harder than concrete."

Schitz extended his arm and mimicking the rebel's accent. "Help me up there, boy."

The rebel sported a wide grin but as he pulled Walters up, he hissed, "You want to go home and tell your mama you got your white ass kicked by a boy?"

Schitz reached into the pocket of his combat vest and retrieved a pack of cigarettes. He tossed the Lucky Strikes towards the aggregation and watched the ensuing scramble.

Kwami, the Katangan brigade commander, smiled. "We need more than your cigarettes, Mister Craig... we need guns."

"Come on," Schitz said. He smacked the side of the truck and looked AIDS in the eyes. "Take me to your uranium mines and you'll have your guns soon enough."

He walked around to the passenger side of the truck. A ragged, foul-smelling elderly woman suddenly appeared and grabbed Schitz by the forearm.

"Whoa now. There are tricks and tracks before you, three apiece and four beside but therein lay the leopard's eye, or Leopold they said would die."

The hag witch doctor drained the lightheartedness from the rebel soldiers. They looked skittish; they looked afraid. Schitz smiled to himself. For centuries, no one had paid any attention to the nonsensical ramblings of the mentally condemned. Even though he was the purveyor of their condition, Schitz had not given their babbling much thought either. But now, given his regular communications with Zinc, the "Schitzo Network" provided a massive tapestry for secret messages. And no one, friend or foe, was the wiser.

Schitz understood the message almost immediately. "Five Angels are moving with Republican forces to ambush the convoy along the route to the mines. Your position has been compromised."

Schitz was not surprised. Angels tracked Demonic movements very effectively. Walters laughed.

"Granny," he said, "it's not even nine o'clock in the morning. Save your drinking 'til the evening and give yourself a rest." He stepped up on the stair on the passenger side. At the last moment, he relieved a rebel of his Kalashnikov. He racked the slide and climbed in.

From behind the wheel, AIDS glanced at his superior. "Trouble follows us everywhere we go, don't it, boss man?"

COLONEL OKWUOHA WAS A built man in his mid-thirties. His men feared him considerably more than they respected him, and they respected him as most people respected God. There were stories of his removing the heart of a Katangese rebel and feasting on it before the victim's very eyes. Most of the tales were true down to the goriest detail.

For Okwuoha, the world was simple; the wealth of the mines, copper, diamonds, uranium was the wealth of the people of the Congo long abused by the Belgians. When the wealth was finally restored to the people, the outlander scum sought to keep it for themselves. The colonel had little inclination toward mercy. He regularly ordered limbs to be severed, heads to be removed, and hearts to be sautéed for his dining pleasure.

The morning sun was as merciless as the colonel, and even to men who knew nothing other than the sub-Saharan heat, the day bordered on unbearable. Sweat glued Okwuoha's olive drab fatigues to his muscular chest but all thoughts of the heat were banished when his men brought news of a captured rebel.

The colonel found the man tied to a tree at the edge of the

encampment. He had been beaten badly and bore the look of a cornered animal. The prisoner spoke in broken gibberish, but Zinc understood the code of schizophrenic speech well. While his men watched the colonel interrogate a man driven mad with fear, Zinc used the opportunity to warn Schitz of an impending ambush.

In return, Schitz acknowledged the message and pledged two Demons vulnerable at the mines after they had repelled the attack.

It will not be a glorious day for either side, he thought, *but isn't that the point?*

Zinc looked at the mass of Republican troops and felt a pinprick of regret. He would lead the Angels and mortals around him into an orchestrated slaughter. Then, once more as he had for the past fifteen years, he steeled himself against his better inclinations.

This is how I survive, and this is how I save the world. A draw means we all see tomorrow.

Upon concluding the dialogue with the captive, Zinc un-holstered his pistol, a silver semi-automatic. The barrel sparkled in the African sun. Zinc shot the man in the face to the cheering of his subordinates.

He ordered his men to move out.

Let them cheer, he thought. *They won't be quite so excited when the same thing happens to them.*

WHEN AIDS ASKED HIS question, it hit Schitz harder than any of the potholes in the miserable road.

"So, when are you going to teach me that language?"

The aging truck lurched violently to the right, then back. Schitz banged his head on the door frame. He hoped his moaning would distract his young colleague.

It did not.

"Schitz, the language?"

"What are you talking about?" Schitz replied. He peeked over his shoulder. The Kalashnikov lay in the far floorboard, just out of reach.

"Seems to me you are conversing with the crazies, passing information or something. You never used to notice those people. Now you go out of your way to talk to them."

Schitz waved his hand in dismissal. "Just getting soft in my dotage," he said. "Starting to feel sorry for the folks who carry my affliction. They're sort of my children."

AIDS cursed and fussed with the clutch. "Well, how do you know when there's going to be action?"

He forced the truck into a lower gear. The transmission protested with a squeal like a stuck pig.

"Better be careful with that clutch," Schitz said. "I do not intend to walk, and you probably don't want to carry me."

AIDS laughed without enthusiasm. "You didn't answer my question," he said.

Schitz let out an exaggerated huff. "You and I have not fought together very often," he said. "I've always warned my pupils about the possibilities of an ambush."

"I just can't figure out how you are always right," AIDS said.

They approached a rebel checkpoint, which gave Schitz all the excuse he needed to cut off the conversation and stretch for his rifle.

"We've got trouble," Schitz said.

AIDS shot him a quick glance. "What? Why?"

"Those men's uniforms do not fit, and I see two bodies in the brush."

He fired three quick bursts through the windshield. Through the shattering glass, they saw the two guards fall.

"Never underestimate the power of instinct," Schitz said.

THE AMBUSH COULD HAVE been played out on the training ground of any military academy of any respectable nation. It came directly from the textbook strategies of Heaven and Hell. Okwuoha commanded an inferior number of troops. He'd suffered significant attrition during his incursion into rebel-held territories. The colonel required little convincing from Zinc to continue his ruthless thrust into the countryside. Owing to a mismatch in force size, Okwuoha abandoned his preferred "steamroller" strategy and resorted to stealth and cunning.

Zinc's trap at the checkpoint was planned meticulously. Two squads of six were arrayed along either side of the road. The men were positioned to create the perfect, crisscrossing angle of fire— no threat of firing into compatriots on the other side of the road. In addition, Zinc placed a three-man team ahead of the front truck to cover the roadblock. If the vehicles tried to bust through, they would drive into another death zone. Two of his men killed the rebels manning the roadblock and donned their uniforms.

He explained to his men. "The trucks will be at full stop. On my signal, open fire."

Zinc took his place in the high grass along the road, a freshly acquired Kalashnikov in his hands. He admired his own strategy. Now he had to trust Schitz.

THE POP AND SNAP of assault rifle rounds carried a distinctly different sound from the rifle fire of the last war. Still, Schitz knew every report heralded the potential for death. He was impressed with the array of the ambuscade and grateful that his Katangan rebels were so disciplined. At the first shot, they disembarked to engage the concealed foes.

One of the faux guards died with Schitz's first shot. The Demon fired again and dispatched the second. Incoming rounds impacted the truck above Schitz's head. He moved around the front of the truck to AIDS's position. The troops from the back of their truck were already pushing forward under heavy fire.

Schitz tapped AIDS on the shoulder.

"Cover me!"

He rushed past and toward the Angel's position, where he spied the telltale aura behind the muzzle flashes. Schitz fired in the direction of the enemy, short bursts of fire. He closed the distance, a lethal gazelle moving towards his victim with grace and ill intent.

Schitz moved farther behind the Republican troops. Fire from comrades zipped over his left shoulder. The nearest Angel stepped out of his host, presumably to avoid being cut down. Schitz fired three rounds into the chest of the enemy soldier and continued. He ignored the Angel in the Celestial. Schitz utilized his mortal host to obstruct the Angel's view of AIDS's approach.

Within the Celestial, AIDS stepped out from behind Schitz and mauled the surprised Angel. Schitz felt the buzz of violent bees zipping past his face. He dropped low and fired into the next Angel, propelling him into a seizure. AIDS rushed past Schitz towards the beleaguered Angel.

"Watch out," Schitz shouted.

The last standing Angel abandoned his mortal host to protect his comrade. Schitz calmly fired and killed the vacant rifleman. He whipped around and fired a single round into Kwami's forehead. The rebel leader's arms flailed into the air, and he collapsed rag doll.

Schitz yelled. "Switch."

Schitz stepped into the Celestial and fired a throwing knife into the throat of the seizing Angel. Blood spurted from the Angel's mouth. AIDS jumped into Craig Walters.

"Let's go," Schitz said.

He drew his short sword from its scabbard with his right hand and held a throwing knife in his left. An inexperienced Angel rushed at Schitz and caught a knife in the thigh for his trouble. The Angel fell to the ground. Schitz crossed over to him and stepped on his wrist. The Angel's eyes darted left and right.

"Do you know who I am?" Schitz asked.

The Angel nodded.

"Good."

He drove his blade into the throat of the foe, retrieved his throwing knife, and turned back towards AIDS. The newly possessed American had mowed down the remainder of the column. The duo broke into a side-by-side run towards the back of the third truck. It was on fire having been struck by a rocket-propelled grenade at the beginning of the engagement. Schitz and AIDS turned the corner of the burning truck and arrived at the right flank of the engagement.

The Katanagan Rebels were still engaging the forward cluster of three. Schitz saw a sole Angel run away. He jumped through the troops, one body to the next, and then into the Celestial.

A junior Demon pointed in frustration. "One got away!"

Schitz shrugged. "How many did you drop?"

"Two."

AIDS fired three well-placed shots and silence descended over the battlefield. Two of the government soldiers had surrendered and stood anxiously with their hands above their heads. Schitz stepped into the body of Lieutenant Asamoah, Kwami's second in command. He surveyed the surviving rebels.

Their morale is broken, he thought.

The lieutenant ejected the magazine of his semi-automatic pistol. He examined it, then removed the remaining bullets. The squad assembled around the two prisoners but never took their eyes off the lieutenant.

"Kneel," he said.

The men obeyed.

Schitz loaded a single round back, then slid the magazine into the pistol. He racked the slide and placed the weapon on the ground between the two men. He put his fingers on the barrel and spun the pistol.

The gun settled with the barrel facing the prisoner to his right. The man looked up at Asamoah and then back to the weapon. Schitz lifted the pistol from the dirt road and handed it to the man. In the most theatrical voice he could manage, he said, "Here is your salvation. Shoot your fellow here, and we will leave you free to go home with your tail between your legs."

The rebels began shouting all at once. "Wait, wait, wait, wait, wait!" They began placing bets.

"Ten says he will do it."

"I'll take that."

"I have fifteen on a headshot."

"No, no... he will shoot him in the gut and make him suffer."

"Fifty says he does the honorable thing and shoots himself."

Money, watches, and rings piled up on the ground. A few of the rebels sprinted over and looted the pockets and wrists of dead soldiers.

Then as quickly as the storm of wagering had erupted, it ceased.

"Okay, okay. You can go on now!"

The man picked up the pistol. His hands shook as if with a palsy.

He looked at Schitz. "What is wrong with you? We are country-men, all of us. This man, he is from my village; his daughters play with my own. Our wives gossip together. How can you ask this of me?"

One of the rebels reached for the pot. "See, I said, he wouldn't do it."

Shouts of protest erupted. When order returned, Asamoah spoke.

"This is the best deal you're going to get. If you turn it down, things will get much worse for you."

Without another word, the man extended the gun and put a bullet in his friend's left eye. The rebels exploded in a symphony of cursing, cheers, and excitement. Grinning men wrested money and jewelry from begrudging losers.

Schitz marveled at how quickly the spectacle had reversed the dread of battle and the fear of losing a close friend. He extended his hand and retrieved the pistol from the distraught prisoner. He reloaded the gun.

"Stand up," he said,

The man complied. A hush fell over the rebels. Schitz's voice boomed.

"Well done, well done... you are fucking cold-blooded. I told you to shoot your fellow. Now, if I were him, I would have hoped you might wound me in the arm or leg, but you obliterated his skull. Damn cold-blooded!"

The prisoner began to cry.

Schitz could not contain his laughter. "I am a literal man," he said. "I did not say kill him. I simply said shoot him. But you kept your side of the bargain, so let me keep mine. As you recall, I promised you would be free to return home," he bared his teeth, "with your tail between your legs."

Recognition dawned on the prisoner's face. "No... please!"

Schitz extended his arm and fired into the man's groin. Blood wisped through the air. The soldier collapsed to the ground. His hands clutched the mangled slop of his manhood.

"Now," Schitz said, "now you have a tail, and it's between your legs. You're free to go home."

The rebels filed back into the two viable trucks and left both friend and foe on the field.

"Savage," AIDS said.

"Africa," Schitz said without a lot of interest. He'd put the incident behind him and was reliving the success of his plan.

They reached the uranium mine. Schitz within Asamoah explained to the human guards about the government's ambush. Schitz pulled two junior Demons aside. He made sure AIDS was within earshot.

Schitz's Notebook

Katangese Rebel

I enjoyed my time in the Congo. The rebel troops make for interesting company. They tend to be bloodthirsty and undisciplined, however, they are ferocious fighters.

"Be alert for the Angel that slipped away."

Schitz and his detachment began a tour of the uranium mine, the purpose of the CIA officer's visit to the Congo. Schitz knew the young Demons would be dead when he came out of the mine. He had not even bothered to learn their names. The newest members of the most recent academy class had barely blooded themselves, and now they would be offered as a sacrifice on the altar of stability. Schitz glanced at them one last time and then turned away.

I knew what I was getting into when I began down this road, he thought.

WHEN SOMEONE FOUND THE bodies of the guards in the mine and the mangled bodies of the two young Demons in the Celestial, AIDS was irate.

"Damn it. How did this happen?"

"I don't know," Schitz said.

He put his hands under the arms of one of the dead.

"Open a portal," he said, "then help me. We need to take them home."

AIDS began the ritual. Schitz looked at the dead youth's face.

Take them home—that's the least I can do.

THE EARLY SPRING DAY failed to bring much warmth to the constricted city. The Ancient shivered, underdressed, and made his way to one of the local favorites, ASK Vorwärts Berlin. The stadium was crowded. By the time they put the ball in play, he was considerably warmer.

The Ancient knew Berlin from its early years as a small town on the crossroads between the East and West when she was barely a hamlet, to the present. He took in the slumbering ruin, a city still reeling from the savagery heaped on her during the last conflict. Yet like all living creatures, the city yearned for life even in its most profound distress. Despite the Wall and its guards, despite the cold and the food shortages, despite it all, ASK Vorwärts Berlin and SC Dynamo Berlin faced off in a local derby, its outcome heightened by the lateness of the season and the fact that both teams were contenders for the title.

He watched the mortals engage in their heated contest and marveled about how much everyone cared about a ball spiraling into a net. The Ancient was slightly amused by his own behavior. He could watch a football match in any city of his choosing: London, Liverpool, Rome, Milan, Madrid, or even a few miles west in the other Germany, the one whose players had lifted the World Cup seven years earlier. He chose to come here, to this sad corner of this sad city, where even on a sunny day in March the wind still bit at one's face; where even at a football match the crowd was mostly hungry; where you would be shot if you tried to travel to another part of town. The Ancient came to the sad, familiar city because it mirrored his own melancholy. Like the city, he carried old scars and long-reaching, painful memories.

The Ancient's reflection shattered. The crowd erupted when an ASK forward buried the ball in the opposition's net. The Ancient smiled despite his lack of investment in the outcome. He did not dislike football; he simply cared less about it than the humans—or any Angel or Demon he knew.

The Ancient marveled at how excited mortals became over a non-lethal contest. These were the descendants of the species that had watched the grotesque pageantry of the Roman Colosseum. The Ancient thought back to those ruthless times when crowds cheered for a decapitation instead of a goal. He remembered larger crowds than this; men and women who rose in unison when a crowd favorite fell under the onslaught of a ferocious lion only to arise, bathed in blood, to conquer the beast. The storm of applause would have drowned out the puny plaudits offered for a historically insignificant goal.

Ripped from his nostalgia, The Ancient turned his attention to some loud strangers alongside him. The men appeared to be arguing about the odds that the game would end in a draw.

"Five to one? Show me your money first. We all know you're broke."

The Ancient laughed and remembered another wager; in another place, at another time. The stadium faded and his memory came into focus.

The sloping hills along the Danube were idyllic beyond measure. The Ancient strode along the banks, bathed in the warmth of the summer sun. His younger brother walked beside him, ever exuberant to be out from under the watchful eye of Father. The grass shimmered in the heat and the birds and insects joined in a rousing vocal tribute to ideal weather.

His brother's voice rang with excitement. "Look! Man!"

The Ancient peered across to the far bank of the river and saw a trio of humans, squatting beside the carcass of a deer. The hairs on the nape of his neck stood. He knew that mankind was the vessel through which the Spirit Walkers did battle. He also knew such forces were incredibly dangerous to his kind.

His brother moved close and whispered. "Let's play a game," he said. "I bet you I can get one of them to kill the other two. If I can, you have to let me explore on my own the next time we leave home."

The Ancient rolled his eyes and sighed. "If you lose?"

He scowled for a moment, unsure. Then said, "I know. If I can't do it, I'll show you how I kill without touching."

"You're on."

The Ancient was certain his brother was incapable of the feat. The river was wide, and the men were fully grown. He had never possessed an interest in the violent arts. He considered himself a shepherd.

"Wait," his brother said. "How do I know you'll keep your end of the bargain; you never lie to Father."

The Ancient squared his shoulders and tried to lower his voice. "You already know that I have taken the oath of maturity. Therefore, I must adhere to honesty when wagering or entering accords. If I break my word, I break my bond to my ancestors and all the gifts they have assigned to me."

"All right then," his brother said, and he bounded for the riverbank.

To The Ancient's amazement, one of the men dressing the deer stood, raised his spear, and plunged it into the midsection of one of his compatriots. The victim howled in agony. He clutched at his stomach. His eyes opened, wide and perplexed. Before the third human could respond, the aggressor lifted a large stone from the river's edge and began to pummel him without mercy. The beleaguered man tried to fend off the ferocious blows, but soon he lay dead in the grass, a dark crimson puddle pooling at the side of his head.

The sole survivor looked about in confusion, then broke down weeping beside the dead deer.

The Ancient felt naked with shock. He watched it all with his mouth ajar.

"See, I told you I could do it," his brother said. "Do you want to know how I do it? I'll tell you even though you lost."

The Ancient shook his head. "Let's just go home."

"What's the matter? They're only humans."

The Ancient fought back tears. He felt an odd kinship with the crying man on the opposite side of the Danube.

His voice crept out of his mouth like an arthritic climbing the stairs. "I would never have agreed if I had thought there was a remote possibility you would succeed," he said.

They walked the rest of the way home in silence.

Later in the afternoon, The Ancient snuck out. He was permitted to be on his own in the world, but he did not want anyone to know his destination. He returned to the scene by the riverbank.

To The Ancient's amazement, the man was still present by the deer and his dead comrades. He rocked back and forth with his head in his hands. His sobs echoed from the surface of the river.

The man stood up, startled by The Ancient's arrival.

The Ancient raised his hand, palm out. "I mean you no harm or malice," he said. He tried to sound calm. His heart raced; he'd never spoken to a human.

"There's no harm you could do to me," the man said through tears. "I have killed my only two brothers and I do not know why."

'I'm very sorrowful for your grief," The Ancient said.

"I hope you never know pain like this," the man said. "I am wounded both by this terrible deed and by my own cowardice. I intend to absolve myself. I am going to jump into the river and die."

The Ancient touched the man's shoulder. "You will not," he said. "Nor will you do anything else to cause your demise." He waited a few seconds, surprised by his reaction. "We will take this mighty stag to your people. Surely you will feel better if you provide for your kin."

The man shook his head. "How can I face them after what I've done?"

"You will tell them that your brothers were killed by the antlers and hooves of this beast. The guilt of your lie will be punishment enough and you will live with it for the rest of your long life."

They hoisted the deer and carried it to the man's encampment.

The feast of the stag was a subdued affair. Everyone was grateful for the meat, but it had arrived at a terrible price. They invited The Ancient to eat. During dinner, The Ancient recognized his deep bond with the murderer.

I am at fault for what he did, The Ancient thought. *Why did I agree to the wager? Why was I so cavalier about someone else's life?*

He looked across the fire pit. On the other side, he saw a serene face of unworldly beauty; stoic deep eyes, an oval face, flowing black hair. Her swanlike neck curved with flawless grace into a fur draped over her shoulders. Her hands were small, her mouth delicate.

Their eyes met and The Ancient shivered. He stood and walked around the stone circle to her side.

"My name is Circades," he said.

"Pulwabi," the young woman replied.

It seemed to The Ancient that they were shouting. Everyone could hear their conversation.

"I would like very much to speak with you privately," he said.

He was gasping for breath like a man who'd run away from a wolf.

"Our customs dictate that you should present such a request to my father," the young woman said. "But my father did not return from the hunt, so you must present your query to my uncle."

The Ancient followed the young woman's gaze to her right and met the eye of the man who had killed his brothers. The Ancient did not need to ask. The man lowered his head and nodded in shame.

The light of the fire gave way to the shimmer of the night sky. They walked in a heavy, awkward silence until Pulwabi spoke.

"Why did you want to take me away from the others, if you refuse to talk?"

The Ancient could have swallowed an ostrich egg easier than the lump in his throat. Finally, he said, "You are the most beautiful thing I have ever seen in all my life."

Pulwabi's laughs pierced the night, high-pitched and feminine. Still, it struck terror into The Ancient's heart.

"Have I offended you?" he asked.

"No one says things like that," she said. "Is such vapid flattery common among your people?"

"Not really," The Ancient said. A blush seared his cheeks. He was grateful for the darkness. "I've never said something like that, but it's true, so I said it."

Pulwabi's smile glistened in the moonlight. "You are very different," she said, "Even though you are a stranger, I am oddly fond of you, at ease with you. Tell me about where you come from."

"There's not much to tell," The Ancient said. "I live with my parents and my younger brother. We practice the old ways, the ways of our ancestors when this world was ours and ours alone; before the Spirit Walkers and before you."

Pulwabi cocked her head. "I don't know much about all that," she said. She laughed again, the sound of silver coins falling against a stone. "I meant more like what do you do for fun?"

Heat tinged The Ancient's face again. "I like to hike," he said. "I've walked along the Danube, this river here by your camp, for leagues and leagues and leagues."

Pulwabi grinned. "I like to walk, too. My people are always moving, following the animals."

And so, they talked and walked beneath the moon and the stars. At one point, Pulwabi lost her footing in the dark. The Ancient held out his hand to steady her; her fingers felt warm and delicate. They held hands from that point on. As the daylight began to creep over the trees, the couple reached the outskirts of the encampment.

"Well, back we are," Pulwabi said. She rested her head against his chest.

"What do you want to do now?" he asked.

She craned her head upwards towards him, and The Ancient felt the flutter of startled birds in his chest. The kiss was tentative at first. It grew in intensity. She opened her mouth, and he accepted the invitation. He drew her close and ran his hands over her strong body. They explored one another until the camp began to stir.

"It would not be proper for us to be found here like this," Pulwabi said.

Circades broke the embrace, reluctant and aroused. He felt an overwhelming sense of grief at the thought of leaving this woman with whom he had spent the night walking hand in hand.

"I will come back later," he said. Frantic fantasies of abandonment chewed at his stomach. "You won't break camp today, will you?"

"Don't ask me to turn away from you," Pulwabi said. Her tear-filled eyes slashed at his heart. "Not even for a day. I want to go where you go and rest when you rest. I don't care that you are of a different kind than me; I want your people to be my own. Your Gods can be my Gods."

The Ancient could not believe her veritable flood of emotion. Unable to verbalize his feelings, Circades grabbed her delicate hand in his and broke into a run along the riverbank. With each step, a sense of gaiety settled on the fleeing couple. By the time they had left the encampment far behind, the duo burst into joyous laughter. The Ancient heaved to a halt and pulled Pulwabi close. He pressed his lips against hers, a love-starved man searching for the nutrition for his lips. The two collapsed on the soft grass along the river's edge. He gazed upon her grinning face, as her chest rose and fell rapidly beneath her furs. The Ancient moved his hands along her body, rewarded by the sensation of her warm, soft flesh as he slipped his fingers underneath her clothing.

"Circades," she groaned, pulling him closer. The Ancient was lost in the passion of discovery.

Later, the day waned as the lovers strolled along the Danube's winding banks. The Ancient felt excited and optimistic about his future. "So, we cannot go to your home?" Pulwabi inquired.

"My father would never have it," he replied, chuckling, "he might even kill you."

"I feel sorry to make you leave your family," she said.

The Ancient stopped walking and turned to face her, releasing her hand so that he could hold her by her shoulders. "Do not regret any part of our life together; I made my own choice because I love you."

"But you just met me," she replied with hesitation.

"Yes," he said. He searched her face, hoping to understand her sudden change in temperament, "but I've seen humans before and women of my own kind, I have never felt anything like what I felt when I saw you."

Pulwabi smiled and embraced him, her thin, strong arms wrapping around his frame. "I loved you when I saw you," she said softly. The Ancient closed his eyes, basking in the warmth of the emotional blanket his lover provided.

When he opened his eyes, The Ancient squinted as he adjusted to the bright morning sun. As quickly as he had been taken back to that hallowed time, he returned to the ASK match. The gamblers behind him had settled their wagers and were enjoying the heightened experience visited on spectators who have skin in the game. Dynamo scored a goal; the betting increased several clicks.

The brief threat posed by SC Dynamo Berlin was short-lived. The contests ended 4-1. The Ancient watched the loser pry open his wallet to pay his exuberant comrades. Circades remembered the bet with his brother.

Never wager with terms you cannot meet, he thought.

Circades had kept his end of the accord by never returning home. He followed the jubilant ASK supporters out of the stadium and laughed at the boisterous men debating about how the team would fair against the likes of Bayern Munich. The consensus was that East German teams, like everything East German, could not compete with their rivals across the Wall.

Soon, he was walking nearly alone and lost in thought. He turned a corner and collided with a woman. He almost lost his balance. She would have careened into the street had he not grabbed her arm.

'I beg your pardon!" he said. "Please forgive my clumsiness."

He had not released her arm. She had shoulder-length blonde hair, grayish-blue eyes, and a cluster of freckles. He did not notice any of those features. What he saw was a beauty more profound than any soul he'd encountered since...

"Pulwabi!"

He'd imagined the scene every day of every year for countless lifetimes. He had fantasized about and rehearsed what he would say; how he would kiss her, the passionate moments they would share.

But, in that moment, he could do nothing but weep. He clutched the woman to his chest and convulsed—great, heaving sobs broken only by the need to breathe. He felt her tears on his neck.

When he composed himself enough to push back a little, she smiled and said, "Greta."

"Sorry?" he said.

"My name," she said with a faint smile, "my name is Greta Lindenmier, but yes, Pulwabi, and a thousand other names, my Circades." The Ancient tilted her head back and eased into a deep, long, soft kiss that had been building for millennia.

THE NIGHT WAS EVERYTHING she could have hoped for from Heaven itself. Circades took her to a humble flat full of working-class charm where he cooked her a delicious meal and served her an even more enticing wine. They laughed and told tales of hundreds of lifetimes, the highlights of a Titan and the tales of a Strain carrier.

There were events they both remembered. In some instances, they had been in the same city mere blocks from each other. Other times, they were half a world away. When the wine ran dry, and the food was gone, and the tales had been told, they made love into the wee hours of the morning. Exhausted, Circades slept with a satisfied grin across his face. Greta closed her eyes. For one peaceful moment she took in all the available happiness the world had to offer.

When she opened her eyes, her contentment vanished.

What happiness can I possibly have in this life? she thought.

She remembered her immediate past life—the romantic encounter with the Demon Schitz, the gunfight on the street, the stray bullet that sent her on a dreadful trip through the River of Reincarnation. She had died in fear, so it was required for her to pass through the River Styx, a torturous sensation of perpetual drowning.

Had she died in a state of peace, she would have passed through the disembodying River of Eunoe. But neither experience pleased her anymore; she had endured both more times than she could recall. She was exhausted from living through lifetimes, suffering illness, rape, and loss. She was tired of hoping she would bump into Circades, her one true and only love. When she finally did, it was in the middle of a most perilous circumstance.

Earlier in the week, she had killed an American spy. Her actions put her in the crosshairs of both Washington and Moscow. Greta slid from the bed and assembled her clothes. Then she remembered something the Demon in Paris said.

When the war is over, we will no longer need to afflict humanity with our diseases. There will just be peace, and we can be together if we make that happen.

"That's it," she whispered. "We could be together forever if there was no more reincarnation."

She slid her stockinged feet along the floor, determined not to wake her lover. Circades stirred, then resumed his slumber. She leaned over him and whispered into his ear.

"I love you more than you could ever know."

He mumbled a reply. "I know."

Greta went into the bathroom and searched through the gentleman's shaving kit on the vanity. The straight razor caught the rays of the rising sun and momentarily blinded her.

Perhaps I can try to live this life with him, she thought. She stole a glimpse of Circades, then closed the door.

She stood by the sink and remembered the forces that continued to hunt her. She could feel the bullet piercing her flesh, the life ebbing from her human body, the strangling sensation of the Styx.

"Goodbye, my beloved," she said.

Starting just below the palm, she dragged the razor along her arm, severing the flesh and opening the radial artery and unleashing a cascade of crimson along the white tile floor. Her wounded hand shook as she transferred the razor and repeated the act on the other side.

The pain disappeared quicker than she'd imagined and was replaced by a creeping cold she knew all too well. She dipped her finger in the bloody basin and scrawled a message on the mirror.

Her legs wobbled and a cloud passed over the light from outside. With what little strength she had left, she traced a heart at the end of her message.

"That's for Greta," she said. "It's perfect."

And she crumpled to the floor.

The flowing water soothed her as she floated just beneath the surface.

It's the Eunoe.

Usually, the river's ponderous pace was mind-numbing, even irritating to those with The Strain. They wanted to get to their next living iteration as quickly as possible. For the first time though, the first time ever, Pulwabi was at peace. Though she had died in a violent, fearful manner, her demise lay within the protective sphere of her true love, the only proof she needed to justify her actions.

In her heart of hearts, she knew Circades would bring about the end of the war between Heaven and Hell. In doing so, he would terminate the cycle of death and rebirth for humans. Then he and she could live forever in the Eden of the highest plain of human elevation, free from the Demons and Angels, free from God and the Devil. He could destroy them and their unending wager forever.

Pulwabi closed her eyes and let the peace she had found in her night with Circades carry her into her next life.

THE ANGELS BEGAN TO tell a story in the days that followed, the tale of a soul so peaceful that though it struck many rocks, no new souls emerged from it. Some heard the account with great approbation, others with dread. What soul was so content that it never partook in the creation of others? When the victory of Heaven was complete, yes, but the same held true if Hell won the eternal battle.

Many an Angel pondered the story and wondered whether it was the harbinger of impending victory or defeat. Then, as most others do, they discarded their concerns of the eternal question and returned to worrying only about their own survival.

EERIE SILENCE MET THE Ancient when he rose from his bed—the kind of quiet indicating complete aloneness. His worst fears were realized when he found Greta in a bloody heap on the bathroom floor.

He did not call for help. Nothing could save his beloved. He collapsed on the tile and unleashed a howl not heard since Heaven's mourning of the Crucifixion.

He considered the incantations he could use to end his own life. The thought offered a sense of solace, but then he saw the message on the mirror.

"Find me in Ragnarok, where we can be together forever xoxo."

The Ancient leaned on the sink. The Angels and Demons spoke of the Apocalypse in a different way from the mortals. The citizens of the Celestial talked about "Ragnarok," the time when human intellect would reach the highest level of elevation and negate the war between Heaven and Hell. A time when humans would be fully aware of the presence of Angels and Demons; a time when the big secret would be known and thereby discontinued.

The world would change because the mortals' role in providing Celestial energy through the Styx and the Eunoe would dissipate. The Ancient knew how fearful the forces of Heaven and Hell were about the final elevation of human consciousness. Humans had come close. They'd evolved from living in caves and grunting to electronic communication and space exploration.

The Ancient stared at the blood-covered mirror, then wiped out the message. He saw his mottled reflection in the smear.

"I will bring them to the final precipice," he said.

The Ancient dressed in his traveling attire: an old suit, a trench coat, and a Fedora. He loaded twin .45 ACP semi-automatics and slipped them into holsters under his jacket.

At the last moment, he looked inside Greta's purse. He raised an eyebrow when he found a silenced Markov pistol. He checked the magazine, verified a full load, clicked it back into place, and stowed it in his waistband at the small of his back.

Without a second look, he left the room.

The Ancient Lasartu, Nebusemekh, Fuyūrei, Expirant, Circades, Le Fantôme, The ol' Haint, La Larva Sombra, **Zil**

Chapter 11

The Destroyer

U ranium II moved from scientist to scientist. Each one wore the same outfit: a white lab coat and sunken eyes. He felt their exhaustion born from working through calculations and relentless tests. He enjoyed imparting his knowledge from one host to the next, revealing the mysteries of radioactivity, fission, fusion, and all manner of wonders.

They will create a weapon akin to the hand of God, Uranium II thought.

He glanced about the lab. It bristled with equipment for measuring, testing, and analyzing all matter of materials and compounds.

We will end all wars with this.

He possessed Oppenheimer, a stork of a man.

When we end the war, nothing will feed the Styx. Then we can pick the Demons off one by one.

The Angel melded his knowledge with the scientist's considerable brain power. The white-coated physicist began scribbling on a pad with the fire of discovery in his eyes.

The mushroom cloud billowed over New Mexico. A flash of light sparked with the intensity of a thousand suns. From behind the welder's mask within the body of the gaunt man, Uranium II trembled at the power he had unleashed.

The mortal whispered, "I am become death."

He was pleased.

URANIUM II GROANED. HE rolled over in his bed. He had not slept well. Worse, now he needed sleep.

The dreams were always the same, memories of the wretched

Manhattan Project. He struggled to his feet and shuffled past a mirror, where he gasped at his reflection. Wrinkles, liver spots, and bulges covered the surface of his skin; all the ravages of age.

No one has seen this form of The Atrophy before, he thought. *If I cannot find treatment, I will be a walking cadaver.*

He released a hollow laugh. *Radiation now helps cure the diseases that my work in the field caused.*

He longed for the simpler days—times when he could touch a mortal and melt away any tumors—mere decades ago when his power was still a mystery.

He splashed water on his face, dressed, and staggered towards the Great Hall. Every joint ached and reminded him of his frustration. He enjoyed his position of power; he had earned it through the sacrifices he had made in dealing so harshly with his family.

He mumbled to himself. "I have perfected my art form. I am a master of combat, and yet they call for me to step aside because of my malady."

He interacted with Zinc far less frequently. Uranium II only healed by exerting himself in the healing of mortals or killing of Demons. Manna did not heal his malady.

Once again, he thought of Zinc. He spat on the ground with the bitter remembrance that his infirmity had elevated his colleague to de facto solitary Supreme Commander.

"I have to fix myself," he said,

He began the incantations to open a portal, one to a Sloan Kettering Institute in Manhattan.

Lord Hydrogen lay still upon the earth, a Demon's throwing knife protruding from his throat. His Angelic blood intermingled with the Russian dirt. Zinc shuddered when he looked into the eyes of his fiercest enemy turned closest friend—white, cloudy, devoid of pupils or color.

Hydrogen reached for him. "You have entered into a confederacy with my murderer," Hydrogen said.

A voice from behind snapped Zinc from his daydream.

"I said, what have you been up to?"

The frustration in Rachael's voice was evident. She leaned against the frame of his bedroom door.

"Ah, Asia. I've been to Asia a lot recently," he said.

"Without me," Rachael replied. "You finally have me back after all these years. Don't tell me you're going to be distant and secretive."

Zinc did his best to hide his inner disgust. Since Kursk, he had reignited his love affair with Rachael, but thoughts of Eleanor continually clouded his mind, even when he and Rachael were having sex. Rachael's huge family didn't help. Even after the loss of several of her Standard Bearer sons, she was constantly interacting with some son or daughter or one of their descendants.

"I'm just exhausted," Zinc said.

"But I am certain we will be together on a campaign very soon," Rachael said.

She kissed him, slipping her tongue between his teeth, clearly interested in something other than battlefield tactics. She pulled back a little.

"When Uranium II is gone, the new Lord Hydrogen will be your fellow supreme commander," she said. "That would be me."

Zinc hoped his smile looked genuine.

"My love," she said, "we will rule over all the Angels together."

Zinc remembered a time when the prospect would have exhilarated him. Now his agreement with the Demon complicated things. Zinc wanted to tell Rachael everything, but she would never forgive him for falling into league with the entity she hated with such malevolence.

"I cannot wait," Zinc said.

"In the meantime," she said, "I know a way to pass the time."

Now Zinc's smile was real.

"You are insatiable," he said.

ONCE, LONG AGO, HELL Academy's training ground had been a small sandpit wherein the neophytes trained with sword and spear, dagger and bow, mace and hatchet. But the evolution of mortal weaponry required an upgrading of facilities. The new space included a firing range where Demons practiced shooting.

Still, the Demons were required to train on Celestial warfare. To that end, the gauntlet had been created, an obstacle-ridden simulation of an urban environment.

Schitz slid a banana clip into a Kalashnikov assault rifle. The Wraiths were very reliable about bringing back mortal weaponry with which to train.

"Let's show these newbies how it's done," Schitz said.

In reply, AIDS, his assistant weapons instructor, pulled back the charging handle of his weapon. The instructors switched on small flashlights suspended around their necks. The lights served as the mechanism by which they signaled that they were in possession of a mortal. To simulate stepping into the Celestial, they simply turned off the flashlight. Schitz raised a whistle to his lips and blew.

The drill swiftly differentiated the instructors from the seven members of the newest class. Schitz and AIDS moved like deadly ballet dancers. They went from position to position; they never failed to cover one another; they slipped between the Celestial and the Mortal Realms and back with ease. Though the mortal bullets had been modified and bounced harmlessly off the Demons, the effect of the AK–47 and M16 assault rifle fire in an enclosed space did a decent job of imitating combat. In a few moments, the instructors had eliminated all the trainees other than MERS, a promising youngster. He was the son of COVID and Borderline Personality Disorder and continually lived up to the reputation of both his illustrious parents.

The youngster turned to flee before turning off his flashlight and doubling back to attack AIDS. The two engaged in a series of blows with their blunted Celestial daggers. MERS defended himself well from several kicks while his eliminated classmates watched with excitement. The instructor and student landed simultaneous strikes.

Schitz blasted his whistle. "A draw!" he said. "Well, done."

MERS stopped strutting when Schitz tapped him on the back with a Celestial weapon and said, "But you ignored your second foe."

He ruffled MERS's hair. "Secure your weapons and head to personal training."

"That one's got a lot of potential," AIDS said.

The colleagues walked along the Styx.

"Yes, he does," Schitz said. "The whole class is coming together quite well."

"How do you balance it all?" AIDS asked.

"What do you mean?"

"Training, strategizing. You maintain joie de vivre."

Schitz stopped and laughed. "Why do I have the sense that you only want to know about the last part?"

"You know me too well by now." Although he smiled, AIDS looked at Schitz with suspicion. "Besides, your success with the ladies is as legendary as your skills in battle. Where do you find the time?"

"If you focus on everything all the time, you never truly neglect anything."

"Meaning?"

Schitz paused. "Well, when I'm fighting, I'm thinking about strategy and how best to train the youth."

"And who next you'll sleep with?" AIDS said, this time with a genuine chuckle.

"Now you're getting it," Schitz said, "although that usually sorts itself out."

"I know," AIDS said. "I'm jealous of that."

AIDS had lost his wife during the Second World War, and Schitz could more than relate to his sense of loneliness.

"Someone you have your eye on?" Schitz asked.

AIDS shifted his gaze from Schitz over to the Styx. "Oh, come on," Schitz said, "you're not an Academy pup. Who?"

"I'm not embarrassed," AIDS said. "I just hate the thought that you've already had her."

"Rift Valley Fever?" Schitz asked. He made no attempt to hide his enthusiasm.

"No, thankfully," AIDS said. "It's Von Willebrand."

"Ah, yes," Schitz said. "She is a cutie, but no, I haven't tasted of her maidenly bounty, but from what I've heard, your sparring mate MERS is heavily interested there."

AIDS raised an eyebrow. "Oh?"

Schitz chucked AIDS on the shoulder. "Buck up, man," Schitz said. "You're older and more handsome. She'll be yours if you work on it."

The morose affliction on his face vanished and was replaced by a look of boyish hope.

"Thanks," AIDS said. "But enough of this foolish talk of the heart. What's up next on the agenda?"

"Well, if you will quit pestering me, I believe I will endeavor to acquire some female companionship."

"I thought they came to you," AIDS said.

Schitz snapped his teeth together and snarled. "Sometimes, my friend, even the biggest wolf has to wander out of the lair."

OVER 53,000 SCREAMING MANIACS made Anfield a veritable football cathedral, lively and raucous. Even though they were destined for the second time in two years to end the season without a trophy, the Reds put six past the Nottingham Forest keeper.

"I thought all you Demons liked the Red Devils," Zinc said from within the body of a burly welder.

"What the fuck do they know?" Schitz asked. He was possessing the tradesman's brother.

Schitz drunk in the ambiance. The hometown heroes were making short work of their opposition.

"Fabulous crowd," he said.

Every voice joined in a raucous song.

We hate Nottingham Forest; we hate Everton too; they're shit.

"A bit different from the opera," Zinc said.

Schitz shook his head. "Not really. Same elements: passion, love, heroes and villains, drama and artistry. You just have to know how to look at it."

"If I compare it to anything, it's battle, not art," Zinc said. "I see the movements of two armies, not so different than our own; attack and defense across a constantly shifting continuum."

"That too—" Schitz broke off to cheer the Liverpool players advancing toward the opposition's goal.

"So, how were you able to get away today?" Zinc said.

"I'm supposed to be getting laid," Schitz replied.

Zinc spit a little beer from his nose and coughed. "Sorry, you're not my type."

"Think of it this way," Schitz said. "Whenever we meet, somebody's getting fucked."

"Good point," Zinc said. He grew serious. "Why are we meeting today?"

Now or never, Schitz thought.

"There is an Angel of considerable notoriety in your ranks who has caused me considerable suffering over the years. I will not bore you with the details. Suffice it to say, I would like to kill her very much."

Zinc stared at the field, but his jawline tightened, and his eyes narrowed.

He knows, Schitz thought.

"Of course, I am referring to the Angel—"

Zinc whirled; his teeth bared like an angry Rottweiler.

"I know who she is," he said. "Rachael is off the table."

"You have not heard my offer yet," Schitz said. "I always offer fair recompense."

Zinc's expression softened a bit, and he returned his attention to the game. "She is the next Supreme Commander, an Ancient Angel, and, as you surely know, very close to me. I will not give her up."

"So, the rumors about Lord Uranium are true. He is too sick to continue his service."

Zinc kicked himself mentally for sharing the intelligence. "She's off the table," he said again.

"Are you not even curious as to the offer I'd make for her? It's big and personal."

Zinc exhaled. "My patience grows thin," he said. "What Demons would you offer?"

"None," Schitz said. "Not a single one."

Zinc turned to the aisle and spoke over his shoulder. "Call me when you have a serious offer about something."

Schitz reached for Zinc's shoulder. At the very first touch, Zinc spun with unbridled hostility in his eyes. Schitz backed away, not out of fear but to emphasize the absence of aggression.

"Bear with me for a moment," he said. "You are Lord Zinc, are you not?"

"You know I am. And you have one minute to tell me whatever you think is so damned important."

Schitz bobbed his head and motioned to the benches. They sat, though Zinc teetered on the edge of the seat obviously ready to leave at the slightest provocation.

"You do not know this," Schitz said, "but many eons ago, I was not a favorite in Hell. Satan had me imprisoned."

Zinc's head swiveled. Curiosity burned in his eyes.

Schitz continued, "During my incarceration, I made the acquaintance of another prisoner—an Angel. He called himself Lord Zinc. I reason he was—'

"My father."

The color had drained from Zinc's face. He croaked his next question. "Is he..."

"Oh, he is alive," Schitz said. The smile of the cobra etched its way across his lips. "Yes, your daddy is very much alive in Satan's prison. And I will deliver him to you in exchange for Rachael."

Zinc's head sank into his hands. Schitz could hear his muffled sobs, his frantic breathing. He patted Zinc on the back. Zinc did not look up.

"How do I know he's still alive," he asked.

Schitz had the answer ready. "I will send your father to the Isle of Neutrality with a trusted friend of mine. Once I have dispatched of... ah... my little problem, your father will be released. If I fail to uphold my end of the bargain, you can warn her. If you break our deal, your father will not leave the Isle alive, and we will pay the price for breaking the oath held over that sacred ground."

Zinc did not hesitate. "I choose my father."

Schitz suppressed a smile and handed Zinc an annotated map. "That's the Mekong Delta region. Rachael will be here (he pointed) on the day and time we select."

The match ended. According to custom, the fans broke into a rendition of *You'll Never Walk Alone*. Schitz and Zinc made their way to the exit along with the crowd.

Schitz shouted over the noise. "Oi, that's us, innit? Never alone."

Fuck you, Zinc thought.

But he said nothing and walked away.

RACHAEL CAME THROUGH THE doorway to what had become their chamber.

"We found him," Zinc said.

"Who, love?" she asked.

She embraced Zinc and kissed him on the mouth.

"The one you have sought for so long," he said. "He's usually meticulous in the field, but I think the mortal's technology has caught up with him. A Familiar who knows his voice heard him speaking through a mortal over a field radio in Indochina."

Rachael's face reddened with excitement. "He's in Vietnam?" she asked. "Let's assemble a team."

Zinc's stomach churned. He felt a slight tremor in his hands. He stepped closer and kissed Rachael hard. He ran his hands over her body, searching for the special spots he knew would unleash her riotous passion.

Instead of responding, she laughed. "Not now, lover," she said. "Once we get back, I will wear you out. But now we have work to do."

Zinc forced a smile and followed her to the Great Hall. With each step, he ran through every scenario by which he could tell her about his collaboration with her nemesis. Then he contemplated the benefits both Heaven and Hell were enjoying because of "the arrangement."

Zinc was certain he could serve up Schitz to her by changing the positioning of the mortal units, or simply by sending additional Angels. Then, he thought about his father, the torture he had surely endured.

He remembered the orgy of violence perpetrated against the Angels who had been exchanged in the Limbo Accord and trembled at the thought of all his father must have experienced.

I owe it to my father to give up everything for his release, he thought.

Rachael roused several members of the Hydrogen and Krypton Houses. Her preparation was precise; her focus unwavering.

I am serving up Heaven's first female Standard Bearer for purely personal reasons. She is a natural leader, a fierce warrior, and a dedicated family member—maybe a more fit leader than I.

The briefing was an orchestrated charade. Familiars delivered manufactured intelligence. Constance Silver arrived with a message that Uranium II and God had summoned Zinc to an urgent meeting. Zinc looked at Rachael.

"Go on. Don't let him slip away," said Zinc. Every word pricked his heart. "If it's quick, I'll join you."

He motioned her away from the assembled group of Angels and Familiars. His voice broke a little. "Be careful."

Zinc kissed her one final time. "I love you," he said.

"I love you, too," Rachael said.

Once away from the Great Hall, Zinc opened a doorway and

was soon on the steps of the old Priory Hospital. Zinc soon found a schizophrenic patient. He stepped into the body of an orderly and relayed the exact numbers and departure time of the Angels.

"Be sure to tell him that Rachael is leading the foray. I am on my way to the Isle of Neutrality."

SCHITZ WAS NOT UNACCUSTOMED to making promises that he was uncertain he could keep. He hoped he had composed the precise responses he would need to secure Old Man Zinc's release from Titus.

The high priest was in a good mood. "Ah, Sir Schitz, it's good to see you," he said. He was hunched over a pile of scrolls and texts laid out across one of the reading tables in Hell's library. Schitz had never liked the reading rooms with their dimly lit, dusty interiors. He yearned to be outside of the cramped confines as soon as possible.

"Likewise," Schitz said. "Ah... researching something?"

"I'm reading about the forest of Limbo," Titus replied. "When it was planted, what purpose it was supposed to serve; anything new I can learn. Who knows, I may find something that would be useful in plotting a Reconquista. A surprising amount of Hell is unexplored: the lands beyond the Southern Mountains, the extent of the Eastern Plains. We are not sure if there are islands in the sea into which the Styx flows. Fascinating stuff."

Schitz scratched his chin. Mistaking Schitz's silence as interest, Titus continued, "Over the millennia, we have been so absorbed with fighting the Angels, we have failed to understand our world very well. Perhaps when the Final Victory comes, we will take the time to map the far reaches of the Realm. But none of this is why you're here. How can I help you?"

Schitz's lips twitched a smile in response. "I hate to be a heel, but do you remember when I gave you my medal as a show of my support—you know, when we thought Satan might kill you?"

"Of course," Titus said. His initial smile morphed into a look of concern. "So, you want a favor."

"Yes."

"Will it get me killed?"

"Most certainly not."

The Priest clapped his hands, a gunshot within the confines of the small reading room.

"Then, I am at your service."

Schitz took a breath. "I need you to ensure the Devil is far away from the Great Hall. Perhaps you can take him to see the battlements at Limbo, you know, to discuss your findings."

"No problem."

"And... ah... I'll need your keys to the cells."

A perplexed look passed across the Priest's face. He peered into Schitz's eyes.

"Do I want to know?" he asked.

"You do not," Schitz said.

Titus handed the keys to Schitz. "I trust you to always act in the best interests of our people, so I will not ask any questions," he said.

After bidding adieu to Titus, Schitz assembled Anorexia, Autism, and AIDS. He briefed them on the situation and sent them to Cần Thơ basecamp in the Mekong. He made his way through the vacant halls of the throne room and various meeting rooms to the dungeon cells. The stench of mold made him shiver. He experienced a brief flashback, a return of the stomach-pounding dread he'd felt all those years before. He pounded on the heavy door beside his old cell.

"Yes?"

"It's me, Schitz. We haven't much time, but we're getting you out of here."

A brief hesitation, then the sounds of feet moving across stone.

When Schitz opened the protesting door, he was staring at someone he already knew. The Angel looked none the worse for wear after centuries of imprisonment.

"You look like your son," Schitz said.

"How do you know my son?" the elder Zinc asked.

"Plenty of time for that later," Schitz said. "Now, we have to get you out of here. This next part is a little tricky."

The Angel's voice was low and pleasant. "You seem very adept at pulling off the impossible. Something 'tricky' should not present a problem."

"Okay," Schitz said. "Are you adept at the meditative practices that can eliminate one's aura?"

"I've had incalculable time to practice every type of mental activity," the elder Zinc said.

"Okay," Schitz said. "Do whatever you need to do, and do it now. Walk as close to me as possible." Schitz draped a black cloak over the Angel.

The walk to the portals filled Schitz with overwhelming anxiety. With every step, he was certain he would encounter a Demon or Priest who would expose his activity. But the trip was uneventful.

Titus was successful in luring Satan away, Schitz thought. *My Lord always insists on taking an entourage.*

As planned, Josephine arrived by the portal at the precise time Schitz opened the gateway to the Isle of Neutrality. She had not been briefed on the details of her mission. All she knew was her assignment: to escort an individual to the Isle of Neutrality, where she would guard him until she was instructed to allow his release.

"Sorry I can't tell you more," Schitz said. "It's for your own good."

"I don't need to know anything," she said. "I always serve willingly."

Despite the effects of aging, Schitz still found the Wraith alluring. He had a momentary remembrance of their coital bliss.

Josephine snapped her fingers. "Back to the present, My Lord," she said with a knowing smile.

Embarrassed, Schitz pointed to the portal. "Stay with him every minute until you get word from me," he said.

She and the elder Zinc disappeared into the portal.

THE CẦN THƠ BASECAMP was home for the 9th Infantry Division. Just past the entrance gate Schitz spoke to a deranged and elderly local.

The hapless senior confirmed Zinc's message regarding the location of the Angelic patrol.

Lieutenant Eisenhower thanked the old man. The mortal walked away from the gate with confidence; he'd been 'in country' long enough to know his way around. He carried a Colt 1911 on his hip and an M16 assault rifle slung over his shoulder. His boots kicked up little mushroom clouds of dirt. He caught a brief glimpse of himself in a parked Jeep's windshield; sleeves rolled above his elbows, tunic unbuttoned for relief from the tropical heat, helmet at a jaunty angle, and several chains of machine gun ammunition draped over his shoulders. He walked past tents and huts shouting the same phrase.

"First Platoon, mount up."

From behind his dark, aviator sunglasses, Schitz watched the soldiers exit their tents and scramble for a line of UH-1 'Huey' helicopters. He spotted Autism and Anorexia within a pair of sergeants and AIDS in possession of a corporal. AIDS was laden down with claymore mines.

Once the troops clambered into the whirling helicopters, they hurtled over the waterlogged fields and lush jungle of the Mekong Delta. Schitz reclined in the Huey's open doorway. He cradled his rifle in his arms and watched the countryside stream along below.

Schitz's Notebook

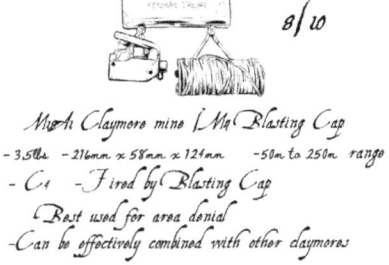

8/10

M16 Claymore mine [M18 Blasting Cap
- 3.5lbs - 216mm x 58mm x 124mm   -50m to 250m range
- C4 - Fired by Blasting Cap
  Best used for area denial
-Can be effectively combined with other claymores

WHEN RACHAEL RAISED THE concealed opening to the Viet Cong tunnel, the light blinded her for a moment. She grimaced from within the body of the young guerilla fighter as her eyes adjusted to the blazing daylight. The warrior she occupied had been studying to be a language teacher before the war and could converse in six different tongues. She was a native of Saigon, but her family had fled to the countryside, and soon, she had found her way into the irregular Communist forces. Rachael admired the young Vietnamese for her courage and intelligence. In many ways, the mortal reminded her of herself.

The VC moved in silence through the thick jungle foliage. They did not like to maneuver in the daylight, and Rachael felt the anxiety within her host's mind. However, they pressed on; there were reports of American activity in the region.

Rachael knew where the U.S. patrol was headed. She arrayed her forces around a clearing and broke into a broad, maniacal smile. In the open, the Americans and their Demons would be sitting ducks.

I will have my revenge, at last.

Josephine had never been to the Isle of Neutrality and was shocked when she was greeted by a young Wraith, a granddaughter of one of her close friends.

"Emily," Josephine said, "everybody thinks you are dead."

Even the older man with Josephine stared at Emily's revealing attire. For her part, Emily did not seem to care—or to mind.

"Will you two be requiring a private room, or will you be taking your liberties within the main chamber," she asked.

"Oh, we're not here to... ah... the main chamber will be fine," Josephine said. She knew she was bright red.

"No judgment here, hon," the hostess said.

The elder Zinc leaned close and whispered to Josephine. "I've heard about this place, but I'm as new to it as you."

"Don't worry. I imagine we will not be waiting long."

A server swished to a halt in front of them. "What can I get you?"

"I never thought I'd say this again," the elder Zinc said. "Do you have any Elixir?"

SCHITZ TRUDGED THROUGH THE thick jungle foliage with a squad containing Anorexia. He had sent Autism and AIDS in the squad that would serve as bait. He and the others maneuvered to the rear of the VC position. The helicopters had conducted numerous false landings along the way to conceal the true LZ.

Schitz's senses were on high alert. He was concerned for those he'd sent into what he knew would be a savage ambush. Their survival depended solely on his timely arrival.

"DOES HE TYPICALLY LIKE to use others as bait?" AIDS asked.

The squad moved into the clearing.

Autism checked the safety on his M16 for the fiftieth time. "Well, look at it this way," he said. "All the responsibility is on those two. All we've got to do is get shot at."

"You should take up motivational speaking as a career," AIDS said.

"Has he ever let you down?" Autism asked.

"Nope," AIDS said. "He's fuckin' solid."

"Right," Autism said. "I've known him my whole life. No one is more reliable. When he asks me to take a risk, I take it."

"Fair enough, but I already feel like someone is sighting me up."

Kalashnikov (AK-47)

Autism shot AIDS a quick look. "My host's alarm is pinging too. Shit's about to hit the fan."

A moment later, rifle and machine gun fire raked the column. Autism's host fell, fatally wounded. AIDS stepped into the Celestial. Crouching next to his seizing comrade and the dying American, he drew his Celestial hatchet and prepared for combat.

RACHAEL AIMED HER KALASHNIKOV in the direction of the muzzle flashes sparking from the tall grass. She fired a burst from her rifle and watched a mortal infantryman fall. The Viet Cong's twin RPD machine guns set up along the tree line pounded the American position. Using the cover fire, Rachael led half her contingent across the field.

Bullets whined past her. A grenade landed near her feet. Rachael made a split-second decision to remain within her host and dove to the ground. Dirt flew and the earth under her chest shook.

There were two Demons in the column.

One of them must be Schitz. With any luck, he was the one who fell with the opening fire.

She duck-walked forward, firing all the time.

SCHITZ SIGNALED THE SQUAD to fan out. He heard the firefight and knew his comrades were pinned. He drew a bead on a VC machine gunner.

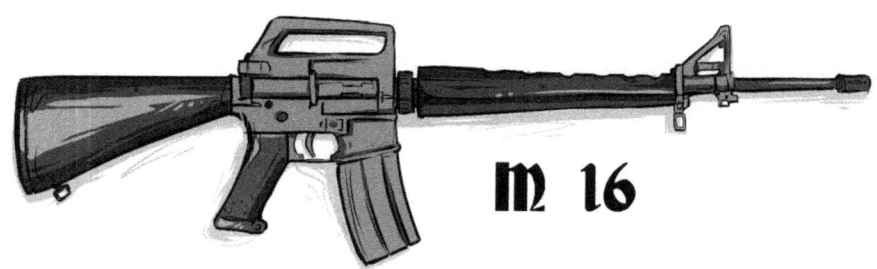

M 16

His host's heart rat-a-tatted along with the staccato fire. He squeezed the trigger. The round tore through the machine gunner's beige helmet, smashing through his skull, and splattering brain matter on the surrounding foliage. With Schitz's shot as a signal, the Americans unleashed hell on the Viet Cong position.

Mud squelched under Schitz's boots as he charged the Vietnamese troops. He stepped into the Celestial and dispatched a pair of seizing Angels with his knives. He jumped into another American and made his way along the tree line. He signaled Anorexia into the Celestial while LAWs and RPGs pounded their opponents.

The VC were sandwiched.

It was a turkey shoot.

RACHAEL'S VIET CONG HOST took a round just below her collar bone. Rachael could feel her agony as she crawled along the muddy ground. Her only salvation was a natural trench that ran across the field, a tiny stream on its way to the river.

Rachael heaved her mortal into the defile. All around, she recognized the screams of Angels being butchered.

That means the Americans who came up on our rear also contained Demons, she thought.

"Fuck!" She held her AK over the top of the trench and fired until it was empty.

How could this happen?

In thousands of engagements, she'd never been trapped so perfectly.

"Nothing left to do now," she said.

She stepped into the Celestial. When she hauled herself out of the trench, she came face to face with Schizophrenia. A female Demon stood next to him within an American woman.

Rachael glanced over her shoulder. On the far side of the ditch, two more Demons stood within the Celestial. The one she had shot at the outset of the engagement had recovered from his seizure. Rachael raised her fists in defiance.

The possessed American raised her rifle and fired into Rachael's former Viet Cong host. Outrage surged in Rachael's heart.

I could not have repossessed her. There was no reason to shoot her. Rachael lowered her arms and reached for a throwing star.

Maybe I can kill him before they kill me. Maybe I can kill all of them.

I'VE GOT YOU, YOU *bitch.*

Schitz knew Rachael could not escape. He felt no fear when he watched her draw her throwing star, the weapon she had used to kill so many of his kin. He looked at her shoulders and saw the cape made of Rubella's skin. He suppressed his anger; he knew it blunted his reactions. He stepped forward and taunted.

"They will kill you," he said, "and they will take your corpse with them to Hell and hang it along the Styx for your brethren in Limbo to see. It will happen, but in the spirit of warriors, I offer myself to you—one-on-one—as it should be."

He saw the raw hatred in her eyes.

The Americans and scattered remnants of the Viet Cong were still shooting it out. The duel would be sanctioned under the Divine Dictum.

"I agree," Rachael said.

She launched the throwing star. He ducked and hurled a knife at her. Before it sailed wide, he'd already drawn his short sword. It had barely cleared its scabbard when Rachael swiped at him with her own blade. The battle was joined. Schitz caught AIDS's eye. While Rachael backpedaled to avoid Schitz's sword, AIDS tripped her. She rolled across the ground, a lithe and gymnastic move. But she could not avoid Schitz's boot. He smiled when his toe connected with the side of her chest. He heard ribs crack.

Still in possession of her sword, Rachael lunged—a final, desperate swipe. Schitz knocked it away as easily as he would have dismissed an annoying fly, then he sliced through her midsection.

The blow did not kill her instantly, but experience told Schitz she would not survive.

He grabbed her by the throat and lifted her from the ground. He stared into her eyes and saw singular, unadulterated hatred.

Rachael smirked. "Your wife called out for you while I was skinning her alive, and you weren't there; always remember that," she said.

Schitz flung the Angel down into the ditch beside her deceased host. He heard her body crumble like a discarded doll. He followed her into the ditch and loomed over her. Her eyes were beginning to dim. He growled into her face.

"You fancy that you have burdened my mind with some suffering because you spoke of my wife. You will not play the role of Shiva in this encounter because I can do you one better. I trapped you here because Zinc served you up. He and I planned the entire thing, the ambush, everything. How convenient that he was called away at the last minute? He is my asset, and I am his. You have been discarded like the pile of rotten meat you will soon be."

Schitz backed away and saw a broken spirit. Tears stained the Angel's face. Blood trickled from her nose and mouth.

"You... have... won. I no long—no longer hate you."

"Now you hate Zinc?"

She groaned and clutched her side.

"No," she said. "I... I don't understand... but I am exhausted of hate. Now I feel," she choked, then spat a torrent of scarlet, "only loss. I doubt you will, but I ask the honor of your knife."

Schitz withdrew his dagger and flipped it. He extended the handle. When she took it, the heft seemed to overwhelm her.

"I will leave you here for your Familiars," Schitz said.

Rachael's tongue lolled in her mouth. Her words were slurred. "If I can't complete it, will you?"

Schitz bowed his head once. "In the old way."

Rachael winked and said, "Goodbye, Scarface."

She plunged his dagger deep into her abdomen. She howled as she dragged the knife up through her innards. Schitz brought his sword down on her neck and severed her head from her body in a clean swipe. Her decapitated crown rolled along the bottom of the trench and her body slumped to the side.

Schitz withdrew his dagger from her body. "Goodbye, Your Ladyship," he said.

With sacramental reverence, he removed the skin cloak from her headless shoulders and cradled the grisly garment in his arms.

"It's over now Bella," he said.

"We're not taking the corpse?" Autism asked.

"It only matters that she's dead," Schitz said.

He surveyed the carnage, then slid what was left of his wife into his pack and signaled his men to head home.

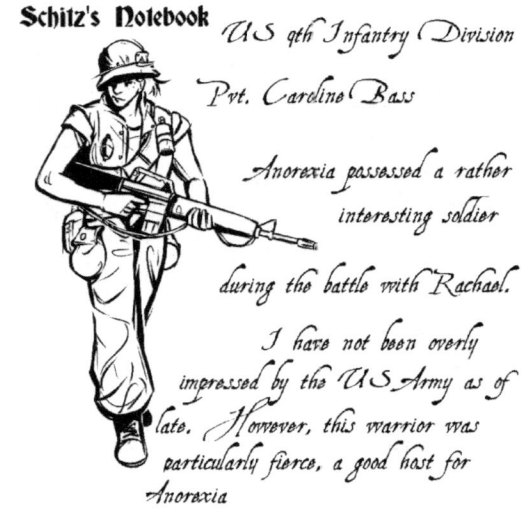

Schitz's Notebook

US 9th Infantry Division

Pvt. Caroline Bass

Anorexia possessed a rather interesting soldier during the battle with Rachael.

I have not been overly impressed by the US Army as of late. However, this warrior was particularly fierce, a good host for Anorexia

JOSEPHINE RELAXED AFTER SEVERAL rounds of Elixir and enjoyed the conversation with the Angel. The hostess came with a note.

"You may return home whenever you like."

Josephine rose to her feet. The room swam and she sat back down.

"Well, I suppose we are now enemies again," she said. Her speech was slow and slurred.

"Be that as it may, I enjoyed our time together," the Angel said.

He stood and walked out while Josephine fell asleep by the fire.

ALL OF HEAVEN TURNED out for Lady Hydrogen's funeral, a fact of little comfort to Zinc. As the incense wafted over the Great Hall where she lay in state, he wrestled with ramifications of his decision. He had chosen his father over the love of his life.

Zinc looked at her, reassembled on a cold, stone slab. A thick, silken white scarf around her neck concealed the butchery she'd endured. There were no accounts of the battle. His treachery had yielded no survivors.

Was it quick and painless? he wondered.

He touched her cold, delicate hand and longed for absolution.

"I had no right to give you away like I did," he said under his breath, "but there will be life in the world of mortals by your death and although that feels to me as though it were me searching for justification, maybe it is a fitting memorial for you."

Bagpipes droned and six pall bearers, Zinc among them, lay Rachael next to Lord Hydrogen. *The Flowers of the Forest* echoed through the Heavenly Halls and across the open countryside.

Zinc felt lonelier than ever.

Odd, he thought. *I am without my lover, I have yet to speak with my father, someone I have not seen in centuries, but the individual to whom I most wish to speak... is Schitz.*

Chapter 12

Organized Chaos

Schitz plowed through the status reports about available forces. The Wraith population was making a comeback after its decimation. Elise, Mephistopheles, and Anubis were gone; Josephine now occupied the lead position.

Perhaps I was too rash. She looked after me... cared for me... nurtured me.

Momentarily overwhelmed, he pounded a fist into the shelf of papers on his desk. "What have I done?"

Then he remembered Elise's interference. He also considered the absolute, unquestioning loyalty he now enjoyed with the Wraiths, and his moment of self-flagellation passed. He looked at the list of Priests.

Titus is a friend and ally, he thought. *He seems disillusioned with Satan. I can count on him.*

The next consideration was Zinc. Schitz regularly weighed the benefits of killing the Angel against the liabilities. He knew he could only execute his fellow conspirator in a massive raid on Heaven.

The juice is not worth the squeeze. Though I got what I really wanted with the death of Rachael, Lord Zinc may still prove useful.

Then to the Demonic forces themselves. Schitz realized the novelty of having no enemies in Hell's ranks. First, there was Vertigo whose death brought on Bubonic Plague's wrath. Spanish Influenza had been ambitious and hungry to surpass Schitz in leadership.

Now, Schitz's primary concern was AIDS, his protégé, a Demon regularly by his side; a circumstance that complicated the collaboration with Zinc. But AIDS provided a sense of friendship Schitz longed for. He and AIDS regularly drank along the banks of the Styx. Schitz saw Conjunctivitis's reflection and Anthrax's shadow in AIDS and felt the fatherly affection he'd had for Rabies.

In rare moments of self-reflective honesty, Schitz acknowledged AIDS was one of his nearest and dearest friends. But Schitz knew he could never divulge his secret alliance to the young, ardent true believer. Despite the horrors of the World Wars, AIDS was still inexorably dedicated to the cause of Hell.

Schitz coughed and sipped on a mug of brew. "If only my young friend were as disillusioned as I."

Schitz realized how long it had taken for him to sink to the bottom of the believers' pool. Time and the death of friends and family, colleagues and lovers.

Schitz considered the roster again—thirty-eight, divided into two distinct groups. Due to his deal with Zinc, Schitz maintained a "roster of the expendable," which included the "price" for each sacrificed Demon.

The second list contained the names of those he deemed essential should his collusion collapse. He would need every one of them if he decided to make a move against Heaven.

Last, Schitz thought about the Devil. His relationship with the Lord of Hell was pockmarked with disasters and highlighted with considerable success. At the beginning, Schitz wanted nothing more than Satan's approbation. Now, he held an intense loathing for the man he called "Master." Still, Schitz could not quite shake a deep longing for recognition.

Schitz glanced down at the medals strewn across his desk. Despite his recent duplicity, he possessed an unconquerable pride in his accomplishments. The Devil would always be difficult; however, he had thrown his full support behind Schitz, and if Angels kept dying, it would remain.

Schitz pushed back in his chair as the odd realization that he had achieved the lasting peace he sought.

I do not need the final victory. I am still strong, swift, and eternal. My foes are vanquished, and I have cultivated support from all the requisite corners of the world: Demons, Wraiths, Priests, Satan, and even an ancient Angelic House.

Schitz

I Corps: Autism

Pancreatic Cancer
Ebola
Endometrial Cancer
Atrial Fibrillation
Alzheimer's
Borderline Personality Disorder
Munchausen Syndrome
Desynchronosis
Vampirosis
Kyasanur Forest Disease
Esophageal Candidiasis

II Corps: AIDS

Lymphoma
Hypertension
SARS
Parkinson's
Marburg Hemorrhagic Fever
Korsakov Syndrome
Sleep Paralysis
Cyclothymia
Chronic Myeloproliferative Neoplasm
MERS
Rift Valley Fever
Haemophilus Influenza

III Corps: Anorexia

Breast Cancer
Anaphylaxis
Metastatic
Cirrhosis
Coronavirus
Narcissistic Personality Disorder

Central Hyperventilation Syndrome
Dyspareunia
Gender Identity Disorder
Von Willebrand Disease
Kawasaki Syndrome

Schitz thought of Zinc. His counterpart presented a unique and interesting case. It appeared that the Angel, too, had seen enough of war to know that he did not want to die in one. In that way, he was a perfect fit as a confederate. He also appeared to be lonely, which meant he was amenable to an agreement designed to provide some semblance of camaraderie.

Schitz looked up from his papers and studied his reflection in a mirror.

"I can live forever," he said. "Not only have I killed those who opposed me, but I have also kept my friends Autism and Anorexia alive."

He smoothed his hair, then pushed away from his desk.

"We can have peace without the final victory," he said. "And I can handle AIDS."

THE EVER-TRANQUIL BANKS OF the Eunoe shimmered in the perpetual sunlight of Heaven. Zinc's family was assembled and enjoying one another's company.

Zinc swelled with pride.

This is my cadre, he thought. *They will follow my every instruction. They are the true force with which I command control over the forces of Heaven.*

Zinc glanced over his shoulder at his perpetual bodyguards. He was never out of sight from Anna Gold or Constance Silver. They alternated between the Manna bakery and his security. His current escort was Constance, his former daughter-in-law.

Zinc turned his attention away from the continually brooding Constance and focused again on his family.

These are the individuals I will never trade to Hell.

Zinc knew that even if no one challenged him, someone would eventually notice how many kills his family had, and how they had sustained almost no deaths. He watched his father meandering through the crowd. They had spoken only briefly since the elder's return, mostly due to the guilt and shame Zinc felt surrounding the exchange.

I will speak to him soon. Right now, it is enough to know he is alive and well.

Zinc missed Eleanor greatly and suffered from the cruel understanding that she had died so close to the inception of his agreement with the Demon.

If she had lived, would I have made the deal? he wondered. He stared at his family without seeing any of them. *The life we lead is full of mysteries; best to limit my thoughts to the things over which I have control.*

His son, Gallium, shoved his shoulder. "Hey, Dad, come back from wherever your mind is. Have a drink." He handed Zinc a flagon of Elixir. "Why so serious?"

"I just miss your mother a great deal on days like today."

Gallium continued to smile, as always. "I do, too," he said, "but she would want us to live as best we can and to remember her in happier times."

Zinc sipped. The mixture warmed him and brought with it a calming sensation.

The Standard Bearer of the Zinc House clapped his son on the shoulder.

I must remain vigilant, he thought. *My deal with Schitz could turn on its head at any time.*

But until it does...

He took another long pull from the flagon, wiped his lips with his forearm, and let out a loud, "Ah!"

WET WITH PERSPIRATION, THE preacher waved his Bible in one hand and pounded the cheap wooden pulpit with the other. His white jacket, long discarded, lay on the metal chair behind him. He loosened his tie and unbuttoned his sweat-stained shirt. Four huge electric fans, one in each corner of the revival tent, droned with the pulsing insistence of airplane engines. The members of the congregation who were not wrestling with overheated, squawking children tried to cool themselves a little with hand-held funeral home fans, which came through the generosity of Fraser's Funeral Home and featured an advertisement on one side and scenes from the life and work of the Blessed Messiah on the other. The preacher's face grew redder with every shouted sentence.

"And when the thousand years are expired, Satan shall be loosed out of his prison, and shall go out to deceive the nations which are in the four quarters of the earth, Gog, and Magog, to gather them together to battle: the number of whom is as the sands of the sea. And they marched up over the broad earth and surrounded the camp of the saints and the beloved city, but fire came down from heaven and devoured them."[52]

"I like this part," Schitz said from within the body of one of the worshippers.

"The part where God smites you with fire from Heaven?" Zinc asked from the person seated next to him.

"You gotta admit, your Lord sounds a lot like mine here." Schitz unleashed his patented smirk.

Zinc refused to take the bait. "Evangelicals like fire and brimstone."

"Roman Catholics, too," Schitz said. "I switched out the King James before the service. Think he'll notice?"

Zinc loosened his mortal's tie. "I was wondering why you picked this for a meeting place," he said, "but I know you are not without your appreciation of irony."

Schitz glanced at the handwritten notes in his mortal's Bible. "Israel wasn't so bad for us," he said, referring to their most recent collaboration.

Schitz's Second Corps went into battle. Sleep Paralysis, Cyclothymia, and Rift Valley Fever, a trio of beautiful young women, never made it back. It had pained Schitz to sell them out, but sacrifices had to be made.

AIDS had not taken the losses well even though twenty-four Angels died in the conflict.

"It was a good piece of work," Zinc said. "We thinned the numbers and maintained the mortal order as well."

[52] Revelation 20: 7-10 (RSVCE)

Sister Sarah began banging out *Have a Little Talk With Jesus*. The congregation joined in. They were enthusiastic and awful.

"Why do Christians all think they can sing?" Schitz asked.

"They all misinterpret the part in the psalm about 'a joyful noise,'" Zinc said. "Amateurs!"

Angel and Demon stood while their mortals bellowed. The Celestial citizens bantered about wins, losses, strategies, and kills.

"Angola, Ethiopia, and Morocco..."

"Whatever happened to that African Angel..."

"Hydrogen... killed at Kursk..."

"Remember that dogfight over Laos..."

"...had to simulate a mid-air collision to get Vampirosis off your Angelic ass..."

"Africa's next..."

"...this time, you lose a Standard Bearer... you got one of ours in Vietnam..."

"I believe you got your father in return."

The hymn ended and the preacher stood behind a wobbly table and lifted a loaf of bread.

"Want to stay for Communion again?" Zinc asked.

Schitz locked him in a withering gaze. "You know that stuff made me vomit last time."

Zinc's shoulders shook with suppressed laughter. "One of the classic moments of all time."

"The only good thing was that I started a chain reaction of barfing. Your Christians have weak stomachs."

They walked out of the tent and Schitz suddenly grew serious. "The sermon was entirely too long today, but I did like one part."

"Which was?"

"When the preacher uttered the line, 'And they marched over the broad earth.'"

"Because?"

"It's what we have done from the beginning; it's what we do now. We march over the broad earth, even if our armies are far less numerous than the sands of the seashore."

THE ELDER ZINC LOOKED at his son. They were walking through a Kurdish village.

"I wondered when you'd come to speak to me," the Elder said.

"I'm sorry, Father," Zinc said. "I meant to—"

His father raised an understanding hand. "I know, I know. I remember how busy it can be."

"It's not that I'm too busy for you," Zinc said. He pillaged through his mind to find the right words.

"Let's talk about the elephant in the room," the Elder said, "the event through which I was released from Hell."

I cannot admit my collusion, Zinc thought.

"I spent a substantial amount of time imprisoned alongside Schizophrenia," the Elder said. "He is the type of enemy with which you can have a decent conversation."

Zinc, ever alert in a Kurdish fighter, looked into his father's eyes. "I will not lie to you after all this time. You have missed a lot. There have been evolutions of Celestial and Mortal warfare that have threatened to cause the Styx to overflow its banks."

Zinc walked past a fellow fighter. He patted the soldier on his shoulder, healing him of a parasitic ailment.

"This," he said gesturing back to the healed man, "this is not enough to stem the tide. And our forces have bled and bled and bled across this vast, rotten globe."

"So, you and he have some type of accord then," his father said without malice or accusation.

Zinc coughed to buy time.

His father continued, "Let me tell you what I think, Son," the Elder said. "I never thought I would see the light of Heaven again. Every day for hundreds of years, I sat in that cramped room and thought I would surely die when the Celestial War was over, regardless of the victor. I had no hope of return. I never thought I would feel the warmth of the sun on my face again or sit by the banks of the Eunoe or walk the halls where my forefathers are laid to rest. You gave that back to me. Now I discover, as

I had already surmised, that my liberty is the product of some illicit accord between you and the enemy. Moreover, I expected to encounter the Houses of Carbon, Iron, Cobalt, and Hydrogen when I returned. They are all gone. The Angels speak of you as though you are their Supreme Commander. They never mention the sickly, Lord Uranium II. Did you and Schitz work to ensure your respective supremacy and survival?"

Zinc stooped to heal another Kurdish fighter, then spoke. "I work with the Demon to ensure my survival and the survival of our kin. I have laid to rest enough loved ones to know that I do not wish to join them, nor do I wish to entomb those still living beneath the floors of the Great Hall. Of course, I can never expel my dreams of the final victory. Through my collaboration with the Demon, I have identified four pillars supporting Hell: Schizophrenia, Anorexia, Autism, and AIDS. If all four of these Demons were to perish, we could achieve the final victory."

The Elder's face yielded no expression. "I imagine the Demon is as cagey as you."

"He is."

"So, I advise that you continue upon your current course," the Elder said. He healed a mortal woman passing him along the street by brushing against her. "You did not achieve anything by chance. This took careful planning and skillful execution."

"I never thought I would hear those words from you, Father," Zinc said.

The tender moment did not last.

"Now," his father said, "fill me in on the dispositions of the Heavenly Houses. I need to be able to recognize friend from foe."

"There aren't many foes nowadays," Zinc said. "I'm rather effective in dealing with those who would oppose me."

The elder nodded slowly and inhaled audibly, then turned over his shoulder to where Anna Gold and Constance Silver walked within the Celestial. "And yet, such beautiful security."

"One can never be too careful," Zinc replied. He relayed to his father the current occupants of Heaven; Lithium (the hoarder of dispensations), the surviving descendants of Carbon (eager to avoid meeting the fate of their father), Uranium (Co-Supreme Commander and leader of the Asian contingent), the surviving descendants of Hydrogen (like their father, mostly concerned with Africa). Zinc informed him of the Houses that were no more; Iron, Gold, Silver, and the others that had been unincorporated. Zinc detailed the Resurrection Project.

"During the most recent global war, God selected a list of individuals who were fiefs and offered them Houses if they were successful during the war."

"I was shocked to hear of female Standard Bearers," the elder replied, once again turning to look at Anna Gold.

Zinc thought of Rachael with great pain and sadness. "It is true," he said, "It was a break in tradition. Yet, I understand it. Some of our fiercest warriors have been women. Why shouldn't they be able to lead a House?"

"Good for them," the elder Zinc said. He once more, looked hungrily toward Anna.

"Those two are allowed to leave Heaven. They have shown themselves to be reliable."

"I see," replied the elder. "Much has changed, and much has remained the same. Perhaps you would do me the honor of awarding me your vassal's hand in marriage?" the elder asked.

He looked at Anna again.

Zinc chuckled lightly and sighed. "I can order her to do anything, but perhaps try winning her over. She is quite fierce."

The elder laughed in reply. "I'm sure I haven't lost my charm after all these years."

"YOU'RE LATE!"

AIDS's voice carried no malice.

"Inspecting the scene outside of Mulondo," Schitz said. "The South Africans hit FAPLA with strike aircraft and artillery. Those poorly armed Angolans had no chance."

"I know," AIDS said. "My contingent was equally effective against the Angels."

They stood in the doorway of a small operations shack and considered the devastation wrought by the bombs dropped by the SAAF's Impala MB-326s.

AIDS jumped up and down with childish urgency. "Look at these!"

He held two long swords aloft. Too ornate for battle, the weapons belonged to Angelic Standard Bearers. Schitz was surprised.

Zinc promised a Standard Bearer... not two.

"Everything okay?" AIDS asked.

"All good." Schitz rubbed his jaw and looked around. "Any casualties?"

"None." AIDS was beside himself with self-congratulations. "Some of theirs tried to ambush us, but I had anticipated that possibility and we turned the table on them."

AIDS handed Schitz one of the swords. Schitz examined the exquisite blade. Other than the name "Xeon," he could not decipher the Angelic characters. He flipped the blade and extended the handle to AIDS. The other weapon yielded no information other than "Curium."

"These are a prize you should display in your room," Schitz said. "I've got a few of those myself back home."

"Most notably the one belonging to Gold," AIDS said. He was beaming. "I'll settle for these."

Schitz questioned the wisdom of a meeting with Zinc; he was not eager for the complaints he would hear. But he wandered over to a local who was attempting to put out a fire caused by the aerial bombing. Schitz afflicted the mortal with his disease, then accessed his thoughts. There was a message from the Angel.

"Your student is becoming a little too powerful. Seems you got your Standard Bearer and an extra. We will need to balance things."

Schitz replied with a single word. "Iran."

"I'm telling you there's a language there."

AIDS came up on his shoulder.

"Nope," Schitz said. "You are just overly inquisitive, just as you were trained. Now come on, there's more work to be done."

AIDS shrugged and motioned for the rest of his squad to follow. Schitz looked at the poor erstwhile firefighter. He'd abandoned his efforts and stood, ranting and raving, while his building burned to the ground.

THE FAJR CALL TO prayer echoed across the dark, predawn landscape.

Allah u Akbar, Allah u Akbar, Allah u Akbar, Allah u Akbar.[53]

The screeching melody scythed through the early morning air. Schitz and AIDS kneeled on their prayer rugs inside the briefing room of the 72nd TFS of the Islamic Republic. The Muezzin[54] continued through the base's loudspeakers.

Ash-hadu alla ilaha illallah, Ash-hadu alla ilaha illallah.[55]

Their hosts were devout, and it was far easier to indulge them in the Morning Prayer than to force them to forego it.
The atonal wailing wafted over the desert trenches.

Ash-hadu anna Muhammadan rasulullah, Ash-hadu anna Muhammadan rasulullah.[56]

Anaphylaxis felt uneasy. He glanced down at his G3 battle rifle beside his prayer rug. His Revolutionary Guard host had set aside his rifle, ammunition, and grenades for his Morning Prayers. Anaphylaxis looked over his shoulder to the rest of his squad. Narcissistic Personality Disorder, Dyspareunia, and

---

[53] God is great, God is great, God is great, God is great.
[54] A man who calls Muslims to prayer from the minaret of a mosque.
[55] I bear witness that there is no God but Allah, I bear witness that there is no God but Allah.
[56] I bear witness that Muhammad is the Messenger of Allah, I bear witness that Muhammad is the Messenger of Allah.

Central Hyperventilation Syndrome were all participating in the Fajr. Further along the trench, Coronavirus was within the body of a less fervent host, reclined against a trench wall smoking a cigarette. Gender Identity Disorder abstained from the prayers and remained within the Celestial. She peered toward the west, twitchy and on guard.

Ash-hadu anna Aliya wali-ul-lah, Ash-hadu anna Aliya wali-ul-lah.[57]

Gallium and his contingent of Angels sat behind one of the Iraqi Army's T-62 main battle tanks. The Morning Prayer echoed over them and their hosts.

Hayya 'alas-salat, Hayya 'alas-salat,
Hayya 'alal-falah, Hayya 'alal-falah.[58]

Gallium knew by the time for dhuhr[59] prayer, they would be heavily engaged with the enemy. He checked his Kalashnikov rifle and spare magazines lying next to the prayer mat. In his head, Gallium could already hear the pop of the rifle and the commotion of combat.

Assalatu khayru min an-naum, Assalatu khayru min an-naum.[60]

Zinc sat alone in the communications room of the Al Hurriya Air Base of the Iraqi Air Force.

Allah u Akbar, Allah u Akbar, La ilaha illallah.[61]

---

[57] I bear witness that Ali is the representative of Allah, I bear witness that Ali is the representative of Allah.

[58] Hasten towards prayer, hasten towards prayer, hasten towards prosperity, Hasten towards prosperity.

[59] Noon prayer time for Muslims.

[60] Hasten towards the best of action, Hasten towards the best of action.

[61] God is great, God is great, there is no God but Allah.

His host was a strict Baathist and had little interest in the morning ritual. But both Zinc and his host paid attention to the transmission that followed the conclusion of the Call to Prayer. Zinc jotted down the positions of the Demonic troops and the vectors of the Demonic flights. It appeared Schitz was once again shackled with his junior, the one known as AIDS, the one who'd been overly eager during the last exchange.

The day's strategy called for a feint on the part of the Angelic infantry. Led by Gallium, they would attack the Iranians at the Demon's location. Plutonium and his retinue would lead Iraqi air support to pulverize the enemy's position before Gallium mopped up. For good show, Schitz and his forces would bounce the Iraqi fighters in an Iranian F-14 squadron; however, the Demons would arrive late, and the Iraqi pilots would have time to cut and run.

Zinc hoped the plan would unfold better than the previous venture.

"WHERE DID WE GET such detailed flight plans?" AIDS asked.

He walked with Schitz toward the flight line of the 72nd TFS.

"The Wraiths," Schitz replied. He made no attempt to hide his irritation.

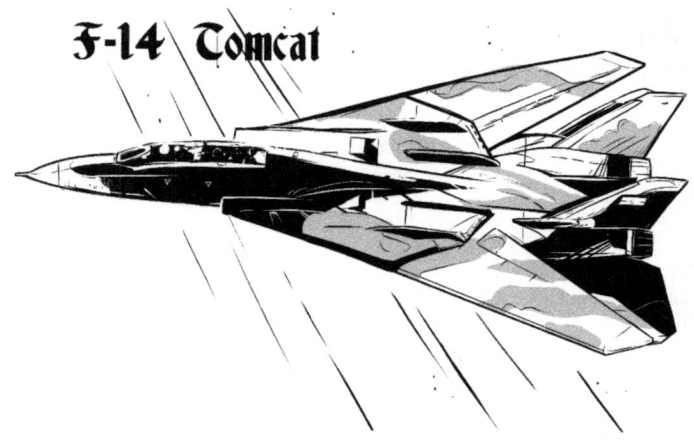

F-14 Tomcat

"Impressive," AIDS said. "Which ones? They should be commended."

Schitz clicked his teeth. *He knows something is amiss.*

"Josephine," Schitz said. "She's tapped into their communications."

"She is something special," AIDS said. "You two have history, right?"

He's trying too hard to sound nonchalant.

Schitz shrugged. "She was a looker when she was younger. The Great War ruined her appearance, made her tougher than a pine now, but back then... well, her innocence was irresistible."

"You're a dog, Schitz."

"A dog of war, for certain."

He was relieved when they reached AIDS's aircraft.

Schitz broke off for his own bird.

"Just watch my back up there, all right?"

CORONAVIRUS, COVID TO HIS friends, had seen his fair share of fighting during the Second World War, but the sight of the mechanized Iraqi units rolling towards his position shook him to the core. He spotted Angels among the infantry, but his primary concern was the Soviet-built tanks that were pounding 125 mm shells. He fired back and shouted to Anaphylaxis.

"Do we need to go into the Celestial?"

The squad leader ducked debris from an incoming shell. "Stay in your host for now. We don't know how many Angels there are."

COVID fired his rifle again and tried to battle back the sensation of inevitable defeat. He was uncertain whether it came from his host or himself, but the doubt... the fear... the terror, were always present.

Suddenly, fire came from above—a flight of Iraqi Air Force MiG-23s. The Floggers were an exceptional ground attack aircraft. Their payload incinerated the Iranian forward trench in a fiery explosion. His host fell and a departure seizure shook COVID, a nauseating paroxysm.

This is it; I am undone.

AIDS PUSHED HIS F-14 to full throttle and closed in on the MiG-23s. Involuntarily, his eyes were drawn to the flickering photo of the pilot's deceased father, a martyr of the war. It was taped to the instrument panel. They were too late to prevent the attack on the trench. The Iraqi fighter-bombers successfully dropped their pay-loads over the front lines and were already exfiltrating the airspace.

Despite his speed, AIDS realized he would never catch the flee-ing fighters. He looked groundward and saw that possessed infantry was assaulting the Demons below. Sustaining a maximum G-force, he threw his jet into a dive. He did not have any ground attack weap-onry aboard, but he opened up with his 22 mm gun.

His control panel screamed a warning; an incoming missile. One of the Mig-23s had fired an R-23 Apex air-to-air projectile.

AIDS screamed inside his host, "Fuck!" then threw his aircraft into a roll and reached to deploy his countermeasures. He knew he was too late.

The missile exploded under his aircraft and tore through the starboard engine. AIDS's experience told him the impact was fatal. A Christmas tree's worth of warning lights confirmed his instincts.

He reached under his seat and pulled the ejection handle. As the plane broke apart around him, AIDS was filled with a sense of certainty that he still had a role to play in the grand scheme of things.

I will survive this, he thought—and then he was rocketed out of the crippled aircraft.

JOSEPHINE HAD BEEN MONITORING the movements of Angels within the Iraqi forces when she observed an Iranian aircraft struck by an air-to-air missile. She watched as the possessed pilot ejected and began the perilous descent to the desert below. Josephine rushed toward the imperiled Demon's location as he landed upon the ground, still within possession of his living host. She recognized AIDS.

"You are lucky to have survived," she said.

"Yeah," he said. He shook his head to clear it and staggered to his feet. "You're Josephine, right?" He had not left his host.

"Yes," she replied, confused. "You should leave this mortal, and I will open a door as quickly as you like. Right now, you're between the lines."

"Weren't you routing us our coordinates for interception?" the Demon asked. "What are you doing out here?"

Josephine wondered if the Demon's brain had been scrambled in the ejection, however, she felt an urgency that superseded his moronic inquiries. "No, nor have I ever routed coordinates" she said. "Now please, we must get out of here. The Angels have us in quite a bad place."

AIDS's face changed—the dawn of understanding. His brow was dark, his voice quiet and malevolent.

"So it would seem."

THE OVERWHELMING SENSATIONS RECEDED from Coronavirus's mind; the departure seizure faded. He sensed an Angel bearing down on him and raised his sword to block the blow. He sliced the Angel across her leg. She fell, immobilized.

Instead of finishing her, COVID fled through the Celestial; he was still a little weakened from the seizure. Thoughts assaulted his mind.

How did they know to have such effective air support at the outset of the engagement?

Typically, either side tried to vector in ground attack aircraft after the presence of the enemy was confirmed. But Coronavirus and his squad had been struck within moments of contact with the enemy.

Were we so sloppy that their Familiars spotted us early?

He grabbed a rough, wooden plank from the floor of the trench and rested it across the gulley. He carved the ancient symbols in the dirt and poured water from his canteen over them. He was relieved when the portal opened, but he could not shake his feelings regarding the ambush.

ANGELIC REPORTS FLOWED INTO the air base's control room, a veritable flood of information and confusion, the controlled chaos of combat. Zinc received confirmation that five Demons had been killed. He also learned about Genevieve's death, Gallium's daughter. Before he had time to process the awful news, he got a correction—severely injured but expected to survive.

Schitz confirmed that AIDS had been shot down over the battlefield and was anxious to ascertain his status. Angelic forces were initially unable to confirm or deny a successful bailout. Later, reports arrived that the Demon had ejected safely and had evaded enemy forces once he was on the ground.

"We almost ended up with the bonus for a change," Zinc said over a secret radio channel.

"Pity you didn't," Schitz replied.

"Well, you can always give him to us," Zinc said.

The Demon's voice cracked through static on the other side of the line. "No, the easiest course is not always the best."

"Fair enough," Zinc said.

A Familiar entered the communications room. Zinc said, "Stay safe, Gallium," and killed the connection.

SCHITZ FIDGETED THROUGH THE Return Ceremony. He was not overly anxious to engage in the post-mission dialogue certain to follow such a brutal ambush. Although he had been forced to serve up a high number of Demons to Zinc, Schitz secretly hoped that Anaphylaxis would rally his squad and fend off the attack. He was glad that he pulled Anorexia from the mission. Before he landed the F-14, Schitz was informed by Zinc that five of the six Demons had been killed. Anorexia surely would have died. Schitz turned when he heard a familiar voice.

"There you are," AIDS said. The younger Demon was storming forward.

Schitz extended his hand. "Glad you're still with us."

AIDS seemed reluctant to shake. "Glad to be here. I was lucky."

"Bailed out, cleanly?" Schitz asked.

"Yes," AIDS replied. "I ran into Josephine on the ground."

"Good fortune for you."

AIDS response was clipped and testy. "Yes, it was, especially since she was the one relaying us the Iraqi's flight coordinates."

"I'm sorry?"

AIDS's eyes never left the commander. "You said that Josephine was sending us intel on the Iraqi fighters' flight plan."

Schitz recovered nicely. "She is never far from my thoughts," he said. "Old memories, you know." He laughed; the chortle seemed forced. "I said her name by accident."

Suspicion painted AIDS's face. To break the tension, Schitz pointed to the statue commemorating his victory on the Plains of Abraham.

"We had better luck on that day, eh?"

"Yes," AIDS said. "I imagine those brave Demons never questioned what was going on around them and simply got on with things."

"Is there something specific you want to ask?" Schitz said.

"Not really," he said. "I just want to know my 6 o'clock is covered."

Schitz dropped his jovial façade. "It was, and is, despite your churlish nature, my friend."

AIDS hesitated, then backed down. "I'm sorry," he said. "I meant no disrespect. It just caught me off guard when I ran into her."

"Forget about it," Schitz said. "It was a rough day for all of us."

Chapter 13

The Amazon

"The Twentieth Century has seen an explosion of medical breakthroughs that can only be described as an age of medical miracles."

Zinc watched his young medical student carve the letters of his fraternity into the composite armrest in the lecture hall while the professor plowed through his presentation with all the enthusiasm of someone preparing for a colonoscopy. Zinc knew from the host's memory that the student had already read the professor's book about the study of novel infectious diseases.

Nothing quite as boring as endless review, Zinc thought.

Zinc turned his attention back to the lecturer. "It is imperative to remain vigilant and to remember the dark ages from which we have emerged. It would not take much for us to find ourselves mired in the depths of another deadly pandemic."

Mortals are completely inept.

Zinc thought about his partnership with Schitz. The mortals had identified his affliction but would never unravel its mysteries while the Demon lived. In fact, they would probably not uncover the secrets of his illness for centuries after his death.

Someone tapped Zinc on the shoulder. He turned to find Lord Krypton.

"They said you'd be here," the young Standard Bearer said.

"What do you want?" Zinc asked. He hated to have his recreational time interrupted.

"I'm looking into the death of my mother," Krypton said.

Zinc showed no expression.

"A tragedy," he said. "But I don't understand your investigation. She was killed in battle. Lamentable, but it happens."

"It's my understanding that she went to Vietnam in pursuit of Schizophrenia," Krypton said.

"Hardly surprising," Zinc replied. "She dedicated large portions of her life to pursuing him."

The lecturer said something about Ebola. Zinc leaned forward. He wanted to hear, but Rachael's son leaned closer.

"Aren't you the one who told her Schitz's location?"

"I was."

Zinc cut his eyes toward the young Angel—a menacing look most residents of Heaven would have recognized as a danger sign. Krypton was undeterred.

"How did you come across the information?"

"How does anyone know anything?" Zinc said. "Familiars." He made no attempt to hide his irritation.

"Which ones?"

"I couldn't possibly remember," Zinc said. "Perhaps you have forgotten, but I am the Supreme Commander. All information flows through me."

Krypton's reply was a hiss. "Well, you're in luck, in more ways than you could possibly know. I have already spoken to all the living Familiars who were covering Indochina at the time. Matthias Gatwick attended the briefing prior to the ill-fated mission. Was it he who provided the intelligence?"

"It could have been," Zinc said, painfully aware that his response sounded lame.

"It wasn't," Krypton said, a hungry cat pouncing on a mouse. "He informed me that he had no knowledge as to the origination of the intelligence. But do you know what's even more interesting?"

"I am sure you are about to tell me," Zinc said.

"Matthias Gatwick, a very senior Familiar, thought it odd that he was unaware as to the origin of the intelligence."

Zinc turned and looked Krypton full in the face. The senior Angel's gaze burned with indignation and irritation. "I speak to scores of Familiars on a daily basis and don't have a need to remember who told me what, just what they have told me."

"Well, I suppose so," Krypton said, "which is why I said that you are lucky. The three junior Familiars who were in Southeast Asia at the time are now deceased. It must have been one or all of them

326 • OVER THE BREADTH OF THE EARTH

that supplied the information."

Zinc shrugged. "I don't see why it matters."

"Well, by itself, it might not, but there are a lot of inconsistencies."

"Inconsistencies?"

"Well, we've covered the murky circumstances pertaining to the origins of the intelligence. Then there is the matter of your absence. I was told that you were called away by one of your lackeys. I didn't bother to question her, as I'm sure she's a steel trap, but I did speak with Uranium II."

Krypton paused for effect.

"Get on with it," Zinc said. "You long ago began to bore me."

Krypton's face was hard. "Well, he didn't have much to say on the subject either. Quite the stone wall. So, what was the meeting about?"

If Uranium II provided a cover story, I might well contradict it if I make one up. That was sloppy.

"If it had been important, I might remember. Since I do not, it was apparently inconsequential," Zinc said.

"How convenient," Krypton said.

Zinc looked at the offspring of his late lover. Krypton resembled a mortal Algerian; he had both European and African features.

He's not my child, Zinc thought. *Hair and eyes are too dark. Good looking lad. Pity I may have to trade him to Schitz.*

Thinking the conversation was over, Zinc returned his attention to the front. He winced when he heard Krypton's voice in his ear.

"Lastly," Krypton said, "there is the matter of the battle itself. My mother was one of Heaven's most ancient and perhaps its most impressive strategists. Seems odd that she was killed, and her cadre wiped out. Odd... almost malevolent."

Zinc did not turn around. He did not think he could hide the pain behind his own eyes. "I think that it was unfortunately her time. If I could change it, I would. I loved her, you know."

Zinc gathered himself and turned. Krypton appeared disarmed by the candor. A lone tear trickled down the younger Angel's face.

"Well, I will not rest until I have uncovered the truth behind her demise. If you loved her, as you claim, surely you would want any subterfuge surrounding her death to be brought to light." As though reading Zinc's thoughts, Krypton continued, "I have already received authorization from God to conduct my inquiry without any other responsibilities. Don't count on sending me on any dangerous missions like my mother."

Zinc without mirth. "Best of luck."

When Krypton rose, Anna Gold and Constance Silver, who'd been watching the encounter from the Celestial, put their hands on their swords. Zinc waved them off, and Rachael's son departed, unmolested by the bodyguards.

Zinc swore under his breath. "It's always something."

He left his distracted, overachieving host and made his way out of the lecture hall.

I will have to deal with this quickly. If I am discovered, Heaven's justice will be swift and merciless.

THE ANFIELD CROWD SHRIEKED with jubilation. The final home match of the 1989-90 season closed out with a 1-0 win over Derby County. AIDS smiled at Schitz from his ecstatic host.

"Nice escape from the routine," AIDS said.

The two colleagues made their way to the street.

"Indeed, it is," Schitz said. "Come on, let's get a pint while we're still in these mortal bodies."

The drinks came and Schitz was filled with a nostalgic feeling of comradeship.

"I've missed these quieter times," he said. He slurped at his dark beer.

"Me too," AIDS said. "Iran was tough, Afghanistan was tougher."

Schitz sipped and recollected the losses. He had traded Korsakoff Syndrome and Haemophilus Influenzae to Zinc by sending them into a Mujahideen ambush. AIDS's grandmother, Hypertension, had perished in an unplanned crash after a Stinger hit her Mi-8 helicopter. Now, II Corps consisted of AIDS and six others.

"I was sorry to hear about your grandmother," Schitz said. "Brave woman."

AIDS tossed back his drink and signaled for another. "Thanks."

"So, who do you want from the most recent class for II Corps?" Schitz asked.

"So much for quiet," AIDS said.

"I figured you'd be happy to take first pick," Schitz said. "MERS has been a pretty good squad member from what I see."

"Yeah, he racked up some pretty good kills in the Gulf War and Panama."

The Gulf, Schitz thought. *I traded Borderline Personality Disorder, Munchausen Syndrome, and Desynchronosis in a tank battle in the desert.*

He could still see the tanks exploding when they were struck by from the shells of the Americans' M1-Abrams. And once the mortals died, Zinc had been waiting in the Celestial to finish off the seizing Demons.

"The new class only has eight Demons," Schitz said. "Autism still has seven. You and Anorexia each have six. I can give you three. Anorexia three, and Autism two."

"Seems fair," AIDS said. "I guess I'd like Epstein-Barr Virus, unless you've slept with her."

Schitz chuckled. "No, I haven't. And since MERS won over Von Willebrand before you could call her your own, then their daughter is the next best thing?"

"It sounds degenerate when you put it that way," AIDS said.

He was mopping spittle and beer from his chin.

"No judgment here," Schitz said.

AIDS leered from behind his mug. "You're not landing the maidens at your usual rate," he said. "Distracted?"

Schitz felt his jaw clench involuntarily.

He's always digging... always looking... always questioning.

"Since you asked," Schitz said, "the football match is today's appetizer. The main course is in a few hours."

"Well, well... the old stallion rides again," AIDS said.

Schitz exited the mortal's body.

"This has been great," he said. "But now, on to better things."

I OVERDID IT, SCHITZ thought.

He watched the subway career down the tracks. He had infected nearly everybody aboard. The train took the turn at full speed and disappeared.

No matter. They'll probably all die in a crash in the next fifteen minutes.

He made his way to the Metropolitan Museum of Art. Zinc was waiting in an exhibition of Egyptian Art.

The conversation went as usual: sarcastic barbs, unemotional planning for the deaths of comrades, and reminiscing about the past.

"What's wrong with you?" Zinc asked.

"Nothing, why do you ask?"

The Angel scrutinized the Demon. "You've just made three consecutive unbalanced trades. I am more than happy to be on the winning side, but I suspect something's up. What gives?"

Schitz bit his lower lip.

Now or never, he thought.

"I... uh... I have... well, I came across an interesting name in one of my reports the other day."

"Yes?"

"Anna... of the Gold House," Schitz said.

"You are investigating my security?" Zinc asked.

"No," Schitz said. "Believe it or not, I had a life before you and I entered into our little agreement—a life separate from this eternal and damnable conflict."

"Go on."

Schitz plowed ahead. "I have considerable interest in the woman. I would like to discuss a trade for her; something along the lines of the one we made for your father."

Zinc's head snapped back. "Why would you want to kill my bodyguard?"

Schitz could not wave his arms fast enough. "No, no, no, I do not want her dead. I want... well... dammit, I want her! I plan to elope with her."

A momentary pause, then Zinc exploded in laughter. "You old dog," he said. "I'd heard rumors about trouble in your past and I know Anna was in Egypt, but I never put two and two together. You and her—"

Schitz snapped. "Do we have a deal or not?"

Zinc was suddenly very interested in a piece by Raphael. His head cocked to one side, then the other as if imagining what the work would look like upside down. He clucked his tongue inside his mouth, a habit Schitz found mindless and irritating but the Demon remained quiet.

"I want the Cancers," Zinc said. "Every last one of them. My wife and several valued colleagues died in a crusade to eliminate them. If you get Anna, I get the Cancers."

"I can make that happen," Schitz said. "It will take some doing; we will need a major conflict since the Cancers are spread out across three separate commands—something in Afghanistan, I imagine. There's always trouble there. The Graveyard of Empires and all that. But it will take time, and I will only arrange this if she is agreeable to reconnect with me."

Zinc doubled over in laughter. "You want me to hand over my bodyguard for your carnal pleasure with the promise you will pay me later?"

For the first time that Zinc could ever remember, Schitz did not have a snarky response or a sarcastic comment. The Demon's eyes watered in what could only be described as genuine emotion.

"We loved each other once," Schitz said. "I would like to have the chance to discover if we love each other still."

Zinc was oddly touched by Schitz's honesty. "Well, you have never failed to honor an agreement. We have a deal. But it may take a while, things are a little hot for me right now."

The Demon took a small pad from his robe and scribbled symbols on it. He handed the sheet to Zinc.

"Two weeks at this location," Zinc said. "I was exiled for a while there."

"As you request," Zinc said. "If we are not there, she has determined not to meet you."

IN THE DEMONIC WORLD, two mortal weeks slipped by in a matter of minutes. But, for Schitz, the fourteen days since the meeting at the MET crawled by with the speed of an arthritic turtle. He tried to appear invested in his work. He assigned the newest Demons to their various postings. He instructed the Academy graduates but didn't bother to learn much about them. They would likely be traded to Zinc sooner or later. He had assigned Epstein-Barr Virus and her brother Anaplasmosis, along with Eileen's Syndrome to II Corps under AIDS. Hand-Foot-Mouth Disease, HAB Illness, and MAC went to III Corps under Anorexia. Autism and I Corps received Hookworm and Deep Vein Thrombosis as a reinforcements.

Schitz was perplexed by how to turn over the Cancers while keeping his friends safe. He did not wish to lose Autism, Anorexia, or even AIDS.

I'll just work something out on the fly.

The night came to travel to the ruined temple deep inside the rain forest. Emotions swept over Schitz in unending waves. Just before he left, a thought crossed his mind.

I told Zinc that I planned to elope with her. What if she expects a wedding; some ceremony?

Titus had been skeptical but agreed to accompany Schitz to the Amazon. The Priest fidgeted for an hour next to a pile of stones in the ruined ancient temple while Schitz disappeared in the jungle.

When Schitz returned, he was draped in the spotted hide of a jaguar. Blood from the freshly skinned kill dripped on the Demon's feet.

"If I didn't know better, I would think you were getting married," Titus said.

His words were still echoing when a portal opened close to one of the temple's old doorways.

From out of the portal, an elegant, lithe figure stepped into the room. Schitz saw Titus's jaw drop. Though Angels usually wore white, Anna's shimmering outfit far outstripped any traditional garb. An elaborate veil concealed her face. Gold earrings fell to her shoulders and gold bracelets adorned her wrists. She walked toward Schitz and the stunned Priest.

Titus recovered enough to whisper out of the side of his mouth. "We are so even now."

Schitz made no attempt to respond. All he could do was smile. Anna pulled back her veil. Her face was as radiant as it was flawless and beautiful. She giggled slightly and threw her arms around Schitz.

He heard her whisper, "I never thought a day like this would happen."

"I know," he said.

Titus cleared his throat. "You'll have to forgive me," he said. "I've never done anything quite like this before. This is slightly unorthodox. I'll have to wing it."

His humor broke the tension.

"Take hands and face each other," Titus said.

Schitz held Anna's hands in his own and gazed into her deep brown eyes. She was as beautiful as the day he had met her in the desert.

Titus began. "We give thanks to... ah, well, let's see... we give thanks to the good fortune that brought you two here today. May you both love one another and remain faithful to each other for as long as you both shall live or eternally. As High Priest, I declare you married, at least as far as the Church of Hell is concerned." He looked at Anna. "You might have to take this up separately with your boss."

Titus bid them farewell and the happy couple stood in silence.

"Let's take a walk," Schitz said. "I know a great place nearby for us to talk."

He led her through the vine-covered, stony ruins until they came upon a pool.

"It's beautiful," Anna said.

"It's yours," Schitz said. "No Demon will set foot in this forest. I can arrange that. You can fight the Atrophy by healing the various local tribes."

Anna grinned. "I will be Our Lady of the Amazon."

"An Amazon for the Amazon," Schitz said.

He moved to kiss her, but she was already disrobing and slipping into the water. He followed.

"How did any of this happen?" Anna asked.

He held her in the water.

"I will explain everything later."

"Good plan," she said.

She wrapped her legs around his waist.

"There have been others," he said.

Anna placed a firm index finger over his lips.

"The only thing I care about is if there will be others from now on. Will there?"

For the first time in his life, Schitz felt certain he could answer honestly.

"Never," he said.

THE DEAL FOR ANNA tipped the scales in Heaven's favor. Zinc shuffled through a pile of reports and stewed.

There will be unauthorized killing. That will wipe out whatever advantage we have gained. And I will be short one bodyguard.

The balance of power did not concern the Angel as much as losing Anna. A fully trusted replacement would be hard to find. Beyond someone who might die to protect him, Zinc needed someone who obeyed orders without question, even when they involved killing other Angels.

My friend Schitz has a thing for Angels, Zinc thought. *Lady Calcium died because of his affections... now, there is Anna Gold.*

Zinc's thoughts turned to his times on the Isle of Neutrality—and Spanish Influenza.

How odd that Schitz never indulged.

The door rattled.

"Who is it?" With an instinct born of more encounters than he could remember, his hand moved to the sword at his waist.

"Afraid of your own father?"

The Elder Zinc moved through the doorway with his reacquired grace.

"Can't be too careful, can I?" Zinc asked.

"You look troubled, Son. What's on your mind?"

Zinc resumed his seat; his father slumped in a nearby chair.

"I need to find a replacement for Anna."

"Ah, part of your dealings with the Devil?" The Elder stroked his trim beard. "How about me? I don't have anything better to do, and no one would be quicker to lay down his life for you."

Zinc shook his head. "You're supposed to be enjoying your retirement. Looking out for me can be dangerous work. Even if there are not many challengers to my supremacy, there are still always issues."

A vivid picture of Krypton's accusing face came into Zinc's mind.

"Nonsense," replied the elder Zinc. "You won't find anybody you can trust more than me, and I need something to occupy my time. One can only heal mortals and tell stories for so long before he goes mad."

Zinc waved his hand in surrender.

"So," his father asked, "what is my first task?"

"Well, since you asked, I am having trouble with Krypton," Zinc answered.

"A troublemaker of the first order. He interrogated me for some time about the nature of my escape."

"What did you tell him?"

"Not much. Didn't see how it was any of his business."

The older man's eyes twinkled. For a moment, Zinc was lost in memories shared by fathers and sons. He returned to the present. "Well, that won't stop him; he's smart, and surprisingly well connected. Somehow he got God to grant him freedom from the chain of command while he conducts his investigation."

"No wonder the little prick was so smug."

"The best thing to do would be to kill him," Zinc said.

He watched for a reaction. There was none other than a quick twitch of an eyebrow.

"My, my, what an Angel you have become," the Elder said. "How do you propose to accomplish his demise?"

They sat in silence for a moment. Outside the window, the Eunoe glistened in the perpetual sunlight. The father broke the stillness.

"If he thinks you are trapped, he will be more aggressive. Give him a reason to believe he is about to discover your secret and he will attempt to outmaneuver you."

Zinc did not know whether to be dismayed or proud.

"You certainly have a mind for this," he said.

His father's voice was flat, matter of fact. "No one lives as long as I have without having a little Demon in him."

"I still can't believe you got Satan's High Priest to marry us!"

Anna was in high spirits. She walked hand in hand with Schitz along the rough trail through the Andes Mountains.

"If I'm honest, it was a last-minute thought," Schitz said. He drew in a deep breath and tried to fill his lungs with the ever-thinning air. "But I thought it would be a nice touch."

"It gave everything a nice, official feel," Anna said. "But I don't want to know what you did to press gang your High Priest into doing that."

Schitz offered his hand to help Anna up a rock formation. She glanced at it with disdain before scrambling to the top on her own.

"Well, if you don't want my help, I guess you're not interested in a kiss either," he said.

"You talk too much sometimes," she said.

She kissed him and pulled him to the ground.

A while later, gasping for breath, they held one another and gazed over the landscape. The Incan trail was steep even within the Celestial. The hike had been arduous; the lovemaking, though brief, intense. They sat until they had recovered. They continued towards Machu Picchu.

The quiet ruins filled Schitz with memories. There is an odd self-voyeurism in returning to a battlefield where one has fought. He could see himself engaged in his confrontation with Gold and Silver.

"So, this is where my absentee father met his end?"

They were making their way up the broken steps of what had been Gold's temple. The skeletal stones had long been picked clean of their glittering ornamentation. Schitz unstrapped the heavy item he had been carrying.

"Yes," he said. "This is where we fought." He unwrapped the sword he had taken from Gold. "From what I am told, this means something to Angels."

He handed her the sword by the handle.

"My father's sword," she said. "In my time, I could have never inherited it, nor would I have due to my questionable paternity, but it is amazing to hold it."

"Keep it," Schitz said, "my gift to you, Lady Gold."

"I've been thinking about that," she said. "I would like to take on your name. Anna Nervosa has a nice ring to it, or maybe Anna Gold-Nervosa. Yes, that's the one."

"Well," Schitz said, "since I am a Sir, you should keep your title as well."

"Nice to know I married so well," she said. "You must have put all that training in the desert to good use, Sir Schitz."

Her face reflected the beauty of the setting sun. "Indeed," he said. "There is no doubt that I owe you my life."

"Well, then it only fits that you have pledged the rest of it to me," she said.

"Speaking of the rest of our lives," Schitz said, "I don't know what sense of normality we'll be able to enjoy."

"You mean since I will be hiding in the jungle, and you will remain in your world of double-dealing treachery?"

"Something like that."

"What you've given me is worth any inconvenience, and I do not mean this sword." She let the blade tumble to the ground. "I am free. I answer to no one. And you are mine. Just promise you will drop in from time to time."

"I do so pledge," he said.

She kissed him. "Good," she said. She nibbled on his lower lip.

Schitz's only response was to step out of his robe.

KRYPTON FOLLOWED SEVERAL OF the Angelic fighters that made their way through the Chechen ranks and ambushed Demons and Russians in the fighting raging around Grozny. In response, the Russians began mass executions. Krypton glanced down into a trench along the outskirts of the city. It was filled with the corpses of those the FSB labeled as collaborators. Most were unfortunate civilians with no ties to the rebels.

The nature of war, Krypton thought.

He had pieced together most of Zinc's treachery. The supreme commander was in league with the enemy. Through this subterfuge, he had secured the release of his father. Krypton did not have all the details of his mother's death, but he knew it involved some sort of backstabbing.

Perhaps she uncovered his duplicity.

He walked past a wrecked Russian tank and tried to figure out how to undergird his theory with proof. He continued tracking the Angels Zinc had sent into battle. Krypton anticipated they would be attacked by Demons, an ambush he hoped would yield some evidence. Ideally, he might capture and interrogate a Demon to determine how the enemy was able to ambush the Angels so easily.

A challenging feat, but Krypton trusted his abilities and his instincts. He was acting alone. Fewer associates meant lower exposure.

If I trust no one, I cannot be betrayed.

Suddenly, there was activity among the Chechen Rebels. The Russian troops had regrouped and were pressing forward. Krypton did not see any Demonic auras within their ranks. A moment later, a Russian gunship whirled past overhead, and Krypton recognized the trap. Within the Celestial several of the Angels turned and rushed toward him.

Zinc has not sent these Angels out to be killed by Demons. He has sent them after me, he thought.

Krypton fled along the dirt road toward the Russian troops. The road was mined, the reason the lead tank had stopped. Krypton scampered up the side of the tank and dove through the commander into the claustrophobic body of the metal beast.

Once he was in possession of the tank driver, he pushed the massive T-72 forward until the treads hit a mine. When the explosive device detonated, Krypton stepped into the Celestial. The blast tore through the compartment and shredded the bodies of the mortal occupants. Krypton was thrilled to see the seizing bodies of the Angels who had possessed the infantry near the tank. Their hosts had been torn to ribbons.

Krypton dispatched the seizing Angels, a slice here—a stab there. He stayed his blade when he reached the last of his attackers, a young male Angel with sandy brown hair. Krypton bound the Angel's hands and feet with Celestial rope. He propped his captive against the hull of the burning tank and slithered back, low to the ground, amongst the Russian troops who were engaged in a fierce firefight with the Chechens.

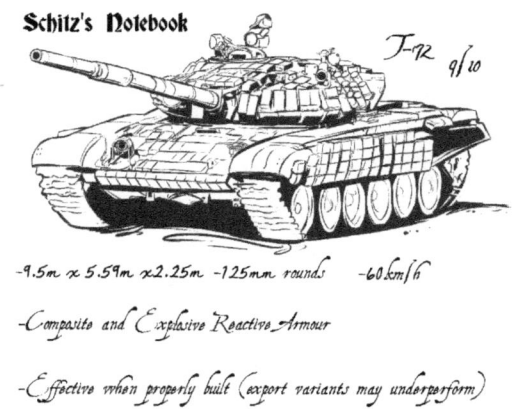

Schitz's Notebook

T-72 9/10

-9.5m x 5.59m x2.25m -125mm rounds   -60km/h

-Composite and Explosive Reactive Armour

-Effective when properly built (export variants may underperform)

Krypton counted four surviving Angels. Sensing a trap, they sent a solitary patsy to rescue their bound comrade. The other three took up positions on the edge of the road. Krypton maneuvered behind them. They had drawn throwing stars and were ready to cover their comrade.

Rain began to fall, its patter helping to cover Krypton's approach. He wrapped his arm around the neck of one and slit her throat. He extended the cutting motion out and to the side, opening a mortal wound in another Angel's chest. Krypton picked up his would-be assassins' throwing stars and stepped onto the road where he dropped the other "guard" and the Angel attempting to rescue his companion.

Krypton raced to the captive and laid a blade against his throat.

"We can do this one of two ways; one will be very, very unpleasant."

The Angel cringed. The Russians continued to fire past them, occupied in their own mortal confrontation. An infantryman collapsed to the ground beside them. His groans punctuated Krypton's threat.

"What do you want?" the Angel asked. He was still in the pains of his departure seizure.

"Who are you?"

"Samarium."

"A resurrectionist?"

"Not quite," the Angel said. "I have not yet been given a House."

"Oh, and let me guess, you were promised one after completion of this mission."

The captive nodded. Krypton felt flush with victory. He had survived Zinc's go at him and would emerge with evidence. He continued the interrogation. "And who were they?" he asked, pointing toward the dead.

"Brothers and sisters of mine. They would have been the foundation of my House," he replied.

"Where did you originate?"

"We were descendants of Boron, unincorporated when he fell," the Angel replied.

"Interesting," Krypton said. "I urge you to respond truthfully to my next question. Who authorized your attack on me?"

"You know I can't say," Samarium replied.

The response means that Zinc did not paint me as a traitor, Krypton thought. *Instead, he established this as an unauthorized action probably to ensure secrecy. That precludes the possibility of reinforcements.*

"Look around," Krypton said, "nobody is coming for you. I can't kill you because you are my only evidence."

Samarium relaxed considerably. Krypton continued, "Don't get too comfortable. Just because I need you alive doesn't mean I won't do some lasting damage to you."

He slid his sword back into its scabbard, then punched the restrained Angel in the face. Samarium's head snapped back into the tank. He moaned. Krypton smiled and reached down into the mud and picked up two teeth.

"Ain't that a bitch?" he said. "I've heard that you can reset a lost tooth with a paste made from crushed Manna and Elixir. I don't know how well that would work for a dick, though."

"Please don't." Samarium's groans resonated with pain. Blood flowed out of his ragged mouth.

Krypton drew a Celestial dagger with one hand and held it between Samarium's legs. "Look, look at me," he said. "I'm going to start cutting things off that Manna won't heal right. Tell me who authorized the hit."

"I can't," Samarium said. "I'll tell you anything else, but please don't do this."

The Angel looked down. Krypton flicked the knife and severed a large portion of Samarium's nose.

"Shit, I bet that hurts," Krypton said with a laugh, "probably less than your balls, though. I will take you back alive to tell God the truth of your story. The state I take you back in is up to you."

"It was Zinc... it was Zinc. Oh, *fuck*, it was Zinc!"

"Good," Krypton said, "And you will repeat this story before God and the Priests?"

Samarium nodded.

"Good," Krypton said. "There's just one more part, and I am sorry, because you're not going to like this, but I was bluffing a little when I said 'look around.' Truth is, I don't know if reinforcements are coming or not. But I can't have you running away."

"No... please... in the name of everything holy... pl—"

Krypton drew his sword and hacked off Samarium's legs, one after the other, just above the knee. The Angel screamed until he passed out.

"There, there, it's all over now," Krypton said. He put Samarium over his shoulder. "Now, you're travel size."

Krypton made his way to a battle-damaged building and opened a portal. He was confident that his arrival bearing such a grievously injured Angel would garner quite a bit of attention. He would use the notoriety and make his accusations against Zinc.

He stepped through the portal and heard the chorus of arrival—music to his ears. His elation did not last.

When he stepped into the Great Hall of Heaven, there were no Priests... no passersby. The hall was vacant except for Constance Silver and the former Standard Bearer, old man Zinc.

Krypton realized his blunder even as the elder Zinc said, "We appreciate your predictability."

Encumbered by his captive, Krypton did not even bother to reach for his sword. He went down in front of the stabbing assault clutching the de-legged Angel like an anxious mother clinging to a child.

The last thing he saw was Constance Silver's beautiful face. The last thing he felt was her hand clutching his hair to raise his chin.

"WELL, THAT'S THAT THEN," the elder Zinc said.

Constance wiped Krypton's blood from her blade.

"That's just the beginning," she said. She turned her attention to Samarium. "This poor fellow's not going to make it."

The legless Angel was too weak either to struggle or protest. He died with only a whimper.

She pointed to a Manna wheelbarrow. "Load them under those sacks."

The elder lugged the bodies and Constance expunged all the signs of struggle.

"Now, we make our way to the river," she said.

"This does not seem to bother you," the elder Zinc said.

"All in a day's work," she replied.

ZINC CALLED THE GATHERING to announce plans for restructuring Heaven's chain of command. His half-baked notion included the Familiars and the Priests. He extemporized his opening.

"If we intend to achieve total victory, we need revolutionary plans."

He looked to the back and saw Constance enter with his father. *It is done*, he thought.

"You've been a tough one to find lately," AIDS said.

"What can I tell you," Schitz said. "I'm a busy man. Need anything in particular?"

There was no one in the Great Hall. The echoes made it sound as if the two Demons were shouting. AIDS lowered his voice a notch.

"I just wanted to tell you Satan has taken an interest in my progress."

Schitz patted him on the shoulder. "Good for you," he said. "You deserve it."

"I can't thank you enough for all you've taught me, all you've shown me," AIDS said. "Since Lushno, you have always been there for me."

"Forget about it," Schitz said. "It's what partners do for one another."

AIDS's face shone with pride and an eagerness to please. "I look forward to the day of the final victory," he said. "Perhaps then, we can enjoy a little peace."

Schitz returned the dazzling smile even while he internally regretted his comrade's naiveté.

"Thank you for coming," God said. "Take a load off."

Zinc inclined his head and sat in an ornate, wooden chair—something constructed to impress everyone in the room except the unfortunate individual sitting in it.

"I'll get right to the point," God said. "I am in possession of a letter from Lord Krypton. The envelope says it should be delivered to me upon his death. Though I have not received any word of his demise, no one can account for his whereabouts. Based on the debacle in Chechnya, perhaps he is dead."

Zinc's throat tightened, but his demeanor remained impassive.

"I am as distressed as you, my Lord," Zinc said.

Every instinct told him to maintain eye contact, but his eyes flicked several times toward the parchment in God's hand.

God's face betrayed deep concern. "I'll be forthright," he said. "He makes serious allegations against you in this document. They are quite damning and are presented in a detailed and plausible manner."

Zinc opened his mouth to protest but was motioned into silence.

God continued, "This would not, however, be the first time an Angel was paranoid or inaccurate, particularly one with aspirations to power. I have initiated an investigation through the Priests of Purity. They are usually busy ferreting out half-breeds, but I believe their talents will be well suited to this matter."

The mention of the ultra-secret division of the Priesthood made Zinc's blood run cold. God was not finished.

"I just wanted to inform you of the investigation and to instruct you not to interfere with it in any way. I'm certain it will all be sorted rather quickly. In the meantime, I look forward to the changes in the structure of the chain of command. That is all."

Chapter 14
HIJACKED

Next to the Dark Lord's private chamber, which no one had ever seen save the women he assaulted at will, there was nothing grander in all of Hell. Schitz gazed around the elaborate room and wondered how the Wraiths had managed to get his old bed through the door.

But he was glad—there were a lot of very pleasant memories attached to the bed. The ménage a trois flicked through his head... the students, most of whose names he could not remember... and Rubella. Guilt wandered into his mind for a moment but was quickly displaced by mental images of her smile, her grace, her body—and her undying affection. Now the bed was empty, and he suspected it would stay that way.

"Well, those days are in the past now," he said to the wall. And he smiled and thought of Anna.

The walls stood as testimony to his accomplishments: medals for valor, trophies from battle, gruesome weapons that formed a timeline of battles won, friends lost, and lives taken. A massive oak wardrobe contained more uniforms than he could count. They ranged from before the days of the pharaohs to the DCUs he wore in the Gulf War. Each outfit was cleaned, pressed, and ready for immediate use.

The pelts of beasts, lions, bears, and wolves, all with bared fangs, adorned his bed and floor. Just beyond a small window Schitz could see the haunting blue Styx, the source of Hell's perpetual twilight.

He thought about the vision of eternity he'd learned from the Priests as a child. The world had been a peaceful place where humans lived like the other animals. There was no disease; there was no fear. When death came, it strolled up in friendship and walked away with you like a cherished acquaintance. But the tranquility was shattered, first by the Titans, then by God and the Angels. They lit the world with the glare of day and infused humans with the knowledge that drove them to challenge the very order of the globe. Sickness and fear rose, the only available means by which to drive humans back to their basic instincts.

"And it's been broken ever since," Schitz said.

He watched the souls pass along the river, the eternal remains of those who had died while in a state of fear, sin, pain, or anger, the fuel of Hell. The Devil and the Priests still spoke of a time when Hell would no longer need the river's energy, when the Angels would be annihilated, when the Demons would assume Earth's throne and rule over humanity.

Schitz believed in the dream for a long time. He had not hated humans; unlike Bubonic Plague, he held no desire to eradicate the race. Neither did he disdain them like Autism. No, Schitz had loved mortal women. The redhead from the Paris candy shop came into sharp focus. Had she not died, he might well have abandoned this whole life.

Well, I've sort of abandoned it anyway, he thought.

He reflected on his pact with Zinc and wondered if he were any different from Gold, a Demon trying to establish his own enclave. No, he was different. He carried no dreams of replacing Satan, or God; Schitz simply wanted to ensure his own survival. Besides, life was much easier to navigate with the information he got from the Angel.

He looked out on the Styx and watched the souls fracture on the rocks. The shards formed new entities for the ever-increasing human population. He was struck by the thought that his agreement with Zinc yielded the noble, albeit unintended, consequence of allowing for the creation of countless new souls. Somewhere in the world, these souls would enter the world for the first time. They would live, and contribute, and then pass through the river themselves for all eternity.

The world will continue, he thought. And he wondered where his Lord, the Prince of Darkness whom he despised, would fit into the ultimate picture.

A folded piece of parchment slid under the door and interrupted

Schitz's musings. He unfolded it: A Summons to Inquisition.

Nothing surprising, he thought. But an odd sense of dread pulsed through him, if only for a second.

He jumped a little when someone knocked on the door.

"Come!"

AIDS entered the room. Though only recently promoted, he wore his authority well. Schitz knew the current inquisition was most likely due to AIDS's digging, a perpetual irritation.

Schitz waved towards a chair.

The slightest wisp of condescension clung to AIDS's voice. "You look a little shook," he said.

"I've been summoned," Schitz said. He sounded like a man announcing his intention to go for an afternoon walk.

"That must be a little nerve-wracking," AIDS said.

"No big deal," Schitz said. "If I am adjudged subversive, incompetent, or unworthy of the Lord's service, I will be executed in a matter of minutes."

He fastened the top button of his black and gray uniform jacket, checked the alignment of his medals, and slipped his Knight's Pentagram over his head.

"So glad we finally ditched the robes," he said. "I look so damn dashing in this."

"You seem awfully calm for a man who could be dead soon."

"Do I have a choice?" Schitz asked. "I know I have not done anything wrong. So, I have nothing to fear; besides, no Demon lives this long without someone taking a run at him. I've traveled this road before."

"When do you have to go?"

"Within a few minutes. Let's go find Anorexia and Autism. I would like my retinue to stand with me when I face my accuser."

ZINC PACED THE MARBLE hallways outside the throne room with increasing anxiety. He wondered what it would be like to die. His religion

claimed there was nothing for an Angel after death, the ultimate motivation to bring the final, everlasting victory. Zinc thought of the moment in the Yak-9 over the Eastern Front; he had been certain he would die then, more certain than ever.

How ironic would it be for me to be executed today because of what saved me back then, he thought. He was more concerned of being unmasked in front of everyone—of being identified and branded as a traitor to Heaven's cause.

His frenzy of foreboding was interrupted by the arrival of his contingent: his father, Constance, and Gallium. As always, he put on a brave face for them.

"About time you showed up," he said with a hollow laugh.

"Who's rushing this snore-fest?" Gallium asked. "It is as pointless as it is insulting."

His father's face was drawn, but his voice remained strong. "Those of us who have survived the great wars should be honored, not questioned, and those who have come after should be cherished as they will be called upon to bear the costs of future engagements."

Zinc pushed against the throne room's door.

"Come on," he said. "Let's get this over with."

SCHITZ WALKED DIRECTLY AHEAD of Anorexia, who was tightly flanked by AIDS and Autism. They walked in grim silence through the eerily quiet hallways of Hell, past the Great Hall, and to the Judgment Chamber. With each step, Schitz felt apprehension fall from his body—leaves from a tree. He was leading his cohort into battle, and although he was a traitor to the letter of the law, his string of personal victories stretched back through to the time when he'd vanquished Vertigo.

I have made every choice of my own free will, he thought. *And my judgment has never steered me in the wrong direction.*

He never paused. He strode into the Judgment Chamber with the attitude of a man completely convinced of his own virtue.

GOD ROSE FROM THE throne. Those in the room were already standing; observers crammed into every corner of the floor and in the galleries above. Zinc and his contingent stood by the witness dock. A procession of Priests entered; two swung thuribles; one carried an ornate scepter, which was presented to the final judge and arbitrator. Although God would not speak during the proceeding, all determination rested on whether he raised or lowered the scepter after the evidence had been presented. The leader of the Priests of Purity spoke, and a hushed silence strangled the room.

"We are gathered in this stern assessment as a reminder that each of us who's in the service of Lord God the Almighty is responsible for his or her actions and that grave vengeance will be visited on those too lazy, incompetent, or treacherous to be considered our Sovereign's Angels."

As was tradition, a panel of Angels had been assembled to select instances from the Priests' inquest to be reviewed. Zinc watched as members of the Houses of Plutonium, Neptunium, and Neon arose and sat at a table on God's left hand, while the Priests of Purity took their place to the right. As was customary, the inquest covered events transpiring within the last hundred years. Zinc anxiously awaited the first question wondering just how secret his pact with Schitz had remained.

A member of the Panel spoke. "Tell us of the encounter between the United States Air Force and the North Vietnamese Air Force in May of 1967."

Zinc suppressed a grin.

Of course, they would start with a situation of collusion, he thought. *Will any question not involve Schitz?*

His voice sounded disembodied. "All through '67 we were having great success joining up with NVA units along the Ho Chi Minh trail; the rugged terrain and the seclusion of the route meant that we would be relatively undetected until we emerged to combat the Demons in South Vietnam. Once we controlled the trails, we kept an ever-constant presence along the route, which kept the Demons out and afforded us influence throughout all of Indochina. In contradiction, the Demons started running flights along the trail, which were coordinated with Special Forces on the ground and intended to dispatch of Angels after bombing runs. We could not risk the destabilization of the Ho Chi Minh trail in this manner. Thus we were in quick need of a response to the American aircraft. The North Vietnamese Air Force was operating MiGs at the time, which were generally on par with the American F-4s and F-8s. However, the American numerical superiority justified a flight of Angels intercede to disrupt the Demonic operation."

Zinc paused for a moment, greatly relaxed by his own testimony. He realized, maybe for the first time in a while, his true influence as an elder Angel. He had assessed risk, devised a plan of action, and carried out the well-constructed strategy that would have broad effects on a large, influential conflict. His undermining of it via Schitz was a separate, higher-level game, which spoke nothing to his effectiveness as a commander. Confidence settled over Zinc.

"I led the flight and selected what I determined to be an appropriate number of Angels based on my assessment of necessity versus risk. We engaged the Americans over the Laotian-North Vietnamese border. It was easy to determine which flight to intercept as our scouts reported American Special Forces on the ground.

Schitz's Notebook

F-4 Phantom II

2,370 km/h   680km range   18,000 m ceiling   210 m/s climb
Air to Air: Aim-7, Aim-9 Air to Ground: Agm Cbu, Cbu
Very effective aircraft. (Decent fighter and good for ground attack.
Capable of carrying nuclear weapons. Vulnerable to SAMs

The Demons, as I stated earlier, would be coordinating with these forces to kill the Angels in the vicinity while they seized from the effects of the airstrike. Upon spotting the American F-4s, it was evident that they had arrived in a flight of nine, three of which were possessed by Demons, which meant that our flight was outnumbered three to one. We had anticipated enemy superiority. At the outset of the engagement, four of the F-4s were brought down by surface-to-air missiles. Unfortunately, none of the Demons were killed by the SAMs."

Zinc remembered how he and Schitz had coordinated the location of the encounter and ensured that the SA-2s were in place.

"The remaining F-4s engaged in a running dogfight. We split up. I was able to down an F-4 via an air-to-air missile. I killed the Demon in the air. His host was killed when the jet went up in a fireball and the Demon fell to earth seizing. Unfortunately, my wingmen were not as lucky. Although he managed to damage an F-4, it was insignificant as it contained a non-possessed pilot. This plane disengaged from the fight and disappeared to the East with another unpossessed F-4, presumably for protection. Both my wingmen were downed in the process of damaging the F-4 I just mentioned and perished along with their pilots. I was then engaged by the two remaining F-4s. Without support, I was forced to develop a defensive posture. Despite my efforts, I was struck by cannon fire. The MiG-21

F-4 Phantom II

was durable, and I managed to score several hits of my own via cannon fire on one of the F-4s. The enemy plane and the Demon died. Debris from this kill clipped his wingman. At that point, I was forced to eject due to a series of cascading failures resulting from the battle damage I had sustained earlier in the engagement."

Infantrymen were generally fascinated by aerial duels, and there had been many witnesses that day. By guiding his plane through the debris before ejecting, Schitz had convinced many onlookers that there had been a mid-air collision between the American aircraft. Exactly where Zinc's bailout occurred in the sequence of events was lost amongst the action.

Zinc continued his account for the Tribunal. "Reports later indicated that the damaged F-4 crashed a few kilometers away. The human pilot was captured, but by that point, the Demon was long gone. That day we sustained a loss of two Angels while killing two Demons. The loss of American aircraft combined with the deaths of these Demons delayed another coordinated assault on the Ho Chi Minh Trail for a long time."

God nodded, slightly, which was followed by vigorous gestures of agreement from the Panel. When a smattering of applause broke out among the onlookers, Zinc relaxed.

This is going to resolve in my favor.

SCHITZ ALWAYS ENJOYED RECOUNTING his exploits, so he was delighted when the Head of the Panel asked him to explain the events in Israel, June 1967.

"Anything involving the Holy Land always gets everybody hot and bothered," he said.

The comment brought a chuckle from the crowd. Schitz acknowledged the spectators with a small wave, then continued.

"We've traded Israel with the Angels so many times I sometimes get confused, but in June of '67, I know they held it, and I know they were feeling the heat from our presence in Egypt, Syria, Lebanon, Jordan, et cetera, et cetera. To the world's surprise, they attacked first. They brought down Demons in the Sinai and the West Bank."

All according to the plans I made with Zinc. I gave him our positions and invasion plans—he provided me with Israel's Golan Heights strategy.

"Those were dark days," he said. He knew when he had an audience in the palm of his hand. "The Angels' offensive completely undermined our intricately laid plans for an invasion of Israel. To regain control of the situation, I redeployed a blocking force to the Golan."

With his careful narrative framing, Schitz deftly circumvented the massive (and intentional) failure in security planning that brought on the loss of Demons at the outset of the conflict. Like a sleight-of-hand artist, he directed everyone's attention elsewhere.

"History will note that the Arabs' tanks were too wide for the narrow paths of the Golan. I assembled two teams, one to possess all leading tank crews and another that I led along the flanks."

Schitz broke down the struggle into short, tactical sentences. In his mind, he could feel the desert heat, the dusty hills, and the burning thirst. He remembered the searing waves of burning tank fuel and the piercing whine of jets overhead.

At Schitz's direction, each Syrian tank contained a Demon, and the Israeli movements he had coordinated with Zinc were followed to the letter. The Angels engaged the Demons in the tank, but when they moved forward, they were struck without warning from their flanks by Schitz and his cadre. Schitz had bathed himself in the blood of Angels and the humans they moved within when the Israelis stalled in the Heights.

"So, how did the Angel's get the jump on us in the first place?" someone asked.

Schitz hung his head for dramatic effect. "The error was mine," he said.

Gasps emanated throughout the room. Schitz thought he saw the slightest crease of a smile flit across AIDS's face.

"I had entrusted Lymphoma with reconnaissance prior to the invasion. I realized too late he was not up to the task." Schitz remembered passing along the time and location for Lymphoma's ambush when he had rendezvoused with Zinc in the Laotian jungle. "The poor lad was caught in a roadside ambush a few days later and lost a contingent of neophytes to the Angels."

The Head of the Panel perused his notes. "Moving on," he said.

Relief swept through Schitz's body almost as if he'd consumed several flagons of Brew.

I have covered every contingency, he thought. *I am in the clear.*

THOUGH SHARKS ROUTINELY PATROLLED the waters just off the beaches, the sea looked inviting. Louis Iraragorri reclined in a white, wooden lounge chair the locals had miraculously located and dragged to the beach. A tall, emaciated Somali clad in all white offered Louis a local tea made with cloves and cardamom pods. Louis took the cup and balanced the saucer on the armrest of his chair. He took a small sip and suppressed a grimace.

Setting the teacup on the saucer, Louis retrieved a cheap metal flask from inside his khaki suit jacket. "There's nothing on Earth that a little Cognac can't fix, Anwar."

"As you like, sir," the man replied politely though his eyes reflected disapproval.

Louis wondered if the man was offended because Allah forbade alcohol or because Louis dared to improve upon his beverage. He concluded it was more likely the latter, for a truly devoted follower of the Prophet would not have been waiting on an international arms dealer, smuggler, and drug runner.

Ah, religion, Louis thought, *how easy it is for us to be disingenuous when it comes to religion.*

Louis Iraragorri was not one to judge—almost nothing about him was authentic. His sports coat and slacks bore designer labels added after his cut-rate tailor in Cairo finished them. The "Italian" sunglasses came from a Karachi bazaar. His clothes only began the deception. While "Iraragorri" implied Spanish origin, Louis was French. He picked up the name from one of the many stepfathers his mother had collected. The name stuck while the man had long ago moved on, presumably to better places than a shabby, over-crowded flat on the outskirts of Paris.

Louis had learned on the streets, L'boulevard, of Les Yvelines, that it was wiser to make friends than to make enemies. The lesson carried him to a high position in a far-reaching oper-ation that spanned from the poppy fields of Afghanistan to the streets of New York, Chicago, London, and of course, his native Paris.

"The Somali's know how to do business," he said aloud. "They always have."

He was in the city of Bargal, a city located on the tip of the Horn of Africa, a strategic location built along heavily trafficked shipping routes. Long ago, the Majeerteen Sultanate negotiated with the British to ensure that His Majesty's shipwrecked crews were well looked after and that wrecks were not looted. The Brits kept these dealings unofficial. They did not want to encourage other rival powers to seek out a similar accord.

Louis's thoughts drifted back to his modern-day concerns. Every link in his carefully manufactured chain remained intact and the money flowed like the waves washing ever closer to his knock-off shoes.

He was in Somalia to solve a problem. A local asset had recently become more interested in a tribal dispute than in moving product. Diplomacy in Africa always took second place to bloodshed. Disputes meant death and Louis hated to lose staff members.

Schitz enjoyed returning to Africa nearly as much as he had relished the memories and thoughts of Monsieur Iraragorri. The possession represented an exotic vacation, the type of holiday that suited the eccentric arms dealer and a disillusioned, double-dealing Demon alike.

If only Anna was here, he thought.

Though he stole away to the Amazon whenever he found a safe moment, he still missed her company. And he was ever aware of the possibility that AIDS might decide to follow him, so caution was the watchword.

Schitz closed his eyes and drank in the calming rush of the waves and the aromatic, mingling of salty seawater and the ever-present breeze. For a moment, he was not concerned about AIDS, or Zinc, or the Devil, or God. He felt free, even if only for the moment.

Blaring French hip-hop emanated from his phone.

"Yes?"

With his typical flair for the dramatic, Ligurius spoke in a breathless tone. "Wherever you are, you need to put on a television 5 minutes ago."

"I am in Somalia. Do you think a television is close by? Just tell me what's going on."

"There's an active war going on in the United States!" Ligurius was shouting.

"In the United States?" Schitz laughed and hoped the senior Wraith was exaggerating. "Who invaded them, Mexico?"

"It's a massive Arab terrorist attack. Fifteen minutes ago, an airliner crashed into the North Tower of the World Trade Center in Manhattan."

"Oh, my Lord," Schitz said.

"There's more." Ligurius was calmer now, demonstrating the calm he'd used to climb to the top of Hell's Intelligence Service. "There are several reports coming in that there are numerous Demons and Angels fighting on several different hijacked planes. It's an active war. Most of the Wraiths managed to create portals and slip out but our fighters are up there, AIDS included."

Schitz groaned. The aptly named Operation Wild Goose Chase had been a less violent means of distracting Heaven and Hell's forces. After Hell and Heaven investigated Schitz and Zinc, both had thought it wise to dial things down a notch. They devised a plan.

Wraiths were ordered to travel via civilian airliners. Angels were typically petrified to board the things. A crash meant instant death; at least military planes came with parachutes. Despite their misgivings, Zinc sent Angels after the Wraiths. Although Wraiths could get out, the incantations and concentration required for an Angel or Demon to open a portal rendered an airliner virtually inescapable. While onboard, Angels were temporarily defenseless.

Schitz tasked several Demons with figuring out why the Angels were suddenly so interested in the Wraiths. *Voila!* Both Schitz and Zinc appeared to be busy with their responsibilities. Still, there would be a temporary, though inexplicable, cessation of bloodshed. The ridiculously convoluted plan gave both Schitz and Zinc a breather and pushed the pause button on their conspiracy.

Why is AIDS meddling in this scheme?

The voice on the other end exploded. "Fuck!"

"What happened?"

"Another plane just crashed into the other tower at the World Trade Center. There's no way any Demons or Angels survived."

"This makes no sense," Schitz said. "What's your assessment?"

"Well," the Wraith said, "AIDS is definitely the ringleader on this one."

"Where's his plane?" Schitz asked.

"Last thing I heard was from a Wraith who managed to get out. The plane is heading west over Pennsylvania; appears to be off course."

"Okay, I'm on it."

Schitz raced down to the water and scooped up a handful of seawater. Louis would have to forgive him for destroying the imitation designer shoes. A mass of frenzied Somalis raced down the street in disarray.

Looking for the closest television.

Schitz spotted a broken-down vehicle that was missing its driver's side door. He bolted into the Celestial where he fell to his knees and began tracing the symbols requisite for Earth and Water. He uttered the incantations with a calm he did not feel, then stepped into the Great Hall.

Pandemonium raged. Demons arrived; everyone was either seeking information or repeating unconfirmed rumors. A cluster of Wraiths stood around Ligurius, clamoring and gesticulating as they reported the information they had acquired.

Schitz ran past the Priests and noted that all other arriving Demons were ignoring them as well. No time for ritual in such moments. As Schitz flew to the departing doors, he was certain of two things: that nobody in Hell knew what was going on or what to do. Schitz knew he might benefit from taking a moment and allow whatever plan was unfolding to take place. He was sorely tempted.

But he knew AIDS was on a campaign to spotlight his involvement with Zinc. Schitz and Zinc had put the Wraiths on the civilian planes, so a voice in his head caterwauled that there was no time, that he needed to find out immediately what was going on. Schitz cursed aloud.

Operation Wild Goose Chase was supposed to suspend all hostilities. Why is AIDS involved in any of this?

Schitz knew exactly where he needed to go.

Otis Air National Guard Base was a simple airfield nestled in the idyllic Cape Cod region of Massachusetts. Schitz stepped through the portal and onto the tarmac. He spotted a group of airmen preparing to board an F-15 Eagle. Schitz rushed across the blacktop and jumped into the senior pilot. He arrived just in time to hear instructions from the commanding officer through the pilot's headset.

"Duffy and Nash are already over New York. You guys are slated to intercept the 757 that's currently in the Ohio/Pennsylvania area and most likely bound for D.C. If it heads to NYC, Duffy and Nash can assist you. Be advised that if it's headed for D.C., Langley just reported that their only option is to ram it. They didn't have time to load up their F-16s. Thankfully we had this B ready for your training flight today. Good luck!"

Schitz climbed into the cockpit of the F-15B. He searched the mind of the pilot and accessed information that could fill any gaps in his already vast knowledge of combat aviation. Schitz ran through the system's start-up and, when cleared, launched the fighter into the skies. Then, with break-neck speed, he sliced westward through the air.

THE PLAN HAD GONE off according to the blueprint. The Angels were so focused on the Wraiths they did not notice when the Demons slipped onto the planes. The Angels did nothing to interrupt the hijackings because the humans were not at war—at least not one they recognized. Al Qaeda and the United States were at war; a fatwa had been issued in 1999. The Demons knew they could kill Angels with impunity. Once they were secure within the cockpits, the Demons focused on opening a portal. They stepped through just when the terrorists had time to hit their targets. The captive Angels died in the conflagration.

AIDS received coded reports from Cleveland's air traffic control. All the Demons had successfully escaped from the flights aimed at the World Trade Center and the Pentagon.

Not a bad day, AIDS thought.

He steered the 757 towards Washington D.C.

There were about ten Angels on each flight. That's thirty to zero in one morning's work. Satan will get the world war he's been hoping for. Fantastic!

AIDS still could not figure out what the Wraiths and the Angels hunting them had to do with Schitz and his treachery. He'd hoped that once aboard the plane, the details of Schitz's scheme would become clear, but the slippery Wraiths unaffected by the turbulence easily made portals in the lavatories and slipped away from their pursuers like rats exiting a sinking ship.

AIDS sat patiently while his confederates SARS, MERS, Epstein-Barr, and Parkinson's overpowered the plane. Then, still possessing Ziah Jarrah, he had taken command of the flight.

Everything is going swimmingly, he thought. *Next stop, Washington D.C.!*

SCHITZ SWORE AND PUSHED the F-15 to the limit.

"Can't this fucking thing go any faster?"

His mind raced. Why did AIDS go after the Angels shadowing the Wraiths? Both sides tried to kill Wraiths/Familiars from time to time, but merely to while away the eons between major wars; a warning shot, a message, "We're still watching you." But why risk sending Demons on a plane. Demons seldom came to the assistance of Wraiths. Why did AIDS track an operation that, in its essence, was meant to preserve parity without unnecessary death?

Schitz slammed his palm on the canopy. Every step he took to preserve the balance was fraught with danger. Now it seemed his efforts would be rewarded with another world war.

He saw AIDS's face in his mind—his protégé, his friend—the Demon determined to bring about his ruin.

I won't go down without a fight, Schitz thought.

He checked the control panel and scanned the horizon as his jet tore through the atmosphere.

ANYONE WHO SAW THE youngest member of the disbanded House of Silver on the phone would have thought he was calling his wife—something anyone would do in such dire circumstances. He was, instead, speaking to his trusted Familiar.

"They haven't said much other than that we're going back to the airport," he said in a hushed voice.

He flinched at the response. "They've tricked you. I don't know who thought a handful of Wraiths was worth putting you all on planes, but they've crashed airliners like yours into both towers of the World Trade Center and into the Pentagon. By all reports, the Demons got out before the impact."

"I love you so much, my darling," Silver said.

He turned to the assembled passengers, including his best friend, the youngest member of the disbanded House of Gold. In addition, there were other sons from various dismissed Houses, Beryllium, Iron, Barium, and Cobalt, and daughters of the Oxygen, Nitrogen, and Hydrogen Houses. They called their clique "The Band of the Disbanded" and often found themselves on less than glamorous missions.

"The news is grim. Terrorists have crashed planes into the Twin Towers and the Pentagon. There's no doubt that ours will be crashed as well."

Several passengers began crying. Silver glanced down the long aisle to the sole Demon standing outside the cockpit.

"How is this possible? This isn't a war zone," Gold said.

"They tricked us," Silver said in disgust. "We're fools." He raised his voice just enough for the others to hear. "If we don't fight back, we will all die."

Silver understood the odds. They could never make a portal in this metal coffin thousands of feet in the air.

He saw a steely resolve build in the group. An unpossessed mortal, a man in a humble suit and sneakers, aged about forty years, sporting round, outdated spectacles, spoke. "Perhaps, we should pray."

In response, another unpossessed passenger, a man in his thirties in a baseball cap and t-shirt, started, "Our Father who art in Heaven..."

Without proof... without direct knowledge, these mortals turn to God in this horrifying moment. Silver swallowed his tears and joined the others.

"...thy Kingdom come, thy will be done, on Earth as it is in Heaven."

THE 757, ONCE A green blip on his radar, came into view—a hulking steel projectile hurtling across the sky. Schitz positioned the F-15 alongside the cockpit and keyed the local frequency.

THE RADIO IN THE cockpit crackled. "United Airlines Flight 93, return command of the aircraft to the crew immediately or you will be shot down. Rock your wings if you intend to comply."

AIDS recognized his mentor's voice.

What the Hell is he doing here? AIDS thought.

He stared at the fighter, then looked back. MERS was drawing the sacred symbols in a pile of dirt (he'd brought it along in his backpack). Epstein-Barr hovered over him, water bottle in hand.

"It's ready, we can open it in a minute with incantations," MERS said.

AIDS felt the tension slide away. Even if someone shot the plane down, they could still make their escape as planned. Suddenly, there was an explosion of activity on the other side of the door. Ungodly screaming was followed by a thunderous impact into the cabin door. The door buckled. MERS stumbled backward and fouled the carefully constructed symbols.

"No!"

AIDS watched MERS straining to re-secure the door. The passengers were battering the door with something, probably the beverage cart. Another concussion from the improvised battering ram shook the cockpit. Epstein-Barr stepped back from the door and looked at AIDS. Terror etched the face of the hijacker and the Demon alike.

Earth & Water

"We're doomed, we'll never open a portal now," she said.

AIDS snapped commands. "Calm down! You and Parkinson's take the pilot and co-pilot's seat and keep us on our heading."

The shaken Demon took the controls. The door rattled with another impact. The door breached just enough for someone to throw hot water from a coffee pot into the eyes of the mortal hosting MERS. The hijacker fell to the ground writhing; the Demon stepped out into the Celestial.

MERS swore. "Fuck!"

"No, it's useful," AIDS said. "Follow me."

AIDS waited, clearly timing the thumps and bangs against the door.

Bang... 1... 2... 3...

Bang... 1... 2... 3...

AIDS yanked the door open. The lead Angel, clearly anticipating an impact, stumbled into the cockpit. AIDS sidestepped the cart and stabbed the sprawled passenger in the throat with a box cutter. MERS finished the job in the Celestial.

AIDS used the narrow aisle to his advantage. He dodged hot

water, coffee pots, and other ad hoc weapons and slashed away with his box-cutter. Whenever an Angel fell, MERS dispatched him or her in the Celestial.

Adrenaline rushed through AIDS.

We could be hit by a missile at any minute.

He leaped sideways, dodged an onrushing passenger, and buried his knife in the man's back. The mortal fell, brave, but no less dead.

The passengers were ardent in their attack. AIDS and MERS slaughtered them without mercy. The combatants came to a stand-still at the partition between first class and coach. The passengers fanned out over the larger space, no longer required to face AIDS one on one. AIDS grasped his box-cutter and threw it with unimaginable accuracy into the throat of the passenger directly in front of him. As the stricken man raised his hand reflexively towards the wound, AIDS bolted towards him. At the last moment, he jumped into the Celestial, leaving the hijacker to tackle the grievously injured passenger. AIDS rushed toward the Emergency Exit.

He glanced over his shoulder to see three Angels in desperate pursuit. MERS stabbed the lead Angel in the back only to be brought down himself by another Angel who came from behind him. AIDS slammed into the Emergency Exit and heaved up on the handle. Instinctively judging the arrival of his enemies, AIDS spun and pressed his back against the exit door. His timing was perfect; he caught the lead Angel square in the solar plexus, just as he was rais-ing his Heavenly weapon to strike. The Angel was thrown back into his fellow, both bowled over by the kick.

After regaining his footing, AIDS turned back to the door.

THE F-15 BUFFETED ABOUT behind the 757. Schitz had dropped back into a firing position. A mechanical whine signified that he had acquired missile lock. The AIM-9 Sidewinder was already armed. It would fly into the airliner's engine. The propulsion-less bird would auger into the earth—everyone on board would die, including AIDS.

Schitz was reasonably certain he could avoid any repudiation from his actions. He would claim he was ensuring success for the mission. After all, putting Demons on an airliner with Angels was practically asking for all parties involved to end up deceased.

Still, in the back of his mind, Schitz was dissatisfied. If he shot down the plane, he would never know what AIDS had discovered or failed to discover. Then it hit him.

If AIDS is in a plane where both Wraiths and Angels are captive, he can interrogate both simultaneously.

"Damn clever," he said. "I never foresaw that vulnerability."

There would not be a smoking gun, but there would be a pattern—at least one strong enough to lead to his execution for treason. The time to hesitate was over.

He readied to depress the trigger. The heads-up display continued to beep. Schitz increased the pressure on the trigger.

Suddenly, the emergency door of the airliner flew open, and a Celestial figure emerged on the wing.

AIDS WAS CERTAIN THAT he had never attempted something so utterly idiotic. He figured the F-15 would be trailing in firing position. He had guessed the correct side. To his relief, he saw the fighter behind the 757's wing, and slightly below.

AIDS leapt.

The sickening sensation of falling filled his stomach. Then he collided with the nose of the fighter jet. He was aware of the sickening crunch of shattered limbs and imagined slivers of bone were piercing his vessels and organs. He shrieked with a final effort, and threw himself into the possession of the weapons officer behind Schitz.

"WHAT IS GOING ON?" Schitz had to shout over the shrieking missle lock alert.

AIDS's voice crackled over the headset. "I'm dying."

"What's happening *on the plane*?"

"The Angels are trying to retake it," AIDS said. His breath came in great gasps. "Light it up."

He had barely finished the sentence when Schitz launched the Sidewinder. The missile burned across the morning sky before detonating within one of the airliner's engines. The massive fireball buffeted the F-15.

"I'm not going to make it," AIDS said. He was fading fast. "I'm sorry, I'm sorry for a lot of different things."

"Shut up," Schitz said. "We're both going home. You'll have some questions to answer, but you will live."

Schitz grabbed a wax pencil and began drawing the ancient symbols on the canopy.

"What are you doing?"

"If there's a hole, there's a door. I did the symbols for Earth and Air," Schitz said.

He unholstered the pilot's semi-automatic pistol. "There's about to be a hell of a lot of air."

He fired through the canopy. The explosive discharge of the firearm in the enclosed space was deafening. Schitz rattled off the incantations and a portal opened.

"Hang on!"

Schitz put the jet in a stall that resulted in a flat spin.

AIDS groaned. "Iran all over again."

Schitz pulled the dual ejection levers. Both mortals died on impact with the canopy.

Earth & Air

Schitz and AIDS catapulted through the portal.

Schitz arrived in the full grips of the departure seizure. He was vaguely aware of the Priests pouring Holy Water from the Styx down his throat and dragging him away. He gasped when he was plunged into the river's frigid waters.

His faculties gradually returned. When he turned his head, his temple felt like someone was inside trying to hammer his way out, but he could see AIDS.

"What kind of idiotic, suicidal shit was that?"

AIDS winced. "I heard you were sending the Wraiths onto the planes and came up with a plan of my own to catch the Angels shadowing them. Nearly came off perfectly."

"Except for the part where you got stuck on an airliner-turned-Kamikaze plane," Schitz said. To his surprise, his protégé clasped him by the hand.

"You saved me, sensei, and I can never repay you," AIDS said.

"But why'd you do it?" Schitz asked.

"I wanted to impress Satan and thought of a way to deliver massive Angelic casualties and trigger a world war. We killed at least forty today."

"How many did you lose?" Schitz asked through ragged breaths.

"Four," AIDS said.

"Well done," said Schitz, "but it's not all numbers."

"SARS, Parkinson's, Epstein-Barr, and MERS. I tried to get them all out. Almost worked."

Schitz patted him on the shoulder. "What's important is that we lived to fight another day."

"Well, there's a bright side," AIDS said.

"What's that?"

AIDS doubled over in pain while he giggled.

"Now you're not the only one dumb enough to jump out of an airplane!"

Chapter 15

Pawns and Kings

Schitz uncoiled from his bed, a languid python. His head still murky from physical exertion and battlefield injuries, he admired Anna's naked body sprawled across their bed of animal hides. Spending passionate moments with her constituted the most enjoyable part of returning to the Amazon after combat.

Her eyes flickered open. "Shall I ready myself for another round?" Her voice rose from the depths of her soul—a purring sound at once soothing and arousing.

"To my great regret, no," Schitz replied, "but give some thought to an appropriate welcome when I return."

Anna giggled. "In your dreams," she said. "The moment has passed."

M249 Squad Automatic Weapon

He leaned for a quick goodbye smooch. She seized him and wrestled him to the bed with a passionate kiss. "I'm kidding, you know," she said. "After you come back, you will not be able to walk for a week."

"I'll hold you to that," Schitz said.

He opened a portal to Hell, then stepped into the hallway that contained the lodgings of the senior Demons. A mortals' song reverberated in his ears. Its rapid percussion and strumming guitars accompanied him down the hallways where he banged on several doors.

> *Death rides a pale, white horse,*
> *A bloated and infected corpse.*

Autism, Anorexia, and AIDS emerged from their rooms and fell in behind Schitz.

"Once more unto the breach,"[62] Schitz said without enthusiasm. Those closest to him heard his next comment. "Iraq is going to be a shit-show."

> *You can't hide when he's coming your way,*
> *Better prepare for the judgment day.*

Schitz looked through the eyes of the United States Marine Corps Staff Sergeant and pointed to a location on the map he held in his hand. "That's where we're expecting them to be," he said to the assault team.

> *He hews mortals down without hesitation,*
> *Harvesting souls for eternal damnation.*

"Wind from the left. I estimate the target to be three hundred meters," AIDS said from within an insurgent. He peered through the scope of an SVD-63 sniper rifle.

"Fire when ready," Schitz said as he perused the American checkpoint through a pair of worn field glasses.

---

[62] *Henry V*, Act III, Scene 1, William Shakespeare.

(Confutatis, maledictis,[63])
Ready to fire at will.
(Flammis acribus addictis,[64])
prepared for the righteous kill.

The shell from M1 Abrams rocked the flimsy stone structure. Before the dust settled, the infantry rushed into what remained of the building. Schitz watched through the tank's periscope as Autism and Anorexia exchanged gunfire with the insurgents hiding in the rubble.

We're young, fearless, and bold; Ready to tear down the stronghold.

Prone on the roof of a residential building, Schitz sighted along the barrel of his M4 carbine. A round from an AK-47 fired by an insurgent with an Angelic silhouette caromed off his helmet.
"Lucky I ducked," he said.

Summon me amongst those by victory saved,
Or Valkyries will lay me down in a glorious grave.
No mercy asked or given, 'Cause no weakness should be forgiven.

Schitz glanced through the canopy of his F-16 and saw Zinc a few feet away in his own fighter aircraft. He keyed his communications and relayed the location of several Demons.

Sigue el rastro de cuerpos, Porque es el Dia de los Muertos.[65]

As the Marines cut down a group of insurgents with fire from their M-249 machine guns, Schitz and AIDS leapt into the Celestial. AIDS landed a killing blow, but Schitz was knocked to the ground from behind by a third Angel.

---

[63] *Requiem*, Amadeus Mozart, When the accused are confounded.
[64] And doomed to flames of woe.
[65] Follow the trail of bodies because it is the Day of the Dead.

"Look out!" AIDS shouted while straddling his victim. Schitz rolled into a defensive posture just before Autism appeared from nowhere and ran the Angel through with his sword. The remaining Angel, now outnumbered three to one, fled down an alley.

"Glad you're still here," Autism said. He hauled Schitz to his feet.

Death rides a horse black as coal, A raucous, stampeding foal.

The whirl of rotors resonating from a line of AH-64 Apache gunships blared across the early morning landscape.

"Stay close behind me," Schitz said from within the body of a helicopter pilot. "Then you can leap down onto any enemies I light up."

"Right behind you, brother," AIDS replied.

He'll bash your head in,
And slash your skin Rider and steed, each a complete savage,
On the prowl for innocents to ravage.

Schitz stepped from under an awning and fired an RPG-7 at a passing Black Hawk helicopter. It sailed wide.

"Can't hit a home run every time," Autism said.

Ava Maria, I won't want to be ya.
When I drink your blood like I'm downing sangria.

Schitz glanced around the semi-circle of American Army Rangers and twitched his head towards AIDS as the chaplain led the assembled in prayer.

"Oh Lord, we ask that you protect us in battle and grant us victory in the name of your son Jesus Christ."

Schitz crossed himself from within the body of the ranger.

We're locked and loaded, Gonna leave your body lifeless and bloated,
Today's the day, a day for death, the day you'll be taking your last breath.

"This is so nasty!" Autism coughed and shoved a mortar shell jerry-rigged with plastic explosives into the putrefying carcass of a dead dog.

"Just hurry up," Schitz said. He laughed when Autism gagged.

> *Mein Durst nach dem Blut ist geweckt,*
> *Verwüstung anrichten und befleckt,*
> *Es ist der Tag der Toten,*
> *Und nichts ist verboten.*[66]

"Clever bastard," Schitz said as he watched an Angel flee through the Celestial and jump into a fellow American soldier a street ahead of him. Anorexia and AIDS glanced over to Schitz for instruction. "Blue on Blue,"[67] he replied as he slipped into the Celestial and moved up the block. AIDS grabbed the radio receiver and called for an airstrike.

> *Death rides a crimson horse; Its hide is battle-scarred, matted, and coarse.*

AIDS kept his voice level and spoke into the radio mic.

"Final attack heading south to north ROE 420, ground commander's call sign Yankee Two-Five."

A moment later, an F-16 dropped a five-hundred-pound bomb on the Angel Schitz was pursuing. Unable to step into the Celestial for fear of Schitz, his human was torn apart by the force of the airstrike.

> *I've got the death-dealer strapped on my waist, and any minute now,*
> *you'll be erased.*

The blast shook Schitz, even in the Celestial, but he pressed on as he grimaced from the rush of dust and the gust of debris. He drew his dagger and plunged it into the chest of the Angel, just above the sternum.

---

[66] My thirst for blood is awakened, wreak havoc and defile, It's the Day of the Dead, and nothing is forbidden.

[67] NATO designation for "Friendly Fire"

There's nothing on Heaven or Earth that can stop me.
There's nothing you could ever do to drop me.

The call to prayer echoed across the barren landscape. Exhausted, Schitz looked up at the evening sky briefly before continuing to load 7.62mm cartridges into a magazine.

It's blood paid for blood, paid back in full,
And I'm itching for the trigger to pull.

The ground shook as Autism fired an AT-4 anti-tank rocket into a building from which they were taking machine gun fire.

Schitz pumped his fist. "Yeah, get some!"

All the Angels in Heaven,
Couldn't stop this Armageddon.
For the time is now, it's the final hour,
And the reaper holds all the power.

Insurgent Banner

The whine of the jet engine howled in Schitz's ears. He scanned the ground through a night vision scope from the solitude of the fighter's cockpit.

"The desert looks so peaceful from up here," he said to himself.

By now, even you fools should see,
Now I am become death, and death has become me.

The music faded in Schitz's ears, replaced by jet engines overhead and bombs shaking the foundation of the stone house. He looked around the bare abode at his fellow Demons and the Iraqis they possessed. The jets faded into the distance.

"Come on," he said. "We've got work to do."

THE DESERT CAN BE a surprisingly cold place. In all the pages and pages of written words and stories of lore, all the tales passed from one tongue to the next, so much describes the unremitting heat that there is little space left for the bitter chill that slinks into the evening like a jackal into the ruins of a ransacked township. When the blazing sun departs, the frigid darkness stakes its claim. The wind carried the night's coolness over the banks of the Euphrates, whipping up small sheets of sand as it passed across the barren expanse between Baghdad and Ramadi.

Khalid had been born a stone's throw from the slow, flowing river but in the dark, restless night, he had never felt farther from home. Even though he had tracked the banks of the river and the barren stretches of land between his father's humble dwelling and the outskirts of the city many a time, the war had transformed this simple patch of earth into a complex killing field. The Americans wielded devastating weaponry: night vision that could detect an insurgent from miles away, laser-guided bombs dropped with the precision of a champion darts player, helicopter gunships whose appearance on the horizon prophesied death and dismemberment for his men.

Khalid strained to see through the enveloping darkness. From his position beside the road, he could keep watch over the men. They were digging a hole in which they would place their IEDs, artillery shells packed with C4 and rigged with a pressure detonator. The men worked with frenetic industry and hoped they would finish before American firepower detected their movements.

Schitz glanced down at Khalid's cheap digital watch. He admired the straightforward youngster who had dreamed of being a footballer a few short years earlier, before the most recent Gulf war claimed his elder brothers. The boy was sharp; the other men looked to him for guidance. Schitz marveled at the kid's meticulous planning. The morning ambush included options for egress and escape. Khalid saw every possible scenario: the lead Humvee propelled into the air by the IEDs, the bombs failing to explode or exploding late, the Americans disembarking from their vehicles or speeding past. He accounted for Coalition air support and instinctively glanced in the direction of a resting RPG-7 propped on the cool earth between him and a childhood friend.

Schitz thought back through time. *How many brave young men have I known who, despite knowing the full terror of battle, still steel themselves for the contest? Countless.*

A jaunty tune of the Red Coats sprang to his mind. He hummed softly.

> *When cannons are crashing, and bullets are flying,*
> *he who would honor win must not fear dying.*

"You and those old songs," AIDS said. He had occupied Khalid's companion. Schitz allowed a half-smile to creep across his face.

"That you would consider that song old reminds me of how truly young you are, my dear apprentice," he said.

Schitz knew from a United States Air Force Pilotless Aircraft commander possessed by Autism that there were no drones over-head. Anorexia's intelligence report indicated no helicopter activity in the area.

The mission was part of his pact with Zinc. Schitz knew the second and third car of the convoy would be carrying a sacrificial lot of Angels, an offering on the altar of perpetual balance. This was the last arranged exchange he had managed to plan with Zinc. AIDS's perpetual watchful eye strangled Schitz's ability to communicate. Schitz was certain that AIDS fancied him a traitor, but what could be done about it?

A pang of worthlessness cut into Schitz. He had not chosen his path for logic or justice. He merely wanted to keep himself—and a select few others—alive. Any derivative benefit for Hell or the world was an unintended consequence.

The roadside ambush went according to plan. Schitz walked through the grisly post-mortem, invisible in the Celestial. The surviving American troops gazed through him and AIDS as they frantically peered through the sights of their rifles, scanning back and forth for any sign of the enemy. The acrid smell of the burning Humvee mingled with the charred odor of incinerated flesh. The stench of death made the air heavy.

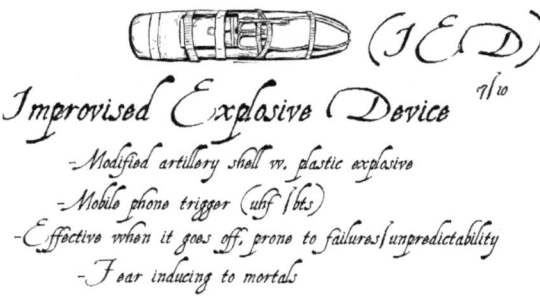

Schitz's Notebook

(IED)

Improvised Explosive Device 7/10

- Modified artillery shell w. plastic explosive
- Mobile phone trigger (uhf/bts)
- Effective when it goes off, prone to failures/unpredictability
- Fear inducing to mortals

The lead vehicle had triggered the roadside bomb in dramatic fashion. A massive explosion rocked the quiet roadway. Shrapnel tore through the truck's compartment and shredded its occupants. When the convoy screeched to a halt, Khalid sighted his RPG on the second Humvee and squeezed the trigger. The moment the rocket left the firing tube, Schitz bounded out of his host. He gazed down at the corpses of the dead Angels.

Caught flat-footed.

The explosive shell struck the vehicle and threw the Angels into a

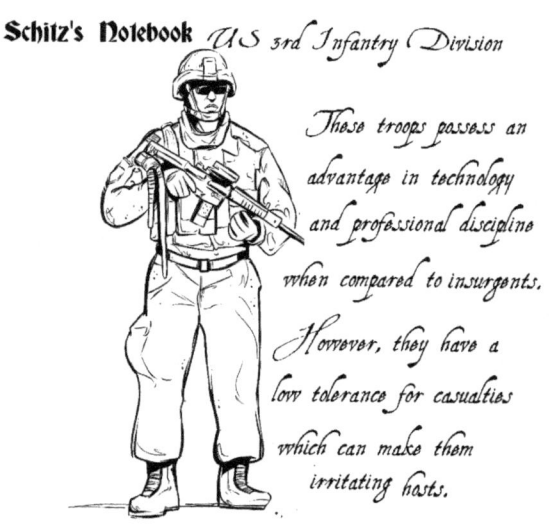

Schitz's Notebook
US 3rd Infantry Division

These troops possess an advantage in technology and professional discipline when compared to insurgents.

However, they have a low tolerance for casualties which can make them irritating hosts.

seizing fit. Schitz slit their throats while AIDS attended to his own victims. The execution was simple, gruesome, and remorseless.

AIDS's voice cut into Schitz's recollection. "Come on!"

The portal was already opened in the wrecked Humvee. The two Demons leaped through the shell of the fighting vehicle and disappeared from the carnage.

Hours after the roadside had returned to normal, the skeletons of the wrecked vehicles were all that remained, the bones of a fallen dragon and shattered knights. Khalid picked through the remains of the battle. The Americans pulled out so quickly they left a few scattered valuables: a magazine of rifle ammo here, a grenade there, baubles for the infidels—diamonds for the insurgents.

Zinc, now within Khalid, saw scattered, random lines carved by a boot upon the sand. To any other eye, the lines would be inconsequential, but Schitz had embedded information temporarily in the Iraqi's brain. Zinc scanned the coded report describing a Revolutionary Guard attack on Coalition aircraft outside of Mosul. Zinc read the conclusion.

"AIDS—only Demon present."

So, *he's finally giving up AIDS*, Zinc thought. *Or is he?*

THE SHRILL CALL TO prayer echoed over the dusty hills surrounding the desolate city of Marivam in Iran.

God finds his way to every corner no matter how barren, Schitz thought.

He leaned against the worn façade of the two-story building, temporary shelter for his members of the 32nd Division of the Revolutionary Guard. He shielded his eyes against the onrushing hues of the morning and saw ten men lounging in the alleyway, equipment strewn about haphazardly. A rifle leaned against the wall. Next to it, a claymore looked lonely and out of place. The parts of a disassembled RPG-7 lay against a tree. Grenades decorated the ground like dandelions in a field. Evidently, the famed discipline of the Islamic Revolutionary Guard Corps was lacking. However, the commander understood. The deployment was both dangerous and seemingly unending. The Americans had committed to a troop "surge," which meant the Iranians were throwing even more Guards units into their self-righteous undermining effort. Schitz fished into the pocket of his drab uniform top and retrieved a loose cigarette, then retrieved a vintage Zippo from his host's ragged trouser pocket.

The orders from Tehran were to shoot down an American helicopter; the Americans felt safe near Mosul, nestled in the breast of their loving Kurd allies. Schitz appreciated the challenge of knocking down yet another Black Hawk, but no, his real concern was Zinc. AIDS knew that Zinc would be there.

AIDS *is damned persistent*, Schitz thought, gritting his teeth.

"Does he know?" a voice shouted in his head, a little too much like the disease he inflicted upon man.

"It doesn't matter if he knows," Schitz snapped. "The Guards have been crossing the border to hit American and Iraqi positions for weeks now. There's guaranteed to be a response. I already know Zinc will be there. I told him to be there only because we need to avoid communicating through schizophrenics."

Now AIDS will surely force the issue, he thought.

Schitz took a deep drag from his dying cigarette and tried to clear his mind. He skipped the butt along the alleyway.

All paths lead to an end. This war in Iraq has given us many opportunities to trade like for like. Both sides are draining blood into the desert sand, but at least now there is a modicum of control.

RPG-7 & Kalashnikov (AK-47)

Schitz saw every face he'd betrayed: Atrial Fibrillation, Lymphoma, Breast Cancer, Metastatic Cancer, Endometrial Cancer, Chronic Myeloproliferative Neoplasms.

He felt good about honoring his promise to Zinc regarding Anna's dowry. The Cancers were falling one by one.

But can I give up AIDS?

He kicked at the dirt—the damnable dirt. He'd lived most of his life in the muck and mire and dust of the earth.

It doesn't matter, he thought. *I can't warn Zinc, that might give me away, and AIDS will not let up. I do not want to lose either of them, but whatever happens, happens at this point.*

AIDS, in the body of first combat leader Desh, reclined with his head on his helmet— the traditional warrior pose. Schitz heard the strains of *Lillibulero* coming from comrade's old earplugs. For a moment, the dust receded from below Schitz's worn boots and, in its place, he imagined shoots of bright green grass. The narrow alleyways of the small border town faded away and were replaced by the open expanse of a rolling, continental field.

The *Lillibulero* echoed across the field and hung in the air over the smoke of cannon and musket fire. Schitz perceived himself in the king's crimson and felt the weight of a musket and his gear. He heard the whistle of shot and smelled burning powder. Arrayed in the distance were the lines of the foe. The music of the fifes and the beat of the drums echoed in his head.

"Are you all right, Guardian Lieutenant?" AIDS asked. "Having another flashback, are you?" He pulled the buds from his ears and looked at them. "The music does bring back old memories, I guess."

"Just ready the men," Schitz said.

AIDS stood up and dusted off his pants. "There's got to be some real action today, right? I mean, we're going right back in again. There's got to be an Angel or two, maybe even the big one."

Schitz struggled to sound nonchalant. "Why would you imagine Zinc might be present?"

"Just the rumor mill," AIDS said. He whirled and shouted in Persian. "Platoon, to arms!"

THE RAGGED MAN CLIMBED the steps of the Union Square subway station with plodding tread and visible exhaustion. He looked more like a ghoul than a human, the product of living on the streets of the sleepless city. His clothes were little more than filthy rags.

Uranium II cursed the heat, cursed his own stench, cursed the people that buzzed past him as though he was invisible. Somehow his ailment not only wasted him, but also turned his hosts into rotten, shiftless drifters and homeless men. With aching steps, he made his way to a small folding table where a tall, thin vagabond sat in one of two folding chairs facing a chess table.

"Care for a game?" Uranium II asked, his voice the rasp of a stick dragged across gravel.

"Sure, old-timer, five dollars to pay ten back if you win."

Uranium II reached into his pocket and retrieved a fistful of gold coins.

His adversary protested. "Not a lot of people take those Sacagawea dollars."

"I remember a time when gold was valuable," Uranium II said. "Maybe you could grant me a small consideration. Paper bills get so filthy in my pockets."

The man rolled his eyes. "Whatever. But you better not stink up my chair. I may be worn but I am clean—and so is my property."

He picked up one of the coins and flipped it in the air. "Heads," he said aloud before it landed in the middle of the board. The man scooped up the coin before Uranium II could see the result. "I'm white."

Uranium II's smile was as crooked as his rotting teeth. "Oh, I think your lineage is much more complicated than that, Ancient One."

THE MEN TRUDGED ALONG in silence under the weight of their weapons and the unremitting sun. Ideally, Schitz would have preferred to cross the border at night. Although their uniforms bore no insignia, the men's features and language would betray them as Persians, should they encounter any locals. However, the brass had ordered them into action without time to spare.

The men marched without expressions. They were not afraid of battle, but no one is jovial at its prospects. Schitz looked over his shoulder at AIDS who returned his stare.

I raised him, Schitz thought, *but I've built something substantial with Zinc.* The argument raged in his head. *I should not have told Zinc to come, but I need to know what the Angel's next move is. With AIDS snooping around, the channels are getting too dangerous.*

"IT'S NOT SAFE FOR you to come and talk to me," The Ancient said. "What game are you playing?"

"It's simple really" Uranium II said. "I want to be free. I need you to teach me how to avoid this Atrophy."

"Why on Earth would I do that?"

"That's the terms of the game," Uranium II replied.

"What do I get if I win?" The Ancient asked, intrigued.

"The keys to bringing about Ragnarok," Uranium II said. He coughed up a little blood. "I've heard you might have interest in seeing that happen."

The humor drained from Circades's face. He moved his hand.

"Queen's Pawn to D4."

"Knight to F6."

"Aggressive," The Ancient said.

Across from the game, a street performer began to sing to the crowd of passing tourists and locals in a clear, melancholy voice. She chose *The Parting Glass.* Her voice hovered over the chessboard like a pleasant aroma.

Of all the money that e'er I had I spent it in good company.

The roar of the rotors and swooshing blades announced the arrival of the choppers before they appeared.

"That one there." Schitz pointed out one of the copters to the man holding a Soviet manufactured SA-7.

"Yes, lieutenant."

The shoulder-mounted tube vomited fire and a sleek, tri-finned rocket. Schitz and his squad took cover. From behind a pair of large, aviator-style sunglasses, Schitz watched the projectile stream towards its target. Then a plume of smoke announced target acquisition, the men broke their typical discipline and shouted. Schitz watched the helicopter fall to its side like a wounded pterodactyl and cartwheel toward the ground.

The mission was a success; the battle had only just begun.

And all the harm I've ever done Alas, it was to none but me.

The Ancient slid a pawn to C4. Uranium II countered with one of his pawns to C5.

"Oh, how, symmetrical the movements of forces can be at the outset," The Ancient said.

And all I've done for want of wit, to memory now I can't recall.

"We should go to the crash site to capture any survivors, sir," AIDS said.

Ignoring his upstart apprentice, Schitz addressed the squad. "Our missile gave away our position. They'll be sending troops from Mosul here and toward the border to cut us off. The crash site is between us and the city, so one prong will go from Mosul through the crash site here to our position. Another will head toward the east. They will not expect us to head farther into the hinterlands, so that is precisely what we will do. We will head west and then north before heading east to the border, effectively cutting behind them and avoiding the chance that we are overrun or caught before the border."

Schitz saw AIDS's mental wheels turning as he reviewed his superior's plan. Schitz knew that he could outrun the responding

Coalition forces to the border. He also knew that if he offered up a swift retreat, AIDS would attempt to force his hand and seek out a confrontation with the Angels. Schitz had subtly offered a compromise. By crossing over the path taken by the Coalition forces, there was still a chance for an engagement—at least a sufficient one to keep AIDS at bay for now.

AIDS nodded as though he had realized that his plan to confront Schitz's anticipated flight for the border had been obviated for the time being. A look of satisfaction grew across AIDS's face.

And why should it not? Schitz thought. *Everything is still in flux.*
So, fill to me the parting glass, good night and joy be to you all.

With disdainful indifference, The Ancient moved his king's pawn to E3. He had yet to move a piece other than a pawn.

"CxD4, the first capture," Uranium II said. He swept The Ancient's pawn from the board.

"Such aggression," The Ancient said. "You are raring for a fight. May the aggressor beware. Once the battle is joined, it cannot easily be discontinued. ExD4."

One of Uranium II's pawns disappeared.

"Didn't the battle begin at the start?" Uranium II asked.

"Oh no," The Ancient replied. "The battle begins only after territory has been infringed upon and blood has been spilled; otherwise, we are just dancing."

Uranium II moved a pawn. "D5," he said. "Only moving within my territory."

"Now it's too late," The Ancient said. His grin could have curdled milk. "Much like your master and your foe's sovereign, there can be no peace once there is blood on the ground. There is no turning back until one king falls."

Uranium II looked into The Ancient's eyes and considered what he had pieced together about Zinc.

"I've lost a pawn, and you've lost a pawn. Surely with parity we can reach an accord that stops the destruction of the remaining pieces on the board," Uranium II said.

Circades batted away the notion with the back of his hand. "No arrangement could ever be strong enough to allow that kind of a balance. C5." He moved a pawn into Uranium's side. "Besides, your suggestion is treason for either side."

"NC6," Uranium II said. He moved his second knight in front of The Ancient's pawn.

"I don't know if splitting the atom scrambled your brains or what," The Ancient said, "but you're coming on awfully strong. Look at me. Have I touched anything but a pawn?"

"I don't have time for niceties."

"As you like," The Ancient said. "Bishop to B5."

Uranium II groaned. His knight was pinned. He could not move it without putting his king in check.

So, fill to me the parting glass, and drink a health whate'er befalls.

The Kurdish soldier stopped and wiped his brow. Northern Iraq was a furnace of sun, sand, and exploding ordnance.

What kind of land will I leave for my children? he thought. *I want them to know air conditioning, modern technology, and peace. Or maybe, dare I dream, that they will know Kurdistan.*

The air burned. He stank of sweat. His skin burned. His lungs ached. AIDS watched the man through the scope of his SVD rifle.

"How many, first combat leader?" It was Ali Falzeise, a private sent by Lieutenant Dai.

"I count three so far, but there are probably more in cover."

Falzeise held up three fingers to the rest of the squad, and then waved his hand side to side to indicate an approximation.

"I wonder why they stopped here," Falzeise said. "There are no houses, no wells, from what I can see."

"I don't know," AIDS said, irritation heavy in his voice. He moved the crosshairs slowly and centered them over the Kurd's chest, then up to his forehead, then back down to his chest.

AIDS was confused. He did not see a single, telltale Angelic aura.

Does Schitz want to fight or not? Does he want to ferret out Zinc or not? Is he being cautious lest his men think him suicidal? If he doesn't want to engage Zinc, why? Self-preservation or treachery?

All intel pointed to a major action directed against insurgents in the area, but the attack on the helicopter happened much sooner than anticipated. Now there was no reason to hang around.

My only play is to put Schitz next to Zinc, then he will have to kill him.

Doubt plagued AIDS's mind.

There's no way Schitz is a traitor. He is a famous and valiant warrior; he is my mentor; he is my friend. But since he is cautious, I will be bold on his behalf.

Falzeise interrupted AIDS's thoughts. "Maybe they saw your scope."

The Kurd's forehead exploded into red mist. The cracking report of the sniper rifle was still echoing when AIDS whispered to Falzeise, "What do you think now?"

AIDS heard the squad hustling towards the hillcrest. He sighted up another Kurd, pulled the trigger, and watched the man ragdoll to the ground spewing arterial spray.

"That's about one hundred and ninety-five meters," he said. He sighted again despite the telltale pop of Kalashnikov fire and the snap of incoming rounds.

Then gently rise and softly call good night and joy be to you all.

"G6," Uranium II said. He moved a pawn forward. "Surely there have been those who have been willing to commit treason in all of the history of this conflict."

"You mean other than yourself?" The Ancient asked. "Knight to F3. I guess there have been some, but in our world, there isn't much incentive. If you are found out, you get put down quickly."

Uranium II moved his queen to A5. "Check. So, what are the incentives?"

Circades moved his knight to C3 with a huff signifying his distaste for a wasted move. "Well, for one, there's love. It's not much of a secret that I spend most of my time, no, all my time, chasing a human through the undying rivers of reincarnation. There have been Demons and Angels willing to break their oaths of allegiance for the love of an enemy soldier."

"I don't think it's love." Uranium II pushed his bishop to G4, pinning one of The Ancient's knights. *I am regaining my balance*, he thought.

"I don't know who could love you," The Ancient said. He let out a choking chortle. "I mean we are talking about you, aren't we? You want to know if there are others who have tried what you tried. Castle."

Uranium II looked at the *swapped* king and rook on The Ancient's side.

Be careful, he thought. *Since the Inquest, you have learned a great deal. Do not give it away. The recent stability between Heaven and Hell and the impact on preventing Ragnarok—that is your only bargaining chip.*

"I'm talking about you," he said and moved his bishop to G7.

The Ancient transferred his bishop to D2. "I'm neither an Angel nor a Demon," he said. "I've made no effort to conceal the neutrality of my Titan heritage. I only remain mysterious because almost all individuals on either side have the sense to know that if God and the Devil see fit to leave me be, I can easily enough dispatch one of their little toy soldiers."

He punctuated his threat by pointing to the chessboard. A shiver ran down Uranium's spine.

"QC7," he said. He put his queen in retreat.

"Withdrawing from the field already?" Circades tssked. "We were just starting to have some fun."

Of all the comrades that e'er I had, they're sorry for my going away.

AIDS *has always been an aggressive hotshot*, Schitz thought. He surveyed the situation and determined there was no longer any time for carefully made plans.

"You five stay here and return as much fire as you can, but remember we only have the ammunition we're carrying. The rest of you with me."

He looked over his shoulder at AIDS while the squad moved out. "Any sign of Angels?"

"I couldn't tell."

"Let's wallop them either way," Schitz said.

"That's the mentor I know and love," AIDS said.

Schitz wanted to throw up.

And all the sweethearts that e'er I had, they'd wish me one more day to stay.

The Ancient moved his rook to E1.

"I take it that survival is another motivation other than love." Uranium II hocked up bloody phlegm and spat. "That's why I need the cure for the Atrophy, after what happened at the end of the war—and because of my injuries. Castle."

"I see," The Ancient said. "You find yourself needing to fortify your position. Believe it or not, I am familiar with the curse that befell you. In fact, I was the judge who issued the sentence."

But since it fell into my lot, That I should rise, and you should not.

AIDS shouldered his SVD and raised his Kalashnikov. He pulled the trigger and watched another Peshmerga Kurd topple. Schitz and AIDS led three others on a decisive thrust through the enemy's position. The Demonic duo moved, sure-footed and steady, as they identified and mowed down targets. There was no need to body swap; their hosts were in little danger.

Schitz found a momentary reprieve in the killing even though, with no Angels present, the Guard regiment could have dispatched the local fighters on their own. Schitz fired two rounds from his assault rifle point-blank into the head of an injured Kurd. He marveled for a moment at the gore that sloped out onto the rocky hillside. Then he waved for the others to rejoin with them.

I'll gently rise and softly call; good night and joy be to you all.

The Ancient moved his bishop to E3. "You know, you are quite clever, too clever for your own good."

"How is that?" Uranium II asked. He picked up his knight and placed it on E4.

Circades responded by capturing a pawn by moving his knight to D5. "Because there is no way of knowing if you can deliver your end of the deal," he said. "You have the evidence that I survive without fighting for any side and don't suffer from the Atrophy; what evidence do I have that you even know anything about breaking this damned stalemate and establishing Ragnarok?"

"I guess you have none," Uranium II said. "Queen to D8."

"Well, then, here is the caveat," The Ancient said. "If you cannot deliver your end of the bargain, I will kill you. Rook to C1."

Uranium II stifled a cough fearful it would show weakness. "If I were you, I'd worry about winning first."

With that, Uranium II captured The Ancient's knight with his queen. Circades sat in shocked silence.

If I had money enough to spend, and leisure time to sit awhile.

After the fact, Schitz always appreciated the quiet before unexpected action. So, when he saw the plume of the rocket-propelled grenade, he knew the moment of victory before this new development should have been that much sweeter.

He heard Khamenei shout. "RPG!"

The private slammed Schitz to the ground just before the Demon's ears began to ring. The hillside erupted in small arms fire. Over the clamor, Schitz heard Falzeise. Shrapnel had torn a large chunk of flesh from his left leg. The man clutched his trembling limb; blood oozed over his filthy fingers. Schitz raised his assault rifle and fired twice into the doomed man's chest. They all knew the rules; if you cannot run, if you cannot keep pace, you were not allowed to be captured. Iran was not involved in this war. The capture of a member of the Revolutionary Guard, uniformed or otherwise, was unacceptable.

Not the first time, Schitz thought.

He issued the order. "Fall back to the east."

He fired a cluster of parting shots, then broke into a run.

There is a fair maid in this town, that sorely has my heart beguiled.

Uranium II watched the opposing bishop glide onto C4.

"Now you're on tilt," Uranium II said.

"Wrong game," The Ancient said. His smile had long since been replaced by a scowl of concentration.

Uranium II retreated his queen to F5.

Her rosy cheeks and ruby lips, I own; she has my heart in thrall.

Schitz's breath came in labored gasps. He crested yet another rocky hill and saw a cluster of one-room dwellings in the distance.

"We'll hold them off there," he said.

In the distance, he saw at least thirty Peshmerga in hot pursuit. There were two telltale shadows of Angels among their ranks. The Peshmerga were outside of effective small arms range.

He held out his hand. "The rifle!"

AIDS, looking equally winded, unslung his SVD and tossed it across the five or so feet between them. Schitz caught the long gun and brought it into firing position. He paid no attention to the incoming rounds that stung the ground around him. Schitz calculated windage and distance, corrected for the change of elevation, and pulled the trigger.

AIDS's laughter rose above the symphony of gunfire as an enemy infantryman collapsed to the ground, a hazy shadow lying beside him. The remaining members of the squad raised a shout of triumph at their leader's expert shot. Schitz turned and led the way down the hill towards the houses.

Schitz's Notebook

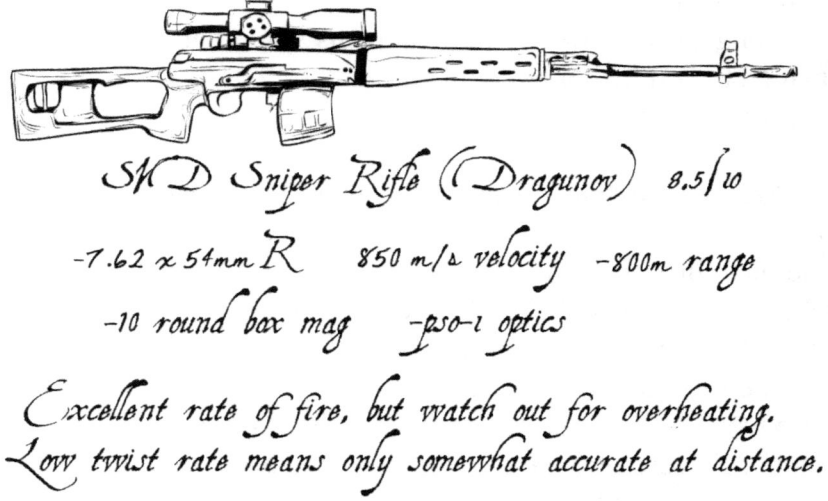

SVD Sniper Rifle (Dragunov)   8.5/10

−7.62 x 54mm R   850 m/s velocity   −800m range

−10 round box mag   −pso-1 optics

Excellent rate of fire, but watch out for overheating.
Low twist rate means only somewhat accurate at distance.

Then fill to me the parting glass, good night and joy be with you all.
The Ancient moved his bishop to E2 in silence. Uranium II countered with his rook to D8. The hustle and bustle of the Manhattan hub faded away; only the warrior and his opponent remained.

Uranium II could not hold back his cough but averted his head to save Circades from a bloody shower. The ailing Standard Bearer did not want to give away his theory; he knew Ragnarok meant his end as well. Uranium II was too tired to fight but too frightened to die. No longer interested in the eternal battle, his sole interest was the bargaining chip he might use to save himself.

Focus.

The Ancient moved his remaining knight to H4. Fire burned in his eyes.

"Get ready for a bloodbath," he said.

A man may drink and not be drunk,
A man may fight and not be slain.

Schitz kicked in the door of the first house and raised his Kalashnikov. He swept the room and was met by the shrieks of a woman clutching two small children to her chest.

He shouted in Arabic. "Up! Up!"

AIDS and half of the squad cleared another house across the small square. Once the others headed out, Schitz ordered the woman and children to stand in the doorway. He kicked over a wooden table and crouched behind it, drawing down on the doorway and the human shields.

A man may court a pretty girl, and perhaps be welcomed back again.

Uranium II captured The Ancient's bishop with his own by moving to E2. Circades captured the bishop with his queen.

But since it has so ought to be, by a time to rise and a time to fall.

The door flew off its hinges. As light flooded into the small house, Schitz and his men fired past the woman and children into the Peshmerga. In the crossfire, the woman collapsed to the floor, riddled with bullets. Somehow, one of the children ran through the doorway and out into the light, unscathed. A grenade thumped across the dirt floor; another followed.

Schitz ducked behind the table and put his gritty index fingers into his ears. The explosion rocked the small room and sucked the air out of Schitz's host's lungs.

When the smoke and dust cleared, Schitz propped himself up on an elbow. The other occupants of the room were dead; he was pretty sure the lieutenant had a collapsed lung. He rose to his feet. When he tried to raise the Kalashnikov, the weapon felt like an anvil—the sure sign his human was dying.

A head poked around the corner of the doorframe. Schitz pulled the trigger and grinned when he saw the man's head explode. The fallen foe's body convulsed and twitched in the doorway. Schitz stepped out into the light turning to the left.

Come fill to me the parting glass, good night and joy be with you all.

Two young soldiers stood against the side of the house. They were too frightened to offer resistance. Schitz shot them both. He slipped in a fresh banana clip and squinted through the burning sunlight.

Schitz saw more Kurds massing for an assault on the other side of the square. Something moved near the town well, a child—the one that had escaped. He... no, it was a little girl... she sat in the middle of the street and wailed. Schitz started towards her. His mind wanted to run faster than his wounded host could manage.

When he finally reached her, he scooped her up and limped towards the cluster of Kurds. Seeing Schitz holding the crying, Kurdish child, all the foes froze, paralyzed by their humanity. Using his free hand, Schitz mowed down all but one.

Just before his human lieutenant died, Schitz dropped the child on her rump and jumped into the surviving Peshmerga. He rushed to the crying child.

He cooed to the child and walked into the shade of a building. "Shush, shush little one."

He put her down, walked two steps, turned, and shot her in the head. One way or another, there would be no available humans into which to jump.

But since it fell into my lot, That I should rise, and you should not.

Uranium II moved his queen to F6. The Ancient retreated his knight to F3. After the flurry of activity, both men surveyed the board.

Uranium II moved a pawn E5.

"Are there still pawns on the board," The Ancient said.

"If you think about it, every piece except the king is a pawn," Uranium II replied.

"All sacrifice for the king," Circades said. He captured the pawn with his own by moving to E5.

I'll gently rise and softly call; good night and joy be to you all.

AIDS stood over the body of a fallen Angel. After plunging his sword into the enemy's back, AIDS looked for a human. Few remained.

Uranium II captured The Ancient's pawn on E5 with his knight. Far fewer pieces remained.

Carnage met Schitz when he turned the corner. The smell of gunpowder and blood wafted in the air. The Peshmerga who had not detached to face Schitz had attempted to hit the village from the rear. They were demolished by AIDS and his men. He poked his head around the corner of the last house.

Zinc and AIDS battled in the Celestial. Each held two daggers, and both were masters with the knife. They whirled, kicked, parried, thrusted. Before either combatant noticed him, Schitz backed around the corner.

What's my next move?

So, fill to me the parting glass, and drink a health whate'er befalls.

The Ancient calmly moved his knight to D4. He muttered unintelligibly under his breath.

"What did you say?" Uranium II asked.

After a moment of silence that hung heavy in the air like the humidity clogging both men's lungs, The Ancient spoke. "Knight to D4."

"Ah, then rook to C8."

Circades deflated and moved a pawn to B4 with fingers suddenly arthritic. He grimaced as he let go of the piece.

Uranium II moved his knight to C6.

"Everything is exposed to everything else," The Ancient said. "Attack and defense, intertwined."

Then gently rise and softly call, good night and joy be to you all.

Zinc grunted and blocked another of the young Demon's thrusts mere millimeters from his face. He had planned on letting the exuberant AIDS tire from his ferocious attack, but in fact, it was he who was tiring. Zinc half-heartedly swung toward AIDS with his left-handed blade.

Overcome with desperation, Zinc head-butted AIDS. He watched AIDS stumble back a few paces with blood running down his face. Then Zinc felt a hot, painful stickiness trickling along his cheek.

So, fill to me the parting glass.

After The Ancient moved his rook to D1, Uranium II captured one of Circades' pawns.

"Knight to B4," Uranium II said.

In response, The Ancient moved his queen to B2 and threatened the offending knight, which was immediately withdrawn to D5. Shooting past the knight, The Ancient's queen captured a pawn on B7.

"Your knight just got out of the way," he said. His voice sounded triumphant. His eyes betrayed melancholy.

Uranium II understood the heartache behind his opponent's gaze. For a moment he considered agreeing to a mutual exchange of information.

No pity, he thought. What's the purpose of escaping the Atrophy, only for him to end the world?

Uranium II moved his knight to E3, and another pawn fell.

And drink a health whate'er befalls.

AIDS grimaced and blinked through the blood.
Where the hell is Schitz?

His lungs screamed for relief. His daggers seemed to be gaining weight. Even in the Celestial Realm, the sun's heat threatened to overcome him. He searched his heart for the motivation to continue.

If I can kill him, I don't have to worry about my mentor's collusion.

Then gently rise and softly call.

The pewter bloodbath continued as The Ancient captured Uranium II's knight.

"Check," Uranium II said. He placed his queen on F2.

Good night and joy be to you all.

Zinc saw the blade flash towards his face. Experience told him to parry but instinct caused him to turn sideways and let the blade run along his own, exposing himself briefly to AIDS's other weapon. The Demon took the bait but was too slow. He missed with his thrust and lost his balance like a man pushing against a door that opens too quickly.

Good night and joy be to you all.

The Ancient moved his king to H1 to escape check but he knew it was only a matter of time before the killer blow came.

"High stakes on the table," he said. "It's one thing to corner the king, another altogether to dispatch him."

"I don't foresee any surprises," Uranium II said.

Good night and joy be to you all.

AIDS fell face down on the ground. Dirt and dust assaulted his face; his grip on consciousness began to slip. He knew the blade was coming to end him. Self-pity gripped his throat. *I played every angle to set this up and still I could not trap Schitz. I cannot even overpower this Angel.*

AIDS rolled over and blindly raised his right-handed sword to protect himself. The blow came but deflected off AIDS's blade, across his cheek, and into the ground. With a supreme effort, AIDS plunged the dirk in his left hand into Zinc's thigh. Zinc bellowed and raised his other sword to strike.

Uranium II captured yet another pawn with his queen at E3. Circades hustled his rook into E1 to threaten. Uranium moved his knight to F2.

"Check."

Schitz pulled the pin and placed the grenade inside his host's shirt. He stepped out of the Kurdish soldier and ducked around the corner of the building. The blast that removed the last human from the equation grabbed the attention of both end-game locked combatants.

Schitz met the frantic gaze of Zinc, dirk impaled hilt deep in his thigh. Zinc's eyes were firm and set, unblinking and hard. Schitz looked down to AIDS. His protégé was frantic and bewildered; one sword protruded from his enemy's leg, the other had just saved his life and was still pressed against the blade that had just creased his face.

Schitz removed a throwing knife from his belt and flipped it in the air. It spun thrice before he caught it by the blade.

AIDS screamed for help. "Finish him!"

Schitz was within five strides. Not even a cadet in the Academy would miss from this distance.

The Ancient's king fled to G1. Uranium II moved his knight to H3.

"Check."

The Ancient moved his king back to H1.

Queen to Q1.

"Check!"

"In the end, even the queen must be sacrificed; anything for survival," The Ancient said.

He slid his rook over and clicked against the queen.

"A fine match, indeed."

Uranium II dropped his knight onto F2.

"Checkmate!"

The knife struck AIDS in the left eye. He began to convulse. Zinc stepped back from the writhing Demon and relaxed his grip on the dirk. The younger Demon's rattling spasm reverberated in Schitz's ears.

"Should I?" Zinc asked.

"No," Schitz said.

He could not tell if the knife had entirely severed AIDS's grasp on the world around him, but perceived the panic spreading across his protégé's face.

AIDS began to stammer. "P... ppp... ppplease... no."

A stranger came upon Schitz—someone... something he'd seldom if ever encountered—regret. But the visitor did not stay long. He pulled the knife from his friend's eye and said, "Goodbye, AIDS," and plunged the blade into the younger Demon's throat.

Zinc yanked the dagger from his thigh with a grunt. "I wasn't sure who you were going to pick."

He looked at the blade for a moment, then handed it to Schitz. "Here, take it."

"Here," The Ancient said after scribbling a series of unintelligible symbols in the margin of a newspaper and ripping the page free. "Put this on the wall with ash while the morning is still dark, then put your hands on either side of the sentence and keep them there until morning's first light has touched it. That will cure you of the Atrophy."

Uranium II's hand trembled and he took the paper.

"There's one more thing," The Ancient said. "The message you have there is different from mine. It..." He paused, thinking how to explain. "It pulls from a different source. If anyone other than you uses it, you will die. So, memorize it and then burn it."

"Sure thing," Uranium II said.

The Ancient pushed onto the back two legs of his folding chair. "What made you think I'd keep my end of the deal?"

Uranium II cleared his throat; it hurt, made worse with every swallow. "I've heard a lot of rumors about you, but three things I've heard consistently. One, you're dangerous. Two, you're obsessed with finding that lady human of yours. Three, you're an honest man with deals and accords."

The Ancient raised his eyebrows and cocked his head. "I wonder which one of those is most true."

"Well, I'll be seeing you," Uranium II said. He hoisted himself up with a lot of effort.

"Better hope not—for your sake."

Schitz drew the symbols he knew worked best for Earth and Air in front of the doorway of the house before sliding AIDS's second dirk into his belt. He exhaled over the symbols and watched as the portal opened. He shouted over his shoulder.

"You got a way out of here?"

"Yeah, I'm good," Zinc replied. "Safe to assume we can go back to using the channels again, huh?"

"Yes," Schitz said. "By the way, you look like shit."

Zinc tossed his head back in a tired laugh. "Compared to you," he said, "I look like springtime in Paris."

Schitz did not reply. He had already entered the portal.

SATAN HAD NOT VISITED the world in eons. He arrived at the meeting early and ordered two pints of Guinness. The Dublin pub was a small, non-descript entity, but it was fastidiously clean. It sat off the beaten path in the middle of a block with a cobblestone street too narrow for cars to run abreast. The irony that he and his vast army fought so hard for a place he did not even visit was not lost on the Lord of the Underworld.

He sipped his dark beer and thought about King John, who ordered the construction of a castle beyond the Pale then never set foot in it. Satan wondered if the world would be his King John's Castle, if he would inherit a place he had struggled to conquer for so long. He took another deep gulp of the drink and smacked his lips in appreciation of its rich, hearty taste, effervescent, pungent, flavorful.

"It is better here," a familiar voice said from over his shoulder.

Satan turned to face his brother and eternal rival.

"How are you, Beelzebub?" God asked. He sat opposite Satan and scooped up the second glass of stout.

"That wasn't for you," the Devil said before draining the last of the pint.

"Oh, well," God replied. "Still, it really is better here on Erin's Isle than anywhere else in the human world. I wonder why that 'tis."

"Did you really request this meeting to discuss the finer points of locally brewed beer or to practice your abysmal Irish brogue? Get on with it. I am very busy, and you are late, as usual."

God drained the pint in a single, long pull. "The remaining Titan has awakened from his slumber."

"I know," the Devil said.

"When our kind was united, we wiped their race from the face of the Earth," God said.

He pounded his mug into the table and signaled the barman for another.

"Nearly," the Devil said. "We obviously missed one."

"He never fought us," God said. "There was no reason to provoke him."

"All he ever does is search for that mortal. She must be one amazing—"

"Don't be crude, Brother," God said. "But the quest seems a little... ah... crazy."

The Devil shook his head. "So, what do you want to do?"

"If we keep fighting each other, he could wipe out all of us eventually," God said. "You know, there was a time when we saw eye to eye."

"That was a long time ago," the Devil gestured for a third round.

"If he waited so long for that woman, think about what he would do to get her back again. I've received reports that he intends to trigger Ragnarok, Megiddo, whatever you want to call it," God said. His eyes were steely, his voice stern.

"I thought only we had the power to elevate humanity's consciousness," the Devil said. He tossed a bill to the waiter. "Thanks!"

"And a good day to ya fine gentlemen as well," the waiter said.

God reached for one of the glasses. "These are not for you," the Devil said.

The server laughed. "There's plenty of pints t' go 'round, I'll bring ya another two. After all, we don't get a lot of fine dressed lads in here."

The server's comment made Satan take note of his brother. God sported a long black overcoat, a black suit, a crisp white shirt with French cuffs and a crimson necktie.

"You look like a mobster," the Devil said.

"Dress for the job you want," God said.

Both brothers laughed.

Satan considered his lame attempt at blending in with the local scenery. Though dressed in a designer suit, he'd opted for a plaid scarf and a wool cap.

"I look a little like a well-dressed, Irish pimp, don't I?"

"Wasn't going to mention it."

Two more pints arrived. This time Satan did not object when God lifted one. They clincked glasses.

"Cheers," God said with his characteristic but often annoying joviality. "To brothers."

"To mutual necessity," Satan said.

"Oh, come, Hades, it's been so long since we sat down together."

"I have a lot of names," Satan said. "Why do you always pick my least favorite?"

"What do you prefer?"

"Well, if you must know, Asmodeus."

God rolled his eyes and took a deep gulp of his beer.

"Well, in answer to your question, yes, only we have the power to elevate humanity's level of consciousness, if we both agree."

"Which we would never do, again," Satan said. "We both know humanity's consciousness is at the very brink of perceiving our kind, which would obliterate all of us and render our contest moot."

"Armageddon," God said.

"Ragnarok," the Devil said.

"The end of times."

"Curtains."

"Goodnight, Irene."

"For us at least." Satan was about to raise his hand again but noticed his brother's disapproving gaze. "What? I'm not driving."

"You always get aggressive when you have a little too much; let's not start anything today, okay?"

"Fine," Satan said. "Anyway, The Strain carriers have very clear memories. And the very religious have very clear visions. We cannot withstand another elevation."

"So," God said, "The Ancient will try to force our hand. He will antagonize us, harry and harass us. He might try to kill us or render our situation so precarious that we risk another elevation of consciousness."

"So, what do you propose? We still have our own wager to settle, or are you telling me you are no longer interested in the World?" The Devil's eyebrows arched in anticipatory glee.

"Oh no, no, no, no! Don't get excited." God laughed so loudly that several patrons stared at the table before resuming the drinking and darts. "I propose that for now, we delegate. He's only one Titan. There's no need for us to fight him ourselves. If we each send an equal deployment to deal with him, neither of us will be at a deficit in our struggle, and we can be reasonably assured of success."

The Devil thought for a moment. "Who do you have in mind?"

God made a pretense at thought.

"You already have someone in mind—you were always a lousy card player," the Devil said. "My best man could never work with one of yours—he's too savage."

"You're right. I know who it is; he will never do. Nor will mine; one is recently recovered from illness, the other too ruthless."

"I'll give you Anorexia," the Devil said. "I'm sure you're familiar with at least some of her work?"

God nodded. "Okay, my side will donate the eldest son of the Uranium House. His name is Hirohisa. He's young, but he shows extreme promise. He was slated to replace his father before his miraculous recovery."

"I like it," the Devil said, "an old hand and an up-and-comer, they should fit well together."

"Do you ever wonder how it is that we're able to sit here like this, and they have to slaughter each other?" God asked.

The Devil shrugged. "It's always been that way; it's the same with the humans. The leaders argue, but the fighters die. The natural order of things."

"I suppose," God said.

He stood, then patted his younger brother on the shoulder. "If you ever grow tired of all the fighting and killing, you can always sue for peace. Maybe I would consider some form of clemency for you and your heathen army."

The Devil brushed the hand away. "Before this is done, you and your ilk will beg for forgiveness, and I promise you will receive neither mercy nor a quick death."

The Devil watched through the front window as a jet-black sedan with heavy tint on the windows squeezed down the alley. The car defied any attempt at subtlety by squealing its tires on the cobblestones. Satan noted the Angelic possessed humans inside the car, a security detail.

He smirked.

We agreed to come alone. I guess he technically adhered to the terms since his men stayed outside.

The Devil left a generous tip on the table and rose to his feet. As he turned for the door, from his periphery, he spied a man in a dark trench coat emerge from the rear portion of the bar reserved for staff. Satan's "best man" had watched everything.

Satan wandered along the streets of Dublin secure in the fact his "six" was covered by Schitz, the most ruthless killer in history.

THE CARTEL BOSS KNOWN in the various reaches of the underworld as La Larga Sombra stood over the elaborate gravestone. He had returned to the Cemetery Dahlem in Berlin to have a headstone erected. It was an expensive work of art, though devoid of the typical themes of Angels. The marble structure was crafted in the shape of a Roman pillar that morphed into a tree trunk.

It is perfect, Circades thought. *We will replace the marble of this world with nature and live as we once did, my Pulwabi.*
The epitaph was etched into a marble scroll.
I have always sought you and I always will,
From the Rift Valley to Vatican hill,
You are all that I've loved from the past,
All that I built knowing it would not last,
And whether healthy or ill,
While I have breath, I will search for you still.

> *At the end of the wheel in my heart I know,*
> *Someday I will find you and won't let you go.*

Circades felt satisfied with the final stanza of his poem. *It is a good end*, he thought.

He stepped away from the empty grave and walked back to his black sedan. The chauffeur opened the door. With one foot in the car, Circades turned to take one last glance toward the tomb.

It is here I bury my search, The Ancient thought. *The world must pay, but she is right. Only in the end of the cycle of births can we have each other forever.*

Several of La Larga Sombra's men had arrived in separate vehicles and remained under the rainy clouds of the dreary Berlin sky.

"I still have no idea who is buried there," Alfredo said. He was one of Circades most trusted advisors, the man who had been instrumental in orchestrating the accumulation of his vast fortune.

"I don't think anybody is buried there," Gustav replied. "I think it is something for him to commemorate the end of his prior life."

Alfredo shrugged. "Either way, it's creepy. Nice, but creepy."

"You are so predictable."

Schitz knew the voice before he turned.

"Oh, am I, Autism?" he said.

He was shocked to see a cold, stern expression on his comrade's face.

"What's the matter, Autsy?"

"I knew I'd find you here," Autism said. "I just didn't know this would be so hard."

Confusion pricked at Schitz's neck; confusion... and fear.

"What's the matter?" he said again, this time with a more serious tone.

"Well, Schitz, terrible business about AIDS, wasn't it?" Autism asked.

"Yes. Although I didn't realize you two were so close."

"Yes," Autism said. "Did you know that the Wraith blacksmiths use standardized tools?"

"I guess," Schitz said. "Never gave it much thought."

"Remember how the Russians struggled when they tried to press into Prussia during the Great War?"

"Sure," Schitz said. "The Ruskies couldn't use their locomotives. The Prussian tracks were a different gauge."

"Right," Autism said. "The Wraiths have their tools and Heavenly blacksmiths have their own, different ones, like the Prussian train tracks."

The smile on Schitz's face faded. He knew where this was going.

Autism chewed the inside of his lip for a moment but never broke his gaze. "You see, based on the width of his injuries, it seems that AIDS was killed by a Demonic blade, not one from Heaven."

Schitz opened his mouth to speak, but Autism beat him to the punch. "Yes," he said. "I'm sure it was a captured weapon, or what have you. I'm sure there is some reasonable explanation."

Schitz was suddenly aware of his sword's weight.

I cannot defect. I cannot cross the river into Limbo. I cannot go into independent business with Zinc.

Autism noticed Schitz's hand touching the knob of his weapon.

"Are you willing to dispose of me to keep your secret—even now?"

Schitz's eyes and voice were flat and hard. "What would you have me do?"

"There is no need to worry," Autism said. He smiled at his own ruse. "I am your friend for life. I simply came to tell you, that if you have lost the path, there is nothing to stop you from regaining it. I have not said anything to anyone, nor will I—ever."

Relief washed over Schitz like the healing waters of the Styx.

"Thank you, Autsy," he said.

His friend saluted, then disappeared into the twilight.

Chapter 16
A LONG WAY TO GO

The Ancient walked through the halls of his picturesque Italian villa. His ivory suit was immaculate, his hair cut neatly and slick with product, his countenance as grim as it had ever been. He had waited and plotted, waited and assessed, waited and thought... and waited. He had waited for this moment, and at last, he was certain that he was ready.

A man who had walked the Earth over untold thousands of years could hardly fuss over a few decades. Yet the days since the ASK Vorwärts match seemed interminable. He withdrew a phone from the breast pocket of his designer suit and turned on the light to the study.

He opened an application and scrolled through the music selections—vast and varied. He searched for the perfect accompaniment to this red-letter day.

"Ah!"

He pressed "play" and the nostalgic tune by Jack Judge and Harry Williams, *It's a Long Way to Tipperary*, filled the study. The Ancient walked to a bookcase and removed *L'Inferno* to reveal a lever.

He pulled it and soaked in the stirring melody.

> *Up to mighty London Came an Irishman one day.*
> *As the streets are paved with gold, sure, everyone was gay,*
> *Singing songs of Piccadilly, Strand and Leicester Square,*
> *Till Paddy got excited, then he shouted to them there.*

Zinc sat in the cramped private reading room of the New York Public Library. He poured over a pile of psychological manuals, all dog-eared to the sections labeled, *Schizophrenia.* His attention shifted to an equally massive pile of the secret texts, opened to various insightful means for dispatching Demons. An alarm beeped through his earphones, interrupting his study music.

It's time, he thought.

He pulled up a contact, "S", and sent a terse text message: 5 mins! The music he'd been listening to returned.

> *It's a long way to Tipperary, it's a long way to go.*
> *It's a long way to Tipperary, to the sweetest girl I know!*

SCHITZ RECLINED IN THE mud and muck along the Afghan road, festooned in the local garb of a Mujahedeen from head to foot. His Kalashnikov assault rifle slung over his shoulder; his CIA laptop balanced on his folded knees. With an accomplished touch, he disengaged the auto-pilot and began guiding the Reaper drone with a small joystick.

His phone beeped.

Ensuring that the drone's path remained level, he withdrew a smartphone from his pocket and read the message preview.

"5 mins!"

He opened a sports app and checked the score while he waited for the convoy from Pakistan to pass—Taliban interlaced with Angels.

Liverpool 1 – 0 Barcelona Agg. (1 – 3), '45.

He groaned.

"Typical."

He began to hum.

> *Goodbye, Piccadilly, farewell, Leicester Square!*
> *It's a long, long way to Tipperary, but my heart's right there.*

THE ANCIENT EMERGED FROM the weapons room and returned to the study weighed down with holstered semi-automatic pistols under his suit jacket, grenades along his leather belt, an assault rifle slung over either shoulder, and a metal ammunition container in his hand. A smile slowly spread across his face. The world was his for the taking, and for the first time ever, he had a guaranteed route to Pulwabi.

He walked through the study, his leather shoes sinking into the lush carpet while the recording continued to play.

Paddy wrote a letter, to his Irish Molly-O,
Saying, "Should you not receive it, write and let me know!"
"If I make mistakes in spelling, Molly, dear," said he,
"Remember, it's the pen that's bad, don't lay the blame on me!"

ZINC SLUMPED DOWN THE stone steps of the New York Public Library, his leather backpack filled to the brim with the books he had checked out. The ambient noise of the Manhattan afternoon filled his ears.

He looked up into the clear sky and wondered which way to go.

He turned toward Grand Central Station and began to grin with happiness. He was alive and in control of his own destiny. Truly the world was his. He slipped his earphones on to mask the cacophony.

It's a long way to Tipperary, it's a long way to go.
It's a long way to Tipperary, to the sweetest girl I know!

ANOREXIA AND HIROHISA URANIUM stood together, looking over a map of The Ancient's known movements. The meeting took place under the towering walls of the Limbo citadel on the Angelic side of the Styx. Each of their squads waited.

"So, for the time being, we will be working together," the young Angel said.

"At least until someone tells us to kill each other," Anorexia said.

> Goodbye, Piccadilly, farewell, Leicester Square!
> It's a long, long way to Tipperary, but my heart's right there.

SCHITZ STROLLED DOWN THE rocky Afghan road. Wrecks of twisted, burning metal and corpses of humans and Angels alike were strewn about the road behind him. With his rifle slung over his shoulder and a jauntiness in his step, he slipped his hand into his pocket and unlocked his phone.

A broad grin spread across his face as he read: Liverpool 4 – 0 Barcelona, Agg. 4 – 3, FT.

He continued down the road, dust slowly rising around him as he went. He was happy for he was alive. He was young, and clever, and free; he was powerful; he was on his way to see Anna. More than anything, he was certain of one thing: the world was his.

He walked away from the smoldering wrecks. As many a soldier has done, he broke into a tune to pass the kilometers of his march.

> It's a long way to Tipperary, it's a long way to go.
> It's a long way to Tipperary, to the sweetest girl I know!
> Goodbye, Piccadilly, farewell, Leicester Square!
> It's a long, long way to Tipperary, but my heart's right there.

MQ-9 Reaper

Epilogue
DO YOU HEAR OUR STEP?

The soldiers' boots struck the ground in unison, a relentless stomp above which rose upward to Heaven and sank downward to Hell the harmoniously discordant sounds of a marching song.

Hört Ihr unseren Schritt?
Fallschirmjäger, Waffenträger,
alle müssen mit.
Bleibe auch du nicht zurück!
|: Bürger lasst euch sagen,
Euch wird man blutig schlagen.
Bürger nehmt die Waffen zu Hand! :|

Mädel lass mich gehen!
Hörst Du sie singen? Schau wie sie springen!
Kann nicht stille stehn.
Mädel, ach lasse mich gehn!
|: Laufschritt, Singsang und Zählen,
Mädel ich kann nicht wählen.
Meine Kameraden ich fand. :|

Führ uns General,
führ uns zur Hölle!
Wir sind zur Stelle.
Fallen wir einmal,
siegen wird unser Fanal.
|: Fallschirmkameraden,

Ihr dürft nie verzagen!
Legt nie die Waffen aus der Hand! :|[68]

---

[68] Do you hear our step? Paratroopers, weapon carriers. All must come with. Do not stay behind! Citizens, let you say, you will be beaten bloody. Citizens take the weapons to hand! Girl let me go! Do you hear them sing? Look how they jump! Cannot stand still. Girl, oh let me go! Running, singing and counting. Girl I cannot choose, my comrades I have found. Lead us General, lead us to Hell! We are there. Let's fall, our end will be victorious. Parachute comrades, you must never despair! Never put the gun out of your hand!

ORIGINAL LYRICS AND POETRY
BY J.L. FEUERSTACK

FROM OVER THE BROAD EARTH VOL. II

TOTENTAG (DAY OF DEATH)

Death rides a pale, white horse,
A bloated and infected corpse,
You can't hide when he's coming your way,
Better prepare for the judgment day.
He hews mortals down without hesitation,
Harvesting souls for eternal damnation,

(Confutatis, maledictis) Ready to fire at will,
(Flammis acribus addictis) prepared for the righteous kill
We're young, fearless, and bold,
Ready to tear down the stronghold.
Summon me amongst those by victory saved,
Or Valkyries will lay me down in a glorious grave.
No mercy asked or given,
'Cause no weakness should be forgiven.

Sigue el rastro de cuerpos,
Porque es el dia de los Muertos.

Death rides a horse black as coal,
A raucous, stampeding foal,
He'll bash your head in,

And slash your skin,
Rider and steed, each a complete savage,
On the prowl for innocents to ravage.

Ava Maria, I won't want to be ya,
When I drink your blood like I'm downing sangria.
We're locked and loaded,
Gonna leave your body lifeless and bloated.
Today's the day, a day for death,
The day you'll be taking your last breath.

Mein Durst nach dem Blut ist geweckt,
Verwüstung anrichten und befleckt
Es ist der Tag der Toten,
Und nichts ist verboten.

Death rides a crimson horse,
Its hide is battle-scarred, matted, and coarse.

I've got the death-dealer strapped on my waist,
And any minute now you'll be erased.
There's nothing on heaven or earth that can stop me,
There's nothing you could ever do to drop me.
It's blood paid for blood, paid back in full,
And I'm itching for the trigger to pull.

All the angels in heaven,
Couldn't stop this Armageddon.
For the time is now, it's the final hour,
And the reaper holds all the power.
By now, even you fools should see,
Now I am become death, and death has become me.

THE WHEEL OF TIME (CIRCADES'S POEM)

Ever since my soul was split,
I've been looking for the other half of it,
I found its reflection in another,
The woman destined to be my lover,
Side by side we would sit,
As the flames danced from the fire pit.

Mankind was new,
And so were you.

I lost you to the flow of time,
Wondering when again you would be mine.

I found you once more in an age of gold,
And in hieroglyphs our story was told,
By the river's winding bend,
I found a princess whose beauty knew no end.
In the shadow of the pyramids bold,
We watched our story of love unfold.

The sands of gold and waters blue.
Could not match the beauty that was you.

I lost you to life's spinning wheel,
All but for the blink of time we could steal.

I found you next amongst a marble hall,
Behind the eternal city's towering wall,
Like the coliseum's staggering height,
Our love grew taller by day and night,

And though the empire would eventually fall,
It seemed but for a moment time would stall.

Antiquity provided many wonders true,
They pale in grandeur when compared to you.

But the wheel of lives once again turned,
And the city we loved to ashes it burned.

I found you in the time of ladies and lords,
At the joust amidst the clatter of swords,
There you stood my princess fair,
Who gave me a ribbon from her flowing hair,
Chivalrous I strove to win your accords,
As I plucked at my loot and sung to its chords.

You were my lady and I was your knight,
In that dark age we found a glimmer of light.

But as the moon must wax and wane,
So life must end to begin again.

Many lifetimes were spent in pain,
Searching for my soulmate only in vain,
I crossed oceans and walked the world,
As over the land new flags unfurled,
I felt in my solitude an invisible strain,
As I crossed mountains and sailed the main.

I've always known my soul was split in two,
And no other lover was made for me but you.

The wheel of life can spin however it sees fit,
And we must be content to play our part in it.

I knew you once in the city of lights,
Alive at peace between the two great plights,
As the strains of a record hissed and popped,
Sat in a cafe I felt as though my heart stopped,
Hand in hand on those bohemian nights,
Below the tower and other memorable sights.

You gave me such peace in a world of strife,
In a moment with you I could live a whole life.

I have always sought you and I always will,
From the Rift Valley to Vatican hill,
You are all that I've loved from the past,
All that I built knowing it would not last,
And whether healthy or ill,
While I have breath I will search for you still.

At the end of the wheel in my heart I know,
Someday I will find you and won't let you go.

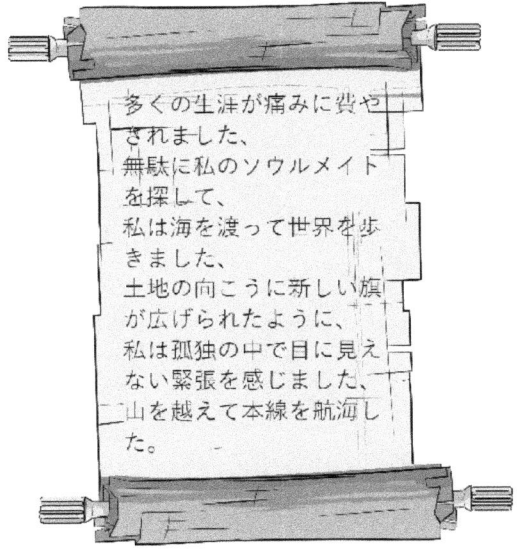

多くの生涯が痛みに費や
されました、
無駄に私のソウルメイト
を探して、
私は海を渡って世界を歩
きました、
土地の向こうに新しい旗
が広げられたように、
私は孤独の中で目に見え
ない緊張を感じました、
山を越えて本線を航海し
た。

ABOUT THE AUTHOR

J.L Feuerstack holds a BA from Washington & Lee University and a MA from Queens College, both in the study of Psychology. He has worked in various investigative and supervisory capacities for the City of New York. He is a diehard supporter of Liverpool Football Club and the German National Football Team.

About the Illustrator

Alana Tedmon has worked as an illustrator since 2012. She graduated with her BFA from the Art Institute of Dallas and also studied illustration under award-winning artists, including Edward Kinsella and Sterling Hundley. She enjoys skiing and cycling around her hometown Philadelphia, as well as spending time with her three pet rats.

ACKNOWLEDGMENTS

The author would like to thank:

My wife Eileen Feuerstack for her unwavering support and encouragement as well as her companionship in traveling to many of the locales featured in the story. And for always listening when I ramble on about this story and others.

Editor, Arthur Fogartie, for his unparalleled skill and patience. His insight and wit were paramount in ensuring that this story was told.

Illustrator, Alana Tedmon, for her talent and dedication. Her creativity was vital for the creation of the characters of *The Saga of Fallen Leaves*.

www.ingramcontent.com/pod-product-compliance
Lightning Source LLC
Chambersburg PA
CBHW070815190726
48292CB00006B/2025